RETURN

K.T. HOLDER

For my Wife

AUTHOR'S NOTE

This book is a work of fantasy fiction, and while it contains magical elements and imaginary settings, it also includes themes that may be distressing to some readers.

I believe stories should be immersive, but also that you deserve to make informed choices about the content you engage with. If you'd like to see a list of content warnings for this and my other books, you can find one linked on my website:

www.ktholder.com

Please be aware that some content warnings may be minor spoilers.

Thank you for reading,
KT Holder

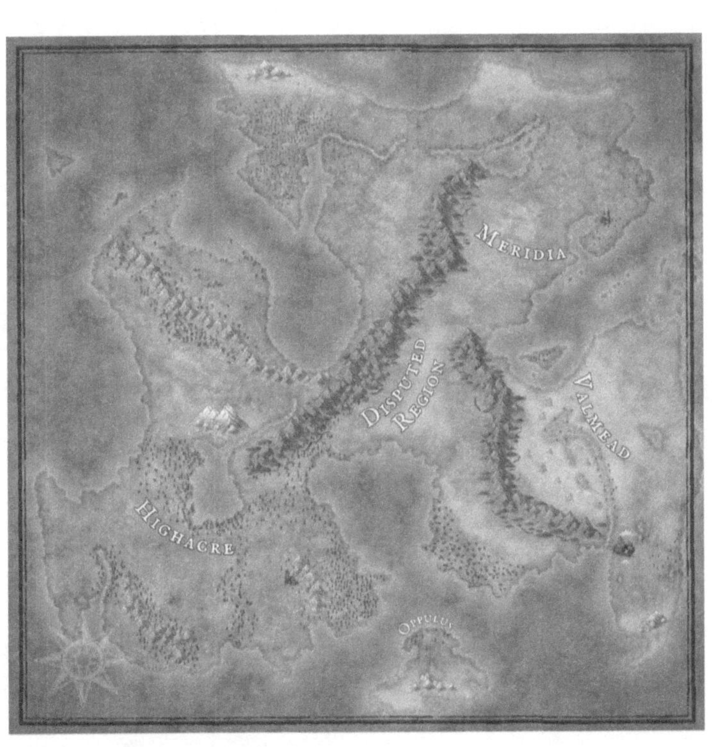

MERIDIA
DISPUTED REGION
VALMEAD
HIGHACRE
OPPULUS

1

"Ow!"

"Get off me!"

"You get off ... no, that's my arm ..."

"Who is touching my butt?"

"Sorry, I'm just trying to ... ow!"

The room was pitch-black. Though this was only Lily's second trip through the interdimensional travel machine, it seemed much clunkier than her first time. Lily and her unwitting travelling companions had been deposited on the dusty floor in a heap. She had no idea where she had travelled to, and her anxiety was through the roof.

Lily's mind was racing through everything that Jenkins, the scientist who created the machine, had told her about the various dimensions that he had visited. Somewhere nearby, an animal snorted, and Lily immediately thought of Jenkins's love of dragons. A nauseous panic settled in her stomach.

Clumsily extracting herself from Ava and Alexei, the Meridian and Valmeadian ambassadors to court, Lily left them squabbling with each other about who was touching whose leg and started groping around in the dark, trying to figure out where she was.

She saw some light coming in from the roof and felt immediate relief that she was in a building and not a weird lightless dimension. Slightly calmer, she noticed a faint musty smell. Her hands then found something familiar; smooth and spiky all at once. It was like a hay bale. No, it *was* a hay bale. Lily realised they were in a barn.

Something clicked, and Lily knew beyond doubt they were in *her* barn. She was home!

"Shut up, both of you," Lily said to the ambassadors, then moved swiftly and easily to the light switch, turning it on and looking around.

Ava and Alexei looked like they had both lost a game of Twister very badly. Able now to see, they quickly disentangled themselves and brushed down their clothes slightly self-consciously.

"That was very strange," said Alexei, looking around at the barn and taking in his surroundings. "This is not the palace."

"Nice work, detective," Ava shot at him. "Thank goodness you're here."

Alexei scowled and rolled his eyes at her. Lily, used to their banter, ignored them.

"Now that we've narrowed it down to 'not the palace', any ideas where we might be? And perhaps how we got here?" Ava asked.

Ava and Alexei didn't know about interdimensional travel. A secret only a few high-ranking officials from Highacre knew about, it was only revealed to Lily when she learned she was actually royalty.

Her biological parents, the king and queen of Highacre, had used the interdimensional travel machine to hide Lily in this dimension when she was a baby. Lily had grown up on her family's farm blissfully ignorant that she wasn't biologically her parents' child, or that her siblings weren't biologically her siblings.

It wasn't until the tragic deaths of her entire biological family that Lily had been brought to Highacre and told of her true heritage. And that she would be queen.

Her advisors must be beside themselves. Lily's heart stopped. Her advisors! The attack. *Were they okay? Were they alive?*

She vividly remembered the gun pointed at her by a traitorous guard. He'd pulled the trigger, but Jason and Naomi had saved her life before hiding her in a side corridor and launching a counterattack at the guard and his accomplices. Closing her eyes, she could still hear the cacophony of gunshots and energy bolts, still smell the singed skin from the fire and electricity hurtled through the corridors of the palace.

If her advisors had been captured, or worse, killed, then no one would be coming for them. Lily considered that Ezra, the Meridian ambassador, might sound the alarm, but he wasn't even supposed to know about the interdimensional travel machine. Maybe he'd keep quiet to avoid any trouble. But he and Ava were close; surely he would want to help her?

"Um, Lily?" Ava looked at her with concern. "What is it? Do you know what's going on?"

Reacting to Lily's blanched face, both Ava and Alexei had adopted more alert postures and were scanning their surroundings.

"Sorry." She shook her head and plastered on a smile. "Everything's fine, we're okay."

Ava and Alexei looked at her dubiously, neither relaxing.

Lily tried to calm her thoughts and order them into an

explanation that wouldn't scare her friends. She swallowed and looked around nervously, her heart pounding. How was she going to tell them that getting home was going to be extremely difficult, if not impossible?

Due to recent unrest in the Disputed Region, an area of land between Highacre and Meridia, namely Meridia taking control of Highacren mines, Highacre had no felixium, the extremely rare mineral needed to power the inter-dimensional travel machine.

Well, there wasn't supposed to be any, but then, how did the cloaked figure power the machine to push us through?

But the machine had been on when Lily entered the room. Perhaps someone other than the cloaked figure had operated it? Could it have been Ezra? But that still didn't explain where the felixium came from.

Either way, they couldn't get back to Highacre until her advisors—assuming they were okay—were able to source more felixium, and she had no idea how they would do that, or how long it would take. And, Lily realized, there was no way for her and her advisors to communicate. She didn't know if they would even be able to tell which dimension they had gone to.

Communicate ...

Something clicked and Lily hitched up the heavy skirts of her dress, groping awkwardly for the pocket in her tights. Fumbling, she managed to withdraw a small metal disk, and held it reverently for a moment. Jenkins had told her it was a communicator. A way for those back in Highacre to communicate with people who had travelled to another dimension. He hadn't yet gotten it to work when he gave it to her, but that was a while ago. Maybe ...

Lily began frantically pressing the disk, gently at first, then squeezing it between her fingers. One click. Double click. She began commanding it to work in case Jenkins had made it voice operated. The longer it went without reacting, the more certain Lily was that it wasn't operational, but she couldn't stop herself from continuing to try.

To their credit, though they cast some odd looks at Lily, neither Ava nor Alexei questioned what Lily was doing, or why. Instead, they simply watched as Lily squeezed and yelled at the tiny, inanimate object.

After Lily gave up, her friends watched her, probably hoping she might offer an explanation or try something else. Instead, Lily lapsed into silence, her mind reeling.

"Lily?" Ava broke into Lily's train of thought, grabbing her arms and shaking her gently from her reverie. "What is going on?"

How am I going to explain this?

Lily looked at Ava and Alexei, who were both staring back at her, expectant, worried expressions on their faces.

"We're at my home," Lily said.

"You live in a barn?" Alexei asked, looking around, confused.

"Not *here* specifically. We're at my family's farm. Where I grew up."

"Oh," said Ava, sounding relieved. "We're in Oppulus." She smiled, having figured it out, then frowned again. "How did we get to Oppulus?"

"This must be the big secret that Highacre has been keeping." Alexei nodded sagely. "Teleportation."

Ava's eyes grew wide, everything clicking into place in her mind. She nodded slowly and started looking around the barn again. "Oooo, cows! Weird cows ... where are their other horns?"

"We're not in Oppulus." Lily sighed, drawing their attention back to her. "I have never been to Oppulus. We're in another dimension."

Ava and Alexei stared blankly at Lily.

"The big secret that Highacre has been keeping is that they found a way to travel to other dimensions. That machine we were pushed through is how they travel. They hid me here as a baby to ensure the succession of the royal line."

Ava and Alexei looked at each other. Lily felt sure that they were thinking she must have taken a blow to the head, but then Ava said slowly, "So, not Oppulus."

"Not Oppulus, no."

Lily did her best to explain to her friends what her advisors had explained to her when she first arrived in Highacre. How the machine worked and the interplay of the multiple dimensions. They asked similar questions to those she had asked, mainly concerned with what was the same and what was different. Thankfully, when this dimension was selected for Lily to grow up in, careful attention had been given to finding as similar a dimension as possible to minimise the shock of change should she ever need to return.

Alexei mulled the information over for a minute and then asked, "How do we go home?"

Lily swallowed thickly. "We can't. Apparently, you're meant to travel with a thingy that interacts with the machine back in Highacre to bring you back, and we don't have it. Plus, you need a mineral called felixium to power the machine, and there isn't any. Well, there wasn't supposed to be any. Anyway, we'll have to wait for my advisors to get some more and then come through and retrieve us."

Silence met Lily's news as both Alexei and Ava considered their predicament. Alexei got up and moved towards the cows while Ava sat on a nearby hay bale and looked at Lily.

"I can't believe we didn't bring a thingy. Who travels interdimensionally without a thingy?"

Lily stared at Ava. She was silently panicking, wondering if they would ever be able to get back to Highacre, and Ava was ... joking?

"That's it? I just told you we're stuck in another dimension and you're cracking jokes?"

"Well, by the sounds of things, there's not much we can do about it. And the other option is that you bumped your head and made all of this up. Either way, I figure that while I'm with the queen of Highacre, there'll be a few people looking for us, so it's only a matter of time until we're rescued."

"About that ..." Lily started pacing, wringing her hands. "The commotion you heard? The one that drew you to the room with the machine? Some rogue guards attacked us on the way to the coronation."

"Lily!" Ava jumped up, scanning Lily for injuries. Lily raised her hands to reassure her friends.

"No, I'm fine. I'm not hurt. Naomi got me away and told me to hide." Guilt washed over Lily. She knew it had been the right thing to do, but she still felt like a coward.

"You did the right thing," Ava said reassuringly.

"Absolutely." Alexei nodded. "They would have been able to fight more freely knowing you were safe."

Lily knew they were right, but it didn't change how she felt. And if anyone had been hurt, or worse ... she shook the thought away.

"The problem for us is, if my advisors are ... if they're unable to help us, then I don't know what will happen. We might be stuck here." Lily resumed her frantic pacing.

Alexei grunted, absentmindedly patting one of the cows.

"Well," began Ava thoughtfully. "It's unlikely that they

were *all* killed, but even in that worst-case scenario, Ezra saw what happened to us. He'll get help, so all we need to do is stay calm and be patient."

"Of course. Assuming the hooded guy didn't kill him," said Alexei unhelpfully.

"Ezra could take that guy, easy," said Ava with a confidence Lily suspected was put on. "And besides, Hooded Guy didn't even have a weapon. Who attacks people without a weapon?"

"Well, clearly he didn't want to kill Lily," said Alexei.

"Exactly," said Ava triumphantly.

"Doesn't mean he wouldn't have killed Ezra."

"The point is," Ava said, glaring at Alexei, "it's extremely unlikely that someone hasn't already raised the alarm. They're probably trying to figure out how to rescue us as we speak."

Lily tried to believe Ava. She wasn't as confident that Ezra would help, assuming he was alive.

Wait—Jenkins saw us!

He would be able to help, and if anyone could figure out where they had been sent, it was Jenkins.

"So, do we stay in the barn and wait to be rescued?" Alexei looked around appraisingly.

Lily shook her head. "We can stay with my family until someone figures out how to find us. They'll be up at the house."

Lily led Alexei and Ava to the door of the barn, and they exited into the crisp night air. Lily looked around and took in the familiar sight of home. She hadn't realised how much she missed it until now. An ache grew in her heart, and she could even feel tears pricking her eyes. The conflicting emotions of being happy to be home and being worried about what was happening back in Highacre were a lot to bear. Taking in a deep breath, Lily savoured the smells and turned to look up the small hill at the house she had grown up in.

She supposed it might not look like much to her fellow travellers, but to her it was home, and she felt such relief looking at it again. The house was a one-storey sandstone building. There were a couple of rooms added on in a light brick that didn't exactly match the main building, but didn't entirely clash with it either. The wraparound porch was also stone, but the wooden deck out the back that her dad had added when she was a baby was sagging slightly and desperately needed a coat of paint.

There were a couple of old cars and other bits of machinery off to the side of the house, near a large shed where her dad and older brother David would work on them from time to time. And she could just make out her mum's vegetable garden in the dim light. Lily smiled. The familiarity of home was just what she needed after the last few months of stress and turmoil. She couldn't wait for one of her mum's bear hugs.

The three of them headed off, leaving the barn behind to the lowing of the cows, and started the trek up the hill towards Lily's house. The lights were on, so Lily was confident that someone would be up to greet them and make sure that there was room for them to sleep. She was excited to see her parents and tell them all about what she had been doing. She had come such a long way, and was proud of her achievements.

Her dad would just smile and nod from his favourite chair by the fire, taking it all in. Her mum would ask all the questions, wanting to know about the people and what everything looked like.

David, the eldest and only son, would no doubt have some input, some advice for Lily about a better way that she could have done something. He couldn't help himself and it drove Lily mad, but all the same, she found that she was eager to hear what it was about her last few months that he would have done better.

Her older sister Elaine would want to hear about all the societal differences and how the people lived, and Lily realised that she would have little to tell her. Her rigorous preparations to learn all about her new country and pass the Trials to become queen had taken all of her time, and she had not been able to get out and about to really see High-acre and its people. No doubt Ava and Alexei would be able to fill her in about their world.

Little April would just sit and listen, grinning at Lily, excited to have her back. When it all quieted down a bit, April would find Lily in her room and ask all the questions she didn't want to ask in front of the rest of them.

They were nearly at the porch now, and Lily's smile faltered slightly on her face. Her family's voices sounded different somehow. Trying to make them out, Lily grabbed the handle and went to enter, but it didn't move and she jarred her shoulder on the door. Lily blinked. Since when did they lock the door?

Lily caught the curious expressions on her friends' faces and shrugged. "We never use this door anyway."

She led them around to a side door. As Lily entered the mud room, her anxiety increased. Something was wrong. Things looked ... different. But she continued forward, as if unable to stop. Lily opened the door to the kitchen. The look of shock on her face was mirrored by the four strangers sitting around the dinner table. The family froze, staring wide-eyed at the intruders.

2

"Er, can we help you?" asked an older man, standing hesitantly from his seat at the head of the table.

"Sorry," said Lily reflexively.

What is going on here?

Lily blinked and tried to get her brain to work. "Sorry, I thought ..."

"What the hell are you wearing?"

"Jenny!"

"What? They look weird. And that dress ..." The teenage girl who had spoken, Jenny, made a face like she wanted to vomit.

Try wearing it.

Lily was still encased in the monstrosity of a dress that she had to wear to her coronation. She had been so fixated on it a few hours ago, and now it was the least of her worries.

"Who are you, and what are you doing in our house?" A middle-aged woman, small but with a formidable presence, stood and approached Lily, Ava, and Alexei. Though projecting confidence, Lily could tell that she was scared. The woman eyed them cautiously and positioned herself in front of her son, who looked about ten and was staring at the group as if they had arrived from outer space.

"I'm so sorry," Lily apologised again. "I thought my family lived here. They used to live here, I think ..." Lily trailed off again, her mind running through possible explanations.

Maybe this wasn't her home dimension after all. Maybe it was a similar one, or they had been sent somewhere else in that multiverse that Jenkins sometimes rambled about. Or it was the right dimension, but her family had moved. That seemed wrong, though. Her father would never leave the farm. Nor David, for that matter. Suddenly, Lily was engulfed in doubt. Could she have been mistaken? It was late; perhaps they had arrived at a different farm? She had felt so sure this was her home, but with the interdimensional travel, not to mention the drama of the attack, maybe she was wrong.

The family was staring at her like she might be a few sandwiches short of a picnic. Then something clicked behind the mother's eyes.

"Wait, it's you, isn't it? The daughter who went missing."

Lily's eyes widened, the blood draining from her face.

"Oh!" The woman's hands flew to her mouth, her suspicion confirmed. She looked at her husband, who echoed her surprise. She reached for Lily's hands and Lily flinched back, immediately regretting doing so.

"I'm sorry. Oh, you poor thing. Your poor mother. Gosh, I wonder how we can contact her ..."

Lily's cheeks burned with shame as realisation crashed down on her. Of course her disappearing for six months would have attracted attention. For some reason, she had been assuming that her family would have noticed, perhaps been a bit worried, but that would be it. Now, however, several things clicked painfully into place. Her family wouldn't have simply sat idly by, wondering where she was and what had happened. There were processes and procedures, the police ...

Having to try to explain what happened to the authorities was the last thing Lily wanted to do. And how would she explain Ava and Alexei? They had no identification, no history here.

The mother had started going down some of the paths that Lily had, and when she suggested they contact the police, Lily distracted her by asking what had happened to her family.

"We bought this farm a few months ago. The family that sold it ..." The woman hesitated, looking for the right words. "They couldn't afford it anymore. The real estate agent told me that they spent all their money looking for their missing daughter. That *is* you, isn't it?"

This wasn't happening. Lily's mind felt fuzzy. She tried to tell herself this wasn't real. But her heart knew. She could feel that this was home. Except apparently it wasn't anymore.

"Do you know where the family went?" asked Ava, putting a comforting hand on Lily's shoulder and peering around her.

"No, sorry," the woman said earnestly. "The agent just said she thought they were moving to the city."

Lily's stomach dropped. She could picture her family moving into a smaller house in town if they had to, but the city? They weren't city people. Her dad would hate it. Not to mention that it was huge. Without something more useful than "the city" to go off, there was no way they'd be able to track them down.

Lily became vaguely aware of the conversation ongoing with Ava and the mother.

"... stay here and work if you like while you look for them."

"That's very kind—"

"Not at all. We could use the help, to be honest. This farming business is not as straightforward as you might think." The mother laughed, seeming embarrassed.

There was a slight commotion back at the table, followed by the father hissing at his daughter to be quiet.

"What? I'd run away with him too." She smiled appreciatively at Alexei, winking at him when she caught his eye. Alexei frowned. "And you've all been, what? At a fancy dress party? Or some weird rave or something?"

"Jenny!"

Lily and her friends all looked at each other, suddenly very aware of how odd their attire was, and how unsuitable it was for anything that wasn't the coronation they had missed.

"I hate to impose," Ava said, smiling at the mother, "but you wouldn't happen to have any old clothes you'd be willing to part with?"

"Oh, I was just putting some bags together to take to the charity bin in town," the mother said, brightening at being able to help. "Jenny, go get the bags."

Jenny ignored her mother; she was too busy smiling flirtatiously at Alexei, who was growing increasingly uncomfortable.

"Jenny."

Jenny winked at Alexei and blew him a kiss.

"Jenny."

Jenny pulled out her phone, snapped a picture of Alexei, and began tapping away, obviously sending the image to all her friends.

"JENNY!"

"What?"

"Go and get the bags of clothes." The mother smiled awkwardly at the strangers in her kitchen. Jenny kept tapping on her phone.

"Now!" the mother yelled.

"Alright, geez. Keep your panties on." She got up and circled the table, going out of her way to ensure she walked past Alexei. "I'm certainly not wearing any," she said, gazing seductively at him.

"Jenny!" exclaimed her parents in unison.

"I might wait outside," Alexei excused himself with a polite nod to the family.

Jenny returned, and upon seeing Alexei gone, her face fell and she dumped the bag unceremoniously at Lily's feet. When her father stopped her from following Alexei outside, Jenny stomped to her room, screaming about how unfair life was and how much she hated it there at the farm.

Lily and Ava quickly rummaged through the bags of clothes, grabbing a few options for themselves and Alexei, and gratefully assuring the mother that they didn't need more than what they were taking.

"Would it be alright if we got changed in the barn?" Ava asked. Lily got the impression that the mother would agree to anything that made her feel as if she was helping. They took the packets of jerky the mother pushed into their hands with apologies that she didn't have a better dinner for them.

Promising to let her know if they wanted to take up the offer of work in exchange for a place to stay while they figured things out, Ava and Lily tried to extract themselves from the farmhouse. With several apologies for barging in, as well as for upsetting Jenny, and much gratitude for the food and clothes, Ava and Lily finally exited the house and went to find Alexei.

3

"Ah, there you are," said Ava. Alexei had been standing in the shadows behind a nearby shed. "I half expected you to be in a tight embrace with Jenny."

Alexei scowled and eyed the bundle of clothes. "You better not have picked anything outlandish for me."

"It's okay, I picked yours," said Lily. "And besides, of all of us, most of what you already have is normal. If you ditched the bling and maybe the jacket, you're basically in business casual."

They turned and headed towards the barn. In the silence, Lily became lost in her thoughts. This was not the homecoming she had expected. Whenever she'd imagined going home while she was stuck in Highacre, it was some variation of her family gathered somewhere cosy and warm, all excitedly asking her about her adventures.

Now that seemed like such a naïve fantasy.

Her going missing had cost her family the farm. Their livelihood. Their home. And they'd gone to the city. The only reason Lily could think that they would go to the city was the greater range of work available, which meant that not only had they lost the farm, but they hadn't made much on the sale. *Or Dad spent it all on trying to find me.* Her stomach dropped at that thought.

Then again, if they were so worried about her, surely moving so far away was counterintuitive. Wouldn't they expect her to look for them at the farm if she returned? Why hadn't they left forwarding information with the new owners?

Ava touched Lily's arm, bringing her out of her thoughts, and Lily found they were back in the barn. She couldn't recall the walk down there at all. They wordlessly went to separate corners of the barn and changed into more comfortable clothes. Ava had to help Lily out of her dress. After a few minutes, they were all in casual attire, jeans and loose tops that were comfortable but smart enough that they wouldn't get kicked out of a restaurant.

Now more appropriately dressed, they all found themselves back in the centre of the barn. Ava and Alexei pulled up a couple more hay bales, and they all sat down.

"So ..." Ava began, looking from Lily to Alexei. "What do we do now?"

"It's getting late. We should probably find somewhere to sleep," said Alexei.

"Sure, but I meant in general. You know, now that we're stranded here in this dimension and we don't know where Lily's family is, or if we're going to be rescued."

They both looked at Lily. Lily knew she should have an answer for them. A plan. This was her home world after all, and she was the one who knew about interdimensional travel. Not to mention she had almost been crowned the ruler of an entire country. It wasn't unreasonable for them to think she might have a way forward. But Lily was still stunned at finding her family gone, and her world felt like it had been turned upside down. Again.

"I think we can probably get away with sleeping here tonight," Alexei offered. "We'll be warm and dry."

"Jenny will come keep you warm," Ava teased.

"That is a risk." Alexei nodded solemnly. "But I trust you'll protect me from her, Ava."

Ava and Alexei kept up their banter as they got up and started shifting some of the hay bales and collecting rugs and tarpaulins. Before Lily's eyes, they set up a little sleeping area that didn't look too uncomfortable. She looked at her friends gratefully, realising how lucky she was that they had been pushed through with her. It might have been unlucky for them, but Lily would be lost right now if she had been on her own. She mentally tried to pull herself together.

"I guess we really have two options," Lily finally said. Ava and Alexei looked up in surprise, having given up on discussing a plan until the morning.

"Alright, what are they?" Ava asked, settling herself down on one of the makeshift beds.

Lily moved over to join them. "Well, we can stay here. I mean, in the general area. Maybe get some work here or on one of the nearby farms. That would let us remain in proximity to the last coordinates that would have been entered into the machine, which is the likely place anyone will start looking for us."

"What's option two?" asked Alexei.

"We go to the city and try to find my family."

The three sat in silence, considering their predicament. The options weren't great. And neither offered a proactive way home.

"I get that you might want to try to find your family Lily, but in terms of potentially getting home, how would that help?" Ava asked gently.

"Yeah, it sounds like it might be worse. Moving away

from this location, and with no way for whoever comes through to find us," Alexei added.

"I'm sure Jenny will be able to find you."

"Shut up, Ava."

"We could make sure these people could contact us," said Lily, cutting off the good-natured bickering. "If we can get a cheap phone in town, then we could leave a number for them to call if someone shows up looking for us. But you're right. It really doesn't offer much in the way of getting home. That said, neither option *helps* us get home. No matter what, we're completely reliant on my advisors fixing things from their end."

"Assuming they're alive," Ava muttered.

Lily looked at her friends. Despite the curveball they'd been thrown, both Ava and Alexei appeared to be taking it in stride and keeping their high spirits. But she could also hear worry in their voices and see the concern on their faces, hidden though they were by shadow in the dimly lit barn.

"Look. Things are pretty terrible right now. We don't know if people back home are looking for us, and if they are, it's not going to be easy for them to come and get us. Which leaves us with what to do with our time here. We may be stuck for a while."

Lily tried to project confidence in the fact that they would be rescued; to present it as a forgone conclusion rather than a distant possibility. Ava and Alexei glanced at each other, sharing a look that seemed to communicate something not meant for Lily. She felt a pang of exclusion.

"I do think we need to maintain a link here," Alexei said. "Whether that's physically remaining in the area, coming back to check, or leaving forwarding details, we need a way to know if your advisors come to get us."

"Agreed," said Ava.

Lily nodded. "Absolutely. The last thing we want is for them to come looking for us with no way to find us. And it'll drive us all nuts wondering if they've showed up." She took a deep breath. "But once we've done that, I really need to try to find my family. I know it's going to be hard. We don't really have anything to go on. But something's gone really wrong here for them to sell and move to the city, and it sounds like it's my fault."

"No, Lily—"

"It is," Lily interrupted Alexei's attempt to make her feel better. "I know I didn't choose to leave. And it's not my fault that no one left any information on where I was or that I was alright. That's on other people. But it was my going missing that has caused whatever happened to my family, so I need to find them and let them know I'm okay, and see if I can help fix it."

Ava and Alexei remained silent, staring at the ground. Ava fiddled with a piece of straw, then took a deep breath.

"I hear you Lily. And I get it, I do. But I really think we need to stay here, at least for a little while," she added hurriedly, sensing that Lily was going to interrupt. Alexei was nodding fervently. "We don't know what happened after we went through. Maybe the machine is still on."

That had not occurred to Lily. How long did the machine work for with each dose of felixium? How much was even needed to power it each time? Or did it need a steady stream of felixium to remain operational? It struck Lily that she was inconveniently ignorant about the operation of the machine. She felt embarrassed, like this was something she should know.

"It's got to have been at least an hour," said Lily, in part to avoid any questions about the machine that she could not answer. "If someone was coming, I think they'd be here by now."

"You said there was a fight," said Alexei. "It's possible that they are addressing the aftermath of that before coming through for us."

"Yeah, and it happening so soon after the terrorist attack at the arena ... I wonder if they are related," Ava said.

"That's the issue though, isn't it?" said Lily, absently rubbing her arm where she'd been shot during the arena attack. "Anything's possible. We have no way of knowing."

"But that's why we should stay put at the moment," said Ava. Lily felt a pang of disappointment in her chest. "It's more likely that if they can get us, they'll do so quickly. We should stay here, at least in the short-term, in case they are able to come for us."

Lily blinked furiously. Tears burned her eyes. She felt sick. She felt guilty enough about abandoning her family in the first place, and that wasn't even her fault. But now that she was back, if she didn't immediately set off to find them so she could tell them that she was okay and help them with whatever problems they now had because of her, it felt like a betrayal. How would they ever believe that she hadn't left voluntarily if she didn't try to find them straightaway? An inconvenient thought occurred to Lily.

"So if they do turn up, we just go straight back?"

"Of course," said Alexei.

Lily looked at him. "Something is very wrong with my family. Knowing that, I can't just ignore it and head back to Highacre and pretend everything is fine."

"Lily." Ava looked at her with a mix of sympathy and something close to fear. "You said yourself that there's a lack of the stuff needed to power the machine. We may only get one chance to return."

"I can't leave without seeing my family."

"We can't miss the rescue. What if they come through

and can't find us and conclude that we're in a whole other dimension? They might never come back here for us."

Now her friends' calm veneers were cracking, and Lily could see the fear, the beginnings of panic. For her, this was home. If she was stuck here forever, she would regret not returning to Highacre, but she would be okay. For Ava and Alexei, they would be marooned in a foreign world.

Lily sighed and looked around the barn as if the solution would jump out at her.

"I mean, I suppose we can split up."

Neither of her friends liked that idea at all, and the three went back and forth, all of them frustrated with the situation.

"Look," said Alexei after an awkward pause that had followed a particularly heated exchange between Lily and Ava. "I know you want to go to find your family right away. But there's no indication that they're in any immediate danger, right?"

"No, but—"

"And you don't know exactly where they are."

"Yeah, but—"

"So perhaps a compromise is that we stay at the farm for a few days—"

"A week at least," Ava said quickly, earning her a glare from Alexei.

"—and we can plan for a trip to the city. At least earn some money. That way, we keep an eye on the likely rescue location, and we can better prepare to find your family. Not to mention procure a phone so these people can call us if anyone shows up."

Neither Lily nor Ava looked comfortable with this compromise. Lily wanted to leave for the city immediately and Ava had voiced her fear of not being near their arrival location in case of a rescue. Ava worried that they would only have one shot, and if they were too far away, they may not get back in time to make it home.

I suppose if Mum and Dad ask about the delay, I can say I needed money for a ticket to the city and that's why I didn't come immediately.

Lily felt instantly guilty for focussing on having an excuse. She knew Alexei's compromise made sense. She would just have to deal with her family if they asked. With another pang of guilt, she realised that there was really no way her family would know when she had gotten back. They didn't seem to talk to the new owners. *But I'll know.* She could suck up her guilt for her friends' peace of mind.

Lily looked at them. Both were making small adjustments to their sleeping setups. Neither looked overly worried. From the discussion, she knew that they were expecting—hoping—to be rescued soon. A few days at most. Lily did not expect to be rescued any time soon. The complete lack of felixium for the six months that she had been in Highacre told her that it was going to take a while for her advisors to obtain some.

If they can at all. Wasn't that half the reason they brought me back?

But *someone* clearly had some felixium, so maybe she was wrong.

"You're right," said Lily, earning surprised looks from Ava and Alexei. "We should stay here for a few days to a week. Earn some money, get some supplies. And if we haven't been rescued by then, we can leave our details here and go find my family."

"Sounds like a plan," said Ava, obviously trying to sound more positive since Lily was open to compromise, though Lily could tell that she was still wary about leaving the location at all. "I mean, why come to a new dimension and not explore, right?"

"How much work do you think we need to do here to make enough to get to the city?" Alexei asked.

"And what do you think they're going to make us do?" Ava added, looking faux-horrified, trying to lighten the mood.

"We can definitely make enough in a week to get us a phone, bus tickets, and probably have a place to stay in the city for a few nights."

Lily absently looked around their current lodgings, thinking that if her friends were okay bedding down in a barn, then they could stretch out their money in the city by staying in backpacker's hostels.

Her eyes fell on her coronation dress.

Giles would kill her.

She smiled wickedly. Ava saw her expression and followed her gaze.

"We can take the gems off my dress," Lily said. "We should be able to sell them for some money. There's nothing much in town, but the city'll have options for us. We might even be able to use them to support us until we're rescued if we're smart."

4

As EXPECTED, Jenny's mother, who introduced herself as Doreen, was only too happy to pay them to work in the fields. She offered a rate that even Lily, who was keen to get to the city as quickly as possible, felt uncomfortable accepting.

When Lily reluctantly suggested that Doreen would be overpaying them, Doreen laughed, embarrassed, and admitted that she and her husband might have bitten off more than they could chew in buying the farm. Neither of them had the slightest idea about how to manage it day-to-day, and they would likely need to hire someone to run it. Doreen was happy to pay a higher price for Lily and her friends to help make the farm look less run-down, which might then save her money in hiring someone who might not realise exactly how little she and her husband knew about farming.

Lily knew that some of the increased payment was sympathy for her circumstances, and perhaps projection. Lily could picture Jenny running away and getting herself into trouble, and she expected Doreen could too, and was treating Lily how she hoped someone would treat her Jenny in similar circumstances.

The idea that they would be helping the family helped Lily swallow her pride and not haggle the price down further. That, and her spiking anxiety about what had happened to her family.

Doreen had been only too happy to let Lily use her phone to try and contact them. Lily had opened the phone app only to realise that all her contacts were saved in her old phone. She was pretty sure she remembered her parents' numbers. They had been drilled into her as a child, and neither had changed them in the intervening years. But an electronic voice told her that her father's number was no longer in service, and her mother's number went straight to voicemail. She left a brief message, apologising for disappearing and letting her mother know she was trying to find them. She gave Doreen's number as the best way to contact her and hung up feeling deflated.

Next, Lily tried email. But her overreliance on the convenience of her smartphone thwarted her again. Unable to remember her own email password, she quickly created a new email account and tried to remember everyone's email addresses.

David had one for work, and Brandon and Gemma would have a school emails. Lily was fairly sure their addresses were their names and then the respective organisations, so she gave them a go, despite a niggling doubt in her stomach that Brandon's email address had contained a number. She had always texted him though, so she wasn't sure. She then tried to remember if her sister Elaine's email was ClassyGrl26 or 27. Hedging her bets, Lily sent an email to both variations.

But the biggest concern was when she logged into her newly created social media accounts—she'd forgotten those passwords too—and searched for her siblings. She knew Elaine and April had accounts, but they seemed to have disappeared. Brandon had stopped using his account last year, claiming it was "how the system controlled you". Lily had rolled her eyes, but his passion had resounded with Gemma, who had similarly stopped using hers at the same time. Lily could still see their pages though, and sent them both messages just in case it would trigger a notification.

But where were her sisters? Closing the pages for her new social media accounts, Lily opened an internet browser window and searched for her name and "missing". A couple of generic news articles appeared, noting that her family hadn't heard from her and was worried. One article detailed her father's efforts to find her—apparently even handing out flyers on street corners and offering a reward for information. Her stomach dropped. That reward money must have been from the sale of the farm.

Guilt consuming her, Lily added "reward" to her search and gasped in shock at the top result. A more recent news article reported that her family had been accused of lying. Someone had tried to claim the reward and had been informed that it was withdrawn as the family no longer had the money. This had prompted an angry backlash where internet trolls had targeted her family, accusing them of making the whole thing up, suggesting that Lily was fine and the story about her going missing was some grab for attention.

Lily closed the internet browser in disgust. Why would anyone make something like that up? There had been no suggestion of what her family was allegedly seeking to gain from the story. She tried to remind herself that internet trolls rarely needed logic, but she bitterly realised why she could no longer find her sisters online.

Lily returned the phone to Doreen, playing up her hope

that the voicemail or messages she sent would prove successful, then headed to the fields to find her friends.

The manual labour was hard going. Lily did not know what happened to the farming equipment her father had owned. Perhaps it had been sold off piecemeal before the entire property was abandoned. Whatever the reason, the new family did not have the appropriate machinery and did not appear to realise that they needed it. As a result, after urging Doreen's husband, Matt, to invest in a tractor, if for no other reason than to save on labour costs, Lily and her friends found themselves ploughing a field with mattocks and hoes.

Blisters reminded Lily that it had been a long time since she had done any physical work, but she found she was enjoying being outdoors, and the manual labour was distracting her from her worries and the nagging feeling that she should be looking for her family.

She could see it was good for her friends too, although she caught Ava regularly glancing at the barn, a hopeful expression on her face.

"If a bunch of palace guards bust out of the barn, I think we'll hear about it pretty quickly," Lily said, trying to reassure Ava.

"I know. But I figure it's good to keep checking. It's possible that if they run into Jenny first, they might retreat into the barn to hide."

Lily laughed. "Well, if they're hiding from Jenny, then we won't see them either."

"You're forgetting." Ava tapped her temple. "X-ray vision."

"Wait," said Lily, stopping digging and gaping at Ava. "Your implant works here?"

"Yeah, why wouldn't it?"

"But ..." Lily turned to Alexei. "What about your enchantments?"

"I'm flattered that you think I could carry the tools and all that fertiliser down here that easily without assistance, but yes, my belt is fully functional." He patted it fondly.

"That's such horse manure. How come your stuff works when my magic doesn't?"

"Wait, your magic doesn't work here?" Ava asked.

"No, Addison told me that it doesn't work in this world. She didn't know why, though."

Ava and Alexei glanced at each other. "So, you haven't tried?" Ava asked, resuming her digging.

Lily followed suit, hacking at the ground in front of her, trying to hide the blush burning her cheeks. Why hadn't she tried? She tried to convince herself that not only was it perfectly reasonable to have taken Addison at face value, but it also wasn't like she'd had plenty of time and opportunities to try her magic out.

"'Cause I'm just saying," Ava continued, "if I've been digging this field when you could have just, like, blown it open, I might feel a little put out."

Lily laughed. "I am unaware of any latent farming magic."

Hesitantly, Lily reached for her power and was relieved to feel it waiting for her. She was so used to it now that she hadn't even realised it was still there. She took a deep breath, trying to stem her frustration. Why hadn't she even tried? Surely if Addison had been right, Lily would have noticed her power being gone when she arrived back home. It would have been conspicuous in its absence, like the sudden loss of one of your senses.

Lily continued to hack at the ground with her mattock while focussing on trying to move some of the smaller rocks with her mind. Her power felt different. At first the rocks didn't move, but Lily kept trying and eventually was pleasantly surprised to see the rocks bounce around, if slightly erratically.

Her magic was there, but it seemed to work differently. It felt like using your non-dominant hand to write—less coordinated and weaker. But luckily for Lily, she had recently been through a magic bootcamp in order to prepare for the Trials. If she practised, she was confident she could bring her powers back up to full speed.

Lily frowned. Had Addison been lying to her? Or was the difference in how magic worked enough that the early scouts had assumed it didn't work at all? Surely if the royal family—her family—knew that magic worked here, they would have left someone to teach her. It didn't make sense to keep her safe as a last resort but fail to appropriately prepare her.

Lily thought about what might have happened if she hadn't been able to learn to use her magic. Highacre would be in the clutches of the prime minister and probably already at war with Meridia.

Have I really stopped that, though? He's probably declaring war right now, while I'm stuck here.

Though gripped with a strong urge to be back in Highacre to fix everything, Lily felt an equally strong pull to go and find her family, to help them too. She had no idea how she could fix the issues plaguing Highacre, nor how she might help her family, but the need to try something—anything—was strong.

Lily stopped digging, stretching her back. Equally strong was a shameful desire to hide. Before her return, she had assumed everything was fine with her family. Part of her wished she had never found out things had gone horribly wrong. A small part of her even wanted to remain on the farm until they were rescued. Her family didn't know she was back—maybe she could keep it that way.

"I wonder where they would have gone," Lily said out loud, trying to banish her selfish thoughts. "My family, I mean."

Ava and Alexei gave noncommittal grunts, their focus remaining on the field.

"There are some nicer houses out in the suburbs. Probably there. I can't imagine them in an apartment. Though that would mean they'd be closer to work ... and that's why they left."

Lily rambled on, but eventually stopped talking. Ava and Alexei kept working, not engaging with Lily's musings about her family. It bothered Lily that neither of them seemed interested. She had made a pretty big compromise in agreeing to stay here—particularly in light of the evidence that her family was in trouble.

Lily began second-guessing herself. Had she deferred to Ava and Alexei too easily? Had she given in to what they wanted, or had part of her wanted that too—to delay finding out what her absence had cost her family?

Lily hacked a little more violently at the ground. She glanced up and saw that Ava and Alexei were similarly lost in their own thoughts. Trying to distract her mind from her impotent frustration, Lily took to practicing her magic while she worked.

The three continued to dig in silence. Gradually, the silence grew charged, like the feeling of electricity before a storm. Lily tried to engage her friends again, asking them how long they should stay at the farm, and how much money they should earn as a buffer before leaving. When that didn't work, she simply prattled on about her family.

They were on her mind and all she could think to talk about, and Lily figured any diversion was a good one.

Lily eventually fell silent again. She sensed her friends were fatigued and worried. They looked toward the barn less, and when they did, despair covered their faces. She realised that they had been expecting a fast rescue. And the longer no one appeared, the more likely it was that no one was coming. The silence stretched out. All of them were spending too much time in their heads, entertaining worst-case scenarios. Lily decided they needed a distraction.

"I think you're both going to really like the city," she began. "If we have time, I can show you some of the things that are different here. We might go to the zoo and the museum. Oh!" Lily stopped digging and looked up excitedly. "The airport! You can see the planes, and I mean, if we can make some money on the gems from my dress, and we have time, we might even be able to take a flight—"

"Can you give it a rest? Please?" Ava said. "We get it. You want to go to the city and find your family. Talking about all these great things for us to see is not going to change our minds about staying here for a bit first."

Lily felt as if Ava had slapped her across the face. "I didn't mean—"

"It's alright for you. They came for you once. You know they're going to try everything they can for as long as they can to come and rescue you. No one's coming for us." As Ava gestured at Alexei, she did a double take. "Well, I guess your dad will come for you. No one's coming for me, that's for sure." Ava muttered the last, hacking once again at the ground in front of her.

"My father may use my disappearance as leverage with Highacre," Alexei allowed, considering the situation. "To gain an advantage for Valmead. But that would be it. And besides, all he would know is that I'm missing. He wouldn't know about interdimensional travel, and I doubt Highacre will tell him. At least Ezra knows exactly what happened to you and where you are."

"Ezra won't—" Ava swallowed her words, then resumed hacking at the ground. She seemed even angrier than before.

Lily stared at Ava. Where had that anger come from? Lily couldn't help but feel hurt by what she saw as an undeserved attack. *Was it undeserved?* She returned to digging and spent a good ten minutes re-examining her words and behaviour to see if she might have somehow upset Ava without realising. Coming up with nothing, Lily decided that it must be the stress of the situation. She was so used to Ava being cool and calm, she hadn't expected her to react like this. But it was perfectly reasonable for her to be stressed with the possibility of being trapped in an unfamiliar dimension.

"Look, Ava," Lily began gently, deciding to forgive the unprovoked attack and try to help her friend. "I know this whole thing is hard—"

"Seriously Lily, would you please just shut up? You can't *fix* everything. And it's not yours to fix. You're not the linchpin, and we're not your—" Again, with an effort, Ava broke off from her rant and managed to stop herself from saying anything more. Dropping her hoe, she turned towards some trees a couple of hundred metres away. "Need to pee."

Lily watched her walk away, blinking furiously to stop her own tears. She would not cry. Ava attacking her hurt. A lot. She thought they were close. Perhaps she was mistaken. Alexei looked as if he was about to say something, so Lily turned and walked away towards the main house.

5

HALF AN HOUR LATER, Lily returned to the field. Ava was back and she and Alexei were working. Lily could hear their voices as she approached, though she couldn't make out the words. They stopped talking when they realised she was coming.

As Lily came up to them, Ava turned, looking calmer and apologetic. "Lily, I—"

"Lunch," said Lily curtly, balancing a tray on the sides of the wheelbarrow. "I suggest we all raise our blood sugar levels before we attempt any further discussions."

Ava and Alexei approached the makeshift table eagerly, and soon they were all munching on the ploughman's lunch that Doreen had put together for them. Lily waited until they had all swallowed a few bites and Ava's mouth was full.

"Look, I do understand that all of this is much harder for both of you. Aside from our positions back home, I'm from here. It's familiar to me. I have people I know who I can reach out to if we're stuck here for … a long time." She stopped herself from saying forever. "I remember how I felt when I was told I was stuck in Highacre, and that was being stuck in a palace being treated as royalty. This is a bit different." Lily gestured to the mud and dirt and manure. Ava looked to be hurrying to swallow. Lily turned to her and continued before she could interrupt.

"I'm sorry for trying to make everything seem okay. It's not. Sometimes things are bad, and you're allowed to be upset or angry that they are. I should have been validating how you're feeling rather than trying to find a silver lining."

Ava smiled at Lily. "I'm sorry for being a bitch."

"You're always a bitch," said Alexei, earning a soft punch from Ava.

Ava took a deep breath, wiping her hands on her pants. "I feel validated now."

"Perhaps we should return to validating the field?" Alexei suggested.

"I validate your idea," said Ava.

As they turned back to their tools, Ava walked over and gave Lily a little squeeze. She returned it, her chest suddenly light, and her stomach did a little flip. Wondering if she shouldn't have had the apricots, Lily picked up her mattock and relaxed back into the distraction of manual labour and magical practise.

A few minutes later, Alexei headed off toward the same trees that Ava had stormed off to earlier, leaving the two women alone.

"I really am sorry," said Ava, stopping digging and looking at Lily.

"It's fine. We were all stressed and hungry—"

"No, I was way out of line," Ava interrupted. "And I'm sorry."

Lily stopped working and looked over at her friend. Clearly there was something more bothering Ava. Ava looked out at the mountains in the distance for a beat before taking a deep breath and continuing.

"A little while ago, I met my biological father. You remember I told you I was raised by my aunt for a bit? Well, according to her, my father was never really in the picture. Mum got pregnant and then couldn't cope and left me with her sister. Then a few months ago, my father turns up out of nowhere. He said he never knew Mum was pregnant. That if he'd known—" Ava's voice caught and she moved over to the fence, leaning on the wooden beam and staring out into the distance, sniffing and giving her eyes two annoyed swipes.

Lily walked over and stood beside her, looking out at the distance too, but leaning in so their shoulders touched. "Ava, that's huge."

"Yeah," said Ava. "I mean, I don't know if that's true. That he didn't know. But maybe he didn't."

Ava sounded so hopeful it broke Lily's heart. It was obvious she needed to believe him. To believe she wasn't abandoned by both parents. Lily remembered the sting of rejection she had felt learning that she had been exiled from her biological family, but at least they had a good reason, and had made sure she went to a loving home.

"Anyway, right before we were pushed through, he and I had a bit of a fight. Nothing too big. He was just thinking of doing some stuff that I think would be a mistake."

"What kind of stuff?" Lily asked.

"It doesn't matter." Ava shook off the question. "But I was thinking that I'd go to your coronation and then go talk to him. That we'd make up and I could talk some sense into him. But now we're stuck here and I feel terrible about the fight and I'm terrified he's going to do something stupid before I can stop him."

Curiosity mixed with sympathy for Ava. Lily also felt frustrated and trapped. She needed to get back to stop the prime minister. To stop the war. And Ava needed to help her father. That desire to help family was something Lily could easily relate to. Lily desperately wanted to know more about whatever issue Ava and her father had fought about, but she pushed that to the side, grateful that Ava had shared this much with her and not wanting to push her too far.

"Thank you for telling me," Lily said sincerely, pushing gently against Ava's arm.

"You deserved to know," Ava said, looking at Lily. "And I really am sorry for snapping at you like that."

"Oh, so I leave for two minutes and you stop work?" Alexei called, mock-angry.

"Uh oh," Ava said in a stage whisper to Lily, "task master is back."

"Sorry Alexei," both women called in sing-song voices, causing Alexei to smile before they all picked up their tools and got back to work.

"I've had enough!" Ava exclaimed, throwing her hoe into the dirt and walking to the wheelbarrow to get a drink of water. They were back in the field after having taken a break from digging for the last couple of days, mending fences and tending livestock instead. "I'm okay with manual labour. I really am. But it's doing my head in that this is pointless. Why can't they just buy a tractor? Or we could do some other task until they buy a tractor."

"Hard work is good for your soul, Ava," said Alexei solemnly, continuing his ploughing. Alexei had done more than twice as much as the girls, which Lily told herself was mainly due to his enchanted belt.

"My soul says they should buy a tractor."

Ava plodded back over to them, sighed, and dramatically wiped her sleeve across her brow, leaning on her hoe as she gulped from her water bottle. It was a hot day, and the field had no shade. The three of them were sweating as if they were in a sauna.

"You should be grateful—"

"Alexei, I swear to god, if you tell me one more time that I should be grateful to be outside and working with my hands ..." Ava trailed off, glaring at him.

Alexei stood up, smiling at Ava, clearly enjoying himself. "I was going to say that you should be grateful to have such a hands-on experience with this alien world."

"This 'hands-on experience'"—Ava gestured widely around them—"is a load of crap."

"I mean, you're not wrong." Alexei nodded. Opening another bag of fertiliser and pouring it around to mix in with the dirt. "You put the manure into the soil and the crops grow better."

Lily took one look at Ava's horrified expression as Alexei explained the smells around them and burst out laughing.

"It's not funny, Lily. Why didn't anyone tell me we were knees-deep in actual shit? This is bullshit."

"Yes," Alexei nodded enthusiastically, pleased she was understanding. "It is."

This resulted in Ava throwing some of the offending matter at Alexei while Lily collapsed to her knees in laughter, trying desperately to breathe. Lily felt relaxed for the first time in what felt like ages. Sure, the work was hard going, but there was something calm about doing a simple task that didn't relate to being responsible for an entire nation. Everything she had experienced lately seemed to come with so much stress and pressure. Digging in a field carried no obligations.

Her stomach fell, and she felt the invisible clamp wrench tight around her chest. Obligations. She *should* be

trying to find her family. They would expect her to prioritise that, and they'd be right.

Ava noticed Lily's expression fall and stopped laughing
with Alexei.

"Hey." Ava touched Lily's arm, bringing her back to the
present. She looked at Lily in concern.

"Oh, I'm alright." She waved Ava off. "It's just … I know
it's not my fault, but I feel so guilty about being away and
then everything seems to have fallen apart for my family.
I'm not trying to change our timeline," she hastened to add.
"I want to help my family, but what if I can't? I'm not even
looking for them at the moment. They all think I'm a failure
anyway. This will just prove it."

"You're not a failure," said Ava gently. "Look at what
you were able to do back in Highacre. You came in as an
outsider, a complete unknown quantity, and you managed
to not only win over your advisors, you showed them that
you were a capable leader for their country!"

Lily smiled, sniffling and trying not to cry. "Well, when
you put it like that, I guess I *am* pretty awesome." They all
laughed.

"But seriously, between that and learning from scratch
how to use your magic? And not only that, to get so good at
it that you completed the Trials? I heard people talking
when Alexei and I were watching. Apparently, no one
remembers anyone ever doing that well."

Lily thought about that. It occurred to her that her advisors had really only started treating her as a true sovereign
when she developed her abilities. Maybe if she hadn't been
able to develop them, or wasn't as powerful as she was, they
would have discarded her, opting to back a different ruler
for Highacre.

"I don't know that I agree with that," said Ava thoughtfully after Lily voiced her concern. "I mean, I think your

power and being able to use your abilities might have given you a confidence boost, but you're so much more than your magic, and your ability to lead isn't reliant on your magic."

"I agree," said Alexei. "My father rules without question. But if you took away the strict rules and discipline, would anyone follow him?"

Alexei kept digging as he spoke. Lily and Ava looked at each other. Alexei rarely spoke about his father.

"I don't know, Alexei," said Lily gently, "I don't know much about your dad, or your family, for that matter. Is he not much of a leader?" She was very curious about Alexei's family, as much because of her friendship with him as Valmead seeming to be a more mysterious country than Meridia or Highacre. But she didn't want to push him or make him talk about anything he wasn't comfortable with.

"I think he just never learned to communicate," said Alexei. "He's always had power and so people do what he says. I suppose he's never had to *lead*, since everyone automatically follows."

Lily and Ava were still as they watched Alexei, waiting to see if he would continue. It was as if they worried any movement might spook him. But the silence stretched to the point that Lily and Ava were readying their tools to get back to work when Alexei stopped and stretched.

"He expects the same of his family. When I was young, it was just my mother and father and me. They were good times, we were all very happy. But when I was about twelve years old, my mother died and my father shut out all that reminded him of her." He picked his mattock back up and continued to work. "Including me. I thought it would get better, but after a few years, he met my stepmother. She wasn't that much older than me. Five years maybe? Perhaps a couple more. Anyway, all my father cared about was making her happy. All she cared about was removing any threats to her position. When she had her first child, a boy, I was so excited to have a brother. Then my other half-siblings came, and I felt like I had a family again. My step-mother was still cold to me, but she let me play with them.

"When I turned eighteen, it was like my father came back to me. He was not like when I was young, but it was as if he saw me again. He announced that I must be trained to prepare to take his place. He would bring me to work with him and take me on trips. This enraged my stepmother. I heard them fighting one time. She was screaming at him that he had promised that her son would be his heir. My father just looked at her and said that his first son was his heir, and that was that. It hurt her to realise that his love for her was not as strong as his love of tradition, but my father is so used to people simply following his orders, it never seemed to occur to him that his change of heart might affect her.

"Afterwards, she limited my time with my siblings. Once, I managed to slip out and visit my brother while he was at soccer practice. I was so excited to see him, but he pushed me and yelled that I was trying to take his birthright away. None of my siblings would talk to me after that. She turned them against me."

Alexei stopped working again and wiped the sweat from his brow. "The ironic thing is, I would have given up my position if I thought that my stepmother would let me have my siblings back." He smiled ruefully at Lily and Ava. "And my father would have happily disowned me for indulging such weakness. Anyway, my stepmother convinced my father to send me for military training. Hoping to get me out of the way, perhaps into a military career and therefore out of her hair for good. But I completed my training and returned to the palace.

"So then she suggested that I lead a diplomatic mission

to the Disputed Region to forge bonds with both Highacre and Meridia. My father was reluctant. There had been outbreaks of violence. But my stepmother convinced him that this would display his strength, and so I went. It was almost as if she was hoping a misfortune might befall me on one of these trips. And I did have a couple of close shaves."

Ava and Lily shared a look. Alexei's stepmother had definitely been hoping that a misfortune would befall Alexei. Lily wondered if the close shaves had been engineered. She didn't ask him, though. Mainly because she didn't want to interrupt, but also because it seemed Alexei didn't really want to consider the idea that his stepmother had likely actively tried to kill him.

"And then she suggested that coming to Highacre as ambassador to court would be good training for me, and my father agreed. I can't say that she could have predicted our current situation, but it does seem like she may have gotten her wish. I may well be out of her hair for good."

"Don't say that, Alexei," said Lily.

"Yeah, we are going to get out of here," said Ava with feeling.

Alexei shrugged. "If we do, great. If not ... I've never really thought about what I might do or who I might be without the expectation that I will become the next Great Leader. I would obviously miss my family and friends back home, but perhaps I might find myself in this new world."

Alexei looked into the distance, a wistful expression on his face. Catching sight of Ava's worried one, he added, "But I can't see us being stuck here for long. So I will be the ambassador to court for the next three years, and then, who knows?" He shrugged, smiled at the women, and returned to working the field.

"Do you want to take over from your father?" Lily asked.

Alexei paused, considering his response. "It's not something that I necessarily feel excited about. I don't really want to be leader just for the position and accolades. But I do think I could do a lot of good. There are things that my father and the leaders before him either didn't want to do, or were too scared to do, that our country needs. I'd really like to be leader so that I could make those changes, then implement the final change, which would be to turn Valmead into a true democracy."

Silence followed Alexei's answer, both women taken with the passion he had for reforming his country.

"You would be the best dictator that Valmead ever had, Alexei."

He stopped working and smiled at her. "Thank you, Ava."

"And if I ever meet your stepmum, I'm going to slap her in the face." Ava hacked her mattock violently into the ground.

"I have never been more grateful that you will not, under any circumstances, visit my country."

"I am definitely visiting Valmead."

"No, you are not invited."

"What? I must diplomatically protest," Ava declared, restarting the manure fight by throwing a clump of dirt at Alexei before hiding behind the wheelbarrow. Alexei bent to pick up another clump as Lily joined in, hitting him on his shoulder. Alexei feigned a throw at Lily, who dove to her left, but instead pegged Ava, who shrieked as it hit her on the back of her head, dirt and natural fertiliser now all through her hair.

"You bastard!" Ava grabbed two handfuls and launched one at Alexei, who successfully dodged, and Lily, who didn't.

"I wasn't even going after you!" cried Lily, scrambling

for some good clumps. As the projectiles kept coming, Lily gave up her search and instead just rushed at Ava, tackling her to the ground and grabbing handfuls of dirt to smear on her shirt. She could feel the dirt raining onto both of them as Alexei took advantage of the situation. Lily sat up, straddling Ava and blocking her hands. She caught an odd look in Ava's eye and suddenly felt a nervous and weird feeling in the depths of her stomach.

"Come on," Lily said, jumping up off Ava and brushing her hands on her clothes. "Let's go get some lunch."

6

Claire hurried up the flight of stairs, shooting a look down the hall as she passed, scanning to see whether it was clear. Upon reaching the next floor, she pulled out her phone, pretending to check it while straining to listen for movement from below. She jumped as a couple exited an apartment to her right. They laughed, relaxed and oblivious to any cares in the world.

Claire turned and slowly started heading up another flight as the couple canoodled their way to the stairs and did their best to descend while keeping their arms around each other. Ignoring her urge to faux vomit at them, Claire paused, surreptitiously looking over the railing until she heard the door to the street close.

Above her, footsteps started down the stairs. She hurried back down to the floor of the lovestruck couple's apartment and walked slowly down the hall, again keeping her head down and thumbs flying across the screen of her phone. She glanced up as the middle-aged man passed the floor she was on without changing speed and was gone.

Heart pounding, Claire headed slowly back to the stairs, mentally re-examining the residents for anything suspicious. Anything to indicate that they were on the *other* side. Reasonably sure that none of them posed a threat, Claire paused at the stairwell, eyes on her screen.

She stayed like that, seemingly engrossed in her phone, for a full five minutes. Satisfied that the coast was clear, she sighed at her phone, put it away, and slowly headed back down to the floor that was her objective.

She was being paranoid. She knew that. But under the circumstances, it was a healthy level of paranoia. The kind of paranoia that saved your life. She would have preferred to enter the building utilising her chameleoning talent and simply blend in with her surroundings. However, the stairs and corridors of this apartment block were too narrow, and if she encountered anyone, there was no way to pass without them realising she was there. And it was less conspicuous to be wandering around visibly than to be busted skulking around, practically invisible.

Claire paused as she reached the landing, eyes scanning for movement and listening for voices, footsteps, or any other signs of life. Remaining alert, she pressed forward to apartment 309. Outside the door, Claire began rummaging in her handbag, as if looking for her keys, and leant her head close to the door, listening again for anything unexpected. She pulled a small tool from her bag, careful to keep it encased in her hand and, with the ease one might use a key, picked the lock and entered the apartment, closing the door behind her.

Claire paused on the threshold, again letting her senses sweep her surroundings and alert her to any danger. Nothing moved. She noted a slightly stale, musty smell that told her the apartment had likely been empty for a while. She gave her ears a minute longer. The apartment was silent, but she closed her eyes and listened for any clicking or buzzing that might signal electronic surveillance.

Satisfied that she was physically alone and not being watched, Claire moved toward the main living area. Almost immediately, a loud noise blasted from her right, and she jumped and squealed before crouching, prepared to vault over the kitchen counter. She saw the source of the noise and scowled.

Typical.

Claire waited, crouched, for a bit more than two minutes.

Standing and shaking the burn from her legs, Claire picked up the farting gnome statue and glared at it. A rudimentary but effective alarm. Embarrassed that it had caught her, Claire relaxed a little. Had there been anyone in the apartment, they also would have reacted to its noise. Or to her squealing.

Resisting the urge to toss the gnome in the bin, Claire returned him to his sentry position and walked slowly through the apartment. The first sweep, as she had been taught during her training, was to ensure the space was empty and to take everything in without disturbing the scene. Claire looked for signs that the inhabitant had been there recently and for anything out of place that would indicate someone other than the inhabitant had visited.

Claire was relieved to confirm the apartment was currently empty, but she also saw no signs that her mentor had been home in a while. After being unable to reach him in over a week, Claire had taken the risk of coming here, worried about what might have happened to him. Grateful as she was to not find him injured, or worse, his absence only sparked more questions, and Claire felt scared and alone.

She scanned the living area and crossed to a well-worn chair by the window. It was clear that he'd spent a lot of time sitting there. She moved behind the chair and leant against the wall, peering out the window without disturbing the lace curtain. It wouldn't be his exact view, but should give her an idea of what he had been looking at.

Claire looked down at the street. The window provided a clear view of the main road. Normally busy with foot traffic, there were less people than usual, but quite a few were still bustling along.

She watched as an HSP patrol entered the street and began stopping the passers-by, demanding to check their newly mandated identity papers. She tried not to resent the civilians for meekly complying and handing them over. Everything was changing so quickly with the prime minister expanding his emergency powers and setting up the High-acre Special Police, his own private band of mercenaries, as alleged protection for the public. And on the back of the terror attack at the arena, the assassinations of the royal family, not to mention the shadow of the last war, the people were scared and tired. They preferred to hope everything would resolve itself than try to force resolution. And in the absence of the queen, what other resolution was there?

Claire pursed her lips as two HSP officers directed a man towards a van. He looked scared, but complied without protest. No, it was unfair of her to expect them to fight the system when the royal advisors couldn't even agree on what to do.

Claire left the window and wandered back towards the guest bedroom. Everything had fallen apart so quickly after Lily was lost. The advisors disintegrated quicker than she would have guessed. There were too many of them seeking to lead and looking at things from their own perspective. And none of them had the training Claire did, or had experienced danger like she had. Well, maybe Jason and Naomi, but with the infiltration of the guards and the attack on the way to the coronation, Jason and Naomi's level of paranoia had gone into overdrive, clearly demonstrating that neither of them were suited to leadership at the political or strategic level. They, like most military, in her opinion, were more suited to tactical operations.

Foreign Minister Juliana Bellingham was a natural leader, but even she had her eyes on the possibility that if they could depose the prime minister, *someone* would be needed to take his place, especially if Lily was still absent. This set off Defence Minister Jeremy Toot, who couldn't see why he shouldn't step into the role instead of her, despite him not having any ideas at all about how to deal with the prime minister in the first place.

And Giles and Addison simply wanted someone, anyone, to tell them what to do. Which was to be expected. As royal household staff, they were meant to take care of the queen, not depose a despot.

At any rate, the only thing that they had all managed to agree on was that it was too dangerous for them all to meet in person and that the palace's "secure communications" had likely been compromised. Unfortunately, they had failed to agree on a plan, or even on tasks for everyone to focus on. And without another meeting set or a means to communicate, they were now all largely operating on their own, based on their individual ideas of what was required, which was ultimately more likely to draw attention to their activities, or ensure that they each interfered with the others' plans.

The guest bedroom in the apartment had been converted into an office. Claire, careful not to touch anything and disturb the thin layer of dust, looked appraisingly at the small desk. Diary, notepad, pens, and assorted stationary littered the surface in a neat-but-used way. But Claire could see no indentations on the notepad, and the diary had only a few appointments listed for the week that was open.

This was staged.

The last entry in the diary was for three weeks ago. Claire looked around the room, wondering what her mentor actually used it for, and what it was hiding. Why stage the room as used at all? And more importantly, where was his laptop? Crossing the room in two strides, Claire opened the closet. Her breath caught and her eyes grew wide as she spotted the hidden room at the back behind the clothes. *This is why I topped my year at the academy.*

Her eyes narrowed again. Far from being seen as a boon, the other royal advisors, upon being informed of her background as a Highacre Intelligence Agency agent and not the etiquette advisor she had pretended to be, had treated her with suspicion. All the goodwill and relationships she had carefully tendered were wiped out, and she was the newcomer all over again. Though obviously not her motivation for taking it upon herself to uncover the plot behind the decline of their country, the look on the royal advisors' faces when she succeeded would be very satisfying.

Claire took a step into the closet. Behind the clothes on the righthand side and propped carelessly against the wall was a large, thin board. Alarm bells sounded in her head.

A false back! Why hasn't it been replaced?

A quick scan of the usually hidden secret area told Claire her mentor's work didn't appear to have been disturbed. Perhaps it hadn't been someone else? Maybe the old man had to leave so quickly he didn't have time to replace the board. She chastised herself for wistful thinking, though she was yet to find any evidence that someone else had been inside the apartment.

The true rear wall of the closet was covered in photographs, maps, printouts, newspaper clippings, and even some building plans. Scattered about the organised chaos were post-its attached to various documents, seemingly at random and posing questions, often single words. Why? When? How? What? Adding to the overall scene was the red string that he had used to make connections between the various pieces of information.

Claire tried to make sense of the madness. It looked like she and her mentor were drawing some similar conclusions. Claire was sure that all of this was political, but she wasn't completely sure whether it was an internal power struggle or an attack by Meridia.

Her mentor, on the other hand, clearly thought Meridia was to blame, though a post-it with *"ENDGAME?"* written in angry red letters indicated he had not uncovered a motive. Claire had similarly been fixated on Meridia, but pushing Lily through the interdimensional travel machine seemed like significantly more effort than simply killing her like the rest of her family. She couldn't see what Meridia gained from keeping her alive. Not to mention that so few people were supposed to know about the machine ...

At the centre of the wall was a large photo of a smiling Ezra Brown. Unable to resist the urge, Claire lightly ran a finger along the string that linked Ezra to a photo of Ava Harrington. They worked together as ambassadors, but were they also partners in crime? She had not really considered that they might be working together to bring down Highacre. That seemed more of Ezra's pet project, and Claire had dismissed their connection as that of colleagues. However, her mentor seemed to put more stock in the idea.

Both were Meridian ambassadors, and both had a background in the Meridian Intelligence Agency. But Ava had been recruited to the MIA long after Ezra had been tossed aside. She supposed it was possible that they could still know each other. Through mutual contacts, perhaps?

Claire considered her own circumstances. Would she consider herself linked to the ex-director of the Highacre Intelligence Agency? She scoffed at the thought. He wouldn't know her from the cleaning staff.

She took a step back and looked at the two of them, both smiling out at her with the same perfect teeth and twinkling eyes. Perhaps she had been too quick to dismiss a link. She considered the entirety of the wall. Though perhaps she also shouldn't be so quick to adopt the opinions of what looked to be a troubled mind.

Claire came out of the closet and was closing the door when it hit her. If her mentor was right and Ava was working with Ezra, Lily could be in much more danger than they'd realised.

7

CLAIRE RETURNED TO THE KITCHEN. If Ava was problematic, there was nothing Claire could do to help until they located the felixium. She couldn't help with that, but what she could do was keep investigating and make sure the Highacre Lily returned to was as safe as possible. Touching as little as possible, flicked through a pile of newspapers. The most recent was from a week ago, but she hadn't noticed any papers outside the door, or downstairs at the mailboxes. Likely, he bought them himself each day. No doubt from different retailers each time.

Don't set patterns.

She looked at the front page of the most recent paper.

Prime Minister Reginald Toth stunned political circles today, including his own party, when he announced the appointment of Ezra Brown as his "special advisor." It is not yet clear exactly what the special advisor's role is, but so far insiders have said that Mr Brown attends all meetings with the prime minister. This is an unprecedented level of access for a non-citizen of Highacre, and has caused much concern.

"It's preposterous," said Foreign Minister Juliana Belling-ham. "The man is the Meridian ambassador and we're letting him sit in our highest level discussions about national security? And whatever happened to Mr Toth's 'Highacre First' line? Why hasn't he given what must be quite a well-paid role to one of our own citizens?"

But Mr Toth seems unconcerned with the criticism. A spokesman for the prime minister said that Mr Brown had relinquished his post as the Meridian ambassador in order to take up his new role without a conflict of interest. Mr Toth himself claimed at a recent rally that 'Highacre First' didn't mean that Highacre wouldn't engage with other nations, and that Mr Brown was simply the most qualified and best suited candidate for the job. The spokesman for the prime minister refused to comment on how many applicants had been considered.

While there is no apparent substance to it, a dark conspiracy has started to gain traction, linking Mr Brown's new appointment to rumours circulating that the sole surviving member of the royal family, Lily Seraphina Brighid Laquisha, has mysteriously disappeared. Palace insiders say that they have not seen the monarch-to-be since her coronation was mysteriously cancelled at the last minute over a week ago. Some suggest that the prime minister has engaged Mr Brown to look into the sovereign's whereabouts, but others claim the special advisor has been brought in to build the prime minister's case that, despite the judges' ruling, Her Majesty failed the Trials and has not been confirmed to ascend the throne. More nefarious rumours suggest that Mr Brown could even be the cause of Her Majesty's absence. For more details of the crown princess's disappearance, see page 5.

Leaving the newspaper, Claire wandered over to the oven. The appointment of Ezra was bizarre and bothered her. She had not seen it coming, nor had she been able to do any better than the local journalists in discovering why he was appointed and what he was doing.

She had read everything that she could find online, and all that had told her was that the prime minister was continuing to use the line about not cutting off other countries to explain his hiring Ezra in mainstream publications, but in more right-wing circles he was boasting about exploiting Ezra for Highacre's benefit. The whole thing was weird. The nationalist prime minister and his Meridian buddy.

She grabbed a dish towel and opened the oven, staring in disgust at the thick layer of gunk at the bottom. As Claire was about to close it again, she saw a thin streak of stainless steel in the front left corner. Something had disturbed the baked-on dirt.

Reminding herself to get a manicure soon, Claire ran her fingernails along the front of the oven's floor. *There it is.* Her index finger found the lip of a small, thin tray. She prised it up, careful to not disturb the thick coating of grease and lard and who knew what else, and retrieved the laptop from underneath.

Claire made for the door, thinking to examine the computer in the privacy of her own apartment, but something stopped her. That tiny streak disturbing the oven debris. She looked around again. She didn't think that anyone else had been in here, but she couldn't be sure.

Placing the laptop on the newspaper that she had already touched, Claire opened it. She sighed in relief when it booted, displaying one thin line of battery power remaining. Still open was an internet browser with three tabs.

As the first page loaded, Claire was shocked to be met with a full colour picture of Minister Bellingham being arrested in front of the Tower, the building where Parliament sat. Her stomach dropped and she searched the header for the publication time. An hour ago—right about the time Claire had entered the apartment complex. She'd had no idea something like this would happen, nor could she realistically have prevented it, but Claire felt guilty. As if she were undertaking an easy job while Minister Bellingham was fighting on the front line.

Clearly, she had not gone quietly. The older woman looked uncharacteristically dishevelled and had been photographed mid-yell, spittle flying out of her mouth. Claire couldn't help the little smile that brushed her lips, thinking how much the now ex-minister of foreign affairs would hate that photo, but the smile quickly left her face as she wondered where Juliana was now, and whether she was safe. Of all the advisors to have been taken out of the game, the removal of Juliana Bellingham hurt their side the most. Claire felt a chill go down her spine. For the first time, she considered the idea that they might lose. Juliana was such a formidable character, and her confidence had given the others a feeling that everything was going to work out. Now, with her gone ...

She scanned the article, trying to find out why Juliana had been arrested. Strangely, the article seemed unable to explain the arrest beyond mentioning that Minister Bellingham had been a vocal critic of the prime minister, and some vague reference to disloyalty to the nation.

Claire frowned. Disloyalty to the prime minister maybe, but to the nation? Perhaps Mr Toth thought that was the same thing. Making a mental note to look up the charges later, she glared at the HSP officers arresting Juliana. For an embarrassing minute, Claire had been tempted to reach out through her connections to look at joining the HSP. She missed the agency quite a bit, and her excitement at the idea of being a part of an organisation again had made her realise just how much operating completely on her own had worn her down. She had told herself that perhaps she could infiltrate it and learn what was needed from the inside. However, something had stopped her, a feeling in her gut. And she had long ago learned to trust her intuition.

She scrolled down the rest of the news website's front page, but it was all new. There was no way to tell what her mentor had been looking at when he opened the tab. If, in fact, it had been he who opened it.

A small story caught her eye. More rumours of the Valmeadian dictator being ill. Just before the advisors had gone their separate ways, Valmead had recalled their ambassadors and had been extremely displeased when Highacre was unable to produce the ambassador to court, who also happened to be the dictator's eldest son. They had since effectively cut communications with Highacre, and there were now concerns they would side with Meridia in any conflict that might break out.

Or be started by our illustrious prime minister.

Claire clicked on the second tab and flinched. It was the parliamentary website that hosted legislation. Claire hated legislation. They had been required to read relevant acts during her training and she had never encountered anything so boring. Bracing herself, Claire tried to see what legislation her mentor had been looking at. A wave of relief washed over her as the page declared that the search had produced no results. However, her joy was short-lived as she glanced at the search bar and saw that he had been looking for the legislation that underpinned the HSP.

There should be legislation and it should be publicly available. Something was very wrong. She clicked back through her mentor's searches. He had begun looking for the legislation on the Department of Security and Home

Affairs's website but found nothing. He had then visited the Department of Defence. Claire allowed that page to load, and her eyes grew wide. The webpage housed frequently asked questions about the HSP, none of which seemed to be answered in any meaningful way. Policing and intelligence was clearly the domain of Security and Home Affairs, so why was Defence responsible for the HSP? And why had Minister Toot failed to mention he was now in charge of the HSP to the other advisors if, for some reason, it did fall under his domain as defence minister? He was meant to be on their side.

Claire clicked on the third tab and was greeted with the same smiling picture of the Meridian ambassador that had beamed at her from the closet. It was an internet search for *"what is Ezra Brown up to"*. Claire smiled wanly. Her mentor had been getting desperate. Rather than spilling Ezra's secret plans to interfere in Highacren politics, the search revealed websites discussing his business ventures, his focus on technological expansion, and his exploits as an eligible bachelor.

She scoffed at the search results, but looked at the preview text nonetheless. Apparently, the "highly eligible" Mr Brown was attending a Meridian National Day Ball at the Meridian Embassy tonight.

Claire smiled. Undercover had been her best subject at the academy. Her smile faltered as she noticed that the little bar at the top of the page indicated it was still loading, despite the page looking to have been fully loaded for a couple of minutes now.

Paranoid, Claire quickly closed all the search windows, disconnected the laptop from the internet, shut the computer down, and pulled out the battery. After wondering whether she was being a little too paranoid, she also pulled out the main circuit board for good measure.

Claire was almost confident that she could put it back together for her mentor.

That's if he ever comes back.

Claire replaced the disassembled computer back in its hidden compartment in the oven and looked around the apartment, checking for any signs of her presence she might have left. She made herself look carefully, even though panic was starting to grip her.

I've been here too long.

She had lingered, comforted by the ghost of her mentor. Not wanting to admit to herself that she wasn't cut out for solo operations, Claire ignored the familiar feeling of hopelessness that was descending and listened at the door. She was just one person, and with no backup or resources. What could she really do against the prime minister with an entire governmental system and a private army at his disposal?

Hearing nothing, she opened the door and stepped out into the hall, quickly scanning her surroundings before locking the door and heading for the stairs. A man suddenly turned onto her floor and she resisted the urge to retreat back into the apartment. He paid her no attention, but bumped into her shoulder as he passed.

Claire entered the stairwell and hurried down into the lobby. Thinking of the continuously loading page and the bump from the stranger in the hall, she shrugged out of her cardigan and with a twinge of regret—it was one of her favourites—discarded it in the bin.

If only I had some help.

Claire pushed the idea from her head as she pushed out the door onto the street. She had always worked better as part of a team. But the only other people that she could trust were Jason and Naomi. Jason seemed nice enough, but he was just so *military*. She always expected him to respond to everything with "yes ma'am". Naomi seemed alright, but she was an unknown factor since she was so new. And perhaps her old agency prejudices were still at play. The HIA had looked down on the military, viewing themselves as precision instruments and the military as blunt weapons. Claire was surprised that the bias was still there. It wasn't like she had really been an agent for that long. But the idea of asking Jason for help was a bridge too far.

Is now really the time for petty squabbles? Who cares if you ask him for help. You need it.

Ignoring the logical part of her brain, Claire hurried across the street and looked into a shop window. Having ensured through the reflection that she wasn't being followed, she allowed herself to look at the display. She couldn't really justify the expense, but if she was going into the lion's den, she may as well treat herself. Claire smiled. The right dress could be as useful as a truth serum. She pushed open the door and entered the store. Time to get ready for a ball.

8

Smiling politely at everyone and no one, Claire lifted a glass of champagne off the tray of a passing server and moved to the side of the ballroom, fading into the shadows.

Still got it.

She was still pleased with how easily she had managed to get past the guards without an invite.

"Oh gosh no, don't tell me I've forgotten it."

"No invite, no entry, ma'am."

"Of course, I understand. It's got to be in here." As she rummaged through her purse, she had allowed the strap of her dress to fall slightly down her shoulder. "I know I put it in here because my boss made it very clear to me I'd be fired if I didn't turn up."

After carefully "accidentally" letting a tampon fall out of her bag and roll towards the feet of the guards, Claire had bent to pick it up, then almost "accidentally" had a wardrobe malfunction with her cleavage and "tripped" into the second guard's arms. As she burst into tears, the guards had let her through after a quick scan with a metal detector.

Claire smiled to herself. Thank goodness they hadn't

been looking at her face. She much preferred to cry her way into places without actual tears, as it saved on reapplying her makeup.

She scanned the room. No sign of Ezra yet. Not having much luck online, this was the best opportunity Claire had yet to try and gather intelligence on the man she suspected was at least heavily involved in everything that was going wrong. He was unlikely to drop any useful secrets in his discussions at a social event such as this, but Claire hoped through observation and eavesdropping to be able to learn more about the type of man she was facing off against. That meant keeping to the shadows and remaining out of the spotlight. He couldn't know she was here.

"Whassa butaful girllik you doinna placethis?" slurred a large sweaty man who had appeared on Claire's right.

She rolled her eyes. *Really?* She turned to move away, and he slapped his large sweaty paw down on her shoulder. "Donturnway when I'm talkinchoo."

The large man now began steering Claire away from the wall and into the centre of the room. She pushed back, trying to remain where she was, but the man increased his pressure, and drunk as he was, he was still strong.

With a split second to decide, Claire determined the attention she would attract by fighting back would be worse than going with him for now. But she needed to slip his grasp and fade away as soon as she could without making a scene.

"Martin! How are you? I didn't realise you were here until Nancy told me." Martin let go of Claire's shoulder and turned excitedly towards the newcomer.

"Nancyssss ere?"

"Oh yes, and she's *very* excited to see you. I was just talking to her over there near the bar, by the ice sculpture."

Martin lumbered off to find and harass poor Nancy, and Claire turned to thank her rescuer. "Oh! Mr Brown!"

Ezra smiled apologetically at Claire. "Please, Ms Jones, call me Ezra. And I'm sorry about Martin."

He glanced toward Martin, who had barrelled his way through the crowd before tripping, then attempted to steady himself by grabbing the head of a cherub on the ice sculpture, which promptly snapped off. He was now trying to convince the bartender to take it in exchange for another drink.

"He might need to go home," Claire said, watching Martin get increasingly angry as the bartender, a skinny young man who looked all of twelve, looked around in alarm for someone to help him.

"Yes. Unfortunately, this is not Martin's first ball and so ... ah yes, here we are."

Two large men in tight T-shirts that proclaimed "*Security*" arrived and helped Martin out of the room to the extreme relief of the bartender and several of the females in the room.

"And yet," said Claire, now turning to Ezra and looking at him. "You sent him after that poor Nancy woman."

Ezra chuckled. "Yes, and if Nancy were here, I would fear her response, but lucky for me, and for Martin, she's safely in Valmead."

They both laughed politely, and Claire took a sip of her drink. How to play this? Her plan had been completely ruined. But perhaps she could still learn something about Ezra before she withdrew. After all, he was here, and he had approached her. Surely, there was no harm in having a chat with him. But she just needed to make sure she wasn't too direct. Not her strong suit.

"I saw that poor Minister Bellingham was arrested,"

Ezra said, saving Claire the effort of guiding the conversation. Claire allowed a worried look to grace her features. She was sure that Ezra hadn't simply "seen" that Juliana had been arrested.

"Yes, I read it in the papers, but I couldn't seem to find out what she was arrested for."

Ezra nodded gravely. "I agree. The lack of information is concerning. I bumped into Addison, and she was quite beside herself about it."

"Oh! How is Ms Grange? I haven't seen her since ... well, in a little while."

"She is well, though obviously worried about Her Majesty." Ezra lowered his voice and bent his head closer to Claire. "As is Giles, poor man. I just don't understand how it all happened."

Claire nodded and scanned the crowd. She didn't want to discuss Lily or the interdimensional travel machine with Ezra, or at all in the Meridian Embassy, which she had no doubt was bugged by all three countries.

"Well, I'm sure the prime minister is looking into it. But of course, you would know better than I. Congratulations on your new appointment, by the way."

Ezra looked appropriately bashful and waved her away. "Oh thank you, but of course, I am simply one of his many advisors and really, my appointment is more of an olive branch to Meridia, I think."

Claire nodded, not believing him for a second. "You must be invaluable to him though, with your intelligence background, and him with a distinct lack of an intelligence capability. What a coup to hire a previous director of the Meridian Intelligence Agency!"

Ezra laughed and looked at Claire, his eyes dazzling, and Claire could see how easy it must be for this good-looking, genial man to gain the confidence of people and access their secrets.

"Yes, I suppose there is that. And what are you up to now? With no queen-to-be to teach etiquette to, you must have some time on your hands?"

"Oh, I'm doing a little bit here and there. To be honest, it's nice to have a bit of time to relax and think."

"It does sound lovely." Ezra nodded and took a sip of his drink, looking around at the crowd. "Though if you were bored, I'd certainly be happy to have someone with your skills on my team. Goodness knows I could use some 'etiquette' lessons!"

He knows. Claire's stomach turned to ice. *Of course he knows, he'd have access to all the HIA records given his new role.*

She smiled politely. "I daresay you have a masterful grasp of etiquette; I'm not sure that I would be able to teach you anything you don't already know."

Ezra smiled at her and put his hand on her back between her shoulder blades. Claire tried not to stiffen at his touch. He leant in closer and said, "A pity. I quite like you Claire, as I liked Minister Bellingham. But I'm sure we'll have plenty of other opportunities to work together." He leant back and added in a louder voice, "Enjoy the party, please excuse me."

And with that, Ezra swept away and greeted a group of people in the middle of the dance floor. Claire's heart was pounding in her chest so hard that she heard it in her ears. Keeping her pleasant expression plastered to her face, she casually strolled towards the ladies' bathroom and entered, checking the stalls in the mirror as she pretended to touch up her makeup.

She was sure that he had just threatened her. But a

small part of her wondered again if she wasn't getting overly paranoid.

You're not paranoid if they're really out to get you.

She shook her head slightly. Would he be so bold? Maybe it wasn't a threat. Maybe ... maybe he was trying to signal to her that he was on her side. The reference to Minister Bellingham might not have been him trying to tell Claire that she could be arrested too; it could have been him letting her know that he would try to look out for Juliana.

She looked at herself in the mirror. Was she really getting that desperate? Even a rookie agent would know that he wasn't on her side. For all she knew, he could be the mastermind behind all of this. But was it a threat?

Certain that she wouldn't be able to achieve anything more at the ball, Claire slipped out a side door and managed to scale a wall in the back of the embassy, walk to the main road, and hail a cab.

Feeling completely alone, Claire checked her phone to see if she had any new emails, but they were all junk messages, spamming her about sales and new products that she didn't want. In slight desperation, she had emailed some of her old colleagues from the academy, but with no responses at all in over a week, she had to start to accept that they would not be getting back to her. Which left Jason and Naomi. Fine, she would call Jason. He probably needed her more than she needed him, anyway.

Glancing out the back window, Claire did a slight double take. She had noticed the blue sporty sedan as she entered the cab at the embassy. But it was a common car. Surely it wouldn't be the same one? Cursing herself for not getting the licence plate number, Claire asked the driver to change course and watched, stomach sinking, as the blue car turned with them. She repeated the process, pretending to be a little tipsy and having difficulty making her mind up about where she wanted to go. The car remained at a discreet distance, but followed wherever Claire went.

Panic grabbed Claire's chest in an icy grip, and she told the driver to stop abruptly, opposite a dark alleyway. Thrusting the fare and a generous tip at him, Claire hurried out of the car and into the shadows. Hidden from view, she blended into her surroundings and scanned for a hiding place. The other car would be there in seconds.

Claire jogged farther into the alley, climbed onto a dumpster, then leapt up, straining to reach the bottom level of a fire escape above her. Her exuberance at managing to catch hold was tempered by the loud clang she made, and as she clambered up and over the railing, she tried to muffle the reverberation as much as possible. She darted over to a metal panel and hid behind it as she heard a car park at the mouth of the alley. She glanced around, making sure her whole body was behind the panel. Her chameleoning would be pointless if they had a powerful revealer with them.

No sooner had Claire ducked down, hidden from sight by the rusted metal panel, did footsteps sound at the entry to the alley. She tried to moderate her breathing and ignore the putrid smell emanating from below. After a pause, the footsteps turned into the alley, and started heading towards Claire. She heard a muffled voice and strained to make out what it was saying. Chancing a glance, Claire watched as two large figures in black slowly paced the alley, looking from side to side and into the various bins and hiding places. One figure pointed to the end of the alley, and with a nod, the other continued the process while the original stopped right underneath Claire, turning slowly and looking around. He touched his ear and started talking in a low voice.

"Revealer deployed."

Claire's heart pounded, and she looked down at her

camouflaged body. If the revealer was more powerful than she was, he would be able to see her, and she would have no warning. She tried to press herself lower behind the panel.

"Alpha team, report ... understood. Bravo? ... Nothing seen either, okay. Charlie? ... acknowledged. All teams continue search. Surveillance team, continue with residence. Any sightings, report to me immediately. Out to all."

Claire's heart sank. She was currently being hunted by a small team of HSP, and from the sounds of things, they had surveillance on her apartment. She had been so looking forward to going home, getting out of her dress and heels, and collapsing into bed. Maybe after a soak in the bath. That was out of the question now.

Claire listened to the men leave the alley and gave them half an hour buffer before she even moved. She stood slowly, letting the pins and needles clear, and shook out her limbs before carefully climbing down the fire escape as quietly as possible. Remaining camouflaged, Claire walked to the opposite end of the alley from where she had entered and the men had left, then shimmied over a wall, dropping silently onto the other side.

She paused, listening for movement, before heading off slowly in the direction of a safe house she had set up, hoping to never have to use. Claire mentally kicked herself for only minimally kitting it out and tried not to be too upset about the loss of her comfortable home full of all her things. They were only things, after all. That was what she had told herself when she set up the safe house and decided that it only needed the bare minimum. She now realised that she hadn't truly contemplated needing to stay there long-term.

She wondered if she should get some groceries on the way, or if she should simply use what she had there before deciding whether she should stay or move on. Sighing, Claire reminded herself that she had at least an hour's walk to figure that out. And besides, she should probably wait to see if her safe house had been compromised before deciding her next steps.

Feeling as low as she could ever remember feeling, Claire darted across a main road and into another alley and resolved to contact Jason sooner rather than later.

9

Lily gazed out the bus window, allowing herself to take some time to switch off and stare. It had been a hectic day, and though there had been plenty of things to catch Ava and Alexei's attention and wonder, nothing had been able to shift the heavy weight of realisation.

No one had come for them.

They had remained at the farm for a week and a day in the end, adding the extra day as a sacrifice to the powers of the universe that might toy with them and have their rescue party turn up the day after they left. But this having failed too, Ava and Alexei had reluctantly agreed that kind of thinking could paralyse them, and that it was time to leave.

Part of Lily's heart had sunk. She had become comfortable at the farm in their routine. The panic she felt upon arrival had worn off, and now she just felt a cool, sick feeling of dread about what she might discover had happened to her family. Half of her wished Ava had put her foot down and demanded they stay a month—what did it matter, after all, if they were to be stuck in this world forever? Lily felt extremely guilty for wanting that comfort.

She needed to find her family. To help them. To apologise for disappearing and to help make up for it. But it would be so easy to leave things as they were. She would return to Highacre, anyway; why put her family through losing her again?

The bus bumped along the old highway. It would be an hour before they reached the main road that was in better condition. She would sleep then. Lily could hear Ava and Alexei murmuring excitedly to each other in the seat in front of her. Ava had bounced over from her seat to watch a crop duster with him, and the two were discussing potential uses for flight back home.

Lily checked the cheap phone they had bought. She had logged into her new email and social media accounts, but there was no reply to the messages she had sent. Disheartened, she called her mother's number again and left a message with her new number, then followed up her emails and private messages with the same information.

She also gave the number to Doreen, who had promised to call if anyone appeared at the farm looking for them. The cowardly part of Lily had been checking the phone regularly for a message from Doreen. If Doreen called to say they needed to return before she found her family, then it was really out of her hands, right? Ashamed, Lily put the phone away and returned to looking out the window.

"Oooh! What are those things?" Ava asked excitedly of no one in particular.

"Alpacas," said Lily. "They put them in there to protect the sheep."

"They're all so ... woolly," said Alexei.

Lily knew she should tell them to keep it down. They had already been given some odd looks from the few other passengers on the bus due to their fascination over relatively mundane things. But she couldn't bring herself to dampen their enthusiasm. Nor did she have the energy. Lily tucked herself into the corner of her seat, balled up her jacket, shoved it between the seat and the window, and rested her head on it. She stared unseeingly ahead, her mind running through endless possibilities of what had happened to her family and how they might react to her sudden reappearance.

After a while, Lily closed her eyes, picturing the reunion. Would her family be happy to see her? Or angry that she had gone in the first place? She imagined multiple reunions, all with different overriding emotions. Common to all scenarios were the questions she would face.

I really need to come up with a plausible explanation for my absence. And for who Ava and Alexei are.

She was pondering the merits of suggesting that she had been kidnapped by a cult and brainwashed before somehow escaping with Ava and Alexei, when Ava bounced into the seat beside her.

"Oh, sorry, were you asleep?"

"No, just thinking."

"Ew, overrated." Ava smiled at Lily, who couldn't help but smile in return. Ava nudged Lily gently with her shoulder. "What were you thinking about?"

"Just ... if we find my family, what am I going to say? You know, about where I've been and who you guys are."

Ava sat back in her seat, leaning over and resting her head on Lily's shoulder. "Yeah, it's a tough one. I suppose we need to be as truthful as possible without sounding completely insane."

Lily snorted. "It's a fine line to walk."

"I walk it every day," said Ava, her face serious but her eyes twinkling. "So, what's the plan when we get to the city?"

"There are some apartments near where I used to live that rent by the week, but I'm not sure how much it costs. We'll definitely have enough with the gems from my dress once we trade them in somewhere." Lily paused, thinking. "I reckon we head to the apartments, check the availability and the cost. We have enough cash to put down a deposit if we need to, and then we can see what we can get for the gems. Once we've got the accommodation sorted, we can start trying to find my family."

Ava nodded and looked past Lily out the window. After a brief pause, she asked, "And *how* do we find your family?"

Lily had been thinking about this. She would keep up her online efforts, but how was she going to find them otherwise? Lily didn't want to go to the police. That would make it infinitely harder to explain her absence, and the lack of identification and background information about Ava and Alexei could be dangerous for them. She supposed she could hire an investigator, but that would depend on the cost. She had no idea how much a private investigator was, but surely it wouldn't be cheap.

Unfortunately, when she then turned her mind to people she knew well enough to ask after her family but trusted not to alert the authorities, only two possibilities came to mind. And Lily desperately wished she could have avoided seeing them, no matter how cowardly that might make her.

"We should be able to track down my boyf—my ex-boyfriend Brandon, or my friend Gemma. They should still be at uni studying, and I reckon they would have been in touch with my family when I went missing. And Brandon was friends with my brother, David. They probably stayed in touch even if he stopped having regular contact with my family when things died down a little."

Ava could obviously sense Lily's anxiety about seeing

them and refrained from teasing her. "Sounds like a good plan." Ava reached out and gave Lily's arm a quick squeeze. "It's going to be okay. I promise."

Lily nodded, and though she wasn't sure she believed Ava, she appreciated the sentiment.

***

Stepping off the bus, Lily stretched and looked around, slightly dazed, trying to get her bearings. Determining where they were from the nearby street signs, she led her friends toward the part of town where she used to live. As they got farther away from the bus station, the streets became more tree lined, the area more residential. Lily began to relax as familiar landmarks popped out.

"That's where I used to live," Lily said, pointing up at an apartment building.

"Nice view," said Ava appreciatively, looking around the area.

"Yeah. My apartment was in the back and had a view of the wall of the apartment block behind mine ... but the area is lovely."

After a little more walking, they arrived at the apartments she was looking for, and Lily exhaled in relief upon seeing a sign indicating that they still did short-term rentals. Only as they approached had Lily considered that it had been over six months since she was in the city, and things may have changed. She would have felt awful making Ava and Alexei walk so far for nothing.

They followed the signs to the reception office and walked in, a small bell tinkling as they opened the door.

"Well hello," a middle-aged woman in heavy makeup greeted them. "How may I help you today?"

"We're after an apartment," said Lily, feeling like she was stating the obvious.

"For how long, sweetie?"

"Um, a week?" Lily said, glancing at her friends. The lady cocked her head curiously. "A week for a start," said Lily more confidently. "We may stay longer, but we're not sure yet."

"How much would that be?" asked Ava, smiling at the woman warmly.

"Well now, that depends on the apartment, sugar! Let me show you what's available."

Lily, Ava, and Alexei listened as enthusiastically as they could manage as the lady took them through all the different variations of apartments that existed before mentioning that, in fact, only two were currently available.

"We'll take the smaller one. Thanks, Jill," said Lily quickly.

"Right you are, darling. I'll need payment up front."

"Er, can we put a deposit down and bring you the rest later today?"

"I'll take one night's rent as a deposit, but you bring me the rest in the morning. I have things to attend to after lunch," she said with a wink. They all smiled politely, unsure of what the wink meant and unwilling to speculate.

Lily handed over the cash and Jill pulled out a wad of paperwork, thumping it on the counter before her phone rang. She turned her back to the group and answered it professionally before devolving into a series of giggles. Ava raised an eyebrow at Lily, who tried not to laugh. Jill murmured into the phone, her voice lower now, and then turned, starting at seeing the three people in her office watching her.

Jill mouthed "First thing tomorrow," while pushing a

key with a large keyring at Lily. She snatched it up and they left, heading off to locate their apartment.

"What was that?" asked Ava, glee in her voice, eyes sparkling.

"I don't want to know," said Alexei.

"Husband?" Lily guessed. "Lover?"

"Boy toy, more like," said Ava excitedly. "I bet our Jill knows these apartments so well because she tries them out with each of her men."

"Okay, okay," said Alexei, gesturing for her to stop. "These are images I neither want nor need."

The girls laughed at him, teasing him a bit more as they located their apartment and pushed open the door.

"Oooh, nice," said Ava, looking around appreciatively.

"One bed," called Alexei from the bedroom. "You two can have it. I'll take the couch."

They spent a little time poking around their new home, discussing the supplies they'd get for the kitchenette and opening various cupboards before sitting on the couch to plan their next steps.

"Okay, so, where do we sell these gems?" asked Ava, who had the bag on her lap and was absentmindedly running her hands through the gems.

"There are a couple of places nearby," said Lily, pulling out her phone and doing a quick search. "I think we try a jewellers first. There's literally nothing like these gems in this world, so we should be able to get a good price. We'll sell a couple at first to cover the week here. Then, as we're looking for my family, we can sound a couple of other places out, see who'll give us the best price."

"Okay," said Alexei, leaning forward, clearly eager to get moving. "So we'll sell a couple of gems, drop the rest back here, and then head to find your ex or your friend."

"Yep. Since they both go to the same university, we can

look there and see if we can find either of them," said Lily, secretly hoping they would find Gemma first.

Feeling positive about the way forward, they freshened up and headed back out into the city. The nearest shops were only a few streets away, and they reached them fairly quickly. Picking a fancy jewellery store, the three trooped in, immediately feeling underdressed and out of place. The security guard glared at them. Two of the shop assistants paused their chatter and looked them up and down—briefly pausing on Alexei—before resuming their discussion. No one hurried over to help them.

Lily walked confidently up to the counter, imagining their embarrassment when they realised what she had to offer.

"Excuse me," Lily said when her presence at the counter didn't prompt an end to the assistants' discussion.

"Can I help you?" one of them asked, sickly sweet with a fake smile.

"Yes. I was wondering if you might be interested in purchasing this." Lily placed a large, dazzling gem in the middle of the counter. The assistant's eyes bulged. He looked up, examining Lily with a new lens.

"Let me get the manager," he said before scurrying away. His fellow assistant smiled politely at Lily, her eyes flicking between the gem and her face.

"Good morning," said a larger man, his tone polite but all business. "I hear you are looking to sell."

"Yes, I am," said Lily. "How much would you offer for this one?"

The manager picked up the gem, examining it, his eyes growing wider the longer he looked.

"I have more," said Lily as he held a magnifier up to his eye, and almost lost it as he reacted with surprise.

The manager examined the gem for a long time, turning

it this way and that. He didn't say a word, and Lily began to oscillate between nerves and excitement. Surely it'd be worth a lot of money.

The manager put down the magnifier and the gem and sighed, looking at Lily and her friends.

"Where did you get this?" he asked.

"It's been in my family for generations," Lily answered truthfully. "It pains me to part with it, but ..." she hesitated, about to say she needed the money but worrying about sounding desperate.

The manager scrutinised her for a minute before seeming to come to a decision. "I'll give you this for it," he said, writing a number on a scrap of paper and sliding it towards her like he was in a movie. Lily's eyes widened. She knew she should negotiate, but—

"Done," she said before her brain could stop her.

"Excellent." The manager smiled. "I'll just need to see some ID." He began pulling out some papers.

Lily's heart sank. Obviously, neither Alexei nor Ava had identification, and her driver's licence was sitting uselessly in a drawer back in her bedroom in the palace.

"Uh, I don't have it with me," said Lily, trying to think of a way to convince the man to go through with the sale without it.

His eyes narrowed, immediately suspicious again. She saw him cast a meaningful look at the security guard, who started to move in what he thought was a casual manner toward the group.

"I can bring it in a couple of days," said Lily, her mind so focussed on wondering how long it'd take to get a replacement licence that she didn't notice how much her plea didn't help.

"Okay," said the manager, surprising Lily. "Why don't

you all wait here? Let me make a phone call and see if we can buy it without your ID."

She watched him move to the back of the store and pick up a phone. He began speaking into it, casting looks back at the group every so often.

Lily turned to Ava and Alexei. "I don't have ID," she explained. "He's checking to see if he can buy the gem without seeing it."

Ava and Alexei stared at Lily, dumbfounded. They looked pointedly at the security guard now standing very close to them.

"Lily, he's probably calling the police," said Ava, getting nervous. "A group of kids dressed like us, trying to sell a very expensive gem and not wanting to provide identification?"

It dawned on Lily how that looked. She turned and looked at the manager. He was still casting them glances, but now it looked like he might be describing them to someone. *Shit.*

Lily snatched up the gem and the three friends hurried to the door, the security guard on their heels.

"Hey!" the manager called from the back of the room.

They ignored him, pushing out the door before the security guard could think to stop them. Alexei led them back the way they'd come, heading toward their apartment, no one speaking as they hurried to put distance between them and the store.

"I didn't even think about that," Lily berated herself, puffing slightly. "Any reputable place is going to want at least ID, if not some kind of proof that the gems are not stolen."

"None of us thought about it," said Alexei kindly. "But then, what are we going to do? If we can't sell the gems, how will we get money?"

Lily thought as they passed their apartment, now simply walking without a clear destination. "We need money fast to secure the apartment. I guess we could try a less reputable place. They might not be as strict about the ID, but we probably won't get as much money." She thought about the figure on the scrap of paper. "We definitely won't get as much money. But if we get enough to secure the apartment, I can try to get my ID replaced, and then we should be okay."

"Well, let's go then," said Ava brightly.

Lily led them back toward the bus station, sure that there would be a pawnshop nearby. As they walked farther, it became clear that they were heading into the bad part of town. Shop fronts were boarded up, and those that weren't were not easily distinguished. Signs, where the stores had them, were broken or faded, and windows were often so grimy that they served little purpose. Lily had never been in this part of the city before, and she could see why. She definitely did not feel safe here.

Lily clutched her backpack a little tighter and felt Ava and Alexei move in closer, all scanning their surroundings and trying to look alert, rather than like scared tourists and easy marks. Lily spotted a pawnshop and led her friends towards it. They remained on the other side of the road, trying to avoid moving close to a group of intimidating men who were sitting on some stairs that led to an apartment, though the entrance had been roped off with what looked suspiciously like crime scene tape.

A small voice in Lily's head suggested that it was not too late to look for a pawnshop that was less likely to see them mugged immediately upon exiting, but she worried that an abrupt change of direction might attract more attention, and she told herself that she could always enter, have a look around, and leave.

The pawnshop was the polar opposite to the jewellers. It was a dingy store that clearly saw no need to worry about advertising or product placement when their main clients were down on their luck, and therefore largely a captive audience. Lily knew the security guard just inside the door was to protect the stock and owners from the customers, but she felt a little better for him being there. Whereas the security guard in the jewellery store had been wearing a suit, this man seemed to be wearing a tactical vest.

Ava wandered off down an aisle, making sure to keep the counter in view, to look at the various gadgets, and Alexei headed towards the gruff man behind the register. They had decided that Alexei should take the lead here, since an imposing man was less likely to be taken advantage of than a smaller woman. Alexei had a few of the smaller gems with him, and one medium gem in case the pawnshop owner seemed willing to negotiate, but the vast majority of their horde was bundled up in Lily's backpack.

After a few minutes, Lily approached the counter to see how Alexei was doing, unable to take the suspense. The pawnshop owner was hunched over the gems, holding a red one and squinting at it through some magnifying device.

"This a ruby?" he grunted at Alexei.

"Sure, I guess so."

"Doesn't look like a ruby." The man's brow furrowed. Clearly, the gem was nothing he had seen before.

"It's a special ruby," said Alexei. "One of a kind."

The man grunted at Alexei and swapped the red gem for a bright green one. His brow furrowed again. He turned it this way and that, then dropped it back in the pile and removed his magnifying device from his eye.

"I'll give you one hundred for the lot."

"They're worth much more than that."

"Sure, but how do I know that? I've not seen anything

like them before. I don't know if there's going to be a market." The man scratched his belly. "Two hundred. But that's it."

"Even if you've not seen any gems like this before, you can tell they're not costume jewellery."

The man grunted and stared at the gems intently, weighing his options.

"And surely you can trade on the fact that they're unique," Lily said, appearing at Alexei's side. "You must have buyers who get off on having one-of-a-kind items?"

The man stared blankly at Lily for a minute, as if wondering where she had come from. Then he nodded and opened his cash register. "Three hundred. Last offer." He began counting notes onto the counter.

"Four," said Alexei.

The owner stared hard at him, but Alexei met his gaze and held it. Not dropping eye contact, the owner dropped another note onto the pile. "Three fifty."

Alexei made to take the money, but the owner slammed a hand on top of it. "ID?"

Lily's stomach sank. *Not again.* She had been sure that a place like this wouldn't worry about regulations. The owner smirked at Lily's expression and removed a note from the pile.

"Two fifty. Now go on, get out of here. And these better not have been stolen," he called as they exited the store.

Lily led her friends out of the decrepit neighbourhood, and once they seemed to be in a slightly better part of the city, she found a nearby cafe and ordered them all some lunch. They sat by the window. Lily looked up and thought she saw one of the men from outside the pawnshop pass by, but she decided that she was being paranoid.

"Is this going to be enough money?" asked Ava anxiously.

"It'll do," said Lily. She had been hoping that they could get enough in one go to pay for the apartment for the whole week. This would only get them a couple of days.

Their food arrived and Lily absentmindedly dipped one of her fries in her mayonnaise and ate it. She had been hoping it would be easy to sell the gems. But this was okay. They had bought a couple of days. She could use that time to try to get her licence replaced and then they could sell the rest of the gems and it would be fine. It was probably better this way, Lily tried to convince herself, considering they should be able to get a lead on her family and might want to relocate somewhere closer.

They ate in relative silence, Ava and Alexei expressing their thoughts on the foreign food, then headed back out into the crisp spring air. Lily led them back toward their apartment to secure the gems before heading to the university to look for Brandon and Gemma. It was early afternoon, so unless their schedules had changed significantly, they should be in class.

"Problem?" Ava asked.

Lily kept looking around behind them. She felt a tingle on her neck, like they were being watched, but she couldn't see anyone suspicious. *Probably just being paranoid.*

"No, I just have a weird feeling. Still spooked from the pawnshop, I guess," she said with a small, humourless laugh. Ava and Alexei started glancing behind them too, the result being that they all looked far more suspicious than anyone following them would have.

They arrived back at their apartment without incident and hid the gems on the top shelf of a cupboard under some blankets. Not the most inventive hiding spot, but the apartment was secure. Heading back down to the street, a man across the road caught her eye. *Could it be ...* No, she was getting paranoid. But she could have sworn it was another of the men from outside the pawnshop. She watched the man walk away toward the industrial area. She exhaled, relieved. He was just a worker heading off to his job. Lily mentally pulled herself together and turned to Ava and Alexei.

"Right, let's head to the university."

10

"Finally," said Ava, stretching. It had wound up being a longer walk than Lily had thought. She had usually grabbed a ride with friends and was surprised at how much longer it took to walk, especially with the "shortcut" she had led them on that had ended in a tall wire fence she hadn't known about and a requirement to backtrack.

Ava straightened up and looked around. "Wait, *this* is a university? I thought you said it was all about learning."

"They are learning physics," said Alexei brightly, pointing to their left. Lily looked over and saw a group of students playing frisbee golf.

"Physics? What's physics?" Ava asked.

"It's one of their sciences," said Alexei enthusiastically. "I looked it up on the phone while you two slept on the bus earlier. They've built all of these theories to explain how things work without enchantments, magic, or cybernetics."

Ava stared at Alexei, a look bordering on disgust on her face. "Why would you do that?"

"Do what?"

"Look up *science*. You have a new world's entire knowledge database at your fingertips. Next time, search for cat videos. You're welcome."

"Anyway," Lily broke into the discussion, "they're not learning, they're playing. Goofing off in between class."

"And where are the classes?" asked Alexei, looking around.

"They have class inside. See those buildings up there? This is a sports field."

"Why are they all armed?" asked Ava.

"What?" said Lily, alarmed.

"Those three have knives in their pockets, and that guy has an electric gun."

"He's a campus security guard, and that's a taser. But they shouldn't—hey, what are you doing?"

Ava had snatched the phone out of Lily's hands.

"This would be so much faster if I could link my implant. Where is that search thingy ... okay, frisbee golf ... oh. Why?"

"Why any sport?" said Lily, distracted. She was trying to get her bearings, not having spent much time on this part of the campus.

"Okay," said Ava, reading Lily's mood. "Where might your friends be?"

"If they're on campus, they'll be in the economics build-ing. It's this way." Lily started off to her right, adding under her breath, "I think."

Lily and Ava got a few metres before realising that Alexei wasn't following. They called to him.

"Sorry," he said, catching up but glancing over his shoulder. "I thought I saw one of the guys from outside the pawnshop."

"Really?" Lily's stomach dropped. "I thought I saw a couple of them earlier, but I figured I was just being paranoid."

"Where did you see them?"

"One outside the cafe where we had lunch and another outside the apartment."

Alexei looked back in the direction where he had seen the man, frowning.

"Not much we can do," said Ava, prodding them all back into motion, heading towards the economics building. "We'll keep an eye out, and if we need to, we can find somewhere else to stay tonight."

"You're right," Lily said. "But first, let's find Gemma or Brandon."

Lily thought they might be in class, trying to remember their schedules, but they circled the economics building twice in case they were waiting for one to begin, or chatting afterwards. Reluctantly, Lily led them inside the building.

Aside from her desire to simply ghost Brandon rather than deal with him head-on, Lily had had no desire to ever be in this building again. For her, the building was full of bad memories and broken dreams. She didn't know what she had thought she'd do with her degree, had she managed to earn one, but when she first arrived on campus, everything had seemed so full of promise.

Now it was as if she had been transported back in time. She could feel the sense of loss when she had realised that this path was not for her. That the course was difficult, and she was not interested enough to put in the effort required to pass. Unfortunately, despite having realised that a degree in business and economics was not for her, she'd had no idea what she did want.

They wandered around the building aimlessly, looking in windows and scanning the faces of the people they passed. Lily didn't know which rooms Brandon or Gemma's classes were in, nor could she see any familiar faces of people she could ask. She was slightly relieved by this. She didn't want to run into anyone who knew her well enough to know she had gone missing, or anyone who would ask awkward questions about what she was doing now.

Well, I'm about to be crowned queen of a country in a different dimension, and in my spare time, I practise magic. You?

Eventually she decided that Brandon and Gemma either weren't in the building, or their haphazard search was unlikely to find them, and, eager to get away from bad memories, Lily led her friends back out into the fresh air.

Thinking Brandon at least might be at the university bar, Lily led Ava and Alexei through the social precinct and into a large, converted library building. Now that classes were almost done for the day, the bar was starting to get busy. A quick pass through the bar, out through the beer garden, and back into the pool hall told Lily that Brandon wasn't there. She hadn't really expected him to be, having realised how futile a plan all this was when they were looking for him in the economics building. Reflexively she checked her phone, wondering if she could ask the university administration department for Brandon or Gemma's contact details or class schedule. Or maybe see if they could somehow pass hers along. Unfortunately, the administration section was closed now. Maybe they could try tomorrow.

Lily turned and shrugged at her companions, who, far from being disheartened, remained fascinated by their surroundings. Deciding not to waste the opportunity, Lily helped her friends order some food and drinks, and they returned to the beer garden, grabbing a table in the back corner that afforded a view of the whole area.

"So, these are your scholars?" Ava said, looking slightly bewildered as two young men engaged in a drinking competition, while another staggered inside in urgent search of a bathroom.

"I guess," said Lily, frowning. "I mean, I suppose it's become more of a business. Education, I mean. Selling certifications that employers can rely on, claiming that these people have a certain level of knowledge or understanding about whatever their degree is in. Don't your countries have universities?"

"We do on-the-job training," said Ava. "And apprenticeships. You learn by doing, but with supervision."

"We have scholar halls," said Alexei. Lily waited for him to explain, but he seemed to think it didn't require anything further and became engrossed in watching a game of beer pong until Lily prodded him and asked for more information.

"Our best thinkers gather and discuss ideas. They read papers from other halls and discuss those, and often send their own thoughts in response."

"Sounds like pointless navel-gazing," said Ava into her beer.

"What they learn is sent out into the world. They are often consulted by magistrates, engineers, teachers, politicians—"

"Oh, I can just see your dad having a deep conversation with some philosopher!" Ava laughed.

"It is not his … favourite part of the job," Alexei allowed, his mouth twitching as he tried not to smile. "But at any rate, not just anyone can go." He watched as two students tried to high five each other, missed, and fell into bushes on either side of their table.

Lily looked around. She had never minded the social side of university, but she certainly didn't miss her classes. And listening to Ava and Alexei, she somehow felt that this mass-produced education missed the point. She felt briefly better about her decision to drop out, before realising that it was a moot subject since she was meant to be the queen of

Highacre and no longer needed a university degree, anyway. *Assuming we make it back.*

Their food arrived, and the trio fell silent as they enjoyed their meals. When they were done and Alexei had delivered more drinks to their table, they settled into some good-natured people-watching and Lily felt herself begin to relax. With all the stress, she felt as if she had been back for months, but in reality, it had only been a little over a week.

Lily's mind drifted to the current problem set. How was she going to track down her family? Especially since she seemed incapable of even tracking down her ex-boyfriend. And she at least knew generally where he should be.

"Hey, we're having fun tonight. We agreed," Ava said, a mock stern look on her face.

"I know, it's just—"

"It's just nothing. Come on, you know there's nothing else we can do tonight. And this was only our first try at finding your friends. It was always going to be a long shot to find them on the first go. And honestly, it wasn't a really good first attempt."

Lily had to admit that Ava had a point. She shouldn't get depressed about failing to find her friends after a few hours of aimlessly wandering around campus. She felt a pang of guilt that she couldn't remember their schedules, before realising that she'd been gone over six months. They would have completely new schedules. Lily felt briefly better for not remembering, before a now familiar hopelessness washed over her. At least if she knew when he had class, they'd be able to target their efforts better.

"And we can always try their apartments."

Lily looked over at Alexei, stunned. *Why didn't I think of that?* The only explanation, other than extreme exhaustion and stress, that Lily could come up with to excuse her not thinking of going to Brandon's flat was that it felt too intimate. Even with her friends in tow. Despite the desperation she felt to find her family, she was still wanting to avoid the difficult conversation that she needed to have with him. It would be bad enough having to explain why she left without a word and where she had been without crushing a happy reunion with a dumping.

Brandon could be quite expressive and Lily would much prefer to have that conversation in public where he'd be more likely to moderate his response. With a flush of shame, she couldn't think of a good reason for not considering heading to Gemma's flat as an option. Maybe they weren't the good friends Lily had thought they were. They had always been different, but Lily had assumed they were close because opposites were sometimes attracted to each other. Now it seemed that they had been friends merely because life had thrown them together. Once their paths had diverged, the connection was gone.

"Again." Ava nudged Lily. "All of this is a tomorrow problem. For now, introduce us to your culture." She pointed at the beer pong table that had just been vacated, and she and Alexei moved towards it.

"Oh no," said Lily, catching her friends and steering them towards the pool hall. "None of us need hangovers tomorrow, and besides, we can't go over the top with the money." They instead found a vacant table and Lily explained the rules as best as she could remember them. Ava snatched up a cue and started, potting all the balls on her first turn and causing the others to refuse to play unless she promised not to use her implant.

In the end, the rules were largely forgotten, and they simply took turns potting balls until a shot was missed. They stopped after two drinks, but were relaxed, laughing and joking and having a great night.

"Lily?"

Lily stopped wrestling Alexei for the cue and turned, grinning, to see who had said her name. Her face fell as she saw Brandon staring at her slack-jawed and holding another girl's hand.

Gemma.

"Hey," said Lily, breaking free of Alexei and moving toward her boyfriend and best friend. "We were looking for you."

Brandon and Gemma looked pointedly at the pool table where Lily and her friends had been cavorting.

"I mean, we came here today to find you, and we couldn't, so we had dinner and then ..." Lily trailed off, and an awkward silence descended.

Brandon shook his head as if to clear it and dropped Gemma's hand, moving towards Lily. "My god, Lily. Where have you been?"

"We've been so worried," said Gemma, moving in and giving her a tight hug.

"I was ... well, I mean ..." Lily's brain failed her. "I was kidnapped by a cult. Alexei and Ava were there too." She gestured to them, sensing them tense at her choice of story. "We escaped," she finished feebly, shrugging.

"And came to the uni bar?" said Gemma, unconvinced. She released Lily and stepped back into her position at Brandon's side.

"No, I went home to find my family, but they weren't there, and the lady who owns our farm now said they moved to the city and so we worked for them until we had enough money and came here to find you two, to see if you know where they are." Lily tried to keep her tone neutral. She was annoyed at having to explain herself. At the implication that she had disappeared and now was simply hanging out with friends and having a good time.

She was also irked that Gemma and Brandon were

clearly together. Even though she had been planning on dumping Brandon, and despite the fact that she had long thought the two of them would make a better couple than she and Brandon did, it bothered her that it seemed to have happened so quickly.

Brandon frowned. "Wait, so you escaped a while ago? Why haven't you called to let us know you're alright? We've all been beside ourselves."

"I lost my phone and I couldn't remember your numbers," said Lily. Though she was sure they would be hard pressed to recall her number without assistance, she noted they both looked offended, and her mood soured further. "I did email you," she said defensively.

Both automatically whipped out their phones and checked all the email folders that might house Lily's message before declaring that nothing had come through.

"Did you use the three?" Brandon asked.

"And they spelled my last name wrong," Gemma added, hurt starting to darken her features. "Don't you remember? We joked about it for ages."

Lily closed her eyes, trying to ignore the feelings of being judged. Of having unrealistic expectations foisted upon her. She had done her best. She knew that her absence had clearly been hard for everyone left behind, but it hadn't exactly been a holiday for her either.

"No, I'm sorry, I forgot. It's been ... it's been a difficult time for me as well."

Lily saw her friends' expressions turn from relief and happiness at her return to suspicion and judgement. Feeling this was utterly unfair in the circumstances, Lily asked, "So, how long have you two been dating?"

Gemma had the grace to blush, whereas the blood drained from Brandon's face.

"Oh no, we're not ... I mean, we didn't ... you were gone

so long, and it just kind of ... happened." Brandon weakly finished his attempt to distance himself from Gemma and play down their relationship. Gemma looked stung, but glowered at the ground rather than cause a scene. Brandon looked frantically from Lily to Gemma, caught in a trap and unable to decide which way to jump.

Lily's anger at her friend dissolved and was replaced by sympathy. It was clear Gemma really liked Brandon, and his uncertainty about her now that Lily was back, and seemingly an option, hurt her.

"Look, Brandon—" she began.

"Lily," he interrupted, as if sensing what might be coming. "I still can't believe you're back. You just vanished, and then we heard nothing for so long. But now that you're back, we can all talk about what's happened and figure out—"

"Brandon, things happen for a reason." She looked pointedly at Gemma. "I think this is for the best. You and I —we were probably over anyway, and you and Gemma seem like a good match."

Far from being grateful, Gemma seemed to resent Lily's words, and Lily had to admit in hindsight that they sounded slightly patronising. "And anyway, I don't know what my future looks like at this point, and so it's best that I'm not with anyone."

A group of students had moved in behind them, asking Ava and Alexei if they were done with the table. Handing over the cues, Ava and Alexei moved to stand behind Lily.

"Your family," Alexei whispered to Lily, reminding her of the point of trying to find Brandon in the first place.

Brandon watched the exchange, seeming to fully take Alexei in for the first time, his eyes narrowing. "Oh. Oh, okay. I get it. You're with him."

"What?" Lily blinked at him, caught completely off guard.

"Don't bullshit me, Lily," Brandon spat, suddenly angry and embarrassed. "Don't give me that 'I need to be alone' line. Clearly you're together. Is he why you ran off in the first place?"

"Oh my god, do not come at me when you've hooked up with my best friend," Lily snarled.

"We're not best friends," Gemma snapped.

"We are not together," Alexei added in a loud voice, interrupting the beginning of a fight and attracting not only the attention of the group, but everyone in the room.

"Good news for me, sexy!" called a voice from over at the bar. Someone wolf-whistled and the room dissolved into laughter.

"Just ask them and we can go," said Ava to Lily quietly, touching her arm reassuringly and calming her down. Lily swallowed her next attack and nodded at Ava. Finding her family was more important.

Gemma clocked the touch and looked at the two women, suspiciously at first, and then a smug, knowing expression spread across her face.

"Look," said Brandon. He was slightly calmer, though his cheeks remained flushed with anger. "I'm just saying that you should be honest about being with him, rather than just trying to make me feel bad for moving on too. I didn't even know if you were alive, and—"

"They're not together," Gemma cut across Brandon, stopping his rant before he could gather steam. "*They* are." She nodded to Ava and Lily.

"What?" Lily looked at Gemma in annoyed confusion.

"It's okay, Lily. I mean, it explains a lot."

"What on Earth are you talking about?"

"You're with Ava. Is that why you ran away? You were afraid of coming out?"

"I—wait, what?" Lily was struggling to keep up with the change of direction. She was vaguely aware of Alexei nudging Ava behind her.

Brandon was looking from Lily to Ava and back, a completely bewildered expression on his face that Lily would have found hilarious in any other situation.

"No, we're—"

"We didn't want you to find out like this," Ava interrupted, putting an arm around Lily's waist and pulling her close. "And you're right. Lily was confused by her feelings. She left to try to figure it out."

"What are you—?"

"Lots of therapy," Ava spoke over Lily.

"I ... no. Lily?" Brandon looked lost, unsure of how to react to this twist in events.

"Brandon—" she started.

"I was good in bed," he stated as fact, seemingly as much for himself as for the others listening.

"What?"

"This isn't my fault. I'm a generous lover."

Lily heard Alexei snort and could feel Ava struggling to suppress her laughter, their bodies still pressed together.

"Do you really think that has anything to do with why people are gay?" Lily gaped at him.

"People like us," added Ava, giving Lily a little squeeze to remind her of their story. "We're gay."

"I'm just saying, it's not my fault."

"Lily needs to come out to her family," Ava blurted before Lily could respond. "But we went to the farm, and they're not there. Do you know where they went?"

Brandon's expression turned slightly alarmed, whereas Gemma had a hint of satisfied malice in her eyes.

"You don't know?" Brandon asked, slightly panicked.

"No, what happened?"

Brandon looked at Gemma for help, but she just nodded encouragingly at him. Lily felt panic rising in her chest.

"I mean, you've been gone for ages. Missing. We didn't know where you were, or if you were alright."

Lily bit back the urge to point out that despite that, he'd hooked up with her best friend. *Stay on topic.*

"We didn't know if you'd ever be back. Your family, they never gave up hope, though. They ran ad campaigns, put up posters. They were even on TV. They put all their money into trying to find you."

Gemma muttered something under her breath, and Lily stabbed her with an icy glare. She saw Brandon squeeze her hand and shake his head.

"They had to sell the farm. They moved here to the city. Apparently, they figured this was the best place to be to find you, since this is where you went missing. And there were better job opportunities so that they could fund the effort to find you."

"So where are they?" Lily was getting impatient. She largely knew all this.

"Uh, I only know where David is." Brandon was now very uncomfortable. Clearly, there was something that he didn't want to be the one to tell her. Lily tried to ignore her worry about what that might be. She could push him, but if he didn't want to tell her, he wouldn't, and then he would leave. Better to get a solid lead.

"So where is he?"

"He hangs out at Goodman's, over on 5th Street. He's there most nights, I think."

Goodman's was a bar near the centre of the city. It attracted the kind of office workers who couldn't afford the trendier bars and clubs. David had never been much of a drinker beyond a beer at the end of a day's work on the farm, but maybe he was working there?

Again, Lily felt jarred by how off everything seemed. Nothing was how she had expected it to be. Nothing was familiar, and she felt more alone and off-balance than she had when she arrived in Highacre.

"We'd better head off, babe," Gemma said to Brandon, clutching his arm and pressing her body against his.

"Oh, yeah. Yeah, we have to go." He looked at Lily, clearly unsure of the protocol for saying goodbye to the girl you had been dating but thought was gone for good, then hooked up with her friend, and who had now just dumped you, apparently for a girl.

"Yeah, we should too," said Ava. "Come on, spunky." She turned Lily's face and kissed her gently on the lips. Thoughts fled Lily's mind and her body tingled. Shocked, she blinked blankly at Ava, who grinned mischievously back.

"Bye, Lily," said Gemma, pulling a gawping Brandon with her. Lily watched as they exited the bar, heads together, quietly bickering.

"Well, that was productive," said Alexei brightly. Lily looked at him, still slightly stunned and aware that Ava hadn't yet dropped her hand, despite Brandon and Gemma having left. "Should we go straight to that bar? Or do we need to decide if we're still staying at that apartment and try the bar tomorrow?"

"Let's go there now. We can do a quick check and try again properly tomorrow."

"Okay," said Ava brightly, leading them out of the university bar. She fell into step with Lily as they took the path through the campus. "You might have mentioned how much of a bitch your friend is."

"She's not," said Lily, instinctively defending Gemma. "Or at least, she never used to be. I probably wasn't the best friend to her. And fair enough that she hooked up with Brandon. She did think I was dead."

11

LILY NEVER USED to go out clubbing much when she had lived in the city. She had told herself it was because it was so expensive, but truthfully, it had just never been her thing. Now, having been largely cooped up in the palace for six months, the sensory overload of the city centre was intense. The lights, noise, and crush of people was too much, and Lily felt her anxiety rising.

Groups of happily drunk students, office workers, and tourists jostled and bumped Lily and her friends, and she was becoming aggravated by the entitlement that led others to take up the entire sidewalk.

Lily couldn't help her mind from replaying the conversation with her friends over and over.

It's okay, Lily. I mean, it explains a lot.

What had Gemma meant by that comment? She knew there were other parts of the conversation that she should be more focused on. Like what Brandon had clearly not wanted to tell her. But her mind kept looping between Gemma's comment and Ava's kiss. And Gemma had assumed she might be scared to come out. So scared she disappeared for six months.

Lily's mind turned this over. Would she be scared to come out if she was gay? She didn't *think* her family would care. Her parents told their children "so long as you're happy" so much it was practically a catchphrase. She remembered David becoming quiet when they were all wondering about the two men who had bought the Reilly's farm a few years ago. But before she'd left to go to university, David had struck an agreement with them to let his cows graze in their bottom paddock.

Not that it mattered anyway, since she wasn't gay. Was she? Lily felt a heightened level of confusion about her feelings for Ava. They were definitely good friends, but Lily had never been interested in a girl before. How did you know if your feelings were something more? And what did it matter, anyway? She'd wandered through life on the default setting of "straight". And it's not like that had been going well for her. Would her life really be that different if she was gay or bisexual? She felt a twinge of conflicting emotions. Anxiety about rejection from those she cared about collided with a strong conviction that anyone who felt differently about her because of the gender of the person she was with wasn't worth worrying about.

Her musings carried her the rest of the way to Goodman's, and when she saw the building ahead, she pushed the thoughts from her mind, eager to get off the crowded street. A feeling of relief washed over her as she slipped through the door to Goodman's, but it was short-lived, her spirits dipping when she saw how crowded it was and realised she could barely hear the music over the rowdy conversations.

"Can you see him?" Ava yelled into Lily's ear. Lily shook her head, though she could barely see past the groups of people crowding around the entrance, so that didn't mean he wasn't there.

"Follow me," Alexei boomed as he squeezed past and began carving a path to the bar. It was an easy task for six-foot-tall, broad-shouldered Alexei, and Lily noticed his job was made easier by most of the women in his trajectory moving to watch him appreciatively.

Ava and Lily hurried to take advantage of his wake before the throngs of people resumed their positions. They carved out some space in the corner where people weren't vying for the harried bartender's attention and looked around.

"Anything?"

Lily shook her head, a feeling of hopelessness descending. She knew she shouldn't expect finding her family to be easy. They had been lucky to find Brandon; it would be too much to hope they would also find David in the bar on their first visit. But Brandon's reaction to being asked about her family had been gnawing at her. What had happened?

They held their ground at the corner of the bar, with Lily scanning the crowd as best she could for another ten minutes. She knew she needed to actually move around in order to see beyond about three people deep, but she was suddenly exhausted, and the idea of squeezing through the drunk, sweaty patrons was not appealing in the least. Knowing that they'd need to do that anyway to exit the bar at this point had her paralysed, even though she knew she needed to either find David or get going. Particularly if they needed to find somewhere else to stay.

"Gross, check out the sleaze in the corner," Ava said, glaring at something in the next room. Lily couldn't see what Ava was looking at from her position. They were in the main bar area of Goodman's, but there were several rooms, each decorated slightly differently, where patrons could gather. The room Ava was looking at was set up like a comfortable lounge area with deep, plush armchairs and couches. Lily shuffled towards Ava, intending to use the momentum to keep going and lead her friends out of the bar.

She glanced in the direction of Ava's gaze, more to be polite and not ignore her comment, but quickly performed a double take. A man was sprawled in a large wing chair, one girl sitting on his lap, one on the edge of his chair, and another perched on a nearby coffee table that looked to have been dragged over so that she could sit closer to the man. He had an arm around the girl on his lap, ostensibly to support her and ensure she didn't fall, though it seemed possessive as well. All his attention, however, was on the other two girls, carrying on a conversation with them while his eyes raked their bodies greedily.

His behaviour wasn't shocking to Lily, who had seen her share of drunken jerks. What did shock her was that the man was David. Her collared-shirt wearing, proper manners, almost snobbish big brother, who had warned her repeatedly about falling in with the wrong crowd when she moved to the city for university, was completely legless and almost slobbering over three girls. They all looked much too young for him, not to mention he was supposed to be engaged. If Simone could see him, she'd be furious.

"Lily," said Ava loudly in her ear, touching her arm to get her attention. "We should probably head out and sort out our accommodation."

Lily was torn. Here was her chance to find out what had happened to her family, and certainly the image before her increased her sense of foreboding. But the man she was watching wasn't behaving like the brother she knew, and she didn't know what to do. Even if she approached him, would he be able to give her the answers she was after in his current state? Maybe she should come back tomorrow. She could arrive early and wait for him. Catch him before he started drinking. But what if he didn't come tomorrow, and she lost her chance?

"Lily," said Ava again, shaking her slightly.

"That's my brother." Lily nodded toward David and his girls.

"Your brother's a sleaze?"

"No. Well, I mean ..." Lily struggled again to reconcile the image of the David before her with her memory of her older brother. "He never used to be."

"What are we waiting for?" asked Alexei. He moved off toward David before Lily could protest, with Ava on his heels. Lily hurried to follow before the path through the patrons closed behind them.

Lily saw David look up as Alexei blocked the light, casting a shadow over him and his girls. He glared up, squinting at Alexei, while his companions eyed the newcomer eagerly.

"What do you want?" David demanded.

Ava moved out from behind Alexei to curious looks from the girls and more interest from David. This distraction meant that when Lily appeared to Alexei's right, no one noticed her.

"Alright, sweetheart, you can join us," David slurred at Ava before glancing back at Alexei. "*You* can bugger off."

"Oh come on Dave," whined the girl in David's lap, her eyes fluttering at Alexei. "They can all stay, right? The more the merrier."

"All?" David said, confused and blinking as he looked about. His eyes found Lily, and the blinking increased. He stared at her, slightly unseeing for a while, his expression that of someone who knows that they should know who they're looking at, but can't quite place them.

"Hi David," Lily said. Her voice was too quiet to hear given the volume of Goodman's, but something clicked behind David's eyes.

"Lily?" David looked at her, awestruck. His face almost broke into a smile before something else seemed to click in his head and his demeanour darkened. "Well, where the bloody hell have you been?"

Lily was now sitting awkwardly to David's left on a chair that Alexei had procured and nursing a drink that Ava had brought her, thinking buying a round for the group might ease the tension. David hadn't asked Lily for answers again. He seemed more perturbed by the interest his companions continued to show in Alexei.

Lily was frustrated that David seemed disinclined to talk, so she tried to use her magic to read his mind. But her grasp on her ability was still clumsy, and it was difficult to concentrate in the pub. She only discovered that David wanted to go to the bathroom, and that he was annoyed by Alexei, neither of which was ground-breaking or useful.

Hearing another bout of ingratiating laughter, Lily turned her attention back to the group. Lily had wondered whether Alexei might excuse himself from the women as he had back at the farm, but he either thought that David might be easier to talk to without the female distractions, or he was enjoying the attention.

"So, where are you from, sugar?" the girl on David's lap asked Alexei, before sipping seductively on her straw.

"Who cares?" snorted David before Alexei could answer. He gave the girl what he seemed to think was a playful slap on her rump, but was rougher than intended and the girl pulled away and shot him a dirty look. David seemed to decide that this was Alexei's fault and glared across at the larger man.

"You're very tall," one of David's other companions informed Alexei.

"I suppose it depends on your perspective," Alexei replied. The girl laughed as if this was the cleverest response she'd ever heard, leant over, and touched Alexei's arm.

"Oh, you're *so* funny. And gosh! Strong too."

Ava snorted and took a quick drink, trying to cover her reaction, but the other girls only had eyes for Alexei. Her snort did attract David's attention though, and perhaps deciding his drinking companions were a lost cause, turned his sights on her.

"And where are you from, beautiful?"

Apparently, at this stage of inebriation, the array of available pick-up lines had narrowed considerably.

Ava rolled her eyes at David, fixed him with a stare that told him exactly how pathetic she found him, and replied, "I prefer women."

Angry, David returned his attention to the girl in his lap, who no longer wanted his paws all over her and stood up, loudly telling him to piss off. Her friends stood too, glaring at David before heading to the bathroom to console each other and freshen their makeup before looking for other options.

"Oh, great. Nice one." David glared at Lily and her friends. "Thanks a lot."

Before Lily could think of what to say, David stood and wobbled away. It took a minute for Lily to realise David was heading to the door and seemed intent on leaving, rather than talking to her. She and her friends hurried after him, squeezing between people and receiving a few glares when accidentally bumping them and spilling their drinks.

"David!" Lily called after him as he staggered up the road. David didn't so much as turn around, but Lily easily caught up.

"Piss off," David muttered, yanking his arm away from Lily, the effort causing him to stumble into the wall. He righted himself and continued stumbling along, presumably going home.

"David, we need to talk. Where is everyone? The rest of the family, I mean." Lily felt silly clarifying, though she wasn't entirely sure that David would have processed who she was referring to otherwise.

"Where do you think they are?" David grumbled.

"I don't know, David. That's why I'm asking."

David slurred something at her that she couldn't quite make out. She looked to Alexei and Ava for help and they inclined their heads, indicating for her to join them, trailing behind David.

"I can't get him to answer me," said Lily, both frustrated and worried.

"Yeah, I'd leave it for a bit," suggested Alexei, watching David with slight revulsion.

"We were thinking maybe we just follow him home. Probably a good idea just to make sure he gets there in one piece, but also so we know where he lives. Once he's home and maybe has some water, he might talk, but even if he doesn't, at least we know where he is, and we can try again tomorrow."

"Good idea," said Lily, watching her older brother stagger into a pole, vomit, wipe his mouth on his sleeve, and continue on his way as if nothing had happened. She felt deeply sad at the change in David, and an anxiety was gnawing at her gut. Her surroundings were familiar, but everything here seemed wrong. Like a parallel universe. A small part of her was clutching at that possibility—perhaps somewhere else her real world was playing out, her family safe and well. But in her heart, she knew this was her home dimension and something was very wrong with her family.

David somehow made it up three flights of stairs in a dingy apartment block, and having dropped and retrieved his keys twice, managed to open his apartment and enter. He slapped at the door to close it behind him, but Lily stopped it with her foot and followed him in.

It was a tiny one-bedroom apartment, with the bedroom separated from the rest of the living space by a wall. The kitchen, dining area, and living room were all crammed into a space that might have made a small yet cosy lounge room, but felt claustrophobic holding the majority of the living space. Lily assumed any bathroom must simply be an ensuite somewhere in the space for the bedroom. They could hear David making use of the facility, and so, however small, it clearly met his needs.

"This is ... nice?" Ava prodded at what appeared to be a strip of lace masquerading as female underwear with her toe.

"This is not David," said Lily defensively. "I mean, it is him, but he's not usually like this. Something is very wrong."

"Yeah, no kidding," said Ava, scrunching her nose at some dishes that seemed to have been in the sink for quite a while. "From how you described him, I was expecting a button-up collared shirt, styled hair, reading some financial magazine kind of guy."

David burst out of the bedroom and started at seeing three people standing in his apartment. Seemingly unsure of what to do about the intrusion, he eventually decided to ignore them and stumbled into the kitchen corner of the room.

"David, where's Simone?"

David snorted. "Simone. Bitch left me," he slurred. "Said yes to the ring, but apparently not so sold on the 'through thick and thin' stuff."

"But something must have happened—"

The three jumped as David threw a mug at the wall, shattering it and showering them with fragments. He glared at Lily, eyes slightly less glazed for the anger.

"Of course something happened! You happened. You disappeared. And where exactly have you been, Lily? Where did you go that was so important that you couldn't tell anyone? What did you need to go and do that was more important than our family?"

Lily opened and closed her mouth, shocked by the sudden rage and unsure of how to respond.

"New friends? That was what was more important? Well, I hope they're worth it." David turned back to whatever he was doing in the sink, muttering, "Screwed my marriage, screwed my life, but I'm sure you've all had a great old time."

"It's not like that," Lily said quietly, blinking back the tears that were pricking her eyes.

"Then what is it like? Huh?"

"I—" Tears tumbled down Lily's cheeks as she fumbled for an appropriate explanation.

David looked at her with drunken disdain. "Well, if you're not going to tell me, then how about you piss off and bother Elaine and April."

"Okay, where are they?"

"They're over in Fernwall." David started towards Lily, apparently over the conversation and keen for her to leave his apartment. "Some converted warehouse or something."

"Are they with Mum and Dad?" Lily asked as David ushered them out the door.

"Mum! Huh. Mum is probably somewhere drowning in

a barrel of vodka, or having a breakdown, or whatever new pathetic broken crisis she's moved onto."

Lily turned, and before David could shut the door, asked, "And what about Dad?"

David glared at her, pain in his eyes. "Dad's dead."

And he slammed the door in her face.

12

"Why not?" Jason was getting frustrated. He needed to go to the Disputed Region, but Minister Toot seemed intent on blocking him.

"It would be frowned upon," said Minister Toot, condescension dripping from his lips.

"Frowned upon by who?"

"Whom."

"What?"

"Frowned upon by *whom*."

Jason stared at Minister Toot, fuming and not quite sure how to say what he wanted to say without swearing. Minister Toot, for his part, simply smiled patiently at Jason, sipping his whiskey and waiting for his response.

"Well?"

"Well what?"

"Whom would frown upon it?"

"*Who* would frown upon it."

Jason bunched his enormous hands into fists, closed his eyes, and forced himself to count to ten. Minister Toot seemed to sense that while Jason might lose his job if he punched a member of Parliament in the head, the more frustrated he got, the more it might seem worth it. Not to mention that Minister Toot might ultimately be the worse off. The minister hurried on, "The prime minister has expressed to me concern that the palace should continue to operate as close to business as usual as possible, so as not to alarm the public."

"If the prime minister is worried about alarming the public, why don't you tell him to rein in his HSP cronies?"

Minister Toot looked at Jason with the disdain the rich reserve for the poor. Jason bit back his next comment. As much as the disdain was mutual, now that the Royal Guard answered to the Defence Minister, along with the HSP, if he wasn't smart about his interactions with Jeremy Toot, his life could get a lot more difficult.

Sensing Jason's defeat, Minister Toot smiled and continued, "There is no reason for you to leave, Jason, and really, you should be here in case Her Majesty returns."

"But I need to go to the Disputed Region to find the stolen felixium so that we can get her back. She can't simply return on her own."

"Yes, but the optics wouldn't be good."

Jason stared at the weedy little man, his mouth opening in surprise. He couldn't tell if Toot was baiting him or if he really was this stupid.

"Excuse me, Minister," Naomi suddenly appeared, cutting off Jason's next comment. "Boss, may I have a word?"

She took Jason's arm firmly and led him away from Minister Toot and out of the operations room altogether. She didn't speak again until they were outside the palace and she was steering them towards the extended grounds.

"A walk will do you good," Naomi responded to Jason's question about where they were going. She cast a worried look behind them. "And besides, it can't hurt to be away from the palace." She leant towards him and added in a whisper, "The walls have ears."

Jason nodded at Naomi. She was right, of course. Following the attack on the way to the coronation, and Minister Toot's assumption of control, they couldn't be sure who they could trust, or what level of counter-surveillance was in place. Jason went to stop, satisfied that they were far enough away from the building, but Naomi pulled him on.

"A little more, boss. You know how I love the gardens, but this time of year there are just too many insects."

"Insects?"

"You know I hate bugs," Naomi said pointedly, rolling her eyes at Jason's lack of speed on the uptake. Jason nodded, abashed. He was having difficulty adjusting to his new reality. He much preferred the enemy to be "out there" rather than hidden in his house. But Jason knew he needed to step up his game. He couldn't keep relying on Naomi to keep him out of trouble.

Halfway through the manicured gardens, they rounded a corner and almost ran into a woman who was moving at pace while talking nonstop into her phone and reading from a tablet.

"... run with that, Jen. Oh! You know what? I'll call you back." She snapped her phone closed, tucked her tablet into a bag, and smiled at Jason and Naomi.

"Hi Paula," Naomi greeted the woman, surprising Jason, who had no idea who she was despite having worked at the palace significantly longer than Naomi.

"Hey Nay." The woman smiled back. Jason was amused to see Naomi stiffen at the greeting, but not correct her. He suppressed a smile and filed the detail away for later.

Naomi, clearly eager to move on, introduced Jason to Paula. Paula was the palace's media liaison, and Jason could now remember seeing her name on emails and other official correspondence.

"Look, I could use your take on something." Paula pulled her tablet back out and handed it to Naomi, who held it so that Jason could see. "We're being asked to comment on this article and opinion seems split about whether we should go with 'no comment' or actually give a response. Do you guys have any input, particularly from a security point of view?"

Jason skimmed the article and grimaced. "Someone" had leaked the discovery of interdimensional travel to the press, and the last few days had seen a media storm as Highacre, and indeed the rest of the world, moved through a raft of emotions in reaction. At first, most articles had lauded the invention, speculating on the advances that could be made in all areas from medicine to technology to different ways of life.

It didn't take long for the tenor to turn, as people realized exactly how long Highacre had been in possession of this invention. They began to condemn those who had kept from the world all manner of life-saving advancements, accusing them of letting people die to protect their own source of power. There had been protests throughout Highacre, and at their foreign embassies. The people were angry, and asking what the intended future use of this technology was. A question that had yet to be answered, and one that Jason had unsettlingly realized had never fully been addressed by the king before his death. At least not in front of Jason.

The prime minister, far from addressing the concerns of the public, had predictably gone from initially confirming that Highacre had developed this capability, and strongly hinting it had been a project directed by himself, through to laying the blame squarely at the deceased royal family's feet and decrying their selfish nature. He had no answers as to the future, and responded to any question relating to this by reminding everyone that it was Lily's family who had hidden the technology, and that he would need to be fully briefed before commenting further.

The article Paula was currently dealing with again featured the prime minister. He had now confirmed that Lily had in fact been hidden in another dimension from birth, rather than in Oppulus as everyone had been told, and that this was where she was now.

Unhelpfully, the prime minister had not offered a reason for Lily's return to the other dimension, though hinted strongly that she was ashamed of her failure at the Trials. As a result, the article was hypothesising everything from Lily being overwhelmed by her new responsibilities and running away, to her being exiled as part of the plot against the royal family. Naturally, "anonymous" sources had lent credence to each of the rumours.

Naomi handed the tablet to Jason as she engaged with Paula about the security risks involved in the various options for response. Jason was only half listening as he scrolled to the comments at the bottom.

A number of people were rehashing the conspiracy against the royal family and wondering whether Lily's disappearance was related. A lively debate had arisen where some readers were echoing Jason's main question, which was: Why would those responsible send Lily back to the other dimension when it would have been simpler to kill her like the rest of her family?

He saw a thread discussing whether she had, in fact, been killed in the terrorist attack at the arena. Comments grew heated as they discussed the attack itself. A not-insignificant number of people seemed to question if the attack had even happened. Jason scoffed. How could they think that when so many people had been there and witnessed it firsthand? It had been televised live, for crying out loud. He was pleased to see a large number of people reminding the conspiracists of just that, but his spirits fell when many of those who agreed the attack had happened hypothesised that the attack had been perpetrated by the Highacren government to create a justification for war with Meridia.

Jason was about to click out of the comments in disgust when he saw one user had posted a picture in support of his belief that the attack had been carried out by Highacre. It was a side-by-side comparison of the terrorists and the HSP. Jason rolled his eyes. The grainy pictures had no real detail and essentially seemed to hinge on both groups wearing black clothing. Still, he hesitated. He couldn't put his finger on what it was, but there was something similar about the two groups.

Shaking himself out of his conspiracy haze, Jason scrolled back up to the top of the page and a link to another article caught his eye. He clicked on the link and found an article detailing the growing nationalist sentiment sweeping across Highacre. A larger number of people than Jason would have ever thought possible seemed to be hopping on board the prime minister's propaganda train, for the most part fuelled by the terror attack at the arena, and there were increasing reports of abuse and violence aimed at immigrants, especially those from Meridia.

Jason snapped the tablet closed in disgust. What was the world coming to? If there was one thing the army had taught him, it was that everyone had something to offer, and everyone died just as easily as everyone else. It didn't matter where they came from.

Paula took the tablet back from Jason, thanked Naomi for her help, then hurried off, pulling her phone back out and resuming her call. Naomi started off for the extended grounds, and Jason had to hurry to match her pace.

"Okay," started Naomi, "so what was all that about?"

Jason sighed, trying to figure out where the best place to start was. Naomi wasn't a royal advisor and so hadn't been at the last meeting.

"I was asking Minister Toot for permission to go to the Disputed Region. At our last meeting, Minister Bellingham told the rest of the advisors that prior to Meridia seizing control of the felixium mines, an entire shipment of felixium had been ready for transport. Apparently, they were able to hide it before things got bad down there. Minister Bellingham authorised a covert operation to recover the shipment, however, something happened to the convoy as it headed towards the border and it vanished, troops and all."

Naomi raised an eyebrow. "Minister *Bellingham* authorised the operation? But isn't Jeremy Toot the defence minister?"

"Yeah, Toot was pissed. I've never seen him that mad. He even yelled at her. I mean, if those two got in a fight, my money's on Bellingham, but he got up in her face, telling her to keep out of his lane and then stormed out."

"Interesting." They walked in silence for a while before Naomi added, "He seems to have gone from placid observer to being highly involved in the prime minister's business. And you saw she was arrested. He hasn't mentioned that?"

Jason shook his head.

"Interesting," she said again.

"It's disconcerting, that's what it is. He's gone to the other side." Jason suddenly felt much safer with Naomi's decision to talk out here in the woods. With Jeremy Toot now in charge of the Royal Guard, who knew how secure the palace or the grounds were. He had been caught off guard by all the changes, focused as he had been on trying to retrieve Lily. Cursing himself for falling behind, he made a note to ask Hudson to check their equipment and see if he had something that could sweep the operations room for listening devices. Hudson's magical ability was an affinity with technology. He could connect to almost anything with his mind. Maybe he could come out and scan the room himself?

"Gone, or was he always there?" Naomi asked.

"You're thinking he might have been the insider?"

"I mean, it fits. Lily's pushed through and suddenly Toot is the prime minister's flavour of the month? He had to have been working with him from the start."

Jason thought for a minute before saying, "The insider was pretty active. That doesn't sound like Toot to me—"

"He's active now," Naomi interrupted.

"Fair," Jason admitted. "It doesn't feel right to me. Toot floats wherever the power is. It was with the royal family until their death. He stuck with Lily, thinking she'd step into the role. And then she disappears, and the prime minister enacts his special emergency powers. Now he's Toth's best friend."

Naomi nodded. "Both theories fit. We'll need to assume he wasn't the insider until we can prove he was."

They walked on in silence for a while, the calm, beautiful day at odds with their thoughts.

"Did Toot say anything about the arena attack?" Naomi asked eventually.

Jason shook his head. He had expected to be involved in the investigation. Not only because the sovereign had been present, let alone Lily's actions in resolving the incident, but because the Royal Guard were always involved in nationally significant investigations. An incident like the attack might have seen him simply kept in the loop, but he would at least be a part of the team. However, when he asked about the investigation, Toot had told him to mind his own business. He said that a terrorist attack was not a matter for the Royal Guard and that if Jason needed to know anything, Toot would tell him. Jason had heard nothing since, which he found alarming.

Not only was Toot apparently firmly on the other side, he wasn't even trying to pretend he was part of their team anymore. What had the prime minister told Toot that had the old man so convinced that he was now on the winning side that he was willing to burn all his bridges?

"And any news on Lady Octavia?" Naomi asked, sensing Jason's mood and switching topics again.

"No," said Jason sadly. Lady Octavia was the detector, a once-in-a-generation power that allowed the user to identify what magical abilities someone might have. She had disappeared right before Lily undertook the Trials, and no one had heard from her since.

"I suppose we should start looking into her disappearance," Naomi prompted.

Jason blew out the air in his lungs in frustration, looking at the ground. She was absolutely right. They should be looking into her disappearance. A sense of shame solidified in his chest.

"We can't, Naomi. We don't have the resources, and I don't trust anyone else with it." Naomi went to respond, but Jason continued before she could speak, "It's brutal, but in all likelihood, Lady Octavia is dead, and right now I need to prioritise the living. I understand there's a slight chance she's been kidnapped, and if that's the case, no one will feel worse than me, but I have to focus on the knowns. We know that Lily's alive and that she's back in her home world."

Following the ambush in the halls and the shock of Ezra's announcement that Lily had been pushed through the working interdimensional travel machine, Jenkins had examined it and determined where she had gone. Jason felt much better knowing she was somewhere safe, likely being looked after by her family.

"So, if you can't go to the DR ..." Naomi dropped the subject of Lady Octavia and brought Jason back to the task at hand. "Then I guess it'll have to be me."

Jason hesitated.

"What? Don't think I can handle it?"

"You know that's not it. You can do this stuff standing on your head. It's just that you don't have the contacts that I do. Most of the guys you're going to need to talk to are military or ex-military. I either know them or know someone who does, which means they're going to trust me easier. You're an unknown, and these guys are usually pretty paranoid. And they're going to be more paranoid if they are up to no good."

"Okay." Naomi thought for a second. "Just thinking out of the box here, so don't shoot the messenger, but would it be worth reaching out to Claire? She does have undercover experience."

Jason tried not to dismiss the suggestion out of hand. If he was honest with himself, he had considered reaching out to Claire to see if she would join forces a number of times. He had dismissed it each time. Her being ex-HIA meant she had skills and abilities that would be complementary and very useful. But in Jason's experience, agents always thought they were so much better than military people, when in fact, they were too busy looking like they were getting things done to actually do anything. Which is probably why they claimed credit for the work of the military.

"I see where you're going ..."

"But you don't want to work with an ex-agent."

"No. Okay, I admit, I am a little biased here. It is a good

idea. We could have her go to the Disputed Region and pose as an ex-military security contractor. The problem is that she still won't have the network. We could just as easily have you pose as a contractor. They still won't trust you because nobody knows you."

"Fair enough," said Naomi. "But I do think it'd be worth reaching out to her. Just to see if she wants to join forces."

Jason grunted noncommittally, reminding himself that he'd actually liked Claire before he learned of her background.

"Okay, so our plan is that I will go to the Disputed Region and see what I can do in the spirit of 'something is better than nothing' and you will remain here and continue the investigation with Hudson and maybe Claire."

Jason kicked at a rock. There wasn't another solution, and he knew it. But he was so much better at doing physical investigations. Interviewing people and looking for evidence. Searching through email records and endless documents was just not his wheelhouse. He was getting agitated by the lack of action.

"Approved. But look, it's important not to push it. See if you can find a way in, but assume you won't. We need to leave the door open in case I can get down there. The last thing we want is for none of them to talk to you, and then they freeze me out."

"Got it." To her credit, Naomi didn't sound the least bit offended at being sent on a mission where she was expected to fail. "I'll head off and get some supplies and hit the road. And don't worry boss, this is a scoping mission. If I can at least get you intel on which organisations are down there and what the structures are, then it should make it easier for you whenever you're able to escape the palace."

13

Naomi darted off before Jason could thank her. He didn't know where he would be without Naomi. She was practical and always put the mission before ego. Now that he thought about it, she was the most competent and effective person he'd ever worked with.

Jason turned and headed slowly back towards the palace. He took the time to enjoy the sunshine on his face and listen to the birds. He was spending too much time cooped up in the operations room. As he walked along the path, Jason took some deep breaths and reminded himself to be present in the moment. He was so focussed on being present that he didn't see the flash of messy white hair moving at speed along the other fork and collided with a small man at the junction of their paths.

"Jenkins!" Jason helped the scientist to his feet. "What are you doing out here?"

"Messy, messy." Jenkins brushed the forest debris from his coat and pants before looking at Jason, surprised to see him there despite having literally just run into him. "Jenkins is ... uh ... going for a ... walk. Yes, a walk." He breathed in exaggeratedly deeply. "Mmmm, fresh air. What are you doing here? A better question. Yes, indeed. Why is the bodyguard in the woods?"

Jason smiled curiously at Jenkins. He had a soft spot for the inventor of interdimensional travel. Jenkins was simply Jenkins. No ulterior motives. No subliminal agendas. What you saw was what you got, and Jason appreciated that.

"Are you okay, buddy? You seem agitated."

"Not agitated, no," said Jenkins, his agitation increasing. "Must go. Nothing to see here. Very busy." And with that, Jenkins hurried away toward the palace, muttering to himself and occasionally glancing back at Jason.

Jason watched him go, wondering what was going on. Jenkins was probably just experimenting with something he either wanted to keep secret until it was done, or that he shouldn't be experimenting with. But it was possible that he was in trouble. Especially with the public revelation of interdimensional travel. Jason had no doubt some people would very much like Jenkins working for them instead.

He looked curiously down the path from which Jenkins had emerged, trying to remember where it led, before turning and heading back towards the palace. He reminded himself to swing by Jenkins's lab and check in on him. The idea that someone might be pressuring or mistreating Jenkins made him mad.

Jason absently wandered back towards the operations room, his head firmly in the Disputed Region, trying to think of anything he could do to help Naomi or make things easier for her. Was there anyone he could call who could help her? He couldn't think of anyone he could trust with the level of information they would need or want before getting involved.

His mind firmly elsewhere, Jason rounded a corner and collided with someone for the second time. His heart sank as he recognised Edmund and helped the younger man to his feet.

"Hi Jason," said Edmund enthusiastically.

"Hello sir," Jason said stiffly, nodding at Edmund before turning towards the operations room. He inwardly cringed as Edmund followed him. Edmund was a good-natured guy, but Jason just didn't have time for him today. He felt guilty, thinking that there were probably a lot of people who didn't have time for Edmund.

"Any news?"

"No, I said I'd call you if there was, sir."

"I know, but I figured I'd drop by and see if I can help."

Jason tried not to sigh obviously. He failed. A flash of hurt crossed Edmund's face.

"What's up?" Edmund asked tentatively, clearly hoping the sigh hadn't been for him.

"Oh, nothing." Jason searched for something to blame as they entered the operations room together and Jason sat down in front of his computer. "It's just that ... there's a task in the Disputed Region. I wish I was heading out rather than Naomi."

"Is she not up to it?"

"No, no, it's not that at all. It's just that I have the contacts from my army days, you know? Naomi will be fine, but she doesn't have that background."

"Sounds like what you've been saying to me. You'd love me to help, but I just don't have the right skill set."

"Yeah." Jason was distracted by an email from Hudson updating Jason on his progress. "Yeah, it's not that she can't do it, but it's the connections and the soft skills that you get from being in the army, you know? There's very little that isn't enhanced from military training."

"Perhaps I could enhance my skills?"

"Sure, yeah." Jason ran his hands through his hair.

Hudson had sent a link to a number of files for Jason to review. This was so frustrating and unnecessary. Naomi would be through the files in a quarter of the time it would take Jason, and with his contacts, he would make much faster progress in the Disputed Region than she would. If only they could switch, they'd be able to figure out where the felixium was. He was sure of it. "This is so stupid."

"What is?"

Jason had almost forgotten Edmund was there. "Oh, sorry mate. I just haven't felt this useless and lacking in control in a while. Makes me miss the army—"

"I feel useless."

"—despite the officers, you know? I don't know, maybe I'm just remembering the good things now that I'm gone, but there was a mission, and a purpose—"

"I'd like a purpose."

"—and you have a team and you're all working towards a goal—"

"That sounds good."

"—the same goal. You build a cohort of people that you can reach out to later in life and—"

"So you're saying I should join the army." Edmund was nodding to himself.

"—they're always there for you, and ... wait, what?" Jason started paying attention to his conversation with Edmund a little too late.

"No, I got you man. I'm picking up what you're putting down."

"Err, what do you think I was putting down?" Jason was pretty sure he had inadvertently told Edmund to join the army. He hoped he was wrong.

"You're saying I should join the army."

Nope. Damn.

"Well, I mean, sure. Uh, like I said, I'm probably just

remembering the good things now I'm gone, you know? And it's not for everyone ..."

"No, of course not. But for guys like us, it's a calling, right?"

"Guys like us ... sure." Jason had no idea how to backtrack without upsetting Edmund or completely destroying him. He was absolutely not the right fit for the army. They would chew him up and spit him out.

"Ah, look, sir—Edmund ..."

"Sorry mate, but I've taken up enough of your time, and I should really get out of here if I'm going to enlist ..."

Jason internally shuddered at the thought of Edmund as a private soldier. He had been having a hard enough time imagining him as an officer. But at least the officer corps was practised at hiding the nobility who insisted on joining. He thought they might even have a whole stream dedicated to them.

"But thanks for the advice!" Edmund trotted happily towards the door, which he tried to sweep out of, but pushed instead of pulled. After two awkward minutes where he tried to force the door and then resorted to turning the lights on and off, thinking the switch was a door-release button, Edmund left.

Jason turned back to his computer, trying not to feel like the coward he knew he was. Why didn't he just tell Edmund that the army wasn't for him? Or at least try to get him to join the air force instead? Surveillance balloons seemed more Edmund's thing.

He pulled up some documents and then remembered he was meant to be looking at Hudson's files. He was scattered. Maybe Edmund would be alright. He'd either get kicked out of basic training or sent to some administration corps where he couldn't do any damage. Maybe he'd even be good at it.

14

Lily stumbled back out onto the street, dazed, half surprised to find nothing had changed.

"Lily? Are you alright?" Ava touched her arm, looking at her in concern.

Lily nodded and then dissolved into tears. Ava grabbed her and held her, and she felt Alexei's hand rubbing her back. They stood together like that for a while. Strangers passed them and, assuming some drunken crisis was underway, gave them a wide berth. Lily's mind gave up on trying to make sense of what David had told her and instead focussed on something it could comprehend and address.

Lily pulled out of Ava's embrace and wiped her face on her sleeve. "Thank you," she looked at both her friends gratefully. "It's late. We should head back to the apartment."

Ava and Alexei exchanged a look, but they didn't challenge Lily's avoidance of the news she had received, and the three began walking toward the apartment in silence. Lily's mind felt like a void, echoing her thoughts without being able to catch any of them to consider properly.

Her father was dead? It didn't seem real. Couldn't be

real. And why were her siblings living separately? And her mother. Where was she? It sounded like she'd had some kind of breakdown, but it wasn't like David was a reliable source.

Lily felt an overwhelming desire to have stayed at the farm and been rescued, never knowing that her disappearance had wrecked her family so thoroughly. Had killed her father.

No; you don't know that. His death could be completely unrelated.

But she didn't believe that. Guilt threatened to overwhelm her.

"Lily, we're here," Ava said gently, grabbing Lily's hand to stop her from walking right past their apartment.

"Oh," she said, staring blankly at the building.

They trudged up the stairs, Lily solely focussed on dropping onto the soft bed and drifting off to sweet oblivion. When Alexei pushed past her, she irrationally thought he too was fantasising about going to sleep and was trying to get in first to get the jump on the one bathroom. And then Ava's hands were holding her back, and she decided they were in cahoots.

It took a minute for her to realise their door was slightly ajar. Alexei approached it cautiously before Ava called out quietly, "It's empty."

Lily's brain, still not operating properly from the shock of the evening, busied itself wondering why Ava was being quiet if no one was there. But she let Ava guide her to the small porch outside their door as Ava and Alexei went inside to confirm it was clear. She leant against the railing, grateful to have such good friends.

With a bolt, she stood up straight. *The gems!*

Lily hurried inside to see Ava and Alexei standing in the middle of their ransacked living room, expressions concerned. She met Ava's eyes and knew the gems were gone. Nonetheless, needing to see, she went to the cupboard. The blankets were tossed carelessly on the floor and the shelf of the cupboard was empty. Lily stared at the shelf blankly. It was too much. It was all too much.

She didn't know how long she stood there, but suddenly Ava's hands were guiding her back to the living room and she was gently sat on the couch, a steaming mug of tea placed in her hands. On autopilot, she sipped the tea, not registering the taste. Slowly, she became aware of a hushed argument taking place.

"... in no state to go after them."

"She'll be safe enough here. Or I can go and you stay with her."

"Neither of us should go after them alone." Frustration was in Ava's voice.

"If we leave it until morning, we'll lose the trail."

"I'm fine," Lily said numbly.

"You're not," said Ava, moving to sit beside Lily, rubbing her back and glaring at Alexei. "Which is okay and completely understandable. We're all exhausted and we need sleep."

"We need to track them while we can," Alexei implored.

Lily's logical mind tried to push through the sludge of grief blanketing her brain. Alexei was right. The best chance they had at getting the gems back was to track them now. But now that the gems were gone, they couldn't stay anywhere as nice as this apartment. Maybe they should make the most of it and get a good night's sleep. But if they got the gems back, then they could stay. Well, not until she sorted her ID—

Lily shook her head, trying to keep her thoughts on track, and caught her friends up on her thought process.

Alexei predictably jumped on her reasoning that with the gems recovered, they would have many nights in the apartment. Ava continued to insist that Lily needed rest.

As they devolved into another argument where Alexei wanted to head out alone and Ava didn't want to split up. Lily's focus jumped around, landing on wondering how they would track the thieves. Her mind jumped to Lady Octavia. Possibly looking for an adult to provide comfort; possibly for a mentor to provide answers. Whatever the reason, her memory sparked, and she was back in the courtyard examining it after Lady Octavia went missing.

A pang of sadness for her mentor and worry about where she was and if she was okay joined her heartache about her father. She closed her eyes, hoping that despite all that was going on in Highacre, someone was looking for Lady Octavia, and then opened them, her focus on trying to reveal the memory of their apartment.

Lily pushed all other thoughts from her mind and concentrated on the living room, which she suddenly noticed had been tidied before she had been led to the couch. A pang of love for her friends mixed with a jolt of guilt. She could mourn later. They needed her now.

Renewing her efforts, Lily reached out with her magic. After an initial flicker, ghostly images suddenly appeared in front of her. Two men, maybe three, began strobing around the room, moving objects and throwing cushions to the floor. She thought men, but to be fair, all she saw were human-shaped blobs. She watched as they moved to the kitchen and began ransacking in there.

"Lily? Are you alright?"

Lily noted Ava's concerned tone and broke from the memory ghost to see both her friends looking at her in concern.

"I appreciate you wanting to protect me," Lily said

warmly, standing and squeezing Ava's hand. "But Alexei's right. We need to act now if we have any chance of recovering the gems."

Ava saw her resolve and nodded. "Okay, but I don't see how we're going to track them. I can't follow with my implant unless I'm there when the object is taken. I suppose we could assume the pawnshop is involved and head straight there ..."

"I can see the memory of a place," said Lily, briefly explaining her ability.

"Okay, let's see if we can track them with your magic. When we get closer to where we think they are, I can start using my X-ray vision. Alexei." Ava hesitated, looking him up and down. "You stand around looking intimidating."

Alexei scowled at the implication that he wasn't useful in the search.

"Perfect," said Ava. "Let's go."

Lily followed the blobs through the apartment until finally they pulled the blankets out, the bag of gems dropping on the floor. Snatching them up, the blobs headed straight for the door, and Lily led the others out of the apartment and down to the street.

They followed the memory of the thieves across the city, none of them surprised to find they were heading back toward the pawnshop. Lily found that using her magic like this, intensely after a period of inaction, was fatiguing, but not in a completely unpleasant way.

About halfway through their quest, she realised it was becoming easier to bring up the location's memory, and in fact the shadowy figures that she was focussed on were becoming more pronounced. Though they had reached more populated areas, it wasn't too difficult to pick out her targets.

It would be much easier to follow them if I could make the figures a different colour.

Lily had barely thought this when a reddish tinge silhouetted the memory ghosts.

Lily realised with a jolt that *she* was in charge of her magic, and not the other way around. It seemed silly now, but she had been treating it as a gift and was grateful for what she had been given. She now realised that it was a part of her, just like any part of her body, and she could use it as she wanted. Deciding to experiment, she concentrated on seeing the figures completely in red and overlaid on her normal vision so she could keep them in sight as they moved, rather than having to pause every few hundred metres to bring them up and check that she was still on their trail. It worked, but was much more draining.

They moved faster now that Lily had increased her mastery of her power, but they still paused regularly to let Ava scan the area. The short pauses let Lily rest.

As they got closer to the pawnshop, Lily found the memories were starting to fade. In the middle of an alley with several doors and exits, the figures faded altogether. Lily mentally cursed herself for delaying the pursuit, and was grateful that Alexei didn't say anything. Ava scanned the area but found nothing useful.

"Though to be fair, there's a lot of interference here," she said, gesturing to the significant amount of trash strewn around.

"The pawnshop is two streets that way," said Alexei, pointing. His tone was clear. They knew where the thieves were headed.

Without another word, the three headed towards the shop, Ava scanning for people now and Lily occasionally trying to find the targets, even though she knew they were gone. The alley they were following spilled them into the main street near an intersection. Over the road on their right was the pawnshop. It was closed, which was no surprise given the late hour.

"Anything?" Alexei asked both Ava and Lily. The two women scanned the area. Lily saw lots of blobs moving around, but nothing useful.

Ava shook her head, frustrated. "I can see lots of stuff in the store, but I can't get enough detail to find the gems."

The group moved toward the shop, as if increasing their proximity would somehow provide an answer. Now directly across the road from the establishment, Lily found she had no better idea of what to do. They were assuming the gems were in there. But even if the pawnshop was behind the theft, there was no guarantee that the gems would be there, rather than stored securely elsewhere. And what were they going to do? Go in and ask?

"Any ideas?" Ava asked in a tone that told Lily she had been thinking along the same lines.

"I mean, with my magic, your implant, and Alexei's enchantment, we could easily bust in and if the gems are in there, take them back. But we would attract *a lot* of attention."

"We'd be fast though," mused Alexei. "I think we could be in and out before the authorities arrived."

"Yeah, but we need to be careful. I don't want to go in guns blazing and take out any guards with our powers, only to find that Ava's implant couldn't wipe the security footage from everywhere it's backed up to, and then have the police start hunting us down. We can't risk being locked up when they come to rescue us."

Neither Ava nor Alexei seemed to have an answer for that, and the resulting silence grew tense. They needed to get the gems, but how?

"Look, I'm not saying we give up. We have to get the

gems back. But we need to be smart about it. I know that means we might be uncomfortable for a while—"

"It's not that," interrupted Ava. "We don't want to spend all our time trying to earn money to live and having no time to find your family."

"Let's have a quick look while we're here," said Alexei. "Just scout out the security. That way we can better plan while we're looking for your family."

They moved quickly across the road, and trying to keep to the shadows, circled the pawnshop. Lily noted at least five cameras mounted on the walls. She'd not been to many pawnshops, but that seemed like a lot.

"What can you see?" Alexei hissed at Ava. She turned to answer him, and her eyes widened, staring into a dark alley behind the shop.

"Well, look what we got here," a voice snarled from the shadows.

Alexei and Lily turned as three imposing men emerged from the alley.

"Wotcha looking at then?" the smallest one, who had a rat face, asked, peering exaggeratedly around them to look at the pawnshop. "Wot you looking at Fingers's store for then? Don't reckon he'd like that, would he, boys?"

Both larger men grunted, shaking their heads.

"Here, you look familiar," Rat Face sneered. "Do we know you from somewhere?"

"No," said Ava in a tone that said she wasn't interested in his games.

"Well," Rat Face leant back, a smug smile on his lips. "I know you ain't from around here. You're on my patch."

There was a threat in his last sentence, and Lily's instincts screamed at her to run. Ava and Alexei were standing their ground, so Lily tried to project a similar level of confidence, but she was sure her hands were shaking. She felt Rat Face's anger rise as Ava refused to be intimidated by him. The sneer left his face, replaced by a barely restrained rage.

"Get 'em."

The two larger men lunged, one striking out at Ava, the other at Alexei. Rat Face went for Lily. Her instincts took over, and she twisted, slapping his arm away and avoiding being grabbed. He lunged again and Lily darted backwards, slamming into the wall and banging her head. Rat Face grinned, showing the gaps of his missing teeth.

"Knew you'd be easy," he said, stalking towards her, running his fingers up one arm and grabbing the other as she instinctively leant away from his touch. He pressed against her, his rancid breath blasting her face as he whispered, "Them gems' ours now. I see you 'round here again, you'll get worse than this."

Lily's heart pounded against her chest, her mind panicking about what "this" was going to be. Suddenly Rat Face was lifted bodily away from her and thrown into an open dumpster nearby. She saw Alexei take two steps and grab Ava's attacker from behind. She could see that Ava had been holding her own. Alexei's attacker was lying unconscious on the ground.

Ava darted in, kicking her now-restrained attacker in the groin before slamming a fist into his face. She nodded at Alexei to indicate she was done, and Alexei turned, throwing the man into the dumpster, where he landed on Rat Face, who had been trying to scramble up and out of the bin.

Alexei slammed the lid shut and moved to Lily, checking that she was alright. She nodded that she was, eyeing Alexei's enchanted belt and offering a generic thank you to the universe that he had it and it worked in this dimension.

"We need to get out of here," Ava urged as she concentrated on the cameras that had been facing the fight. They all moved away, quickly but cautiously, scanning their surroundings as they headed back towards their apartment. Only when they were close to home and Ava had satisfied herself that literally no one was around them did they relax a little bit and stop glancing around nervously.

"Are you okay?" Ava asked, falling into step beside Lily.

"Yeah, just frustrated," Lily said. "I spent so much time learning my magic back in Highacre, but I get back here and it's like I forget I have it. I shouldn't have needed Alexei's help back there."

Lily had been stewing on it for most of the walk. Pleased as she was to have retained some of her hand-to-hand lessons, she was pretty sure that a simple blast of magic would not only have had those men running for the hills, but might also have intimidated them so much that they would leave them alone whenever they did go back to try to recover the gems.

"I mean," said Ava reasonably. "If you'd incinerated them, that may have attracted more attention than we'd like."

"True," Lily admitted. "But I could have singed them a bit. They'd be scared of us, and it's not like anyone would believe them if they said anything."

"Though like you said, if the cameras showed you shooting fireballs from your hands, we'd have much bigger problems," Ava said.

Lily nodded. "Were you able to erase the footage?"

"I think so, but I guess we'll find out when we go back."

Lily worried that, regardless of the footage, there would be issues when they returned to the pawnshop. Surely the three men they'd just beaten up would warn the other guards and the shop owner that they were sniffing around for the gems.

"I don't think they'll mention it at all," said Alexei when Lily voiced her concern. "They're not going to want to admit that two women and one man beat them."

Lily wasn't sure, but with no way of knowing until they returned to the shop, she tried to put it from her mind.

Entering their apartment, the three fell onto the lounge setting, slumping in their seats, utterly exhausted.

"What did you see when you scanned the shop's interior?" Alexei asked Ava.

"A whole lot of trouble," she said with a yawn, waving at him. "But let's debrief in the morning. I'm shattered."

15

Lily fell into bed and slept like the dead. She awoke to find the comforting mass of Ava gone. The sound of running water indicated she was in the shower. She rolled onto her back, and memories of yesterday rushed back like a punch to the stomach.

My dad is dead.

She turned, doubling over, clutching herself around her waist, trying to suppress a low moan that wanted to escape her. It wasn't that she had forgotten, but the realisation that her father had died had moved to the back of her awareness, and when it emerged again, front and centre, it was as if it hit her again, the pain fresh.

Lily didn't know how long she stayed there, but eventually she was interrupted by a gentle hand on her back.

"Lily?" Ava said softly.

Lily wiped at her face with her hand. "I'm okay," she said thickly.

She felt Ava settle on the bed behind her, enveloping her in a firm embrace. They lay there together, Ava murmuring words of comfort and rubbing Lily's back. Lily cried softly now, rather than the racking sobs that had grabbed her before.

When Lily seemed calmer, Ava pulled back slightly, propping herself on her elbow and looking down at Lily. Lily smiled gratefully up at her, embarrassed at her display, but thankful that Ava had no judgement in her eyes. Returning her smile, Ava leant down and kissed her on her forehead. She looked at Lily, an unspoken question. Lily nodded, letting Ava know she was okay for now, and ready to get going. Ava gave her shoulders a rub and left the room, allowing Lily to get up and use the bathroom.

Refreshed from her shower, Lily padded out into the living room and sat next to Ava on the couch. Alexei was sitting in the armchair.

"So what do we do now?" he asked after the usual morning pleasantries were exchanged.

"We have two main issues," said Ava, saving Lily from having to take charge and trying to make it sound like they had challenges to overcome rather than insurmountable problems to face. "Finding Lily's family, and resourcing. Resourcing comprises funds and survivability. Food and accommodation," she explained, seeing Lily's expression. "I think we need to consider all the options available to us."

"Okay," said Alexei thoughtfully. "I get it. You're saying that trying to recover the gems would be one way of addressing the issue of funds, but not the only way."

"Exactly. And it may be that we can recover the gems, but it could take a while, so we need to look at how to manage in the meantime."

Lily stared at Ava, wondering when she'd had the time to plan ahead. All Lily had been able to do was sleep and cry.

Ava shrugged. "I didn't sleep much."

"We have the money we did get from the pawnshop," Alexei mused.

"It'll cover a couple of nights here," Lily piped up, forcing herself out of her funk. "Or we could look for somewhere cheaper."

"I think we scope out Fernwall," said Ava. "We can head out and I'll fill you both in on the pawnshop's security as we walk. Spoiler alert—it's not going to be easy. And then when we get to Fernwall, we can look for a place to live, scope out opportunities for money, and make a plan to find Lily's sisters."

Summarised like that in Ava's upbeat voice, it was easy to imagine things were fine, or at least, that they would be. But Lily's mind pulled the broad suggestions apart, pointing out how any one of those things was going to be next to impossible to accomplish. How were they ever going to do it all?

"Sounds good," said Alexei, equally upbeat as he stood and began packing their backpack. Lily got the distinct impression that a pointed look from Ava had prompted his positivity.

The thin man behind the desk was smoking despite sitting directly under a *"No Smoking"* sign. His white singlet was stained in many varied colours, none of which Lily wanted to know the origins of. He scratched himself as Lily asked about available rooms, slamming a key on the desk before she finished.

"Money up front," he grunted.

Lily pulled out enough for a week, trying to ignore the voice in her head screaming that this was a bad idea.

Not like we have anything worth stealing anymore.

They followed the man up the rickety stairs as he led them to their new home.

But we can still catch whatever multitude of viruses and infections this place has on offer.

Lily snatched her hand away from the handrail as she touched something sticky. They passed several doors before they reached their own. Banging, thumping, screaming, and groaning sounded from behind them, as if the doors and walls weren't even there.

"Bathroom's down there," the old man pointed unhelpfully behind them. "Room's as is." He shuffled off quickly, lest the group ask him to do anything.

Alexei put the key in the lock, and the door opened without him turning or pushing. He raised an eyebrow at the women, but pushed forward and they followed him in.

The room was tiny; about the same size as their living room in the other apartment. A lazy fly droned in circles above their heads. The couch looked broken and as stained as the old man's singlet, as was the carpet. A large rust-coloured blot pooled in a corner. It looked suspiciously like blood.

"Well, this is ..." Ava was clearly trying to remain upbeat, but even she failed to find the words to put a positive spin on the filthy room.

"We can still go sleep in the park," Alexei suggested hopefully.

"I don't know that this place entertains refunds," said Lily, cringing at the bedding and trying not to gag.

"I might be willing to pay that much *not* to stay here," Alexei quipped.

Ava cocked her head, her attention caught by some of the noises of their new neighbours stopping. "I think we might have been able to pay for this room by the hour."

Alexei pulled some blankets out of the backpack and draped one over the couch before sitting on it.

"Alexei! Did you steal those?" Lily said, appalled.

He blushed. "It's compensation. For the terrible security at the apartment."

"Good call," grinned Ava, sitting next to him. "Oooh, terrible couch." She jumped back up. "But a great reason not to hang around here. Let's get going."

***

"So cameras everywhere; alarms on the doors, windows, and display cases; deadbolts and chains; and three armed guards," Lily confirmed.

"I mean, I say 'guards', but think less proper security guards and more armed thugs," said Ava.

Lily mulled over Ava's description of the pawnshop's security. It was going to be very difficult to get in there.

"Should we head over and confirm they even have the gems?" Lily asked.

"I think we need to be prepared to do it all at once. If we show up again, they're probably going to move the gems, if they haven't already. We need to confirm they're there right before we break in."

"Do we just focus on work, then?" Lily asked, reluctantly voicing something that had been becoming more and more apparent to her. She had been looking at the gems as essential. As if there were no other way to survive. And she knew a large part of that was because she knew that if they needed to work to survive, that would take a large chunk of time away from looking for her sisters.

But the gems were almost taking on a life of their own now. And there was still hope they'd be rescued soon. What if they spent all their time trying to get the gems back and then Doreen called to say people were there for them and they needed to leave? Could she do that? Could she return to Highacre without finding her sisters? Especially now ...

Lily forced the thought of her father away. It was still too raw. Too painful.

"What do you think, Alexei?" Ava asked.

"I feel really creepy," he complained.

The three of them were standing across the road from a high school and Alexei had very decidedly *not* been staring at the students, and looked significantly more uncomfortable than either woman. Lily and Ava had been scanning the students, trying to locate April. Alexei didn't need to be scanning the students, not being in possession of magical powers or a cybernetic implant.

Having declared that what he could bring to the endeavour of trying to find Lily's sisters seemed to be the ability to lift heavy things, he had taken to providing moral support and trying to keep out of Lily and Ava's way.

"Here, look at the photos; then you could keep an eye out," Lily offered, holding out her phone and trying to make Alexei feel useful.

"I think it's better if I don't ogle the schoolgirls," Alexei said. He moved off to scour the side streets, though since he hadn't looked at the picture, Lily wasn't sure what he was looking for.

Ava sighed heavily, turning away from the school and moving toward Alexei. Lily reluctantly followed.

No one said that their efforts were being wasted, but that was the general feeling. Lily tried to think of another way to find her sisters, but the only thing she was sure of was that April would still be going to school.

"I'll go back to David's place tomorrow," said Lily, checking her watch and deciding it was too late today to be certain he'd be sober. "He's got to have better contact details than a suburb." Lily's tone indicated she was uncomfortable at the idea of another run-in with her older brother.

"We can come with you," Ava said.

"No," said Lily reluctantly. "Much as I would love that, we can't afford to waste time."

"Maybe we split our efforts in general," Ava suggested. "There are three of us. No reason why we can't look for your sisters *and* earn some money."

"We shouldn't split up," Lily said again, the same panic gripping her chest as the last time Ava had suggested it. She put it down to a reaction to her father's death, but the idea of splitting up gave her an intense feeling of impending doom. As if splitting up would result in never seeing them again. She had thought to buy two more cheap phones, but without the gems, that seemed excessively extravagant.

"And besides," Lily added, trying to sound more certain than she felt, "once I speak to David, we shouldn't need to search for my sisters."

"Of course," said Ava gently. "But on the off chance David can't help us, I figure since Alexei's not looking for April anyway, he could go and look for work? We need to eat," she added softly to Lily, seeing her face fall.

"That is a great idea," said Alexei, straightening up and looking like he might head off immediately.

"We have a home base now, for what it's worth. We can meet back there at the end of the day—"

"We should have lunch together," Lily insisted. The idea of going a whole day without seeing them was too much. What if something happened to Alexei in the morning and they didn't even know he was in trouble until evening?

"Sure. We'll pick a park, somewhere central to our efforts, and meet there," Ava said.

Lily could tell Ava didn't like the idea, preferring to

spend all their available time focusing on their tasks. But she relented, balancing the mission with Lily's current emotional state.

"I will head off now," said Alexei.

"How are you going to find work?" Lily asked, alarmed at the idea of Alexei marching off into the city at random.

"I will find the warehouses. As Ava keeps pointing out, my main asset is that I can lift heavy things. I'm sure people will be happy to pay for cheap hard labour."

"I mean, the good thing is that with your accent, they'll probably assume you're not legally able to work, and so asking for cash in hand won't raise too many eyebrows," said Ava.

"So long as they don't report him," said Lily.

"I can handle it," assured Alexei. "If anything looks bad, I'll make a run for it. I'm not going to take unnecessary risks."

As Alexei headed off toward the industrial district, Ava and Lily started off toward the next high school. A sinking feeling in Lily's stomach kept saying that she and Ava were wasting time, but she had no clue as to a better way to search for her sisters.

16

Claire moved quickly but silently up the stairs, eyes scanning for anyone who might notice the movement despite her camouflaging into her surroundings with her chameleon ability. She was mentally rehearsing what she would say and how she would make sure it was Jason asking for her help and not the other way around.

She didn't quite know why this was so important to her. Why couldn't she just walk in and suggest that they join forces? There was no weakness in that. Was it her pride? Maybe it had to do with her feeling like she had something to prove as the only HIA agent still trying to protect the queen. She shook the thoughts away and ran through a few zingy one-liners she could use to let him know who was in charge.

Pausing outside the door and taking a few deep breaths, Claire steadied herself to ensure she would appear calm and not flustered. She focussed on exuding confidence, and, after returning her breathing to normal, swept into the operations room. The door seeming to open by itself clearly startled Jason, which satisfied her immensely. She took in the scene and noted Jason looked stressed.

"Hello, Jason." She materialised in front of him, making him jump. He recovered himself maddeningly quickly.

"Hello Claire. Come to slum it down here with us, are you? To what do I owe this esteemed honour?"

"I thought it might be useful to come and see your ... capabilities." Claire looked around the operations room in polite disgust. "How nice that you kept your old ops room. I'm sure having an abandoned space like this gives you ample time to get away from it all and have some peace and quiet."

Jason looked confused. "Old ops room?"

"Yes, it's so quaint and rudimentary. Naturally, you would have upgraded years ago." Claire was wandering slowly, examining the room as someone would look around in a museum. She was keeping a close enough eye on Jason to see the annoyance register. After suppressing a smile, she paused her perusal and looked back at Jason in mock surprise. "Wait, this isn't ... is this your *current* ops room?"

Jason sat back in his chair, crossing his arms and glaring at Claire. "Yes, and it's perfectly functional. Some of us don't need fancy equipment to supplement any lack of competence."

Both of them jumped as a young guard entered the room. She startled, not expecting to see Claire, then braced in front of Jason, throwing a snappy salute.

"Relax. What is it, Quinn?"

"Sir, we're still locked out of the system, and Minister Toot says you're not to ask again and that you'll have access to what you need when you need it. Sir."

"Thanks Quinn, off you go."

The guard snapped a salute, about-turned, and marched out of the room. Claire watched Jason run his hands through his hair, exhaling loudly in frustration.

"Things not going well then?"

"Look, Claire—"

"I wasn't having a go," Claire said, raising her hands in surrender. "Things are pretty bad at the moment for me, too."

They looked at each other, sharing sympathetic, tired smiles before remembering themselves. Jason slumped in his chair. "Not that I don't enjoy your company, Claire, but I do have work to do. Why are you here?"

Claire noted that Jason's question lacked the usual bite. In fact, was that a hint of hopefulness she heard? Maybe he wanted to join forces too?

But if that was the case, why didn't he just say that?

She had made the first move in coming here. Was holding out the olive branch, so to speak. It was his move to take it, to suggest that they join forces. He clearly wanted to, so what was holding him back? *Stubborn grunt.*

"Well, I figured, since we're both essentially working on the same operation ..."

Jason sat up straighter, eyes lighting up and darting to Claire. She watched as he caught himself and pretended to be interested in his computer screen. "Are you suggesting that we work together?"

"No," Claire said quickly. "But if you think perhaps we should join forces?"

"Of course not!" Jason scoffed. "Is that what *you* came here to ask?"

"No, I ..."

The door opened, causing both of them to jump again, and Naomi marched into the room. "Boss. Claire," she said, nodding sharply at both of them.

If she was surprised to see Claire in the ops room, she didn't show it. Jason and Claire both goggled at Naomi, wrong-footed by her sudden arrival. Naomi sat heavily in the chair next to Jason and slammed her feet on the desk, crossing her legs.

"Such a terrible drive from the Disputed Region," she complained. "Remind me to take more supplies next time. Reduce the trips back." Rubbing her face, she took in the scene. "Am I interrupting?"

"No, not at all." Jason hurried to respond before Claire had a chance to. "Claire was just visiting to ask us something."

Glaring at Jason, Claire added, "Actually, I was just checking in because Jason is—"

"Oh, good," Naomi interrupted. "You two have realised that we should all be working together and have finally grown up and stopped waiting for the other to be the one to suggest it first." She looked at the two of them, her expression slightly menacing. "Right?"

Jason and Claire both muttered their agreement, shrugging and looking like naughty schoolchildren. Naomi suddenly glanced around, looking worried.

"Nothing builds a team like fresh air. Maybe we should—"

"It's okay." Claire pulled a small metal cube from her pocket. "Disrupter. No one can hear us."

Naomi looked suspiciously at the device, but remembering Claire's background, didn't challenge its efficacy. "Great. Well, where are we at?"

"Well, er, Hudson and I have done quite a lot of vetting and research while you've been away," said Jason, shuffling his papers and looking for a document. "And we've discovered, uh, that Giles did not have anything to do with Her Majesty being pushed back through the portal."

Claire watched as Naomi stared blankly at Jason. He looked back at his subordinate, his posture that of the head of the Royal Guard, but there was something in his eyes. A plea of some kind. He was probably trying to make it seem as if he had made more progress than he really had, to avoid losing face in front of Claire.

"Um, good. That's good." Naomi removed her feet from the desk and sat up a little straighter in her chair. "I didn't get too far down there, to be honest. I think I've made some good contacts, but they don't trust me enough yet to tell me anything about the theft of the felixium." She turned and looked at Claire. "How about you?"

Claire moved around behind them and pulled up a chair so that they were in a small huddle. "I've been looking into Ezra Brown. Something's off there. He knows too much and the prime minister appointing him as his special advisor is weird. And ..." Claire hesitated. Somehow, telling them about being followed felt like admitting a failure, but she reminded herself that she needed to trust Jason and Naomi. She couldn't do this alone. "I'm being followed. I think they're HSP. They're staking out my apartment, and I think they've tried to bug me at least twice. My wardrobe can't take much more. Especially since I'm living in my third safe house and only have two more jackets."

Naomi ignored Claire's weak attempt at humour. "Were you followed here?"

Claire cast her a withering glare. "If I was followed, I wouldn't be here. There's no way I'd bring them to you and let them know we're working together."

"No, of course. Sorry." Naomi looked embarrassed.

"Sorry Claire," echoed Jason, "it's just that things have been bad here, too. We're pretty sure the palace is bugged and our secure communications systems have been infiltrated. Toot being in charge of us should have made things easier, but now that he's working with Toth, we're being hamstrung at every turn. I've been shut out of the palace surveillance system—"

"What?" Naomi was shocked.

"Yeah. That's what Quinn was here about before," Jason explained to Claire. Then, turning to Naomi, "Toot's shut all guards out while the system is being 'upgraded'."

Naomi swore.

"Yep."

A morose silence enveloped the group.

"If you need a place to stay, I have a spare room," Naomi offered Claire.

"Thanks," Claire said warmly, meaning it. "It's probably better for us to all remain separate, though. That way, if one of us is compromised, there's still two to continue."

Naomi nodded and brought the focus back to the mission.

"Alright, so you suspect Ezra, but you have no evidence. We know at least one advisor is dodgy—"

"Other than Toot," Jason interrupted.

"Yeah, other than Toot. We ruled him out as the insider. But we can't find evidence as to who the insider was. And a shipment of felixium was stolen, but we don't know who did it," Naomi summed up.

"Yep, that's about it." Despite the dire state of affairs, Jason clearly felt buoyed by Claire joining the team. "Okay, Naomi. I know you have an opinion. What should we do from here?"

The door opened suddenly, jolting them all again. Giles shuffled into the room, looking dishevelled, which was to say that his tie was slightly crooked and there was a single scuff mark on his right shoe.

"Oh, hello." Giles seemed surprised to see them gathered there.

"Hello, Giles. What can we do for you?" asked Naomi kindly.

Giles looked around the room as if searching for the

reason he had entered in the first place. "Oh, nothing, I expect." He smiled weakly. "Just looking for Jenkins. But I suppose he wouldn't be in here." He laughed weakly.

They smiled sympathetically at Giles. He was at such a loose end without a royal family to take care of. And he seemed so nervous. Perhaps he wasn't spending much time with other people these days. Claire made to stand to talk to Giles, but the old man turned and headed towards the door.

"Sorry, can't stay. Much to do," he said, exiting quickly and leaving them in an awkward silence.

Claire stared sadly after the old man. When she joined the royal advisors, he had been such a large part of the team. In fact, sometimes he had rivalled Minister Bellingham for de facto leader of the group. Now he just seemed like a lost old butler.

Her paranoia spiked at his timing, entering the room so soon after she had employed the disruptor, but she forced the thought from her mind. If he was up to anything, surely he would have stuck around to see what they were discussing.

"Right, well." Naomi drew their attention back to the task at hand. "Claire, I think you need to run point on discovering the identity of the insider and figuring out how Ezra Brown fits in. Are you sure he's involved?"

"Yes, definitely. I actually think he's connected to the insider, though I suppose it's possible that he's running a completely different game. Maybe he's using the political distractions for his own purposes, and the insider is reporting to someone else entirely in connection to the overall plot."

"What other game would he be running?" Jason asked.

"I mean, he is a businessman. Maybe there's an opportunity here that he's looking to exploit for financial gain, rather than political."

"You're not maybe too focussed on him because of your background?" Jason asked.

"No, but I think my background helps me think like him. His background in intelligence makes it more likely that he's involved in the actual plot. Once you've played 'the game', it's difficult to stop. He's likely developed a wide network of connections. Those connections could lead us to the insider, and maybe even to whoever is behind all of this."

"The prime minister?" Jason asked. He seemed like the most logical suspect. No one had gained as much from everything that had happened as Reginald Toth. Claire shook her head at him.

"No, he's more likely to be a pawn. He has gained a lot, but he's not ..." Claire searched for the right word. "He's not sophisticated enough to be running the show."

"Well, if it's not him and it's not Ezra, then who is it?" Jason was clearly getting frustrated.

"That's what Claire is going to find out," Naomi cut in, breaking the circuit before things overheated. "Hudson might be able to help you with IT and searches and stuff."

Claire nodded gratefully. "That would be good. I don't have access to a lot of the databases that I used to have, and some of my old contacts have gone missing."

Jason sat up at that. "Missing? Who?"

"My old mentor, for a start. I can't reach him anymore and he hasn't been back to his apartment in weeks. Also, a bunch of our support staff from the HIA. Analysts, IT gurus, and gadgetry experts. Suddenly they've all gone silent and I can't raise them."

"Could they have gone to ground?" Jason asked.

"No, I'd still be able to find them. There's always a trail, even if it goes cold. It's like they've all just disappeared."

Jason frowned, a troubled expression shadowing his face.

"Some of my contacts have gone quiet, too."

Claire felt her stomach drop. Despite her bravado, she had been hoping that her contacts had just been better at covering their tracks than she'd given them credit for. That they were lying low with this new quasi-police state they seemed to be living in. She was going to have to consider that things were every bit as bad as she thought they might be. And maybe quite a bit worse.

"Sounds like we all need to be careful," said Naomi. "Particularly Hudson. I'll reach out to him and send him a message to lay low." She looked at Jason. "You need to lead the felixium investigation. Obviously you can't go to the Disputed Region yet, but you can still use your contacts and try to open some doors for me, and help me plan the investigation."

Jason nodded, though Claire could sense his frustration. He struck her as a doer, and she could imagine sitting back in the palace while the women were doing the doing was driving him a little crazy.

"You're the leader here." Naomi said. Claire tried not to bristle at the comment. "Claire and I will go and gather the information and bring it back to you. We need you to put it all together, to make sure that we're not missing the connections as we focus on our own tasks. And you need to figure out what we're going to do with all the information."

"I'd rather be out there," Jason complained.

"I know. But of all of us, you're the only one with experience in leading an operation. Correct me if I'm wrong, Claire, but from my understanding, you were a junior agent. You went and carried out the operations; you didn't plan them."

Claire rolled her shoulders back, but had to admit that

Naomi was right. She had not been involved in planning missions. And if it was a choice between her and Jason to gather the intelligence, it wasn't really a choice.

"Agreed. Jason is the best one of us to plan and have overwatch."

Jason couldn't keep the surprise from his face, but Claire's vote of confidence seemed to help Jason accept his role, despite his desire to be in the action.

"Okay then, Naomi, you get your supplies and head back down to the DR. I'll reach out to some of my contacts down there and have some meetings set up for when you arrive. And Claire?" He paused, hesitating slightly. "You do whatever it is that you do, but focus on figuring out the insider. I know Ezra is fascinating, but he's only useful to us insofar as he helps us bust the insider. Until we know who it is, we're sitting ducks."

Claire nodded, and they all stood up.

"Be careful," Jason said as the women headed towards the door.

The door flew open just as Claire camouflaged herself, and in strode three guards. She saw Jason tense, surprise and concern on his face. He didn't know why they were there. Had they somehow detected her? Claire was certain her disrupter was working. Maybe they were here for Jason? Was he going to be detained?

The guards fanned out and stood in the imposing fashion of people providing security for someone important.

"Hello Jase," drawled a voice from behind the three men.

"Richard! What are you doing here?" Jason gaped at Richard as he strolled in, one hand in his pocket, lazily looking around the room.

"I've come home, old chap." Richard smiled, a hard look in his eyes. "I'm your new boss."

17

CLAIRE WAS PRACTISED at standing still. As a chameleon, the quickest thing to give her away was movement. So, when she was a child, she had practised for hours, sometimes simply to avoid detention, but other times she'd listen in on conversations. It had surprised no one when she announced she was joining the HIA.

Claire was currently leaning against the trunk of a tall tree, surrounded by some shrubs and flower bushes. The trick was to find a spot among the bushes, but not in them, where you would be constantly brushed or insects might crawl onto you. You had to ensure nothing would tickle you, or cause you to move. Finding something to lean on helped with the stiffness, and anything nearby that might move in a breeze would help cover the small movements one must make to remain limber, in case you needed to leave or fight.

The outdoor cafe Claire was watching was only mildly interesting. It was quieter than she remembered, but not so quiet that she would stand out. And the vibe was tense. But that was true of most places in Highacre at the moment.

Her thoughts turned to her investigation. She had, as requested by Jason, turned her mind to who the rogue advisor might be. However, unwilling to discard her suspicions about Ezra, she was starting her investigation with those advisors who might be linked to the former ambassador.

Jason had mentioned loose ties between Austin and Ezra, but if Austin was involved in the plot, he was clearly a lackey. He had a strong military background, which Claire associated with someone following orders rather than masterminding a coup. She noted her bias and ignored it. In this case, it felt right. Either way, her instincts told her that there was something off about Austin.

Even when she first met him, she'd felt it. So far though, all she had managed to find—beyond what Jason had given her—were a couple of receipts that showed he and Ezra had attended a few of the same conferences. Self-help and leadership conferences. "Being a better you" type stuff. Not usefully called "How to assassinate a royal family and assume control of their country".

The main person with a connection to Ezra was Addison. But it was a blatant one and seemed to be purely a friendship.

Possibly misguided on Addison's part.

But there were no financial ties, no evidence of having known each other before he came to the palace. And there was nothing that would indicate that Addison was seeking to gain anything other than some friendship, a companion of a similar age with whom she could relax and chat with over a cup of tea.

And just what did you both talk about?

Maybe there was no real connection there, but Addison may have inadvertently leaked information that Ezra could have exploited.

Claire looked up as Addison appeared, as if summoned by Claire's thinking about her. She didn't really think the older woman was the palace insider, however, it would be remiss of her not to at least question the woman. But Claire had another reason for meeting with Addison. She was hoping to recruit her as a source within the palace.

Following Richard's surprise return, Claire had found herself suddenly cut off from the team she had just joined. She had slipped out of the ops room at the earliest opportunity after Richard's arrival, then waited to hear from Jason and Naomi, becoming increasingly paranoid as the hours turned to days.

Finally, an email came from Naomi, carefully crafted to deliver a message that only Claire would be able to decipher. Claire had been begrudgingly impressed at Naomi's abilities. Seemingly a gossipy complaint about a terrible day Naomi had at work, the email had told Claire that with Richard's reappearance, neither she nor Jason would be able to communicate with her in the foreseeable future. Naomi indicated they had their IT expert, Hudson, working on a fix, but until then, Claire should not reach out to either of them unless it was absolutely necessary.

Signing off, Naomi had let Claire know they would look to catch up with her when Naomi returned from the DR. Claire had felt an unexpected pang of disappointment and loneliness. Reluctant as she had been to join forces with Jason and Naomi, having done it, she had felt a huge sense of relief, and of belonging. It had seemed like things were perhaps getting back on track, and with the support of her new partners, everything would be alright. Naomi's email had severed that connection somewhat, and Claire felt alone again. It was possible that this had some influence on her decision to use Addison as a source. Whether or not she was able to provide useable intelligence, she was someone on her side who Claire could talk to.

If she is on my side.

Returning her focus to Addison, Claire realised the woman looked haggard, and she had lost weight. No longer the self-confident and bubbly house-mum of the palace, Addison sat nervously at a table and fidgeted with her rings, occasionally looking about with a worried expression.

She didn't have the paranoid focus that Claire had developed; she wasn't scanning her surroundings for threats, but mostly just seemed anxious. Claire remained hidden from view, watching to see if Addison had been followed. As the minutes ticked by, Addison relaxed slightly, perhaps thinking that Claire was not coming after all. Claire continued to watch, now less focussed on any tails Addison may have collected, and more on whether Addison herself may be communicating with someone else.

Though, if she told Ezra she was meeting me, he would have told her not to let me know that, and not to talk to him again until she left the cafe.

Just as Addison seemed to have decided that she had waited long enough, Claire decided it was safe, ducked behind some bushes to rematerialize, and hurried over to Addison's table.

"So sorry I'm late," she gushed, sounding out of breath.

"Oh, not at all, I'm glad you could make it," lied Addison unconvincingly.

Claire tried to engage Addison in some small talk, but Addison was clearly distracted.

"Addison, how are you? Really?" Claire asked quietly, leaning towards the older woman.

"Oh, I'm ... well, it's just—" Addison started picking her paper napkin to pieces. "Claire, I think I've done something terrible," she hissed.

Claire leant farther forward, briefly touching Addison's arm to show sympathy, but said nothing in the hopes that Addison would continue.

"I think I might have—it's just, I know I shouldn't—but I didn't think—" She took a deep breath, trying to blink back tears. "I *know* better. With my training—so *stupid*. And after the assassinations—now Lily—"

"Hands where I can see them!" a man clad in black demanded, pointing his assault rifle at Addison as if she were a dangerous criminal.

Claire looked around, stunned that several similarly dressed and armed HSP officers had managed to sneak up on them. Screaming erupted from around the cafe as its patrons panicked and tried to flee. On instinct, the HSP officers turned their weapons on the crowd, demanding that they remain in place. Claire took advantage of the distraction, camouflaging herself before sliding to the ground and crawling back toward the bushes she had hid in earlier.

Feeling guilty for having arranged this meeting with Addison, only to abandon her to the HSP, Claire told herself that it did no one any good for her to be caught too, and slowly raised herself into a position where she could observe what was happening.

"Target secured," she heard the man she assumed was the team leader say into his radio. "Secondary escaped."

Claire listened to the man give the responses of someone who had clearly disappointed his superior as she watched them lead a handcuffed Addison over to a black van. Addison gave no resistance, but glanced around, perhaps wondering where Claire had gone, or possibly whether she had been a part of this operation.

Claire painstakingly withdrew from the area, not relaxing at all until she was several blocks away, in a side alley, the likes of which were becoming disturbingly familiar to her. Her mind replayed the arrest.

Secondary escaped.

They had wanted to arrest her too. Any wishful thought

that the HSP were simply surveilling her evaporated. She needed to be more careful.

Claire took pains to ensure that her route back to her latest safe house was both one she had not taken before, and completely illogical for someone returning from the cafe where Addison had been arrested.

Here and there on her journey, she saw others also traversing the alleys and wondered whether they were, like her, avoiding the HSP. Halfway home, Claire saw two men out of the corner of her eye. One looked familiar, so she moved closer to get a better look.

Claire almost walked into a trash can when the man moved into the light. It was Austin! She didn't recognise the man he was with. Curious, she tried to get into a position where she could hear what they were saying.

"—must be keeping you on your toes," Austin was saying.

"No kidding. Bugger, do not let me forget to pick up some whiskey. He will kill me if I forget it again. He hates using his power to make drinks for other people."

"Better you than me. That's why I prefer freelancing. I could not put up with catering to Toot."

"Yeah, gun for hire suits you."

"That's what they tell me. So, the Patriot wants to know if ..."

"Ooof." Claire had walked straight into a baton that blasted the air from her lungs.

"Using magical abilities to avoid a checkpoint is a class one offence, ma'am."

Claire slowly straightened herself and looked at the officer who had stopped her, trying to keep an eye on her targets. Blissfully unaware of Claire's presence, or her current predicament, the two men strode quickly down the street.

Claire's eyes flicked to the officer's shoulder patch.

HSP.

She had literally walked into the very people trying to arrest her. Suddenly less concerned with losing Austin, Claire scanned the area. The HSP had set up a checkpoint about a hundred metres to her right, down a different street. They were checking people's identity papers. She saw a lady burst into tears as two officers led her to a van.

Claire glanced at the officer who had stopped her. He didn't seem to realise who she was. She needed to keep it that way.

"Oh, no." Claire smiled her most innocuous smile. "My apologies, Officer. I wasn't trying to avoid your checkpoint. I'm meant to be in a meeting in ten minutes. I sometimes use my ability to avoid running into people I know and having to chat when I don't have time." She turned her smile part apologetic, part embarrassed, hoping the HSP officer was also the type to want to avoid annoying acquaintances.

"Uh huh." Apparently he was not. "This way, ma'am."

Claire cast a quick glance down the street and saw that Austin and his companion were already out of sight. At least he hadn't noticed that she had been following him. The officer escorted Claire over to a line of people and directed her to the end. Without another word, he walked back over to the end of the street and started scanning.

A revealer. And a powerful one, too. Claire turned her attention to the checkpoint. It was unusually quiet for a group of people this large. No one was complaining or chatting. Everyone was standing in lines compliantly, anxiously awaiting their turn. She watched the officers for a couple of minutes.

Claire had to give it to the HSP. They were running a well-oiled machine. Most people only waited a minute or two before their papers were checked and they were on their way.

Claire's eyes drifted to the far end of the street. That was the entry to the checkpoint, and she saw a couple of officers waving pedestrians through to various lines to have their papers checked. She saw a small family walking towards the checkpoint. They turned to go down a side street. From Claire's perspective, they didn't seem to be trying to avoid the checkpoint, but nonetheless, four burly HSP officers yelled and ran towards them.

The woman picked up her small son and pulled her pram protectively towards her. The man stepped in front of them. Claire felt a sudden pang of loneliness. There was no one to step in front of danger to protect her. No one for her to protect. Given the circumstances, the disbandment of the HIA that she had sacrificed so much for, and the implosion of society, maybe she shouldn't have prioritised her career over her family. That did *not* mean her mother was right, though.

She refocussed on the scene. The officers' voices were getting louder, the man and his wife more panicked. The man was shaking his head and backing away from the men in uniforms, his arms raised as if surrendering.

Claire let out a small gasp of surprise as the four officers lunged at the man, throwing him on the ground and kicking him, his wife now screaming for them to stop and his two children crying. One of the HSP officers stopped beating the man and advanced towards the woman, who shrank back, protecting her children and shaking her head.

The officers picked up the man, who was now bleeding and unconscious, and threw him in the back of a vehicle. They then turned to the woman, who was crying uncontrollably but still managed to pull out some papers while ensuring that she remained between the officers and her children.

An officer snatched the papers, and she flinched. He asked a question, and she shook her head, clearly unable to answer coherently. Another officer slapped her across the face. Claire heard herself exclaim, and the man standing in front of her in line turned and glared, shaking his head for her to be quiet. His eyes were full of fear as he shuffled a few steps away from Claire.

Claire returned her attention to the scene in time to see the officer throw the woman's papers back at her and yell for her to leave. The van with her husband was driving away.

It all felt so unreal.

You have not evaded them for this long only to be caught by a random checkpoint.

Claire mentally pulled herself together. She checked her pockets for her doctored papers, hoping that she had done a good enough forgery. She took a deep breath and concentrated.

Glamouring had always been her weakest skill; she could usually barely change the colour of her eyebrows. But if she could alter her appearance a little, it might let her by. Or at least create enough doubt to let her talk her way out. She felt her nose tingle and resisted the urge to scratch it.

"Papers," an empty voice demanded. Claire handed her fake papers over and somehow managed to concentrate enough to answer the man's questions.

"Name?" the HSP officer demanded.

What was happening? What had Highacre become? Had the country really fallen so far, so quickly? That poor family. Obviously, they weren't the only ones suffering. And she had just stood there and watched it happen. Claire felt slightly sick.

"What is your purpose for being in this sector?"

She had always thought she was the kind of person who would step in to help others in a situation like that. But she hadn't. She tried to tell herself that it had happened so fast that there was no time to intervene, but the thought rang hollow. In truth, she hadn't even thought to help. She was so shocked by the whole thing, she had felt paralysed.

"Go on. Next."

Surprised by the reprieve, Claire hurried home, head down, ignoring everything and everyone. She felt a flood of relief as she turned into the street of the little townhouse she had borrowed; its owners were abroad on holiday.

"Oh, excuse me, sorry!"

A smiling young woman touched Claire's arm reassuringly as she jumped. "Didn't mean to startle you, sorry," she apologised again sincerely.

"It's fine," Claire said, reminding herself to smile.

"I'm Helen," said the woman, offering her hand. "We've just moved in over there."

She pointed to a townhouse diagonally opposite Claire's temporary home. Its windows would be able to see into her front rooms.

"Welcome to the neighbourhood," Claire said warmly.

"Thank you, everyone's been so lovely here." She beamed. "I hate to be a bother, but do you have an allen key by any chance? The movers didn't put everything together and, of course, the one box that's missing is the one with the tools."

"Of course," Claire sympathised. "Isn't that always the way it goes? I'm afraid I'm not much help. I broke up with my boyfriend a month ago and he took everything that he decided was his, which included all our tools. I've been meaning to get some replacements, but part of me is hoping—"

"That you'll be able to make up?"

"That he'll realise he's being petty and bring them back."

Both women laughed airily.

"Oh well, thanks anyway," said the woman. "No doubt I'll be seeing you." She pointed unnecessarily at her house and went inside, waving at Claire from her door.

"I doubt you will," Claire said under her breath, smiling and waving back.

Reaching into her bag for her keys, Claire pulled out her phone and pretended to take a call. Making a show of telling the person she'd just gotten home, she dropped her shoulders as if resigned to her fate, then turned and headed off down the street, putting the phone away as she rounded the corner.

Hurrying now, Claire navigated to the farthest of the three potential new safe houses that she had been staking out. It made her feel better to put as much distance as possible between her and the old one, and she was the most certain that this apartment was vacant.

Entering the apartment a couple of hours later, she locked the door behind her and secured the chain. She sat heavily in a chair and wept silently, feeling hopeless as hot tears rolled down her cheeks. She was not the woman she had thought herself to be, and she was scared.

Claire sat there crying silently for a while. Eventually, she wiped her cheeks and went to the bathroom to wash her face. She looked at her puffy red eyes in the bathroom mirror and saw her gaze turn from fear to resolve.

She had not been the woman she wanted to be in that moment at the checkpoint. But she would be that woman now. She would not stand by again. And for now, she could help her country and her people best by figuring out this conspiracy. That was more use than rushing in and getting herself arrested.

Her eyes grew doubtful.

Is that a convenient excuse for my lack of action?

Claire shook herself. No, she would learn from that mistake, and now she would be smarter and faster. No more time for tears. She needed to figure out who was involved and what was going on. She needed to be on the front foot, taking action instead of reacting.

Claire's eyes narrowed, her resolve hardening.

She had work to do.

18

Jason ate his lunch in strained silence. Taking a bite of his dinner roll, still warm and oozing butter, he felt resentful that he wasn't able to enjoy the food, which was always amazing. He let his eyes rove around the room, but refused to make eye contact with anyone in particular.

The guard's mess was essentially an old dining hall. It was located within the original palace castle, and while it had been updated, the modernisations had avoided touching the architecture and aesthetic. High stone walls extended overhead to the cathedral roofing, and beams in the roof held banners of various military units, and of course, the Royal Guards.

The stone walls similarly displayed tapestries and coats of arms, and several suits of armour stood guard around the perimeter. Long wooden tables filled the room, with bench seating on either side. Due to the shift-work nature of their job, there were always people in the hall, eating and chatting and playing cards and other various time-filling games. Jason loved this room. It reminded him of the best parts of being in the military and managed to give him a nostalgia hit.

"Must remind you of your military days," said Richard, irritatingly reading Jason's mind. Jason grunted in response.

"Come on now, you're not still giving me the silent treatment, are you? It's been over a week."

Jason bristled at being told he was essentially behaving like a small child. And while it was true that he hadn't been conducting the handover of his position with the level of grace he perhaps should have, he certainly hadn't behaved as poorly as he suspected Richard would have in his position, especially given the tantrum he had thrown when Jason brought Naomi in.

An uncomfortable thought about karma entered Jason's mind, but was dismissed. His current behaviour, in his view, was more in response to how Richard was acting. Jason had expected Richard to be gloating, proudly telling everyone they had to meet with that he had been chosen to replace Jason, strutting around and basically taking pleasure in Jason getting his just desserts.

Instead, Richard had adopted a sympathetic tone that implied a separation between Jason being replaced and Richard being the one replacing him. That the higher-ups had been looking around for a replacement and he just happened to be the one selected for the role. This was worse for Jason, as it implied some unknown screw-up by him, and better for Richard, as he was able to appear to be on everyone's side, including those who might have remained loyal to Jason. Jason had underestimated Richard, had been blinded by his assumptions based on Richard's background. And he was angry at himself for it.

"Look," said Jason, deciding that he needed to deal with his circumstances and start making them work for him. "You knew the job already, and you've been well briefed in to the current situation. I think it's time I got out from under your feet. It might be good for me to actually be out of the picture for a bit."

"You want to take some leave?" asked Richard, looking surprised. "Of course, I mean, you've definitely earned it, and are probably long overdue. Naomi's due back today, right?"

"She is, but actually, I was thinking I might head to the DR with Naomi when she goes back. Help her with the investigation down there."

Richard frowned, considering the request. "I can't spare both of you. But if you wanted to swap out with her, that would be okay with me."

Jason brightened. Getting away from his current humiliation would be great, and he was itching to work on the investigation. He knew Naomi would be able to work her magic here to make sure she had space to operate, and he had a feeling that she and Claire would make a formidable team.

"Only thing is, I don't have the final call on that."

Jason's heart sank. "What do you mean?"

"Toot's told me he needs to personally approve any and all guards 'working in the field'. But if you can convince him, you can go. Oh, and it's your lucky day. Look who just walked in."

Jason turned in his seat in time to see Minister Toot just inside the entrance to the mess, glancing around and clearly searching for someone, distaste plastered all over his face. He spotted Richard and started in their direction. Jason stood and strode out to meet him. He wanted to ask without Richard in earshot.

"Minister Toot, may I have a word?"

"Er, yes I suppose, Mr ... er?"

"Jason McFarlane. You might remember me from all of those royal advisors meetings." Jason glared down at the defence minister. Such a small, ferrety man, Jason had always found him irritating, but now it was all he could do to keep his temper.

"Of course, yes, forgive me. I meet with so many people, you see? What can I do for you, McFairland?"

"Richard, the head of the Royal Guard—"

"Yes, yes, I know who Richard is."

"—tells me I need your permission to go to the DR."

"Quite right."

"Well?"

"Well, what?"

"Can I go to the DR?"

"Whatever for, man?" Minister Toot looked at Jason as if he had asked to go and live in the sewers.

"To replace our officer, who is down there investigating."

"Investigating what? You're supposed to be guarding the palace."

Jason decided not to argue the merits of guarding an empty palace. "The Royal Guard is leading the efforts to find Her Majesty—"

"Well, you'll hardly find her in the DR!"

"No sir." Jason gritted his teeth. "But we will need felixium to recover her."

"The felixium has been stolen," Toot told Jason, now speaking to him as if he were a very simple person.

"Yes sir," said Jason, clenching and unclenching his fists and trying to count to ten in his mind. "I want to go to the DR to investigate its theft, recover it if possible, and then use it to recover the monarch."

"Well, you might have started with that, McFadden." Toot sighed, as if thinking there should be people to deal with the riffraff for him, and downed the last of his whiskey.

"Look, I don't know what your man in the field has told you, but—"

"My man in the field is a woman."

"But ... er, what?" Minister Toot was surprised by the interruption, clearly distracted by the idea that a woman was conducting the investigation.

Jason stared menacingly at Minister Toot, daring him to say anything disparaging about Naomi because she was female.

"Oh. Well. In that case, I completely understand, McFarlton. Yes, you should have her replaced. Good luck with your investigation, and safe travels."

Jason opened his mouth to correct Minister Toot's sexist assumption, but before he could say anything, an angry man bustled up and poked Minister Toot in the chest.

"You told me she would be safe!"

Jason's jaw dropped. He'd never heard Giles raise his voice before, let alone imagine him confronting a government minister publicly like this.

"I never said—"

"You assured me. That was the exact word you used. 'Assured'. And I did what you asked." Giles was clenching and unclenching his fists, blinking rapidly. "She's been arrested," he hissed.

Minister Toot glanced about, clearly upset at the attention Giles had attracted. "My good man, I don't know what—"

"You promised she'd be safe!" Giles yelled.

"Giles, what's going on?" Jason asked, deciding to step in.

"Yes, thank you McFarlane. Take care of this, will you?" said Minister Toot hurriedly before turning away, clearly hoping to escape the emotive butler.

"He's had me watching you," Giles said, addressing

Jason but raising his voice, causing Toot to halt. "He said if I reported on your movements, he'd make sure Addison was kept safe. But they arrested her."

Jason looked at Giles, shocked, and the old man dissolved into tears.

"I don't know what you're talking about." Minister Toot whipped around, leaning in and hissing at Giles menacingly. "But if you don't shut up, you'll be seeing your friend again very soon." He glared up at Jason, making sure the larger man understood the threat applied to him too.

Before Jason could recover himself, Minister Toot strode away toward a bewildered Richard, grabbing him by the arm and sweeping out of the hall.

"Giles—" Jason began.

"I'm so sorry," Giles sobbed.

Aware of the many ears listening to them, Jason ushered Giles out the opposite door to where the minister had exited and escorted him out into the grounds. He sat the older man down on the edge of the pool surrounding the fountain. The running water was loud and should conceal their words.

While Giles was collecting himself, Jason's phone buzzed. He ignored the call from Naomi. She'd be calling to let him know she was back. He sent a quick text with his current whereabouts and asked her to meet him.

Giles eventually stopped crying and began cleaning his face with a perfectly pressed handkerchief and taking some deep breaths. "I'm sorry," he said again, quieter this time.

"Oh no, what's happened?" Naomi jogged up to the pair, throwing an arm around Giles's shoulder.

"Addison's been arrested," Jason said.

"What? Oh no, I'm sorry Giles."

Giles nodded, but looked uncomfortable.

"And apparently Giles has been spying on us for Minister Toot," Jason added.

Naomi flinched as if wanting to remove her arm from Giles's shoulder, but left it there, looking at Giles instead and waiting for his explanation.

"He said he'd keep Addison safe," Giles said again, this time sounding disillusioned, like a child who'd discovered Christmas wasn't so magical after all.

"He's been blackmailing you?" Naomi asked. Jason thought the description sounded more lenient than what he'd use.

Giles nodded. "He came to me a few weeks ago. Said we were all in trouble. That it was only a matter of time. He said the prime minister wanted us all arrested."

"And you didn't think to tell us about that?" Jason asked.

"He said if I let him know what you were up to, then he could run interference. He could show the prime minister that he had you under control, and he would keep Addison and I safe in exchange. But, but ..." Giles started crying again.

"Was she hurt?" Naomi asked Jason quietly, confused by how devastated Giles was.

He shook his head and opened his mouth to answer, but Giles looked at Naomi and responded first. "I thought I was doing the right thing. That I was helping. But instead, she's been arrested anyway, and all I've done is betray you both."

They let Giles cry, rubbing his back, but at a loss as to what to say. He had betrayed them. It had come from a good place, but Jason couldn't understand why he didn't tell them what was happening.

"Giles, I know you're upset, but we need to know what you told them," Jason said firmly.

The old man shook his head. "I didn't tell them anything. Not really. Just locations, or anything that I thought was benign or something they would already know.

That's why I've not been around. I didn't want to learn anything that I might need to hand over."

"Giles," Naomi began, urgency in her voice, "You saw us with Claire the other day—"

"I didn't say anything about her being there. I told Minister Toot that the two of you were in the operations room talking about the investigation in the Disputed Region. That's all, I promise."

Jason glanced at Naomi, who gave a slight nod. Naomi could detect lies, but Giles was telling the truth.

"Okay, Giles? We believe you. I know you thought you were doing the right thing, but I need you to promise you'll tell me next time. If anyone approaches you like this again, you need to let me know," Jason said.

Giles looked up into Jason's eyes as if he'd been given a reprieve from the firing squad. "Oh yes, of course."

"And now Naomi and I will need to keep our distance, just for a bit. Given how many people saw you yelling at Toot, we can assume it will be known that you told us you were spying on us. We'll be expected to be mad at you. But if you need us, give us a sign and we'll meet you out here."

"I'll swap the crests outside the barracks. The little ones beside the door? The correct order is the king's crest on the left, the queen's on the right. If it's the other way, then I need to speak with you."

"I've never noticed the crests," said Jason, straining to remember.

"Then it's a perfect signal," said Naomi, smiling at Giles. "And if you need us more urgently, complain that the pond is dirty again. If you can, make it seem like you're complaining to yourself."

"I can be subtle," Giles nodded enthusiastically. "Thank you. Thank you both for your understanding."

"Of course," said Naomi giving him a quick hug.

"We're in this together," assured Jason, clapping a reassuring hand on Giles's back.

Smiling at them both, Giles scurried off, back toward the palace.

The two Royal Guards watched him go, Jason thinking Giles was the last person he would have expected to betray them. If Giles was compromised, could they really trust anyone?

19

"WHAT DO YOU THINK?" Naomi asked as soon as Giles was out of earshot.

"We'll have to monitor him. Make sure this isn't just a story."

"If it is, he believes it," said Naomi. "It's more about what the real purpose was in having him report on us."

"If he was as bad at reporting on us as he says he was, maybe that's why they arrested Addison," Jason mused. "Let him know they aren't playing around. Use it as more leverage."

As if by unspoken agreement, the two stood and headed into the extended grounds.

"Toot's given me permission to head to the DR," Jason said.

"Oh thank goodness," said Naomi. "No offence, but I'm sick of dealing with macho, arrogant military, and military wannabes."

"Tell me what you really think," laughed Jason.

"They're all just so patronising. And the contractors are the worst. And you were right. Without the contacts, no one is going to tell me anything. This will be much better. You can go and talk about manly things, and I'll stay here and work with Claire."

"We need to check that she's okay," said Jason, frowning. "I was in the ops room when the report of Addison's arrest came in. Richard sent me off on a task pretty quickly, but the reporting I heard indicated a secondary target. I think they mentioned chameleoning."

"That's not good at all," said Naomi darkly, her expression concerned.

"On the upside, I think I'd have heard if she'd been arrested. On the downside, they're clearly after her."

"I'll need to get myself a crappy assignment that no one cares about. Then I can go and see if I can help her. She may not be able to help us anymore, you realise that?"

"I know," said Jason morosely. For all his reluctance to work with Claire, she was an excellent operator, and the idea that they had lost her skills so quickly after gaining them again was depressing. He also found he was worried about her. He liked Claire, despite having discovered she was HIA, and the idea of her in danger, especially when he wouldn't be able to help, was upsetting. Jason kicked himself for wasting so much time not teaming up.

As they walked slowly through the woods, Naomi briefed Jason about her investigation. She had visited the scene of the theft, but that was just a stretch of road where the convoy had lost contact with the control room—or "gone dark". Naomi had spent a few hours scouring the area and found nothing. Anything that may have been left behind had long been driven into the dirt or dispersed by the heavy traffic. And the storm that had blown through the area the week before she arrived hadn't helped.

Naomi didn't have Jason's tracking skills, but she could read the emotional memory of places. She could confirm that it was the scene of the ambush, but only because those emotions had been so strong. Everything else had dissipated.

The most Naomi found was some high ground nearby that would have served as the perfect overwatch spot for the ambush. It had a clear view of the area where they lost contact with the convoy, as well as good visibility of the routes in and out.

Jason was impressed that she had found it, but as Naomi said, all she found in that position were a couple of what might have been boot impressions. Unfortunately, everyone in the Disputed Region wore boots, so that wasn't overly helpful.

Next, Naomi had gone to Bomberra, the Highacren barracks town that had grown up around the base. With the base and the town, it was like one big military community, and everyone seemed to know everyone. Which made it hard to break in and get people to talk.

"I felt like I went back in time to a frontier town, but where people were wearing sensible clothes," Naomi said. "The men all seemed like bikers in a bar, all in their various gangs, and not willing to snitch on a rival gang to an outsider. And the women were all the tough, weathered types who wouldn't dream of snitching on their men and hated me for posing a threat."

"How are you threatening?" Jason had seen Naomi work enough to know that she could appear to be very disarmingly sweet and naïve if required. It was quite unsettling.

"For some, it was threatening their safety and freedom, asking too many questions about something they either knew their men were mixed up in, or knew they could have been. For others, I think they thought I might take their men, and that was the bigger threat."

"Well, at least in that respect, I'll be less threatening."

"You might be more so." Naomi smiled sweetly at Jason, who took a beat to get her meaning and then found himself blushing and feeling quite uncomfortable.

"So." Jason cleared his throat and turned the conversation back to who might have been involved. "You mainly spoke with the soldiers and private security contractors?"

"And the miners, and the construction workers." Naomi continued at seeing Jason's confusion, "The miners obviously knew about the felixium. Even the ones who mine for other resources. They're all friends and live in the same part of town. It wouldn't be hard for them to all know what was going on, and they all had access to the relevant equipment needed to move the felixium if the plan was to ditch the original trucks."

"But we never found the original trucks, did we?"

"No, and that's the other thing. Where would they be hiding two big trucks of felixium? I thought maybe they could have hidden them down one of the mines. Or maybe in plain sight within the mining fleet. We'll have to get someone to scan them. I couldn't get close enough to check."

Jason was again struck by just how good an investigator Naomi was. Annoyance rose within him that the main reason she hadn't succeeded on her mission was because she was female.

"The construction workers were a bit of a long shot," Naomi continued. "But they have equipment and the ability to hide and move large quantities of materials. I don't really think they were involved. My gut, from being down there and talking to people, is that it was probably some of the private security contractors."

"Why is that?"

She shrugged. "They're dodgy."

"Right. Well, I'll have them all arrested."

Naomi nodded. "Good plan, boss. Case closed. Nah, they're a bit removed from the other groups down there. Most people seem to dislike them. They feel the contractors give them a bad rep. The contractors also seem to think that they're better than the others, which adds to them being on the outer. Ultimately, the result is that no one else knows what they're up to, and it's difficult to get them to talk. Of course, you'd think that would mean everyone else would be happy to tell me what the contractors had been up to, but while the contractors are outsiders, they're still more 'in' than I was."

Jason and Naomi had looped around and now found themselves closing in on the palace grounds. A figure was walking towards the palace from the gardens. The man spotted Jason and Naomi emerging from the extended grounds, turned, and began striding towards them.

Oh no. Richard.

Jason began running through possible explanations for being in the woods.

"Jason," Richard said, with a nod to acknowledge Naomi. "Glad I caught you before you left. You'll have to delay your trip to the DR slightly."

Anger flared immediately and Jason began to protest, but Richard held up his hands as if surrendering. "You can go, I just need you to do a job here first."

"What job?" Jason asked obstinately.

Richard's face fell into a solemn expression. "Lady Octavia's body has been found," he said in a low voice. "I want you to lead the investigation. She's been missing a while, so I don't need you to drop everything, but you will need to view her body at the morgue, and maybe go and view where she was found before you head off to the DR."

Jason felt suddenly wrong-footed. He had been so focussed on finding the insider and the felixium he had almost forgotten Lady Octavia was missing. Guiltily, he realised he had already written her off as dead, and while he had respected her, he'd needed to direct his efforts towards the living. He was also thrown at Richard wanting him to lead the investigation.

"Do we know if—had she identified her replacement?"

"If she did, she doesn't seem to have told anyone." Richard looked ruffled, and Jason wondered if the task Richard had been given was to find the new detector and ensure they were on the prime minister's side. "Once you've finished the investigation, if we haven't found her replacement, I might put you on it."

That last comment didn't ring true, confirming Jason's suspicion. He decided to test the waters a little. "Um, thanks. Look, this level of ... it's something I would normally have taken myself. You know, as head of the Royal Guards."

"Which is why I want you on it," said Richard reasonably. "You have experience, I don't."

Jason blinked. This was not the Richard he had been expecting. He felt like the younger man was playing him.

"What about Naomi?" Jason suggested, having almost forgotten she was there. "She could lead it. I can't recommend her highly enough."

Richard looked apologetically at Naomi, but addressed Jason. "She just doesn't have the background. Look, I want you to lead, but how you go about it is up to you. If you want to do the preliminary stuff and get Naomi to carry on the investigation in your absence ..." Richard shrugged with an air of someone telling someone else how to do their job, but not wanting to appear to be telling them how to do their job.

"Right. Well, we'll get on it," Jason said, still looking at Richard with suspicion.

"Excellent. Make sure to do a good job." Richard turned

and headed for the palace, calling over his shoulder, "High-profile investigation like this, fingers will point if you stuff it up."

Jason and Naomi stared at Richard until the new head of the Royal Guard had entered the palace.

"A cynical person might think he's setting you up," said Naomi.

"Maybe he's trying to find a way for us to work together," said Jason, not believing it for a minute. The two looked at each other, then began walking back towards the palace, following in Richard's footsteps.

"Look," said Jason, stopping and looking at Naomi, mind returning to their plan. "If Claire's still operational, great, but we need to be careful. She can still be helpful doing online research with Hudson if going out and about is too dangerous. You might need to make that call if she's too keen to keep going. I support your assessment one hundred percent."

"Got it. Thanks, boss."

"And whatever happens, you be safe. I'm serious," he said, cutting off what he knew was going to be a joking response. "Last thing we need is both of you out of the picture, and I like Claire, I really do, but if it's a choice between both of you, I need you, Naomi."

Naomi looked touched. "I won't do anything stupid, I promise. And if any buses even look to be coming our way, I'll be right behind Claire, pushing her in front of them."

He smiled, but was relieved to see in Naomi's eyes that she understood the seriousness of the situation.

"Hey," Naomi called as they went to part ways. "You be careful too. I don't want to get stuck working for that Richard bloke forever."

20

THE NEXT FEW weeks passed in a blur of routine, one day bleeding into the next. The three headed off each morning, Alexei to find work and Ava and Lily to scour Fernwall, hoping to happen upon one of Lily's sisters.

Long having given up on schools, Lily and Ava were now attempting a systematic search of the area. Progressing through the streets was offering a sense of accomplishment, and this kept morale high. Neither gave voice to the fact that clearing a block one day did not mean that Lily's sisters wouldn't appear there the next.

Lily was beginning to think finding her sisters was a lost cause. She had returned to David several times, however, each time her hungover brother had slammed the door shut in her face.

To distract herself, Lily tried desperately to come up with a better cover story than the one she had given to Brandon and Gemma. She doubted the reunion with her sisters would provide a similar distraction from the weak fabrication, and she knew her sisters would interrogate it more, if only for wanting to know what Lily had been through. So far, nothing had occurred to Lily, but with the lack of success in finding them, her anxiety at creating something believable had begun to dissipate. It seemed more and more unlikely that they would just bump into them on the street.

Despite the anxiety that, while this was their best hope of locating her sisters, it was a largely pointless endeavour, Lily enjoyed being with Ava, and looked forward to their mornings together. She was struck again that being around Ava felt effortless. She didn't have to try to be anyone but herself, and Ava seemed to genuinely enjoy spending time with Lily.

Some days they would create backstories for the people they observed, each becoming more ludicrous than the last. Other days, they would sit and watch the people and share stories from their own pasts or talk about their hopes for the future. Lily learned Ava was thinking of leaving her government job after her stint as ambassador to court.

"I don't know what I'll do, but I'm just sick of all the bureaucracy, you know?" Ava said, idly snapping a small twig into tiny pieces.

"Oh yeah," said Lily, remembering her brief stint as an intern.

"It's a double-edged sword, really. The pay and benefits are really good, so it's comfortable. But in return, they own you. I just want to feel like my own person again."

Lily looked at her friend. Ava had a faraway look in her eyes, clearly somewhere else mentally. Lily understood the feeling. The obligation that she had felt while preparing to be queen of Highacre sometimes seemed to dwarf the perks of being royalty. She wondered what Ava was thinking about, but before she could ask, Alexei appeared.

Each day, around lunchtime, Alexei would meet them with sandwiches and they would take a break, eating and updating each other on what the morning had brought.

Alexei was doing quite well in finding work. He was fast, efficient, strong, and relatively cheap. By this stage, he had managed to find a couple of warehouses that were happy to give him repeat work.

The afternoon would either see Alexei head off to any work he had teed up or remain with Lily and Ava, laughing and joking and helping keep their spirits up.

Adding to the weight in her chest was the increasing concern about getting back to Highacre. She continued to worry about her advisors. What was the outcome of the attack? Were they okay, or had some been injured? Or worse ...

Lily worried about Kevin. She missed her tiny pelotromo friend and fretted that no one would be looking after him. Everyone but her seemed scared of the little fluffball and she couldn't imagine Giles tucking him in at night. But she reminded herself that her little friend was independent. He could somehow get into and out of the palace on his own, and she supposed he could take care of himself.

She also missed Highacre, which had begun to feel like home when she was there. That feeling was magnified by the starkly different home world she now found herself in. More and more, the guilt-ridden thought kept crossing her mind that things were so bad here, all she wanted to do was to escape back to Highacre.

Lily could tell being stuck in this dimension was weighing on Ava and Alexei too. Though they were keeping upbeat and remaining interested in any and all differences —they still looked up excitedly whenever a plane or helicopter flew overhead—the longer they were marooned here without any contact from their home world, the more Lily caught them lost in their private thoughts, looking worried.

Today, however, the three friends were in a different park from their usual one and were sitting at a picnic table, enjoying the soft sunlight as it shined through the trees while they ate their lunch.

"Not that I don't like them," said Ava thickly, her mouth full of sandwich, "but what's with the same sandwiches every day?"

Alexei swallowed his mouthful before responding. "They're cheap and we know we like them. Why go to the trouble of trying to find something new when it could be more expensive and might not taste as good?"

Ava watched Alexei suspiciously. He had kept his eyes on his sandwich as he answered, examining it in his hands as if it were fascinating. Ava leant closer to Lily on their bench. "I bet he has a thing for the sandwich shop girl."

Both women stared at Alexei, who remained fascinated by his sandwich and didn't respond.

"He does!" said Ava with glee. "Alexei's found himself a pretty little shop girl. Are you even working in the warehouses, or are you just chatting her up each morning?"

"He must be working. He brings in all the money," said Lily, taking pity on Alexei.

"Maybe he's working in the shop with her!"

"Well, if he did pick the shop for the girl, at least the sandwiches are good."

"Oh yeah, Alexei loves her sandwiches," Ava said suggestively, wiggling her eyebrows at Alexei. He scowled at Ava, but continued to refuse to comment on her accusations.

Lily smiled to herself later that evening, lying awake on the lumpy bed, recalling the banter and trying to ignore the pungent smells that no amount of cleaning seemed to touch. The smile faded as her mind returned to what was keeping her up. She had mentioned that Alexei was bringing in all the money to try to defend him from Ava's teasing, but it had stuck with her. She wasn't really helping in the search for her sisters. Her magic wasn't useful for the task. The likelihood of someone who knew her sisters wandering in front of her for long enough that she could penetrate their mind was extremely low.

She knew she should have followed Alexei's lead and found some work. She could even accompany him. Use her telekinesis to help with his manual labour jobs. She could stock shelves pretty quickly. So why hadn't she?

Lily worried for a beat that it was because she was lazy. But that wasn't it. Lily was many things, but she'd never been lazy. She considered it might be the need to find her sisters. She felt that at least being out searching for them increased her chance of finding them.

Finally, it dawned on Lily, as if her mind had pulled back a curtain to reveal what had always been there.

She was enjoying spending time with Ava.

Lily had never had a friend like her before. Ava was funny and smart and always had a way of looking at things that hadn't occurred to Lily. Being with her was soothing. Lily's worries about finding her family, and what had happened to them, not to mention about getting home to Highacre, were somehow dulled when she was with Ava. Though she knew she should be doing something that contributed to the team, she didn't want her time with Ava to end.

Sighing and rolling over as best she could, Lily resolved to do the right thing tomorrow. It wasn't as if she'd never get to spend time with Ava again, she told herself. They were together every day. And in reality, Lily was probably going to be less attractive as a warehouse worker than Alexei was. Which meant that some days she would find herself without work, and could go and support Ava's efforts. Lily, trying not to feel guilty for being excited at the idea of getting out of work she hadn't even found yet, allowed herself a smile, thinking that she might be able to both contribute and still hang out with her friend.

On the precipice of sleep, Lily sighed and got up, trying not to wake Ava, who was sleeping next to her on the lumpy mattress. She slipped on her shoes, unwilling to let her bare feet touch the dirty carpet, and headed to the bathroom.

A strange static crackling sound came from the pocket of her jeans that were bundled in the corner.

"Ah, that's it. Right. Need to tell someone. Who though? Not Jason. Intimidating. Also, geographically inconvenient."

That's Jenkins!

Lily fumbled at her pocket, racing to pull the small disk out. Jenkins had got the communicator to work. Thank goodness she had the small disk on her when she was jettisoned through the portal.

"Jenkins! Jenkins, it's Lily, can you hear me?"

But as suddenly as it had sprang to life, the small disk fell silent. Lily stared at it in her palm. A wave of panic threatened to overwhelm her. What if he couldn't make it work again? Lily took a deep breath, and, still grasping the disk, returned to bed. He had made it work once. Jenkins would get it going again. She would just have to be patient.

21

THE NEXT MORNING, Lily told her friends excitedly about the communicator working, but after staring at the small disk, which remained obstinately silent, Ava and Alexei's enthusiasm waned.

"It's okay, Lily," said Ava, trying her best not to sound patronising and looking at the unimpressive disk with distaste, "we all wish your little disk thing would work."

Lily realised that they thought she'd imagined it.

"Either way," said Alexei loudly, cutting across the budding argument between Lily and Ava. "It's not working now, so we'll just have to wait until it works again."

Feeling unsatisfied with the conversation, Lily accompanied Alexei deep into the warehouse district. She felt very out of place and was grateful to be with Alexei, whose stature and focus on his task meant that while they attracted looks, no one felt comfortable calling out or approaching them.

They arrived at the warehouse where Alexei had a job lined up for that morning.

"Wait here," he instructed Lily.

She watched as he approached an older man wearing a hi-vis vest over his flannelette shirt and a beanie pulled down, covering his ears. She saw Alexei point to her, and the older man started to look annoyed, shaking his head. Alexei put his hands out, placating him, and then started gesturing, apparently explaining Lily's worth. After much back and forth, the man shrugged and pointed at Alexei, then walked away.

"That looked like it went well," Lily said dryly when Alexei returned.

Alexei shrugged. "We got there in the end. You won't earn any extra for helping me today, but once we show them what you're worth, they'll be happy to hire you for more work."

Lily understood the concept, but the knowledge that she was essentially working for free did not spark her enthusiasm, especially when Alexei led her into the storeroom and she saw exactly how much stock was in there.

Alexei explained the task to her, and they split the work by the weight of the items. Alexei would take the heavy stuff and move it to the bottom shelves. With his enchanted belt, he looked like he was picking up empty boxes. For her part, Lily would take the smaller boxes and use her telekinesis to stack them on the higher shelves. This also gave Lily a welcome opportunity to practise her magic, and she decided that once they were done, she might see if she could lift any of the heavier objects. Back home, she could easily manipulate smaller objects, and even move several at once, but heavier objects had eluded her abilities. It felt jarring to be in her home world, performing such a mundane task, but using magic to do it.

Eventually, they found their groove and relaxed into the work. Though she missed hanging out with Ava, having something useful to do was boosting Lily's mood. Plus, she enjoyed Alexei's company too.

"So Alexei," began Lily, floating some boxes of what looked like dish soap up to a shelf near the roof. "I don't think I've asked you—having lived there for a while now, what do you think of Highacre?"

"It is a very beautiful country," said Alexei automatically, picking up another heavy box as if it were light as a feather.

"Yeah, yeah. But really. If—when—we get back there, I'm going to be in charge. Tell me, from your perspective, what I need to know."

Alexei walked back to the pallet and picked up another box, glancing at Lily as he went. "You really want to know?"

"Of course." Lily smiled at him. "I want to learn all I can about Highacre, but so far most of my information comes from people who were born there and have lived there their whole lives. You can give me an outsider's perspective. Not to mention an insight as to how Highacre is viewed by her neighbours."

They continued unpacking and stacking while Alexei considered his answer.

"Highacre has good intentions," Alexei finally said. Lily decided this ominous beginning did not bode well for his opinion on her country.

"You know what they say about good intentions," Lily said, smiling.

"No. What do they say?" Alexei asked, genuinely curious.

"Oh, sorry. It's just a saying here. 'The road to hell is paved with good intentions'. It means that ..." Lily paused, thinking. "It either means that it's no good having good intentions if you never act on them, or that people can mean well, but still do bad things."

After a slight sojourn down a rabbit hole where Lily did her best to explain the concepts of heaven and hell, and religions in this world in general, she gently led Alexei back to the topic at hand.

"Yes, sorry. I think your saying is apt here. Highacre means well, but sometimes its actions have bad consequences. I think Highacre believes we're all lucky that it is the dominant power in the world because they view themselves as a benevolent power. However, as any country would, they wish to maintain their dominance, which means that some of their actions can be detrimental to others. Which, again, is understandable, but I suppose this image they try to portray of being the 'good guys' then feels hypocritical."

Lily concentrated on floating some cans of food up to a shelf second from the top. Ignoring her initial pang of defensiveness for a country she now felt was her own, Lily could see how what Alexei said might be true. Certainly she had seen that at play in this world.

"I don't know that this is necessarily a trait of Highacre itself. Surely whichever country was dominant would do the same," Alexei continued reasonably. "But living there now, I can see similar behaviour focussed inward."

"What do you mean?"

"For some people, being powerful means being in charge and having control. And if you have power and you don't want to lose it, sometimes you increase that control to ensure you don't lose it, or that no one takes it from you." He walked to their small pile of belongings in the corner and pulled out a bottle of water. Offering it to Lily first, who gratefully took a gulp, he took a swig.

"I suppose some people also want to increase their control to increase their power. Anyway, Highacre seeks to control engagements with other countries to maintain their dominance, and I feel like, more and more, your prime minister is trying to increase his control to maintain his position."

Lily stopped what she was doing and stared at Alexei. "I think you're absolutely right. Toth definitely is trying to increase his power." She hadn't thought about it like that before. "Do you think some of what he's doing is coming from a place of fear then?"

"Fear of losing his position? Absolutely. It would seem that your return, for instance, upset his plans of taking the role of the monarch. It also disturbed his control of the government and made him worry about losing his grip." Alexei picked up another box, returning to his task. He didn't say anything for a while, and then said, "My father has a lot of control. He uses it to maintain his power. People describe Valmead as a fascist regime, but sometimes I don't see that much difference between what he does and what your prime minister is trying to do. In a way, my father is just more open about it."

Lily remained silent, thinking about Alexei's views. She agreed with him, but wondered if the reason she was so ready to agree with him was because she really didn't like Reginald Toth.

"Do you think it works? Your country's system, with a dictator."

"Yes, and no. Having one person in charge can be very efficient. Decisions can be made very quickly, and sometimes it's easier to get things done. But how do you make sure that one person has the right ideas about what should be done? It seems having one wrong person, or having too many people try to run things, are equally bad systems. But then, how do you find the right balance?" Alexei shrugged at Lily with a smile. "When I am in charge, I want to do everything I can to improve things for my people. A large part of that is going to be reducing the Great Leader's power so that it can't be so easily abused by the wrong person. I'll have to balance the improvements I want to make with reducing my power to make sure I get the changes through before I lose the ability to do so."

"That's a very noble ambition, Alexei. But I see what you're saying. It's all so tricky. So, does Meridia have the right idea then? Aren't they sort of in the middle?"

"The soulless businessmen?" Alexei snorted derisively. "Meridia is too focussed on making money. Everything is a deal, and everything is about the bottom line. I'm sure that when they're dealing with disaster relief in their own country, they're still weighing up how much money it will cost to save lives and debating whether it's worth it."

Lily was surprised, not by the content of Alexei's outburst, but by the disgust he seemed to feel for Meridia. "Gosh Alexei, I thought everyone hated Highacre, but it sounds like you dislike Meridia more."

"Highacre at least has passion. Meridia feels too cold and calculating. It's like they've calculated the humanity out of their decisions."

Lily recalled Addison telling her about a trade agreement between Valmead and Meridia, whereby Valmead provided resources to Meridia to make medicines, and then Meridia sold them back to Valmead at what seemed like a pretty big profit margin. Lily had asked why Valmead signed such a lousy deal, and Addison had told her they needed the medicine for their people. They weren't prepared to let them suffer and die painfully. Lily frowned.

When she had first arrived in Highacre and needed to learn about her new world so quickly, it had seemed that Valmead was some nefarious totalitarian regime, and

Meridia, by comparison, was a progressive country that embraced advancement. It was jarring to have her stereotypes challenged, but she had no time to reflect further, as Alexei was still talking.

"... not all bad. Ava is a kind and genuine person, for example," he paused. "Don't tell her I said that. But then you take someone like Ezra Brown. He's too charming. I don't trust anyone who is that charming. He has big plans, and you can bet that the person they benefit is him."

"Yeah, at first I thought he seemed nice. But then ..." Lily thought about Ezra knowing about the interdimensional travel machine. "I just feel like he's up to something."

"Someone like Mr Brown is always up to something. It's just a matter of if he drives the bus over you on his way to where he's going." Alexei stacked his box and turned to Lily, a worried look on his face. "Don't mention this chat to Ava. She is very close to Mr Brown, and she'll get defensive."

"Of course, what is discussed in the warehouse, stays in the warehouse."

Alexei smiled, and they both returned to their tasks, falling back into silence. Lily's mind stayed with Alexei's desire not to tell Ava that they were suspicious of Ezra. It did seem odd. Ava was such a nice, genuine person, whereas Ezra was shady. Now that she thought about it, the warmth of Ezra's smile didn't extend to his eyes. Behind the mask, she somehow knew he was cold and calculating. Why would someone like Ava be so close with someone like him?

Maybe she was exaggerating things in her mind, seeing conspiracies everywhere because of the stress she was under. Ezra had been a perfect gentleman whenever she saw him.

Except for that time with the top-secret machine that he shouldn't know about.

She shook the thought away. Ava knew him better,

having worked so closely with him. Maybe he wasn't so bad. She smiled briefly, thinking of some of the odd pairings back at her old job. There were some bosses she knew of with terrible reputations, but when people she had trusted worked directly for them, they couldn't speak highly enough of them.

***

Soon enough, the shelves were stocked, and Alexei left to find someone to check their work and pay them. Lily looked at what she had achieved. It was difficult at first, like exercising a muscle after neglecting it for too long. But she had settled back into it, and after a while it felt natural to use her magic again. She longed to practise some of her other powers, but doubted now was the time to start launching fireballs around the warehouse, or call down lightning, which, on such a clear day, might raise suspicions.

The supervisor followed Alexei into the room, grumbling at being disturbed. The cigarette dropped from his mouth at seeing the task completed so quickly. He looked from Alexei to Lily and back, first amazed, and then slightly suspicious.

"We're hard workers," Alexei assured him, his voice firm, his hand outstretched. The supervisor stared at him a beat longer, weighing something in his mind.

"I'm just paying for you. I don't care how many did the work."

Alexei nodded, and the man relinquished the money.

"She was a bonus today," Alexei nodded towards Lily. "To demonstrate her value. We're available for more work, but she earns as much as me."

The supervisor looked like he was about to argue, then looked at the shelves again, nodded, and left.

As Lily walked with Alexei towards the sandwich shop, she felt strangely satisfied. Everything seemed a little brighter, and she enjoyed the sun on her face and the slight breeze, which kept the temperature pleasant. She breathed deeply and ignored the smells of the city. Lily hadn't realised how much she missed being useful; achieving something.

Who knew stacking shelves could feel this rewarding?

They walked in comfortable silence, but as they approached the sandwich shop, Alexei slowed his pace. Before they reached the door, he turned to her.

"I'll go in. You should stay out here. Enjoy the fresh air."

"It's smoggy." She looked at Alexei, confused. "And I've had plenty of 'fresh air' on our walk here, and will no doubt enjoy more of it when we find Ava. Why are you acting weird?"

"I'm not acting weird," said Alexei defensively, blushing and fiddling. Alexei never fiddled. Suddenly, Lily remembered Ava's teasing.

"Oh! You *do* have a thing for the sandwich shop girl." Lily smiled and playfully pushed Alexei. He tried to look annoyed, but a huge smile broke across his face. He repressed it quickly and began to protest.

"It's okay, Alexei. I'll wait out here so you can flirt."

Alexei grinned at Lily and practically bounded into the store. Lily loyally faced the street, her back to the shop to give them privacy. She imagined Ava's annoyance when Lily told her she hadn't even stolen a look at the girl's appearance. Despite her intentions, she could hear the interactions in the store, and before Lily could move away, she heard the sandwich girl greet Alexei.

"Well, hello hot stuff. The usual?"

"Yes please. You're looking particularly beautiful today."

The girl scoffed, clearly pleased. "I look the same as every other day. But thank you."

"You know, I won't change my order. You could always pre-make them to save yourself some time."

"But then how would I drag out our time together, handsome? How has your day been?"

Lily was stunned, frozen in place. Not because of the flirting. But that voice ...

She entered the store, vaguely seeing the look of disappointment on Alexei's face, but was completely focussed on the sandwich girl, who stopped what she was doing when Lily entered.

"Lily?"

Alexei whipped around. His look of disappointment turned to confusion at the sandwich shop girl's use of Lily's name.

"Elaine. Hi." Lily was still in shock at the sudden discovery of her older sister. She mentally kicked herself out of her reverie. "Er, I've been looking for you."

Elaine looked as if she were about to drop her sandwich implements and run to Lily, excitement and joy sparking behind her eyes. Then, as if remembering something, a shadow fell and Lily saw anger staring at her.

"Where the hell have you been?"

"It's a long story," Lily said apologetically. "I saw David. He said Dad ..." Lily couldn't finish the sentence and Elaine dropped her eyes, her face falling. It was this reaction from her older sister, more than anything, that told Lily it was true. Any dim hope that David was just being drunk and cruel was extinguished, and Lily felt like she had been punched in the stomach. She struggled to regain control.

"Can we—"

"Elaine!" A short, middle-aged man with huge bushy

eyebrows burst into the shopfront from a back room. "What have I told you about having your friends around?"

Elaine went to answer, but her boss wouldn't let her get a word in. He barrelled on, oblivious to the tense and sombre mood. "They can come in if they're buying, but they leave when they've been served."

"But I haven't—" Elaine was gesturing at the unfinished sandwiches, but her boss interrupted, undeterred.

"Last warning." He pointed at her, dipping his head slightly and raising his eyebrows, then exited back through the door he had emerged from.

Elaine swore under her breath and started slapping the rest of the sandwiches together quickly. "Look, you need to go—"

"But Elaine," Lily protested, suddenly panicked at potentially losing her sister as suddenly as she had been found.

"Go, or I'll get fired." She thrust the sandwiches into Alexei's hands. "Here is my address." She scribbled furiously on a paper napkin, thrusting that at Alexei too. "Come round at six tonight. Don't be late. I only have an hour there before I have to get to my night job."

Alexei bustled Lily out of the store as Lily thanked her sister and babbled something about being happy to have found her.

The two started off towards the park where they were to meet Ava, both engulfed in a stunned stupor.

"I didn't even ask about April," Lily said out loud, feeling horrible not to have asked after her younger sister, and half tempted to double back to the store.

"I'm sure she'll be there tonight," said Alexei distractedly.

They continued in silence for a bit.

"Maybe we should pop round to Elaine's place now. See if April is there."

"Wouldn't she be in school?" asked Alexei.

"Oh ... yeah, I guess," said Lily, glancing at her watch. It was just past one thirty. It felt like ages until they could meet Elaine, and doing nothing until then seemed wrong somehow. As if it lent credence to the idea that she had run off and left on a whim, and caused her family all this pain with reckless abandon. She felt a strong need to actively seek them out, as if that would somehow prove that she hadn't left voluntarily.

"Problem at work?" asked Ava upon seeing the looks on her friends' faces. She took her sandwich and sat at a picnic table in the park.

"We found Elaine," said Lily dumbly. "Well, Alexei did I guess ..."

"What? How?" Ava looked excitedly from Alexei to Lily, then her face fell seeing their mood. "Didn't go well?"

"No. I mean, yes, it was fine." Lily's head was swimming, and she was finding it difficult to concentrate. Ava looked questioningly at Alexei, who took a seat opposite Ava and focussed on unwrapping his sandwich.

"Will one of you tell me what happened?" Ava was clearly getting frustrated.

"Elaine is Alexei's sandwich shop girl."

"She's not *my* sandwich shop girl," muttered Alexei.

"Wait, you've been crushing on Lily's sister?"

"I didn't know it was her sister."

"We have her address, but we can't meet her until six tonight." Lily looked at her watch in frustration.

Why is time moving so slowly?

She glanced around the park as if looking for something to do.

"Hey," Ava called to Lily, bringing her attention back and patting the seat next to her. "Relax. Have some lunch."

Lily sat reluctantly. "I just feel like I should be *doing* something."

"We probably should have done this a while ago, but perhaps we should use the time to come up with a story to explain where you've been," suggested Alexei.

"You're just keen to make sure we match our story to whatever you've been telling her to impress her," Ava teased.

"It's a good idea," said Lily. Her reeling mind locked onto this new task. What could she tell them? The cult story was still at the top of her list. But though she wanted something that demonstrated she didn't vanish willingly, she felt guilty lying about a nefarious kidnapping. Real people were victims of such crimes and she felt dirty using it as cover to make herself feel better.

Of course, I was taken against my will.

Lily dismissed the thought. It just wasn't the same thing.

"Just going out on a limb here," Ava said, breaking into Lily's thoughts, "but how about the truth?"

"Tell my sisters that I was taken to another dimension where I was taught magic and declared the legitimate queen of a country? How are they ever going to believe that? I'll sound crazy. At best, they'll think I'm lying, and at worst they'll think I've gone nuts. Either way, it'll sound like I'm not taking things seriously, and with Dad really being dead ..." Lily broke off, her voice cracking.

It still did not feel real. In her mind, he was on the farm, working with a big smile on his face. At home on the tractor, or leaning on a fence, watching the livestock. She tried to picture him cold and still. Or his headstone. But she just couldn't.

"It may sound far-fetched to them. But you *can* demonstrate that you have magical abilities. That would lend credence to your story," Alexei suggested.

Lily looked at her hands, considering. She blinked, wondering why that had not occurred to her. It would alarm her sisters, but being honest was Lily's preference.

And it'll explain why I have to leave if we get rescued.

When we get rescued.

22

THE THREE FRIENDS sat awkwardly in the cramped living room of Elaine's apartment. They cradled chipped mugs of weak tea as Elaine bustled in and out of the room, putting things away that she had used that day and gathering things she would need for the evening. April, who Lily had been excited to see and hugged tightly, was lukewarm and looking anywhere in the room but at Lily. Lily was trying to be reasonable and see things from her little sister's point of view, but she couldn't help but be stung by the chilly reception.

"Okay," sighed Elaine, sitting heavily on the couch next to April. She looked completely worn out and glanced at her watch, disappointed at what it told her. "We're going to have to make this quick. I've only got forty minutes left."

Lily tried not to be annoyed at the implication that it was she who had wasted twenty minutes. She sat up, preparing herself to speak. Elaine got in before Lily could begin.

"So what happened? Where have you been? And why didn't you bother to contact us?" Both her sisters were staring at her, a mix of hurt, resentment, and hope in their eyes.

"This is going to sound really far-fetched, but please hear me out," Lily began to a narrowing of Elaine's eyes. "I promise I can back it up."

"Okay," said Elaine, glancing at her watch again, "let's hear it then."

It took a mere ten minutes for Lily to tell her sisters how she'd been taken, without warning, from the conference room at work, found herself in another dimension, and had been told she was the heir to the throne of Highacre. Lily told them about the political turmoil, both internally with the prime minister's dangerous ambition, and externally with the threat of another war looming.

When she told them about her magical abilities, Elaine had scoffed. Perhaps the only thing keeping her from leaving at that point was that Alexei wasn't acting like this was a joke, and kept his eyes on Lily, encouraging her sisters to similarly listen to her tale.

Lily finished slightly anticlimactically. Once she got through describing the ambush in the corridor on the way to her coronation, she lost her momentum, simply stating that they'd been pushed through the machine only to find that her family had left the farm and so they had come to the city to find them.

"And, well, here we are," Lily added, indicating to her sisters that her side was over, and now it was their turn. April, who had listened with a look of fascination, now glanced at Elaine for guidance on what their reaction would be.

Elaine stared at Lily, unsure of what to make of what was, to anyone who had not lived it, an outrageous explanation for being missing for six months. Not seeing any inclination that Lily was going to back down from her story, Elaine exhaled loudly and rubbed her eyes. "Geez, you sound just like Mum," Elaine muttered, almost to herself.

"I can prove it," Lily said, hoping desperately that with evidence, her sisters would believe her. "Don't be alarmed, but I can do magic here, too. If it's okay?"

Elaine looked at Lily almost pityingly but nodded as if tired and eager for it to be over.

Lily readied herself and focussed. Three small balls of flame emitted from her hands and she set them circling in front of her as if she were juggling them. April gasped, eyes wide, awed by what she saw.

Elaine swore loudly.

"And I can move things," Lily said brightly, keeping her fireballs moving while summoning Elaine's keys from the entry table. She was showing off, but somehow it felt like if she could win them over with her magic, everything would be okay. She caught the keys and put them on the coffee table, then extinguished the fireballs. Her sisters were still staring, mouths open, unsure of what to say.

"So ..." Elaine opened and shut her mouth, trying to think of what to say. "So you're a princess?"

"Yes, and I need to be crowned queen so that I can stop the prime minister from starting World War ... I don't even know how many wars there have been."

"Five," offered Alexei. "This would be World War Six."

"But we were sent back here," Lily brought them back to the point. "I think to keep me out of the way so that the prime minister can shore up his hold over the government."

"But surely it'd be easier just to kill you?" Elaine asked matter-of-factly.

"That's what I keep saying," said Ava happily.

"Anyway." Lily chose to ignore them. "Now we're stuck

because Highacre doesn't have enough felixium to power the machine."

"Well, I'm sure there are worse places to be stuck," said Elaine, shooting a smile at Alexei, who blushed and became very interested in his tea. "And now you're home." She smiled at Lily and Lily's chest filled to bursting. "We've missed you, Lily, and goodness knows I could use your help."

Lily's smile faltered. "What happened? You know, after I ... left."

Both her sisters' faces fell, and they stared at their cold mugs. Silence descended and Lily began to feel uncomfortable. It was April who broke it.

"I went to find you," she said in a small voice. "'Cause we were meant to spend the weekend together, remember?"

Lily heard the pain in her sister's voice. Given everything that must have come after, it tore at Lily's heart that April was still hurt at feeling forgotten by her big sister.

"But you weren't at your place. So I went and found Gemma, but she hadn't seen you, and we all tried to call, but you didn't answer. She let me stay with her that night, and I called Mum and said I couldn't find you. She said I could try again tomorrow, but if you didn't answer, then I needed to come back to the farm."

Lily could picture her sister's disappointment. April and Lily had always been close, as a couple of years separated them from their older siblings. When Lily moved to the city, April had been heartbroken, but Lily made sure to have her visit often, and April always looked forward to those trips and their time together. As did Lily; she loved her little sister.

"I'm sorry I wasn't there," Lily said. April nodded, indicating she'd heard, but she still wouldn't look at Lily.

"When you still didn't answer after a couple of days,

and Gemma and Brandon hadn't seen you, Mum and Dad went to the police," Elaine took over the story. "They checked your place and talked to the people at your work and then declared you a missing person. But the police weren't really interested." Elaine sounded angry now.

"They didn't have much to go on," said April reasonably.

"Yeah, but they seemed to think you must have just done a runner. They said since you had dropped out of uni and didn't like your job, that perhaps you'd just gone overseas on an adventure or something. So they didn't seem to be doing much to find you."

"Mum wasn't worried about it," said April, looking at Elaine.

"Mum was trying to calm Dad down," Elaine told April before addressing Lily. "Dad was beside himself. He was convinced something bad had happened to you. That some psycho had taken you and you were tied up in his basement or something. And with the police not taking it seriously, or as seriously as he thought they should," Elaine added as a concession to April, "he took it upon himself to try to find you.

"He went to the city and asked around. He put up posters. He went to the newspapers and TV stations and got them to run campaigns. But there were no leads. Lots of bogus calls and suggestions, but nothing useful. It was like you'd just vanished off the face of the Earth. Which ..." Elaine looked thoughtful. "I suppose is accurate."

"David tried to manage the farm," April said, bringing them back to the story. "But Dad was spending more than the farm was bringing in. And the farm wasn't doing the best to start with."

Elaine saw Lily's face fall, guilt written all over it.

"I mean, the farm hadn't been doing well for a while, so

even without this, they probably would have had to look at selling."

Lily appreciated Elaine trying to make her feel better, but she still felt terribly guilty.

"But yeah, they sold it and we all moved here to the city, into a little townhouse that Dad rented. Mum, David, and I looked for work, but it was hard. None of us had many useful skills for the city, you know? Dad wouldn't do anything but look for you."

Elaine stared unseeing across the room, lost in memory.

"They fought a lot," said April quietly. "Mum and Dad. She wanted him to stop spending all his time looking. She said it was unbalanced, unhealthy. And he was drinking."

"Yeah, and he thought she wasn't looking enough." Elaine took over the story again. "He was mad at her. Felt she had just given up on you. And in his mind, you were still being tortured in a basement somewhere. The money didn't last as long as we'd thought, and that added to the stress. When we couldn't pay the reward and the internet trolls came after us, things were at breaking point."

April's face darkened at the mention of the trolls and Elaine patted her hand comfortingly. "He didn't even have any information," Lily's younger sister said angrily.

"It was rough," Elaine said to Lily, throwing an arm around April's shoulders. "Some of them were really nasty."

It was impossible for Lily not to feel guilty. Though she hadn't chosen to go to Highacre, she had been living a luxurious lifestyle in a palace while her father was worried sick and her family had lost all their money, their home. Her older siblings had needed to find jobs to help support their father's search for his daughter, who was being looked after by an entire palace staff.

She looked around the room at the dirty secondhand furniture and lack of anything that wasn't functional. Her sisters were still suffering, and she thought of David with a sick feeling in her stomach. Still hurt by his behaviour towards her, she could understand it more now. Maybe she deserved it.

"We weren't expecting the heart attack." Elaine brought Lily back to the present with a jolt. "I mean, yeah, he'd been stressed and was drinking too much, and I guess none of us were really eating well. But I mean, he seemed fine, considering. He went out like usual to go looking for you. He usually went to the uni or near your work and handed out pictures, asking anyone passing by if they'd seen you.

"He wasn't home for dinner, but that wasn't completely out of the ordinary. Mum was cooking something. Well, reheating. I think it was some ready-made thing from the supermarket. Anyway, the police knocked on the door. I think we all thought at first that they were there about you. I thought to myself 'Dad's going to be mad he wasn't here to hear it for himself'. They were sombre, and I think we all thought they were going to tell us you were dead." Elaine sounded slightly apologetic.

"When they said it was Dad, it took a while for all of us to get our heads around that. He'd had the heart attack in the morning. He'd been dead most of the day without any of us knowing. It took them all day to track us down."

A heavy silence fell on the room. Lily could see it all in her mind, like a split screen. Her dad, under a white sheet, being taken to the morgue while the rest of the family went about their day. She pictured Elaine and April laughing and joking while they put her dad in a freezer. Or would they have done an autopsy? She shook her head, trying to clear the morbid thoughts.

Elaine started and looked at her watch. "Bugger, I'm going to be late. Do you have somewhere to stay? You're all welcome to crash here if you need to. I mean." She gestured around the small apartment. "There's not much room, but if that's okay with you, you can stay." She grabbed a bag and crossed to the door in a couple of steps. "And if not, I have a break at ten tomorrow before I start at the sandwich store. I'm usually in the park across from the store. You can meet me there if you like." And with that, she was gone, hurrying off to whatever her night job was.

Lily turned to April, who seemed uncomfortable to find herself alone with her sister and her friends. Before Lily could say anything, April stood.

"I have school tomorrow and a bunch of homework to do before bed." She left quickly and Lily heard a door close toward the back of the apartment.

"This is sooooo much nicer than our place," said Ava enthusiastically. She patted the cushions before pulling one up, seeming to consider whether to leave it on the chair or make a bed on the floor.

"You think we should stay?" asked Lily.

"Don't you?" Ava looked surprised.

"Yeah, I guess." She looked down the hallway towards April's room.

"Maybe leave it for tonight," said Ava gently.

"She doesn't want to talk to me," said Lily, fighting to keep her voice even. "I thought ... I don't know what I thought," Lily muttered, busying herself with her backpack.

"She's hurting," said Alexei. "And probably doesn't know how to balance her hurt at you leaving with her happiness at having you back."

"She doesn't seem happy," Lily said. She knew she was being unfair. April was sixteen, and her whole world had been turned upside down. Her sister went missing, she lost her home, and then her dad died. Lily could hardly expect April to put all of that aside and throw her a parade. Alexei was right. She probably didn't even know what to feel.

"It's a lot for her to process," said Ava, echoing Lily's thoughts. "I don't think either of them even registered that you don't have the same biological parents. Give her some time and try again in the morning."

Lily hadn't even thought about that. Would her sisters feel differently about her when they did realise she wasn't related to them? Would it make things different somehow? There was already a gap between them. Elaine and April had lived through the trauma of the disintegration of their family together, and Lily ... well, she'd been the trigger for everything that happened.

Somehow, Ava worked some impressive cushion Tetris and turned a bunch of cushions into a couple of mattresses that, after so long in the shady apartment, looked positively comfortable. They all curled up, Ava and Lily next to each other and Alexei toward their feet. Soon, Lily heard her friends' breathing change, telling her they were asleep. Neither seemed to have difficulty drifting off. Alexei had tried to teach Lily the trick he had learned from his military training, but it just didn't seem to work for her.

Trying not to toss and turn for fear she'd wake Ava, Lily tried to lie still, willing sleep to come. After a few hours, she eventually gave up and crept to the kitchen in search of water. Having filled her glass from the tap, Lily turned and jumped as the door opened and Elaine appeared, closing and locking the front door as quietly as she could behind her.

"What are you doing up?" Elaine whispered.

"Couldn't sleep. How was work?"

Elaine shrugged. "Gives me money. That's all that matters."

"You must be tired," Lily said.

"I will be. I'm always a little buzzed after the night shift.

I usually have a cup of tea to wind down before crashing. Want to join me?"

Lily nodded, and Elaine moved silently around the kitchen preparing the tea. Giving Lily her mug, Elaine motioned for her to follow and led Lily into her small bedroom.

"I like to sit out here," Elaine said, opening her window and climbing out. "Pass me that." She indicated to her mug of tea that she'd put on her side table. "And yours. There we go."

Lily found herself on a rusted fire escape and had time to wonder why Elaine would want to sit out here before she realised Elaine was climbing some stairs that led to the roof. She followed Elaine up, across the roof, then joined her sitting on the opposite edge to where the stairs had finished.

"Oh, wow."

Before them lay the city, lit up with lights of every colour. The sounds of traffic and people on the street below floated up to them, the faint honking and sirens telling Lily that the city centre was very much awake.

"It's not the farm, but for some reason, I still find it peaceful," said Elaine, staring out over the city. They sat in silence for a while, watching and listening and sipping their tea.

"I'm so glad you're back Lily. It's been ... rough without you."

"I'm so sorry Elaine."

Elaine shook her head. "No, it's not your fault. I mean, your story's nuts, but I believe you." Her eyes darted to Lily's hands, as if expecting more balls of fire to erupt from them. "It's just been a lot to take care of on my own. I used to be so jealous of you, you know?"

"Jealous? Of me?" Lily was shocked and completely distracted by that comment. She had been about to ask about their mother, but—how could her older sister be jealous of her?

"Oh yeah. You've just always been so adventurous. You want to try something, you try it. I just sit there going over all of the possible things that could go wrong before I either talk myself out of it, or the opportunity has passed. I should have gone to uni like you. Or at least moved to the city on my own. I'd have been set up properly here. Not scrambling to keep my head above water. You've just always been so confident."

Lily laughed. "It may have seemed that way, but I'm anything but confident. I was feeling so lost. So unsure of what to do with my life. I was about to quit my job, but I had no idea what to do instead, before ..."

"Before you were whisked away and declared queen?" Elaine suggested with a smile.

"Yep. I wanted to know what to do with my life. Be careful what you wish for."

They resumed watching and listening to the sounds of the city below. A couple passed by on the opposite street, clearly fighting, and a few blocks away, a dog barked.

"I need your help, Lily," Elaine said quietly.

"Of course," said Lily without thinking.

Elaine beamed at her, tears shining in her eyes. "It's just, I don't know if I can keep this up. All these jobs. I don't want April to have to drop out of school, but I just don't know how much longer I can do this." Tears spilled down Elaine's face and Lily shuffled closer, putting an arm around her older sister's shoulder.

"It's okay. I'm here now." Lily ignored the feeling in the pit of her stomach that told her she needed to make sure Elaine knew she may not be able to help forever. She held her sister while she cried silently, and when she regained some strength, Lily wiped Elaine's face.

"Elaine," Lily said gently. "What happened after Dad died? What happened to David, and where's Mum?"

Elaine blew out her breath, thinking of where to start.

"There's no nice way to put it," Elaine said finally. "Mum had a breakdown. She couldn't cope with losing Dad, especially after losing you. She was talking all kinds of nonsense and she kept disappearing. We'd find her and try to bring her home and she'd start screeching about needing to find it."

"Find what?"

"I don't know, something." Elaine gestured, trying to remember. "A gateway? I don't know, it didn't make any sense. But she couldn't keep disappearing and wandering around the city like that, and none of us could stay home to take care of her. So we had her committed," Elaine said guiltily.

"Like, put in a mental facility?"

"We were worried about her," Elaine said defensively. "I thought maybe they could give her some medication and she'd calm down."

"And did they?"

"No," Elaine stared bitterly out at the city. "They assessed her and decided she wasn't bad enough to keep locked up, so they let her go."

"What? They didn't even tell you?"

"Nope. She's an adult, so they just released her. I went in that evening to visit and they said they'd let her out in the morning. We had no idea where she'd gone, and the police said the same thing—she's an adult, she can go where she wants and if she chooses not to tell us, then that wasn't their problem.

"We looked for her for a bit, but we needed to work. David stepped up at first, tried to run things. But he made some dodgy friends at work. They kept asking him to go out at night with them. Kept telling him he was entitled to a life. To kick back and party. Eventually, he lost his job. He was so ashamed that he didn't tell me for a while. I found out because we got evicted. My salary only covered half the rent. If he had just told me, I could have found something to cover the other half."

"Couldn't *he* have found something else?" Lily couldn't help but be angry with her brother for letting their sisters down. And it was easier to blame her brother than consider her role in the whole situation.

"He didn't quit the partying, so he was in no state to get another job. When the landlord told me we needed to be out by the end of the week, I found him drunk in the lounge room. We got into a huge fight. He kept screaming that he was allowed to have a life. I asked him whether I was allowed one too, and he just stormed out saying that wasn't his problem. I haven't seen him since."

Lily didn't quite know what to say to that, so she simply told Elaine she was sorry. Elaine shrugged, wiping at her eyes, and the two sisters lapsed into silence once more.

Something was nagging at the back of Lily's mind, just out of reach. Like a word on the tip of your tongue. She mentally ran through what Elaine had told her, trying to prompt the thought into the light. Dad died, David's drunk, Mum's ill ...

"Elaine, what did you mean earlier? When I told you where I'd been, you said I sounded like Mum. Did you just mean raving about things that didn't make sense?"

"I mean, yeah, but it kind of sounded the same. She was muttering about magic and a high tower and medium being the enemy. And she just kept saying she had to get to the backup gateway thingy."

Backup gateway? Maybe she meant portal? Excitement buzzed in Lily's chest.

Elaine leant over and gave Lily a tight squeeze. "We should probably get some sleep. I need to be up in a few hours." She pulled back and beamed at Lily. "I'm *so* glad you're back."

Lily could see the relief in her sister's eyes, and pangs of guilt pricked her chest.

"I'm glad to be back," she said, not entirely honestly.

23

Though Elaine and April breakfasted and left the apartment quickly in the morning, Lily felt as if it took them forever. Feeling bad, she returned Elaine's smile after promising that she and her friends would look for work. She told herself that she didn't try to engage April because her little sister needed more time; besides, April had school to focus on. This did not entirely quell the guilt.

In truth, she was just eager to speak with her friends alone.

"Okay, so where shall we start?" Ava asked as they packed up their makeshift bedding, returning the lounge to its usual function. Lily then ushered her friends onto the couch and relayed the conversation she had with Elaine. She was frustrated when they weren't as excited as she was. "Don't you see?"

Ava and Alexei stared at her blankly.

"What Elaine remembers Mum muttering about. A *high tower* and *medium* being the enemy? A *backup gateway?*"

"Lily—" Ava began gently.

"She *knows*," Lily said emphatically. "Think about it.

One of them had to know—my parents," she clarified for Alexei's blank look. "Unless I was dumped in a basket at their front door and they just never told me I was adopted. I'm telling you, my mum knows I'm from Highacre."

Ava and Alexei glanced at each other sceptically. Lily knew it sounded like a stretch. Especially given all that had gone wrong, it was easy to think she was trying to find something positive.

"Think about it," Lily urged again. "What if she is from Highacre? And what if there was a way for her to go back? Surely that's worth looking for."

"Absolutely," said Ava gently. "But Lily, if there was a way back from here, why didn't they use that to bring you to Highacre? Why send guards to grab you? Wouldn't they have had your mum sit you down and explain everything to you? Maybe even bring you back herself, so it wasn't such a shock?"

Lily hated when Ava made sense. And it did make sense, now that Ava laid it out like that. That version would have been much more preferable to being snatched and having her world turned upside down. Not to mention it would have been better for her family ... then again, maybe that's why her mum hadn't been as worried when she went missing. *But why didn't she tell the rest of them?*

"You're right, there's a lot of unanswered questions. But isn't it worth looking into? I mean, what are we going to do otherwise? We can stay here, working and helping to support Elaine and April, waiting around like damsels in distress until we're rescued, or we can try to help ourselves."

"You do realise Elaine thinks you're staying for good?" Alexei asked quietly.

Lily dropped her face into her hands. This was all too much. She needed to keep moving. Working towards a goal kept all the uncomfortable thoughts at bay. If she stopped, she'd need to deal with all of it, and if she broke, she didn't think she could get back up. Images of her dad smiling and laughing, chasing her around the paddock, broke into her thoughts. Unprovoked, her mind replaced the image of her father with a grave. How long had he been gone now? She stood, expelling the images of what her father's body might now look like from her mind.

"I will make sure she understands. Look, we don't know when we're going to be rescued. I would like to help my sister in whatever time I have here, and I would like to find my mum. It just so happens that finding Mum might also lead to another way home. I think that's worth checking out. But I get that most of that is about me and my family, and that's not your problem. So, I don't want to put any of that on you. Both of you are welcome to hang out here, or go back to the farm, or even to go and look around and explore this world while you're here."

"We want to help, Lily," said Ava. Alexei nodded behind her. "We're just worried about you."

"I appreciate that," Lily said genuinely. She knew how lucky she was to have two such good friends with her. "I know you're both worried about what I'm going to do when faced with the choice about whether to stay and help my family, or return home and help Highacre. I can't pretend I really know what I will do, but I can promise that I will ensure you both get home, regardless."

Ava and Alexei looked slightly relieved. Lily exhaled loudly, thinking about the task in front of them.

"I have no idea where to start looking for Mum. I suppose I could ring around mental facilities. Elaine said they had her locked up at one point."

"You might try April," said Ava. "When Elaine was talking about not knowing where your mother is, April squirmed. I think she knows where she is."

Lily hesitated. That meant biting the bullet and fixing things with April.

Haven't you been pushing to find your family so you could fix things?

Lily realised, uncomfortably, that a large part of her had been hoping that her family would be so relieved to see her, that she would be forgiven for anything they resented her for. Why couldn't April realise Lily hadn't stood her up and forgive her? *Maybe because she's sixteen and her dad just died ...*

"How about we head out job searching and discuss how to find your mother on the way?" suggested Alexei, breaking into Lily's thoughts.

"Perfect, let's—"

But Lily was interrupted by a metallic feedback sound from her pocket.

The communicator!

Fumbling, Lily pulled out the small metal disk and placed it on the coffee table.

"Lily? Lily, are you there?" Giles's voice emitted from the disk, clear as if he were in the room with them.

Ava and Alexei's faces were perfect masks of shock, and Lily confirmed they really hadn't believed her about the disk working before. She looked at Ava and Alexei, a smug expression on her face. The two were leaping out of their seats, scrambling to get to Lily's side and closer to the disk.

"Oh yes, Giles, I am. Say, are you communicating with us through this disk thing?"

Ava and Alexei were too excited to say anything, though Ava rolled her eyes at Lily. Their eyes were glued to the disk, which, for the moment, was doing nothing out of the ordinary other than projecting Giles's voice from another dimension. Lily was struck by exactly how hard being away from home had been for both of her friends. They were generally so upbeat. But watching their reaction, she realised they were both genuinely scared that they would never get home.

"If I just push this button," Jenkins's voice replaced Giles's through the disk.

"No, don't touch that, we need to ..."

The three listened to Giles and Jenkins bicker back and forth for a bit, and then suddenly the disk emitted a beam of light and the two men appeared in front of the trio, projected into the middle of the room.

"Ah yes, there we are. It is good to see you all." Giles looked warmly around the room, his eyes eventually resting on Lily. "How *are* you, Your Majesty?"

"I'm good Giles, we're all well. Just a little, you know, trapped."

"Yes, my apologies, Your Majesty. Rest assured, we *are* working on it."

"Giles!" Lily sat bolt upright as the thought struck her. "The attack in the corridor. What happened? Is everyone okay?"

"Yes, yes, Your Majesty, we're fine. There were a few very minor injuries, but otherwise your advisors and guards got away unharmed. It's a miracle it wasn't a disaster."

Lily slumped back with a sigh. *Thank goodness.*

"So, when do you think we might be able to come back?" asked Ava, taking advantage of Lily's relief.

"Yes, well," Giles coughed uncomfortably. "The issue is the felixium—"

"I don't mean to be rude," said Ava, cutting Giles off, "but I don't need to know what you're doing to get us back, just your best guess at how long."

Lily looked at Ava, taken aback by her bluntness and the urgency in her voice.

Giles was fiddling with a handkerchief and briefly

glanced at Jenkins as if the other man might help him. Jenkins was bouncing slightly on the balls of his feet, whistling.

"Miss Harrington," Giles's voice was low and devoid of emotion. "I can't see us having access to felixium for at least another month or—"

"A month? Just to get some stupid mineral? What, are you picking it out of the mountains with the world's tiniest little pickaxes?" She indicated using something smaller than a toothpick. "Bing, bing, bing. Oh no, I have a finger cramp. Better call it a day and come back tomorrow."

They all stared at her in awkward silence, and eventually she sat back in her chair.

"Sorry, but I mean, come on. We've already been here for a month. How long can it really take to get this stuff?"

Giles looked put out and said snappily, "Well, we wouldn't be in this position at all if Meridia hadn't illegally stolen our mines and likely the last shipment of felixium."

Ava sat forward to respond, but Alexei put a hand on her shoulder and shook his head. Lily took advantage of the opening.

"What shipment?"

Giles softened as he returned to addressing Lily. "After you left, Minister Bellingham informed all of us that there had been a shipment of felixium that left the mines, but didn't make it out of the Disputed Region before the attack by Meridia. The shipment was hidden so as not to be captured or harmed during the hostilities. She tried to have the shipment extracted from the Disputed Region in the days following your disappearance, but unfortunately it appears that the convoy was, er, taken."

"Taken? What do you mean?"

"Well, we don't really know what happened to it," Giles admitted. "It just sort of disappeared. There was no immediate sign of where it might have gone, or who might have stolen it. Jason is investigating what happened to it as his top priority. The sooner he can find it, then obviously the sooner we can retrieve you."

"Why would someone take the shipment?" Alexei looked at Lily. "You are the only ones with a machine, right? The only ones who need this"—he gestured, trying to remember the name—"felixium."

"Probably the same person who pushed us through." Ava looked over at him. "No point in pushing us through the portal if we can just come right back."

Alexei shrugged, acknowledging her point. "True. I would have just destroyed the machine after pushing us through. Much more difficult to get us back then."

"Giles, they didn't, did they?" Lily asked quickly. She hadn't even considered that possibility.

"No, no, it's here. It's fine," he reassured them.

"Thank goodness, that would have been really bad."

Everyone pondered Alexei's comment. Lily felt slightly sick at the thought, but also wondered why they hadn't done exactly that. If they wanted her out of the way for a long time, or even permanently, destroying the machine would have been the way to go. If they didn't want to just kill her, which, as everyone kept pointing out, would be simpler. Again, Lily found herself baffled about what her adversaries actually wanted. None of their actions seemed to make sense.

"Oh yes," Jenkins broke the silence, addressing Lily and seemingly oblivious to the delay of his response. "That would have taken many months to fix. Maybe a year." He nodded enthusiastically. The rest of the group looked at him, shocked.

"But my point is," Alexei continued, "I thought your machine and how it works were meant to be a state secret.

Who would know to steal the felixium? Who would know how to use the machine and what pushing us through would do?"

No one had an answer. Lily realised the gravity of the situation. Whoever was out to get her knew about the machine. That meant it had to be one of her closest advisors, or ... or someone knew about the machine who should not know about the machine. And not only that, knew enough to be able to use the machine. But now that she thought about it, people *did* know about the machine who should not know. Ezra had somehow known about it, and whoever had been writing her those notes that had appeared in her room did as well. She felt a pang of regret that she had delayed telling Jason about the notes. Maybe if she had told him earlier, they wouldn't be in this position.

"Giles, what's happening back there?" Lily asked, looking for a distraction from those depressing thoughts. "How is everyone? Have there been any more terrorist attacks?"

Giles's face fell. He took his glasses off and began polishing the lenses.

"No, no more attacks. But it has been ... a little difficult back here, Your Majesty," he said. "Things have taken a turn for the worse in Highacre. The prime minister is using his new special police to turn the country into a police state. They are terrorising the citizens and enforcing his complete control over the country."

"Is Minister Bellingham fighting him?"

Giles paused. Jenkins stopped whistling.

"Can't fight from prison," said Jenkins. Giles hissed at him to shut up, but Jenkins was lost in his thoughts. "Prison? Or is it jail? Can never remember which. Hmm, should send her some cigarettes. Currency." Jenkins nodded and pulled out a small notebook, making a note for himself.

"She's been arrested?" Lily asked Giles.

Giles nodded sadly, his gaze dropping. "Addison too."

"Addison! But why?"

"I don't know, Your Majesty." Giles looked lost, and strangely, a little guilty. "I've asked everyone I can find, but no one can tell me. Not even Toot."

Lily looked at Giles, stunned. He'd nearly spat Toot's name, and not once had she ever heard him refer to one of the politicians without their title.

"Perhaps he doesn't know—"

"Oh, he knows," said Giles, angry now. "He told me he'd keep her safe. And then even though I ... well, but they seem to have forgiven me ... still, I'll never forgive myself."

"Giles? Forgive yourself for what?" Lily was struggling to make sense of Giles's ramblings, but his stark change in demeanour worried her.

"What? Oh, never mind. We can discuss it when you get back."

"You were talking about Minister Toot?" prompted Ava.

"Ah yes. Risen the ranks, our Jeremy Toot. He's in charge of the HSP, and is Toth's new best friend. I've never seen the man so industrious. Never lifted a finger as your father's advisor."

"Could Jason look into why they arrested Addison?" Lily was more worried about her friend than Jeremy Toot's new social status. Worry bubbled up, and she felt she was grasping around in the dark for a solution to a problem she couldn't see. She felt so powerless stuck here while her friends and country were clearly suffering.

"Jason is no longer the head of the Royal Guard, Your Majesty."

"What? They fired him?"

"No, no. Mr Berryman has been brought back to replace him. Jason has been retained, but I believe he now has a much lesser role."

It took a while for Lily to realise Giles was talking about Richard, Jason's previous deputy. With Minister Bellingham and Addison arrested, and Jason sidelined, Lily wondered if Giles's estimation of their rescue might be optimistic.

She listened as he continued to paint a stark picture of the current situation. Key people arrested, disappeared, or killed. Increasing requirements for citizens to submit to information gathering or tracking protocols. New identity papers were required to move about freely, and even shop for food. And he'd heard that internment camps were being set up for Meridian and Valmeadian citizens present within Highacre, as well as people deemed Meridian or Valmeadian sympathisers.

Severe punishments were being handed out for noncompliance or breaches of the prime minister's new regulations. Most were extrajudicially applied by the HSP with little to no oversight. And Highacre was on the brink of war with both Meridia and Valmead once again.

Lily sat back, shocked beyond words. Highacre had been, in her mind, an idyllic place. Beautiful and magical, full of bright colours and happiness. She knew that was not the reality. The whole reason for her return was evidence enough of that, but still. She felt as if a beautiful garden had fallen into darkness, and was now being strangled by fungus and thorns.

Ava and Alexei took advantage of Lily's silence to ask about their countries.

"Not much information is coming in these days, I'm afraid," said Giles apologetically. "But the little I have heard indicates that Valmead is preparing for conflict. Restrictions are being applied to basic food and goods. And the draft is in effect again—"

"What is the minimum age?" Alexei interrupted.

"I had heard eleven, but I could be wrong," answered Giles sadly. Alexei paled and sat back.

"And Meridia?" asked Ava.

"Meridia is definitely readying for war. The Disputed Region is being reinforced. More troops are arriving every day, and reports are coming in about electronic barriers and machines popping up. All trade between Highacre and Meridia has ceased, and Meridian nationals were recalled about a month ago. I haven't heard anything about conscription, but we hear less from Meridia than Valmead. The prime minister has decreed that Meridian propaganda is banned, and that means we don't get their news reports."

"They wouldn't conscript unless war had been declared," said Ava absently, becoming lost in her own thoughts.

Lily suddenly remembered she needed to tell Giles about Ezra. He had been in the room with the interdimensional travel machine before she was pushed through. Only a handful of people were supposed to know about the machine, and as the Meridian ambassador, he certainly wasn't one of them.

Lily opened her mouth to speak, but Jenkins suddenly piped up. He got part way through explaining that the communications link may cut out at any second when they were cut off, and the image of Giles and Jenkins disappeared.

The three friends, alone once more, sat in silence, lost in their own thoughts. Lily wondered whether Jason would even be able to locate the felixium and bring them home. It seemed more important than ever to find out if her mother had a way back to Highacre.

"My brother is eleven," said Alexei.

"He'll be fine," said Ava dismissively. Alexei glared at her.

"What?" she said defensively. "The son of the dictator? Of course he'll be fine. They'd never conscript him."

"They conscripted me," said Alexei quietly.

"At the end of the war," Ava shot back.

"I was eleven, like my brother, and they didn't know the war was about to end."

"Oh of course they did Alexei. And even if they didn't, it was for show. They'd never have put you in any danger."

"Arrogant Meridian!" Alexei shouted, suddenly on his feet and balling his fists. "You know nothing of my country or the dangers my family faces."

"Stupid Valmeadian!" returned Ava, facing off against him. "What are you going to do? Hit me? Typical Valmead. Violence is always the answer, isn't it?"

"We fight because you attack us! Such arrogance. You all think you're so much better than everyone else."

"Hey," interrupted Lily, standing now too. "We all need to work together."

"Says the Highacren who's about to declare war on both of us," said Ava bitterly.

"Woah," said Lily, surprised by the attack.

"My friends will be on the front line of your war," said Ava. "And for what? Why are you all so selfish? Why do you hoard technology that should be gifted to the world? Something like interdimensional travel should be available to everyone."

"Hey, Meridia's not innocent in all this. Your people blew up the arena, in case you forgot? Killed a couple hundred people? If that's not provoking us to conflict, I don't know what is," Lily shot back.

Alexei's temper burst too. "My family will fight. My

cousins, and despite what you think, my brothers. My father will sacrifice them to show that we are Valmead's people. Already there will be rations in place; people will be starving. Meridia will withhold medical supplies like you did last time. People will be suffering, dying in the streets."

Ava looked shocked and slightly ashamed. Lily knew it was true that Meridia would be withholding supplies, even if only for their own use and not as a punitive measure, but she could see that Ava had not considered the effect of this on Alexei and his people.

"Well, we'd have to limit the supply of medicine," said Ava, recovering, "because Valmead will have stopped providing us with the supplies needed to make them."

"Because we need to pull people out of the factories to prepare them for war!"

"That's not our fault!"

Lily's face burned as she realised her country was at the crux of the conflict, and she was the sovereign.

"This is why we need to stick together," she tried to get in before her friends both turned on her. "When Jason gets some felixium and brings us home, we are going to need to work together to stop all of this."

Both her friends scoffed and shrugged her off.

"Jason will never be able to get the felixium if it's in Meridian control," dismissed Ava.

"Then we need to help ourselves. Come on." She looked pointedly at her friends, who were quickly losing steam and beginning to look embarrassed for their outbursts. "We're all stressed and worried about home. But we can't take it out on each other. We're going to have to work together to get home and when we're there, we need to stay tight so that we can fix things."

Ava and Alexei nodded and apologised to each other. By the time they headed off to the warehouses, the tension had lifted and the easy banter was returning. Lily joined in, but an uneasy feeling had settled in her chest. Ava and Alexei were so close, but hearing of the preparations for war had brought them to each other's throats so easily.

If the two of them were so ready to fight each other, what chance did their countries have for peace?

24

THE DOOR to the apartment opened, and April entered cautiously, looking around. When her eyes landed on Lily, her face fell slightly, and she dropped her head before moving quickly for her room, muttering about homework.

Lily's heart sank at her little sister's reaction. She had left Ava and Alexei cleaning a particularly dirty warehouse break room, the three having agreed that Lily might have better luck mending fences with April if it was just the two of them. Lily had been hoping that at least part of April's reaction was her feeling uncomfortable with strangers in her home.

Taking a deep breath and readying herself, Lily stood, walked to April's door, and knocked softly. There was no reply, but Lily, thinking her sister may be wearing her headphones, opened the door and peered inside.

"Hey," she said, smiling.

"Hey," said April, clearly uncomfortable. She turned back to her open textbook.

Lily took this as an invitation to enter and slipped inside, closing the door again behind her. She looked around the sparsely decorated room. April's room at the farm had been covered in pictures and photos. It was bright and warm and mirrored the bubbly teenager her sister no longer seemed to be. Lily sat on the bed next to April, who instinctively pulled her feet back away from Lily.

Lily resented the flinch, and that April apparently wasn't going to meet her halfway. She took a breath and reminded herself that she was the adult here.

"I'm really sorry. About everything. Standing you up, not being here—especially with everything … the way it is. I hate that you're hurting."

April peered at Lily over her textbook, eyes softening slightly.

"But you do get that it wasn't my fault, right? I didn't just take off. I didn't have a choice."

Lily could have kicked herself as April disappeared back behind her book. Why couldn't she just leave it at an apology? Clearly, April needed it. Why did she have to prioritise her need to have her family not blame her? In the grand scheme of things, it wasn't important if Lily wasn't at fault for what happened. She was a part of it, and April needed validation that she had been hurt as a result.

"April, I'm sorry—" she began.

"It's fine," April cut her off without looking up.

"No, it's not. I didn't mean to—" Lily broke off, looking for the words. "I'm sorry you've been going through such a truly awful time, and that I haven't been here with you."

She felt a slight thawing from behind the textbook, but she knew that she'd lost too much ground with her justification. There was no way April was going to open up to her about their mother right now. She'd have to build the relationship more.

Lily felt dirty, reminding herself that she wanted both to repair her relationship with her sister, and to find her mother. But her impatience for finding her mother made her feel like she was playing her sister, only making up with her to get the information.

Feeling like a terrible person, she concentrated, penetrating April's mind, and gently looked for any thoughts about their mother. Unfortunately, April decided at that moment to cut Lily some slack.

"There's this girl at my school who is, like, the love child of Stinky Mahoney and Cat Lady Burgess from town," said April, her eyes lighting up. She began telling Lily about the girl, with liberal reminiscing about the two characters from their old lives who had somehow managed to be the town jokes while also engendering a fierce loyalty from those who lived there. They were the town's weirdos, and no outsiders were to poke fun.

Lily tried to concentrate on the story while continuing to probe April's mind. She tried to make all the appropriate noises and laugh at the right times, and look *at* April rather than at the rings of energy that she saw when mind reading.

As April began to explain exactly how the strange girl at school had wound up as a viral internet sensation after dancing to the beats of the routine alarm testing, Lily saw April did, in fact, know where their mother was. Unfortunately, she couldn't get the location. April had been visiting her regularly, but hadn't told Elaine for fear that Elaine would tell her to stop. With a punch of sadness, she saw that April felt guilty—she thought that if she had time to visit her mother, then she had time to get an after-school job, to take some pressure off Elaine. No kid should have to sacrifice time with their remaining parent to help put food on the table.

And here she was, trying to get information that would ultimately, hopefully, let her go home rather than working to earn money so that April wouldn't have this dilemma.

She was using her sister so she could escape the misery from which April had no escape herself.

Lily's face fell, and immediately she knew that not only was that not the appropriate reaction to April's story, but she had missed a few cues.

April's expression darkened, and she shut her book loudly.

"Sorry April, I was just—"

"I really need to get my homework done."

"I was listening, I just—"

"Can you get out of my room? Please?"

Hesitating slightly, Lily got up and moved to the door. She looked around, but April was not ready to hear Lily's apology. *Your latest apology.* Feeling like a terrible sister, she left the room and returned to the couch.

Would she have felt better about upsetting April if she had managed to get a location? She wasn't sure. But she didn't think she felt as guilty as she should about her plan to follow April tomorrow, when she went to visit their mother after school.

25

"And he found nothing? Not on the body, and not where she was found?" Claire called through the bathroom door to Naomi, who was putting the finishing touches on her disguise.

"Nope. Clearly there had been a struggle, but the HSP report is claiming it was a mugging. No way Lady Octavia was taken down by a simple mugging."

Claire frowned. It was tempting to think larger-than-life figures were immune to the daily tragedies of regular people, but they could die as meaninglessly as anyone else.

"But Jason said the good thing about the lack of evidence is that I can use that investigation as cover for our work," Naomi said. "And in even better news, Giles spoke to Lily."

"She's okay?" asked Claire urgently.

"She is," said Naomi reassuringly. "She's in the dimension she grew up in."

Claire considered this briefly, trying again to understand the motive behind Lily's exile. "Well, she should be safe there. Now that we've located her, we really need to get the felixium back."

"Yep," said Naomi. "Jason's heading to the DR as soon as he can. What do you think?" Naomi asked, exiting the bathroom and presenting herself to Claire.

"My goodness! I don't even recognise you, and I know it's you." Claire couldn't keep the admiration out of her voice. She was quite good at disguising herself, but clearly, Naomi had a gift.

"Thanks babe," said Naomi, slipping easily into the accent of a Monkronian. Those native to the northern coastal Highacren city tended to elongate their vowels more than those from the capital.

Claire checked her own disguise in the mirror. It was nowhere near as good as Naomi's, but it just needed to get her through the crowd in the courtyard, where she wouldn't be able to employ her magic due to the volume of people expected. She adjusted her wig, frowning slightly. It wouldn't stand up to scrutiny from someone who knew her, but it would do.

"When does the rally start?" Claire asked Naomi for the third time that day.

"Six, but people should be turning up from around four to mingle and chat about how terrible foreigners are. We should look to be there at about five thirty. That way, we can make sure it's still safe to go in, and we'll be in position to get inside while they're getting the rally started."

Claire and Naomi had managed to track Austin down and put him under surveillance. After watching him for a little over a week now, they had confirmed that he was heavily involved in the nationalist movement, but had discovered little else. Upon learning that a rally was to be held outside the building that housed the administrative offices for the movement, Claire and Naomi decided to use the distraction to try to break into the offices and see what they could find.

"Okay, we should probably start heading that way," said Naomi, putting the finishing touches on her makeup. "Do you remember the rendezvous point?"

Claire rolled her eyes. "This is not my first mission, you know."

"I know," said Naomi, turning to look at Claire. "But it is mine. My first time undercover. And it'd make me feel better to confirm we are both on the same page."

Claire relented. She could tell that Naomi was a little nervous, but she got the impression that Naomi was more worried about putting Claire in danger. Claire had changed safe houses another couple of times since she and Naomi began working together, and she knew Naomi was worried for her safety.

"If we're separated, we'll meet at the King's Garden in Garrand Park."

"Right, and if one of us gets into trouble, the other is to leave and head there. We don't try to help each other—better one caught than both. Right?"

Naomi was looking fiercely at Claire. This was the part of the plan that Claire felt most uncomfortable with. She was happy to think Naomi would get herself safe if Claire was caught, but could she just run away and leave Naomi if she was in danger? Naomi had been emphatic on this point. And Naomi was worried about leaving Jason to deal with everything alone.

"He's better with a partner," she had said. Claire had been touched by Naomi's loyalty to her boss.

"Right," Claire had finally agreed, obviously not entirely convincing Naomi, but the other woman dropped it.

They moved through the streets largely in silence, speaking only to alert each other to HSP patrols and areas that could conceal surveillance. Finally, they reached the building from which the nationalist movement ran their operations. It was a run-down building in the warehouse district. It had likely been a small storehouse or offices for a larger operation back in its day.

There was a building the size of a large, one-storey house in the back left corner of a large paved area that used to be a loading zone. There was a raised platform where the podium was being set up for the rally that Claire suspected trucks used for loading. The whole area was enclosed in a six-foot brick wall. A large archway, big enough for trucks to drive through, was the only way in and out, and the gates were currently open.

Two burly men manned the gates. There seemed to be no real method to their scrutiny of those wandering in. Anyone who looked out of place to them was pulled aside for questioning, but in the twenty minutes that Claire and Naomi watched, no one was refused entry.

"Okay, I'll go in first and scan for magic. If we're all good, then I'll return to the gate area and wait for you just inside." Naomi pointed to an area visible from where Claire would be waiting. "If there's an issue, I'll come back out."

Claire nodded, grateful. Naomi was a powerful revealer. She could identify people who, like Claire, could hide themselves through invisibility or chameleoning, but she could also detect all magic. She would be able to sense if there were other revealers placed in the area who might be able to see if Claire used her powers, and also identify any other magics that might pose a threat to their plan. Claire had never met a revealer as powerful as Naomi before. She was glad they were on the same side.

She watched Naomi walk through the gate with a sense of purpose. The guards glanced at her, but neither seemed inclined to stop her. Claire waited for what felt like forever, watching the people entering, trying to get a gauge on the type of people attending the rally, and also making sure there was no one who might be able to identify her.

Finally, she saw Naomi appear inside the compound behind one of the guards. Sighing with relief, Claire made her way to the gate, emulating Naomi's sense of purpose and looking to stride through.

"Excuse me, miss," said one of the guards, blocking her path.

Of course. Claire fixed a look of annoyance on her face. "Yes?" she said impatiently.

"Random ID check. You know how it is, can't be too careful." He was grinning at her, enjoying the small bit of power his role afforded him. Claire dove into her bag, giving off an air of being put out, and began rummaging for her fake identification documents.

"Bonita! Come on," said Naomi loudly. She was standing just inside, her phone pressed to her ear and waving impatiently at Claire.

"Sorry Mary, these *gentlemen* want to see my ID."

"You *are* kidding?" She walked over to the guard, glaring up at him. "My assistant needs to get everything ready for my speech. How pleased do you think your superiors will be if everything is delayed because of you?"

The guard squared up to Naomi and began talking about the importance of security, matching Naomi's points about the success of the rally with counterpoints about safety. Claire kept her head in her purse, ostensibly still looking for her ID, but she saw the other guard roll his eyes.

"Go on through, miss," he said, and Claire hurried past.

"What'd you do that for?" called the other guard, furious to be undermined.

Both Claire and Naomi hurried away before they could be detained further. They made it to a corner of the courtyard and turned to examine their surroundings.

"There are a couple of revealers, but neither is powerful enough that they should be able to see you, and they seem to be focussed on the crowd," said Naomi, keeping her eyes on the courtyard. "I can't sense any others inside, but there are also some ghosts here."

Claire nodded, thinking. Ghost was a slang term for a person who could turn completely invisible, as opposed to the camouflaging Claire could do. If Naomi wasn't concentrating, they could easily sneak up on them inside the building.

Or watch us.

Claire froze. She had been so fixated on planning for being caught that she hadn't considered someone might find them but simply watch to see what they were after. If they weren't careful, a ghost could find out what they were there for, and even follow them home.

She whispered her fear to Naomi, who nodded with the air of someone who had already thought of this.

"That's why you're doing most of the searching. I'll be keeping an eye out, and when we leave, we'll stop a couple of times along the way so that I can scan. I've not identified any trackers, so we're in luck there."

"Yeah, but you'd only know about them if they used their power, right? And they're not likely to do that until they need to track us home."

"Which is why we'll be stopping a couple of times along the way. If anyone's tracking us, I'll sense them and we can deal with them," Naomi said patiently, particularly since this was the third time they'd talked about this.

They kept watching for a while longer, keeping smiles

on their faces and pretending to be discussing politics when anyone was in earshot.

"Okay, that gateway there." Naomi pointed to an arch on the wall to the left of the podium. "It's our way in. Luckily, the gate is open, but the guard has low-key lie detection."

Claire looked at Naomi suspiciously. "Are you sure you're not Lady Octavia's replacement? I thought only detectors could identify powers and revealers just knew if magic was being used."

"Revealers sense magic, and with my power, I can identify the magic being used. Not every revealer can do that. But I can't tell what other powers he might have." Naomi nodded at the guard. "He's using his lie detection whenever someone he doesn't recognise tries to go inside."

"Well, how are we going to get past him then?" Claire was already scanning the rest of the building, looking for alternate entry points.

"You can camouflage yourself behind those boxes, and I'll just have to be a better liar than he is a detector."

Naomi started off before Claire could argue. It seemed brash, but having worked with Naomi closely for over a week, she knew Naomi wouldn't risk something like this if she wasn't confident. Still, it took more of an effort than usual for Claire to put herself in character as they crossed the courtyard.

One thing Claire had noticed when scanning the crowd was the lack of women. Including Naomi and herself, there was probably one woman for every ten men present. This wasn't really a surprise to Claire, but what she also registered was that they had styled themselves in a more severe manner than she and Naomi had, and as such, what should have been a brief walk across the courtyard became elongated by Naomi trying to avoid anyone who seemed interested in them, and punctuated by short interactions with eager men she couldn't bypass in time. Naomi handled these well, mostly excusing them to go to the bathroom and promising to be right back.

As they approached the crates behind which Claire was to engage her magic, she muttered to Naomi that they should have pretended to be a couple.

"Some of those sleazes would probably have tried harder. Now, game on—wait for my signal."

Naomi strode purposely forward, once again completely in character. She went to enter and looked at the guard in annoyed surprise when he didn't move.

"Excuse me," she said accusingly.

"Not seen you before," he replied, unmoving.

Naomi sighed. "I'm here from Monkronia. Austin asked me to give a speech. You know, let all of you Burlaronians know what the movement's doing on the front lines? Where we're actually *doing* something? Other than drinking coffee," she muttered the final comment, causing the guard to stand up straighter, ready to defend his role.

"We do stuff," was his reply.

"Oh, you *do stuff*, do you?" Naomi allowed herself to get heated, and as she berated the guard, accusing him, on behalf of everyone in the city, of not pulling his weight, she took a few steps towards him, causing him to step back and away from the arch.

Brilliant. Claire quickly blended in with the background and hurried forward, squeezing through the arch. Claire could hear some voices at the other end of the corridor, where the offices must be. Seeing a bathroom to her right, she ducked in there and listened for Naomi to come through.

Less than a minute later, Naomi strode into the bathroom and to the sinks, looking around the room in the reflection and quickly spotting Claire. Claire jumped; even though she knew Naomi was a powerful revealer, she wasn't used to being seen when she didn't want to be.

"There are people in the offices still," she informed Naomi.

"The rally will start in about five minutes, so they shouldn't be long. We can try to see if there are any empty rooms we can check in the meantime. Remember, stay close to me."

They paused at the door, listening. Claire looked at Naomi, impressed by her performance.

"Where did you learn to do that? And so well as to get by a lie detector?"

"As a female in the Royal Guards, I have learned many useful soft skills. Like how to be a hard arse."

They exited the bathroom, Claire trying to walk as closely behind Naomi as she could without stepping on her heels. The first few rooms were empty, but they were also devoid of anything useful, seemingly occupied by lower-level members who were probably out taking care of the mundane tasks to get the rally going.

"People coming," Naomi hissed at Claire, who froze while Naomi moved behind the door. Chatter filled the hallway as what seemed to be the rest of the staff exited to hear the speeches.

Satisfied they'd passed, Claire and Naomi hurried down the hall, now looking to start with whichever office looked the most important. They found a large office in a corner with a solid-looking desk, as opposed to the flimsy tables everyone else seemed to use.

Claire entered while Naomi kept watch. There were folders all over the desk, sheafs of paper in trays marked *"in"* and *"out"*, and several filing cabinets. Claire opened a few of the files, scanning headings to see if the information was pertinent, and deciding it was, called Naomi in to help.

"This is Austin's office," Naomi commented with a note of surprise as she looked through a folder. "I knew he was high up here, but it just seems so …"

"Businessman?"

"Yeah."

Claire knew what she meant. Austin was always training in the gym or the yard. Occasionally he was inside discussing strategies with Jason, but this office seemed too uptight for the man they knew.

"Lots of references to a Patriot," commented Naomi.

"Yeah, I think he must be important. He's mentioned a lot here, too. Capture what you can."

Both women had a pair of Claire's glasses with cameras embedded in the frame. With a handheld button, they could take photos of whatever they were looking at.

"I think this is important," said Naomi as Claire froze, thinking she heard footsteps.

"Hide," she hissed, moving out of the line of sight of the doorway, vaguely noting Naomi diving under the desk.

"What are you doing, Brett? We're going to be late," came an impatient voice.

"I sense something," Brett replied.

"It's just going to be all the people outside," the voice whined. "I don't want to miss Austin's speech."

Brett opened the door and looked around the room suspiciously.

"Okay, I'm going," the voice said again. "I don't want to get caught in Austin's office. You know how he is about that."

Reluctantly, Brett closed the door and followed the voice back down the corridor.

"We probably need to—" Naomi began.

"Yeah, let's go," agreed Claire.

Their reconnaissance had revealed a back door into the building, and they headed for it so as to avoid trying to get away through the throng of people in the courtyard. The building was empty, and hopefully the noise of the crowd would cover their escape.

They exited the back door and were turning to head towards the smaller gate in the wall when they collided with someone coming the other way.

"Shit, sorry," said Naomi, looking up at the man and freezing.

Austin.

Claire edged out of the way, still camouflaged and not yet noticed by Austin.

"No, I'm sorry, wasn't looking where I was going," Austin smiled before cocking his head. "Have we met? You look familiar."

"I don't think so." Naomi smiled. "I'm from Monkronia. But maybe we've seen each other at other rallies."

"Monkronia? You guys are really getting some wins for the movement." Austin looked impressed. Naomi must have seen the question form behind his eyes, as she quickly spoke.

"One of your friends asked me to do a speech. I said I'd think about it, and I came back here to rehearse." She nodded to the gate. "Figured if I decided against it, I could do a runner."

Austin laughed. "Well, now, I can't have that. It would be good for our people to hear from someone actually in the action. Our guys are still hurting from the attack on the arena. Meridian bastards blow us up, and there's no way to get back at them. Not yet, anyway. And don't worry." He put a hand on the small of Naomi's back, guiding her back inside, "I'll be right there with you, so if you don't want to do a speech, we can just have a chat on stage."

Claire watched Austin lead Naomi away, feeling incredibly guilty for just standing there. She knew that was what they'd agreed—better only one got caught than both—but she felt like a coward. Fleetingly, she considered following and trying to help Naomi get away, but she knew how mad Naomi would be, and tried to put herself in the other woman's shoes. Somehow knowing that she wouldn't want Naomi to come back for her didn't help her feel any better about not going back for Naomi, but Claire made herself move, heading out through the gate and making for Garrand Park.

Though camouflaged, Claire ignored her training and paced around the statue of the dead king that stood in the centre of King's Garden. She tried to avoid looking at her watch, but the longest she'd been able to leave it was three minutes.

They'd agreed to wait an hour if separated. Naomi had wanted to limit it to thirty minutes, but Claire won out by informing Naomi that she would wait sixty. As it approached that time, Claire now felt sixty had been too little and hadn't really accounted for travel time.

Having burned up most of her nervous energy, Claire was now just worried. She wandered towards some bushes where she'd have a good view of the statue and sat with her back against a tree.

"I thought we said only an hour," came Naomi's voice accusingly.

"It's only been"—Claire looked at her watch—"two hours. What happened?"

Naomi helped Claire to her feet, and they began the trek home.

"I waited until he got on stage to open the rally and then said I needed a nervous pee. They escorted me, but no one wanted to miss his speech, so my escort waited outside. I climbed out a tiny window near the ceiling and got away."

"Nice work," said Claire, relieved Naomi was okay.

"Before he got on stage, I was able to talk to Austin. He's so proud of being the boss there, he's happy to brag, and he must've really believed I was who I said. He was talking about how he's got a direct line to the Patriot."

"Did he say who it is?"

Naomi shook her head. "No. He wants people to think he does, but it was pretty clear he doesn't have a clue himself. I'm not sure any of them know who it is, but from what he was saying, this Patriot is behind the entire movement."

"Interesting," said Claire, itching to start looking at the photos they'd taken. "Clearly, we need to find out who the Patriot is. The nationalist movement is connected to all of this somehow, I'm sure of it. Which means the Patriot is involved. It's unusual that they're remaining anonymous, and even more unusual that not even the top players seem to know who they are. It's possible that they're protecting their identity because they're involved in all the rest. Could be one of the advisors. And if so, maybe they're behind the lot. The assassinations; Lily being pushed through; whatever the prime minister is up to."

"Agreed," nodded Naomi. "I'll continue surveillance— just as soon as I put together another disguise. You focus on going through what we found. Try to find hard evidence linking Austin to the Patriot and then see what you can uncover that might identify the Patriot. Maybe work with

Hudson? You should have enough in the photos to do some targeted searching in his systems."

Keen as she was to do exactly that, Claire looked suspiciously at Naomi.

"Are you sidelining me?"

"Of course not." Naomi smiled. "You're the best for that job. That you just happen to be able to do it in the relative safety of your latest safe house is an added bonus."

26

The fire crackled, reflected in the old man's eyes. Those eyes were all that gave any hint of his true age. Most people put him at about fifty until they looked into his eyes, and then they would flinch, sensing something unfathomable. He heard the light footsteps, but did not look up.

"They found her."

His eyes closed. You never got used to losing friends.

"Well, we knew they would eventually." He motioned the girl to take a seat opposite him by the fire, and she obliged, feet dangling, unable to touch the floor. She sighed heavily.

"I saw it happen—in the oracle's dreams—but still, I had hoped ... silly, really." The girl waved her hand and a mug appeared, its contents steaming. Cyril's eyes narrowed imperceptibly. The girl saw him looking and gestured, offering him one, but he shook his head.

She may be the most powerful detector yet.

He returned his gaze to the fire. Everyone seemed to be getting more powerful. Like a storm gathering momentum.

"Lady Octavia thought Lily was 'the one'," said the girl conversationally, taking a sip. "From the prophecies?"

Cyril kept staring at the fire. The girl glanced at him, checking he had heard her before trying again. "She went through most of the prophecies, actually. Was maybe a little obsessed." She paused again. "She thought Lily was the subject of quite a number of them."

Cyril could tell the girl was getting annoyed by his lack of response. He didn't have many visitors and was out of practise. It was often so long between visitors, Cyril sometimes forgot that people wanted interaction, rather than just coming straight out with what they wanted. He could remember the dance. For a time, he had been quite good at it.

"That's why she thought Lily was the one," the girl said, her voice revealing her frustration now. Her impatience. "Lady Octavia?"

"Yes." He said it more to let the girl know he was listening to her, and to encourage her to get to the point.

"It's just, *is* she really 'the one'?"

"Lady Octavia thought so," he echoed the girl's comments, but his tone indicated that Lady Octavia's opinion was good enough for him.

"Yes," the girl said, then hesitated, taking another sip. "It's just ... with all due respect to Lady Octavia, and I did respect her—I do ... but ... she wasn't always right."

Cyril tore his eyes from the fire and looked directly at the girl, who blushed automatically. He could tell the blushing made her mad. Perhaps because it betrayed her emotions. Perhaps because she wanted control.

So much power and a desire for control.

Cyril had a sudden pang of longing to talk to Lady Octavia, and then sadness that she was gone, followed by regret that they hadn't had longer together.

Almost one hundred years, yet barely a moment.

Cyril casually wondered whether he needed more social interaction. His eyes returned to the fire.

"Is Lily 'the one'?" he recapped, both to let the girl know he intended to answer her question, but also because sometimes people forgot which question he was answering. Time moved much differently to Cyril, immortal from all but unnatural death. Seconds seemed like such a tiny measurement. "Maybe. It's either Lily, or it speaks of someone who will exist five hundred years in the future."

The girl froze, her mug halfway to her lips. She put it on the table next to her.

"That seems like a pretty big margin for error. How will we know?"

A smile flashed on Cyril's lips, then was gone. People were so obsessed with knowing.

"I think it best we assume it is Lily, so that the world doesn't end. And if it turns out not to be her ..." He stood, joints creaking like old wood. "Well then, I'll sort it out in a few centuries."

27

Jason looked around the combined mess hall fondly. He couldn't help but think back on his time during the war. Whenever he had been sent to one of their larger bases for some respite, he and his mates would spend all their meals together, and sometimes linger afterwards, playing cards or just chatting when they weren't required for other duties.

He looked around the hall that was effectively the dining room for all the factions from Highacre who worked in the Disputed Region. It was roughly the size of a gymnasium, and everything looked relatively new. Much fancier than what he was used to. Jason supposed that came from the mess being run by the private security contractors and not the military. The companies could give their employees whatever they wanted, whereas the military had to account for all of their spending. Convincing citizens that their taxes should buy the soldiers a pancake machine was difficult, even when they were fighting a war. He poked and prodded the pancake machine. Who even knew that was a thing?

He turned slowly, taking the whole room in. He saw other, what he would call luxury items, such as an ice cream machine, a load of free protein bars and snacks, and in a corner there seemed to be some video games. Whoever was funding the contractors was loaded.

They're all being paid more than me. Much more. Why am I doing this again?

Jason shook the thought from his head. He wasn't cut out for private security work. He had joined the military because he wanted to serve. Because he wanted to give back to his country. That was also why he had taken his current role. He couldn't be a mercenary. Still, a few years here and his house would be completely paid off ...

Jason's thoughts returned unbidden to Lady Octavia's battered body. For such an imposing figure in life, her body had looked tiny and broken when he'd viewed it in the morgue. She had been killed because of her service to her country. No, Jason lived to serve. No amount of money could pull him away from doing a job that had meaning.

Of course, Richard now has your job. Bitterly, Jason looked down at the free snacks, pocketing a protein bar. *Never say never.*

Scanning the room, Jason located who he was looking for. Upon arrival in the Disputed Region, Jason had gone straight to Camp Warchek, the Highacren military base. Though massive during the war, it had been scaled back during this time of relative peace. That was saying something about its previous size; it was still about the size of a small town.

One of his old commanders was now in charge of the base, and over a few beers, Jason had managed to get the lay of the land down here. He had also managed to acquire a room in the barracks, which was lucky. As head of the Royal Guard, someone had always made such arrangements for him. No longer afforded that level of administrative support, Jason had driven to the DR without a thought for where he might sleep.

The commander had told him that the private security companies, or PSCs, essentially ran things down in the DR. There was no real role for the military with no war—all they were supposed to do was hold their ground and be visible so that the Meridians didn't get any ideas.

The PSCs, on the other hand, were out running missions for their corporate bosses every day. They saw themselves as the front-line troops putting their bodies on the line and looked down on the military. Jason's old commander admitted he didn't even know what they did half the time, but did tell him that some of the guys from their old unit had joined up with the main PSC and that they spent most of their downtime in the mess hall.

Jason wandered over to the table, noticing Adam, one of his old teammates, clock him and lean into the group and whisper something before they all sat back, trying to look relaxed. Chris looked up as Jason got close and reacted in surprise, as if Adam hadn't just let them know Jason was here.

"Maaaaate! Hey guys, it's Jase!"

They all stood up and enthusiastically shook his hand and clapped him on the back. Jason took in his old comrades. Though they had been part of the same unit, Jason would consider Adam, Chris, and Pete more work colleagues than friends. They had all gotten along and occasionally up to mischief together, but they weren't close enough to hang out away from the job. That said, fighting a war together grew a bond that was stronger and more intense than what "colleagues" implied. It was confusing. Jason wouldn't necessarily want to go for a beer with them, but if they were in trouble, he'd have been there in a heartbeat.

Sitting down again, Pete asked Jason what he was doing in their neck of the woods.

"Ah, you know. Possible trip down here by some politician, so it needs to be scouted for security and photo opportunities. Decided to volunteer myself to see what other opportunities might be available for a guy like me if I got sick of scouting locations for politicians."

"I thought you liked your gig. Serving the sovereign and all that. Especially after the arena."

"Yeah, but it's the same red tape that we had back in the military. And without the opportunity to do anything about the arena attack. Not to mention, the pay's terrible. Serving the sovereign doesn't make sure my family has a house. From the look of things around here, you guys must be on a pretty good wicket."

The three men shared a look, and Chris took a swig of his beer. "Yeah, we do alright."

Chris was the biggest of the group. Tall and built like a mountain, he had gotten even bigger since he left the military. Jason remembered him as being fit, but now he looked like he was focussing more on *looking* fit. He vaguely wondered if Chris was supplementing, and whether he was doing it legally.

"I suppose it must get a bit boring though, eh?" Jason said. "Same thing day in and day out. And taking a contract, you wouldn't be able to take any short-notice higher-paying jobs that come up."

"It's not too bad," said Pete, spitting another sunflower seed shell into a bottle. Pete had been happy with guard duty in the unit, so Jason didn't necessarily believe him. "And nothing stops you jumping on something juicy if you can find a mate to cover for you."

"And people will cover for you?"

"Oh yeah. If you cover for them later."

"Or cut them in," added Adam with a grin. Whereas Chris had ballooned with muscle, Adam had remained what Jason thought of as functionally fit. He was clearly strong, but could touch his nose without his biceps getting in the way. Pete, on the other hand, was a runner. Shorter than the others, he made up for what he lacked in bulk with speed, and Jason wondered whether that was why he thought of him as wily. Chris seemed like he was in charge, and liked to think he was, but in the old days, Pete was often the one pulling the strings.

"Don't tell me you're interested in joining us, Jase?" Pete looked surprised. "You love rules. This work might be a little too ... grey for you."

"I'm more comfortable with grey these days. And besides, the jobs will be done whether or not I do it. Why shouldn't I cash in?"

The three men shared a look. They didn't believe him.

"Look, maybe you're right. Maybe it's not for me. But it's worth looking into, right?"

"Yeah, fair enough," said Adam. "It *is* good money." They all laughed.

"I knew it, you dodgy bugger!" Jason flicked a bottle cap at Adam, who blocked it, causing it to hit Chris in the head. A small, good-hearted fight broke out with everyone flicking whatever was on the table at each other, and Jason was reminded of the easy times with the guys back in the day.

"Alright, alright," Jason put up his hands in surrender. "So, help me out. Do all your tasks come through the company, or can you get jobs from other sources?"

"Mainly through the company," said Adam.

"I suppose some guys get jobs from outside." Pete was still eyeing Jason cautiously.

"But you don't?"

They all looked at each other. "I mean, if something good comes up, we'll take it," said Chris. "But it'd have to be pretty good."

"Like what?" Jason pressed. "Can you tell me about any jobs?"

"Aw, you know. Finding lost stuff. Escorting people places. Acquiring things. Nothing spectacular."

Acquiring things. Like felixium?

Before Jason could ask anything else, they stood.

"Anyways buddy, we'd better head out. Good seeing you," said Pete.

"Yeah, and if you need us to hook you up with the company, hit us up," said Adam, shaking Jason's hand again.

"Cool, thanks," Jason said, standing and walking out with them. "Appreciate it, guys. I'll be in touch."

Jason walked out of the mess hall and took a lazy route back toward his vehicle through the PSC compound. He walked slowly, but projected a sense of purpose, looking around as best he could without raising suspicion. It was a large compound, but not as big as the military base. He spotted a couple of structures that could fit the stolen trucks, but with the amount of vehicles that would be required by the PSCs, it was unlikely that there was much extra space. And certainly not enough where a significant number of people wouldn't notice some suspicious trucks parked in the corner.

Deciding to try to come back to the PSC compound as much as possible while he was in the DR to try to rebuild the relationship with his old colleagues in the hopes of getting a lead, Jason got in his car and made the short trip back to the base, then headed to his room.

Jason closed the door and sat heavily on the small bed. The room was spartan in appearance, but was reassuringly familiar to Jason, and he felt himself relaxing. He pulled out his phone and called Hudson, who answered on the third ring.

"How's the DR?" Hudson asked without bothering

with preliminaries. He was one of Jason's friends from his military days. His magic let him connect with technology and, following the loss of his legs, Hudson had used that to build his business. He was very sought-after in the technology world. Despite the fact that he must have been making a significant amount of money, he had found the time to help Jason and Naomi with their investigation. Jason had a lot of respect for his old friend.

"Peachy. Just ran into some of our old buddies." Jason told Hudson about their brief conversation and Hudson scoffed.

"Bloody mercenary bastards. I'll run some searches. You like them for the felixium job, right?"

"I was thinking that," admitted Jason. "I'd bet they at least know who did it. How's it been going up there? You keeping out of trouble?"

With the expansion of the HSP and correlating diminishing freedoms, Jason was particularly worried about Hudson, who was known to take risks.

"Oh sure," said Hudson unconvincingly. "I'm working with Claire, looking into that Ezra Brown bloke."

"How's that going?" Jason asked, thinking that with Ezra's new role, cyberstalking him might be a bad idea.

"Really good," said Hudson, brightening. "She's pretty smart, isn't she? And I like the way she thinks."

Jason smiled. It would seem his friend had taken a shine to Claire. "I meant the searching."

"Oh," said Hudson, completely unembarrassed. "Nothing really useful, at least not yet. I mean, there's no handy email titled 'how I stole the felixium and why', but there are a few weird emails to Ava and about Ava that I'll flick through to you. Nothing major in them, but they just seem a bit odd. Otherwise, I'm helping her look for anything on this 'Patriot' figure that's running the nationalist movement."

"Figured out who he is yet?"

"Or she," Hudson corrected Jason, a smile in his voice. "Nah. I'm letting Claire run with that one at the moment. Giving her access to what she needs and letting her look around."

"That all sounds good. But please make sure both of you stay below the radar. No unnecessary risks, got it? At this point, there aren't enough of us to risk sacrificing anyone."

"Awwww, he cares," teased Hudson. "Don't worry about us. We're keeping it safe. You need to watch your back, though. If our old friends didn't pull off the job, they'd still do you over for some cash. And if they did steal the felixium... well, no one's heard from the guys who were driving when the trucks went missing, have they?"

28

"Favourite ice cream?"

"Mint choc chip."

"Eww."

"Not 'eww', it's delicious," said Lily, faux offended.

"It's not, it's gross," said Ava.

"Well, what's yours?"

"Fairy fudge fundae," said Ava, without hesitation.

"What's that?"

"It's caramel ice cream with—wait, where'd she go?"

Lily and Ava looked around for April, who they'd been following across the city for the last hour.

"She turned here ..." said Lily almost to herself, looking around for where her sister might have gone. "You don't think she saw us?"

"Nope, this way," said Ava from the mouth of a side street. "She just turned down there."

Lily hurried over to see where Ava was pointing. They both moved quickly to the next turn before peering around the corner cautiously. This part of the city was much more suburban than the area where April and Elaine lived, but it had small foot paths that wound between the houses and buildings and were often almost hidden by trees. It was much more relaxing than the hustle and bustle of the city centre.

Ava resumed the twenty questions game they had been playing. Lily was enjoying her company, glad that she had opted to help her tail April rather than go to work with Alexei. Lily knew that Ava's decision was likely based on preferring not to clean another break room, but she hoped some of it was wanting to spend time with Lily as much as Lily wanted to spend time with Ava. The official reasoning was that it would be easier to track April with both of their special skills, and Lily had to admit that she might have lost April without Ava's help. Though admittedly without Ava, she might have been paying closer attention.

"Blue, like a really deep blue. Hey, you don't think this was selfish, do you? The two of us following April while Alexei works?" Lily looked at Ava, her eyes seeking reassurance.

"Not at all. If your mum has a way for us to get home, we need to secure it. I mean, if it's a way home that can be used whenever, then we could even plan the return. Stay here an extra couple of weeks to get your sisters sorted and then go. Plus, we're really doing Alexei a favour." Ava's mouth curled into a sly grin.

"How do you figure?" asked Lily, her mind on how dirty the last break room had been.

"We probably won't be back for dinner, which means he gets time with Elaine. Alone." Ava wiggled her eyebrows at Lily, who laughed and playfully pushed Ava away.

"They won't be alone. April will be there."

"Will she though?" Ava looked at her watch. "With how long it took to get here, and then she's going to visit with your mum ... I bet she's told Elaine that she's studying at a friend's place. That or your return is just too much, and she needs a break."

Lily frowned at that, but had to agree with Ava. If April visited her mother regularly, she might even have a standard "study date" in place.

"Looks like we're here," said Ava.

Lily looked at the building April had entered. The mental health facility was essentially a large house, but it was surrounded by a tall, secure fence. The building didn't look fancy, but it was certainly not falling apart. It looked clean and cosy, and Lily wondered how her mother was able to afford to stay here while Elaine was working herself into the ground. She couldn't imagine any of them currently had health insurance, though her parents used to have yearly plans. Maybe her mother's was still active.

"Well," said Lily, looking at the gate, "wish me luck."

"Good luck," said Ava, giving her arm a comforting squeeze. "You'll be fine. Are you sure you don't want me to wait for you?"

"No, follow April. Please," she added hurriedly. She had asked Ava to tail April after she left and Lily went to talk to their mother. Mainly to ensure she got home safely, but in part because if she was lying about visiting their mother, she might be hiding something else.

"You got it," said Ava, who wandered over to a gap between two houses and disappeared from sight.

Lily looked back at the mental health facility, took a deep breath, and pushed the gate open.

"Oh! Your sister just arrived," smiled the receptionist after Lily explained who she was. "Just sign in here."

Lily concentrated on the large blue book asking for her information.

"Your mum is going to be so excited. It's usually just your sister visiting."

Lily didn't know if she imagined the note of judgement in the receptionist's voice.

Maybe I'm just feeling guilty.

"I know, I've been away. I came back as soon as I could. How has Mum been?"

"I can get one of the nurses to talk to you if you'd like?"

"That would be great, thank you."

Lily wandered around the reception area looking at the pictures on the walls until a short, serious woman in pink scrubs approached her.

"Lily? You're one of Belinda's daughters?"

"Yes, hello."

They shook hands, and the nurse started walking towards a door to their left.

"Belinda's physically very healthy," she began, leading Lily through a warren of corridors. "But mentally, since she's been with us, she's been uncommunicative."

"She doesn't speak? At all?" Lily was surprised. Clearly Belinda was talking when Elaine had her committed the last time. And if she wasn't communicating, why was April visiting? She felt guilty for that last thought, but given everything else going on, surely April would prefer to be at home with Elaine.

But Elaine is always at work.

Lily frowned to herself, which the nurse took to be concern.

"She turned up one night, and all she said was 'they're all gone' and since then, nothing."

"And when was that?"

"Gosh, two months ago? No, probably closer to three now."

They rounded a corner, and Lily found herself in an expansive backyard. It had been landscaped to create several nooks and crannies so that patients could enjoy it, but have some relative privacy. Lily saw April sitting next to their mother on a bench in the rear of the garden, under a tall tree. Lily stopped, and the nurse looked at her in surprise.

"Er, I might just let them have their time together first," Lily said. "Sorry, can you tell me, how is my mother's care being paid for?"

The nurse raised an eyebrow but said, "Her health insurance at the moment. But her coverage lapses next month. Your sister said you're all looking into it and will decide whether to pay for continued treatment or take her home and care for her there."

Lily thanked the nurse, who bustled off to attend to other matters. Wandering over to a corner of the garden where she could keep an eye on April while remaining hidden by a hedge, Lily wondered what April was planning. There was no way that they would be able to pay for her treatment. And she was hiding her visits from Elaine. Was she just going to take their mother back to the apartment and surprise Elaine when she got home from work one night?

She moved closer and could make out some of what April was saying. Her little sister was prattling on about her day, telling their mother stories about school, while Belinda stared into the distance at nothing and didn't acknowledge that her youngest child was next to her.

Lily felt sick. Poor April. This was all too much for Lily —how was her sixteen-year-old sister handling it all? She resolved to fix things with April, and properly this time.

On a whim, Lily focussed on her mother, reaching into her mind and trying to find her thoughts. She had resigned herself to trying to talk to her—she was here now and had come all this way—but perhaps she could do so without being obvious about trying to get information from her.

Information that it looked like Belinda couldn't give her, even if she wanted to.

Frowning, Lily probed some more, and thought she saw Belinda twitch. Nothing. She remembered a time that felt like years ago now, when Claire had let her test her mind reading powers on her. She had let her mind go blank and Lily had felt like she was in a void. This was similar, and Lily wondered if it was because her mother's mind had truly gone. She could believe that to be the case, watching her sitting, oblivious to her daughter sitting there, yearning for connection.

After about forty-five minutes, April began to wind up the visit. Lily felt shame at how impressed she was, knowing that, were their situations reversed, Lily wouldn't have spent so long with their catatonic mother. She watched April cross the garden and enter the house, then gave it another five minutes for good measure, just in case April had forgotten something.

Standing slowly and stretching her numb legs, Lily walked over to her mother and sat beside her. Belinda barely blinked.

"Hi Mum. It's me. Er, Lily," she said awkwardly. "I'm back. I mean, obviously. I'm here and all. Not that you seem to realise it," she muttered, glancing at her mother, who hadn't moved and was still staring into space.

This is stupid.

Lily exhaled slowly, wanting to leave but telling herself that if April could do this once a week, Lily could talk to her for half an hour. Twenty minutes, at least.

"It's a bit of an unbelievable story. How I went missing. Makes me sound crazier than you," she teased before she realised the joke was in extremely poor taste, and she glanced at her mother to see if she was upset. But Belinda still hadn't moved. "It has to do with dimensions and stuff.

Oh, and I'm a princess, apparently. Did you know that? That I'm the heir to the throne of a whole country in a different dimension? They took me back to make me queen, but someone pushed me back here when I was on my way to the coronation and now I'm waiting to be rescued."

"So it was all for nothing then," said Belinda.

Lily stared at her mother, open-mouthed, wondering if she had imagined the words. "What?" she asked dumbly.

Belinda sighed, her body relaxing slightly. "If you're going to be queen, dear, you will need to ask more articulate questions."

Lily continued staring. Her mother was definitely talking, but she maintained her spacey demeanour.

"You can talk?"

"I suppose that's better, but I was thinking something slightly higher level. And please stop gawking at me. You'll draw their attention."

Lily snapped her mouth shut and looked around. No one was paying them any attention. She relaxed her posture and sat back on the bench, her mind beginning to catch up. She felt a sudden flame of anger.

"Wait, you've been faking? Why? And why the hell aren't you talking to April?"

She felt her mother take a deep breath, though she didn't see her move.

"When I first came here, I was ... I wasn't well. I'm not proud of it, but I just wasn't coping. When Elaine and David put me in the hospital, I thought I was fine. I was angry that they'd locked me up. I left the hospital wanting some space so I didn't yell at them. I figured I'd stay in a cheap hotel, get set up with a job and then come back and ..." Belinda's shoulders shrugged. "I don't know. Everything would be fine and we'd go back to normal."

Lily could hear Belinda's voice cracking. She wanted to

reach out and comfort her mother, empathy replacing her anger instantly, but she saw the nurses with other patients on the other side of the garden and worried about attracting attention.

"It's okay, Mum," she began.

"No, it's not," said Belinda, her voice hardening. "When I sat on my bed in my room, alone, essentially stopping for the first time in months, it all just hit me. You'd disappeared, we lost the farm, and then Bruce—" Her voice caught and she took a moment to regain her composure.

"I just couldn't think properly. Couldn't operate. I was crying all the time. I thought a day had passed, but it was a week. I realised I needed help. I couldn't help my children until I was better. So I came here. I was so tired, I didn't really answer them at first, and then I realised I didn't have to. As it turned out, not talking helped me get my spot with the insurance—I didn't lie," she said defensively, though Lily hadn't said anything. "They just assumed and then ... well, I realised correcting them would look like I was getting better and then I'd have to leave. I still wasn't well enough to work, and Elaine was already working so much just to support herself and April. I didn't want to be a burden."

"You couldn't have found a way to let April know you were alright?" Lily asked, thinking of her little sister, abandoned by everyone.

"Not without the staff finding out. And I didn't want to put that on her. She's already keeping her visits secret from Elaine. Why make her a part of the lie?"

Lily couldn't argue with that, and a silence settled over her and her mother. Eventually, Belinda moved slightly.

"So, you've been in Highacre, then?" her mother finally asked.

"Yeah. It was a bit of a shock to be kidnapped, taken to

another dimension, and told I was royalty. You already knew, I take it?"

Belinda just grunted.

"Couldn't you have given me a heads up?"

"I know I should have. I always meant to. But when you were little, I thought I shouldn't because you'd just tell your sisters or your dad. And then when you were a little older, you always felt slightly left out, and I thought knowing would aggravate that. And then suddenly you were about to leave home, and it just felt too late. There was never a right time, and, well, to be honest, the longer it went without anyone from Highacre coming to take you back, the more I thought maybe … I thought maybe I'd get to keep you."

Lily heard the emotion in her mother's voice and wanted desperately to grab her hand. Instead, she kept an eye on the nurses, hoping that they wouldn't interrupt. She needed to hear this.

"When they gave you to me, I tried to keep myself distant from you. Tell myself that you weren't mine. To not get attached. But you were just such a sweet little thing, and you loved your brother and sisters. And Bruce loved you as his own. I couldn't help it. You were my daughter. *Are* my daughter," Belinda said fiercely.

"How did I … when did you get me?"

A nurse glanced over at them and checked her watch.

"We won't have much more time," said Belinda. "Can you mind read?"

"Yes."

"Good, quickly, here—look at this memory."

29

Belinda was washing dishes in the sink, and every so often gazing out the window at the beautiful day and her husband and two small children playing in the yard. She sighed in contentment. Sure, it was a hard life at times on the farm, but she didn't mind; she was with her best friend, and they were doing it for their kids.

A knock at the door startled Belinda out of her daydream. Shaking the suds off her hands, she wiped them on her apron front and headed down the hallway. They weren't expecting anyone, or any deliveries. Maybe it was their neighbour Olive, who had become just a little too needy since her husband left to take up fly in, fly out work to supplement their farm.

Belinda paused before opening the door and took a deep breath. *Please don't be selling something.*

"Addison! What on Earth are you doing here?"

"Hello Belinda." Addison smiled. "Long time no see."

Belinda looked around anxiously. Had anyone else seen Addison? Was anyone watching them speak now?

"Come in—no! Wait, around the back, hurry."

Belinda ushered Addison around the side of the house, away from her family.

Still too open.

She kept moving, keeping Addison close. Addison was smiling as if this was funny, which just made Belinda angry.

"Okay, this will have to do," Belinda muttered. "So, what are you doing here?"

"Oh Belinda, you have such a lovely family!" Addison gushed, looking over Belinda's shoulder.

Swearing, Belinda pushed Addison out of sight behind the water tank and ordered her to stay put. She walked towards her husband and kids, who were still playing and oblivious to the visitor who was causing Belinda so much angst.

"Darling," Belinda called, "I'm just popping into the store for a bit. Just want to restock the shelves for tomorrow."

"No worries, love. Need a hand?"

"No no, uh, I'm actually looking forward to the peace and quiet."

Belinda's husband, Bruce, laughed easily. "I'll bet! No worries, love. We'll be here." And he turned his attention back to the kids, chasing them and causing squeals of delight. Belinda watched for a second, smiling. She couldn't believe how lucky she was to have such an amazing family. Her face darkened as she remembered her visitor, and she hurried back around the water tank, half expecting Addison to have vanished.

"They're so sweet Belinda, you're very lucky."

"Yes, I am. Come on." Belinda grabbed Addison's hand and led her to the family's store, where they sold produce from the farm and the various things that Belinda made, such as jams and hand creams, when she had the time.

"Ooooh, this is nice," said Addison, looking around the store with interest.

Belinda ignored her, rushing to the front door to make sure it was locked and slamming down all the blinds over the windows. She turned to see Addison looking at her with amused interest.

"Addison, what are you doing here?" Belinda asked.

"Good to see you too, old friend," Addison quipped. "You knew one of us would turn up at some point. Are you really that surprised to see me?"

Belinda scowled and moved towards the back of the store and into a small break room. She walked to the kettle and gestured, offering Addison a cup of tea, which Addison accepted. Addison sat, and the women were silent for a time while Belinda busied herself making the tea.

Belinda tried to calm her racing mind. Addison was right. This shouldn't be a surprise. Belinda had known when she accepted this mission that at some point, the agency would call on her. But it had just been so long, and she had become comfortable. Belinda froze. She realised with a shock that she had gone completely native, believing her cover. Living her cover. She was completely compromised.

"I'm not here to bring you back," Addison said quietly.

Belinda whirled around, fixing her eyes on Addison. That was exactly what she would say if they were going to extract her and needed to keep her calm. Automatically, Belinda's mind examined her mental map of the area, plotting routes if she needed to escape, each one taking her past one of the many caches she had planted around the property. When had she last checked and restocked them?

"Belinda!" Addison stood and gently placed her hands on Belinda's arms, looking her in the eye. "I'm not here to extract you. They'd never send me, you know that." She clocked the suspicion in Belinda's eyes. "And no, I'm not here to distract you from the extraction team." She sighed and sat back down in her chair. "Bel, we need your help."

Something about Addison's tone made Belinda believe her, that she wasn't here to extract her. She knew her friend well. Something was wrong.

It was Addison's inability to cover her emotions and intentions that had seen her do poorly at the academy, and Belinda's ability to hide hers effortlessly that earned her the prize for best new agent. Despite being so different, when they had met that first day, both dreaming of being an agent in the Highacren Intelligence Agency, something clicked, and they quickly became inseparable.

After graduation, Belinda was sent on her first assignment, and Addison was offered a position as a desk officer. Again, Belinda had excelled, and got sent on more dangerous and deeply undercover missions, whereas Addison was clearly not suited to the HIA as an organisation. She was much too friendly and enjoyed gossiping a little too much. These traits ensured she knew someone who knew someone, and in the same conversation where the agency explained that she just wasn't the right fit, Addison was offered a position in the royal household.

Inevitably, the two had drifted apart, talking and writing less, though Belinda realised she would still count Addison as one of her best friends, despite not having seen or spoken to her in over a decade.

When Belinda accepted her current assignment, she had known that it was long-term, deep undercover, but she hadn't realised it would be her last assignment. Belinda was selected as one of only a handful of agents to go through the new interdimensional travel machine and live in one of the other worlds that had been discovered. Her mission was to assimilate into the culture and feed information back to the

HIA about the world in general, with a focus on technological advances and weaponry.

Belinda had dutifully carried out her mission. With the resources provided, she had bought a run-down farm and used that as a base, then travelled around, hanging out at universities and looking for work in government agencies. At first, someone from the agency had come to the farm to get her intelligence every three months like clockwork. Then she was told that they only needed her report yearly, and then she was informed that "it might be a while" before anyone came as resources were tight. She never saw anyone from Highacre again.

Belinda had kept up her efforts at first. But then, eventually, she had to admit to herself that something had gone wrong. She became distracted and slightly panicked about the idea of being stranded in this alternate world. And then she met Bruce. She fell in love, and they fixed up her farm and started a family. Belinda had put Highacre behind her. And now here was her old friend. Asking for help.

"Addy, are you okay?" Belinda suddenly became worried that it was Addison who was in trouble.

Addison looked up at her old friend. "Yes Bel, I'm fine. It's the royal family that's in trouble. That's why they sent me."

Belinda handed Addison her tea, and Addison told Belinda all about the threat to the family, the attempts on their lives that were being kept from everyone, and the fact that the HIA was clueless as to who was behind it.

"You need me to come and investigate," Belinda said. She steeled herself. She could do it. She'd tell Bruce that she needed to go away for a while. He'd understand. He was so good to her. *But what if I can't come back?* Belinda shook the thought away. She'd get back. Mission first, then home.

"No," Addison broke into Belinda's thoughts, and her plans disintegrated.

"Oh. Well, then what?"

"Belinda, it's been decided that one of the king's children should be hidden to preserve the royal line. We're hoping that you'll take care of him or her. Bring them into your family and raise them as your own."

Belinda stared at Addison, stunned. Of all the scenarios that she had run through in her head, nothing close to this had come up. Raise a royal?

"To what end?" Belinda asked. "Raise them to go back at some point?"

"Well ..." Addison looked slightly uncomfortable. "Possibly. This was the subject of much debate. The plan is that if something happens to the rest of the royal family, then the prince or princess would be extracted and returned to Highacre to ascend the throne. But if everything is fine, or at least one of the other siblings survives, then there would be no need for the child to return. It has been decided that it would be less disruptive to leave them to live here."

Belinda stared at her. "So, let me get this straight. You want me to take a royal child, raise them without telling them about Highacre or that they're royalty, give them no training to be royalty or to use their magic, and then they may or may not go back and become the sovereign?"

"Yes."

"Right."

"Belinda." Addison reached for her friend, grasping Belinda's hand. "The plan, well, the hope is that the hidden heir will not be required. They are confident that they can protect the family such that at least one heir in Highacre is safe, and therefore they mean for the hidden heir to remain here forever. With you." She smiled at Belinda. "I'm also to tell you that this will be your last assignment. Raise the child and keep them safe. That's all we ask."

Belinda thought of her husband and children, playing by the house, blissfully ignorant as to how their lives were about to change. Of course she would take the child. There was no way she could say no to that. She would come up with a cover for Bruce. Some friend or distant relative who was in trouble. Of course he would agree to help. He was such a sweet man.

"You know I will," Belinda said quietly.

"I do know." Addison smiled back. "That's why I said I would come. It didn't matter who told you, you were going to say yes. I just wanted to see you. One last time."

The two women embraced and cried, remembering their youth together, their hopes and dreams. How differently their lives had turned out compared to what they had both imagined back then. Too soon, it was time for Addison to go. Belinda was told that in a couple of months, the queen would arrive to have her baby. They said their goodbyes, and Belinda walked back to her family.

"You're a Highacren *spy*? Wait, what are your powers?"

"Mind reading and lie detection."

This explained a lot about how her mum knew what she was up to as a kid. And, she realised with a jolt, why she couldn't read her mother's mind earlier. She must have put up a powerful barrier.

"And you can use your powers here? Why does everyone back in Highacre think they don't work?"

"They work differently here," Belinda said impatiently, obviously conscious of their time running short. "By the time I realised I could use my magic, Highacre wasn't really checking in with me anymore."

A nurse started crossing the garden towards Lily and Belinda. Both women tensed, but another nurse stopped the first, asking her something.

"Look, Mum, things are *really* bad back in Highacre. We need to get back as soon as possible. Elaine mentioned something you said—she thought you were rambling—but it sounded to me like you might have an emergency portal or something? A way to get back?"

Belinda hesitated. "I do have a way back," she admitted. "But Lily, things are really bad here, too. Elaine and April need help."

"So *you* help them," said Lily, suddenly angry and resentful. "People are dying back home."

Belinda flinched slightly when she called Highacre home.

"Highacre forgot about me," Belinda hissed, unable to hide the hurt from her voice. "They eventually came back again when it suited them, but they were happy to ditch me here and move on. I have no loyalty to Highacre anymore. My loyalty is to my children."

"Your *real* children," Lily hissed back.

She could tell that hurt Belinda, but her mother seemed to have no comeback.

"Look," Belinda said eventually, eyes flicking to the nurse who had turned back toward them. "Your sisters need money. You can help them get back on their feet, and then I'll give you the device and you can go and help Highacre."

"I don't have the time to work here to get enough money for Elaine—"

"If you were on your way to the coronation, you were in that ridiculous dress. The gems are worth a bundle."

"They were stolen," Lily admitted.

"I have every confidence that the true queen of High-acre, rumoured from birth to be more powerful than anyone we've seen before, and her friends the Meridian spy and the Valmeadian pretty boy, can track down and retrieve the gems."

"How do you—"

"April told me. From the sounds of things, you're all more than capable of robbing a pawnshop."

"They've probably sold them by now," Lily muttered, annoyed and thrown that her mother was encouraging her to break and enter.

"Then steal the money," hissed Belinda, equally frustrated.

"What a lovely day for you Belinda!" said the nurse loudly in the happy voice reserved for vulnerable people. "Two daughters visiting!"

Lily felt judgement in the nurse's eyes as she beamed at Lily.

"Visiting time is over now, but perhaps your daughter will come back again?" she asked Lily, though ostensibly speaking to the catatonic Belinda.

"Oh yes," said Lily, standing and looking down at her mother. "I'll be back again. Soon."

30

Jason stood in the middle of the intersection where the ambush happened. If Naomi hadn't told him where it was, he might not have found it. He had to admit, he'd known she was a powerful revealer when he'd hired her, but he'd had no idea the extent of her power. Revealers could sense magic to different extents. That was how they could tell if an invisible or chameleoning person was nearby. But Naomi could sense where magic had been used in the past. And unused as this intersection was, she had been able to pick up the faint remanent of the attack.

The intersection looked like any other intersection down in the DR. The road was typical for a remote area; run-down but wide enough for trucks to pass each other comfortably. Both intersecting roads had been laid in the middle of relatively dense bushland. Trees bordered the highway, but with the width of the roads, a large truck could probably still pull off a U-turn in the intersection. Especially if this was the usual traffic tempo. Jason hadn't seen another vehicle for over an hour.

It was hard to believe that this used to be the main highway through the DR from Meridia to Highacre. Both sides had upgraded infrastructure during the war to get their troops and vehicles to the front line, but after the war, a new highway was opened. It seemed no one came this way anymore.

Unless you're covertly moving a truckload of a rare mineral.

Clearly, someone had leaked the convoy's movements. No one had been waiting at this intersection by coincidence.

Having scanned his surroundings, Jason went into tracker mode. For him, his ability was like having secondary information and colours highlighted in his vision. Looking around the intersection, some broken glass off the road's shoulder glowed a light blue, and some dull reddish footprints showed up. But the brightest colour was a green off in the bush. He'd start there.

Pushing through some bushes, Jason found the traces of a trail. He could see a set of footprints following it, some heading out wherever it led and some heading back towards the road. His ability didn't really give him detail; he wouldn't be able to tell the size of the person's shoes, or whether it was multiple people, or just one person taking multiple trips. But he could only see one set of prints each way, so he was comfortable assuming it was probably just one person making both trips.

He followed the path, winding up and up until the dense bush parted and he could see he was on a cliff. In the distance was the military base, and farther out, the mines. In the foreground was the intersection. He had a perfect view.

Jason squatted down and examined the area around his feet. Nothing. He lowered himself until he was prone on his chest. He could still see the intersection from that position. Again, he scanned the ground. This time, something very small glowed off to his right. He shuffled over and picked it up. A sunflower seed.

Pete.

He could almost feel Pete there, in the same spot, watching for the convoy. Jason stood and scanned the area again. He was going to need significantly more than a seed and a feeling to link Pete to the ambush. But it was a start.

Jason had returned to the PSC compound on both of the last two days. He hadn't seen his friends again and was suspicious that they were avoiding him. Now he felt certain that was what was going on. He glanced around nervously. Avoiding was one thing, but could they be watching him?

Jason walked slowly back out of the overwatch area, still scanning the ground at his feet. A dull glow appeared off to his left. He scratched at it. Something metal was buried beneath the leaves and dirt. A small pin. Jason used his thumb to nudge the dirt off the face and saw his old unit insignia. His feeling intensified. It was a common pin, and not something exclusive to the unit. Thousands of them had been made, maybe more. They were sold for charity fundraisers for injured veterans. Still, as far as coincidences went ...

Jason walked back down to the intersection to look for more clues. Either his old mates were behind the ambush, or someone wanted him to think they were. For the next twenty minutes, Jason followed each individual set of footprints that he could find at the intersection. Some gave him nothing. Possibly truck drivers who had pulled over and relieved themselves in the bushes. But slowly, he managed to plot out the positions of four people in addition to the person in the overwatch position.

Scanning the intersection again, he frowned. Five people was not many for an ambush. There had been ten special forces soldiers escorting the goods, not to mention the drivers for the trucks and escort vehicles. Unless ... how had he forgotten? They had all loved going on patrol with Adam. If they could get him close enough to the enemy, he could paralyse up to three people and significantly slow the movement of another six on top of that. If it was his old comrades behind the theft, Adam alone would have evened the odds exponentially.

A fallen tree lit up in Jason's peripheral vision. It was partially hidden by some underbrush. That was not where it had fallen. Concentrating, Jason could see faint drag marks. They had used it to block the convoy, forcing the trucks to stop, then overpowered the soldiers and stole the felixium.

Killed or captured?

Jason looked for signs of a struggle or of injuries. There was no blood that he could see, but that didn't necessarily mean anything. He had worked with a number of soldiers who had abilities that could kill someone without leaving a trace.

Jason returned to his car and sat, staring at the intersection, trying to imagine what had happened. The convoy would have entered the intersection, but stopped, its path blocked by the tree. Some guys would have gotten out to check the hazard, and he couldn't imagine that they wouldn't have been suspicious. Which means more of them would have exited their vehicles, but they should have been on heightened alert.

By the look of the tree, the convoy didn't have anyone with telekinetic powers. They must have prioritised offensive and defensive abilities. Leaving some keeping watch, they would have tried to move the tree. The vehicles should have had a winch. Perhaps by this time the soldiers would have been alert, but more relaxed, assuming any assault would have happened by that point.

Pete and his buddies probably let them move the tree. It would have saved time on the getaway, as they wouldn't have to move it themselves, and no one else would happen upon a suspiciously blocked road. Then they would have struck. Adam would have fixed the guards keeping watch, while the others addressed those still in vehicles.

Chris could make you feel heavy. If he focussed just on one person, they'd feel like they were made of lead and couldn't move. It weakened the more people he tried to affect, but if he focussed on the people in the vehicles, they would find it difficult to raise their weapons. Even to get out of their vehicle.

Pete sowed confusion. He would have overlaid a fog of uncertainty, ensuring that they couldn't mount a cohesive defence.

Jason saw it as clearly as if he were watching a recording. Even with just the three of them, they would have had a good shot at pulling it off. Who knew what abilities the other two people had. He leant back in his seat and rubbed his face. The big question was, where had they taken the felixium? There were four options. They probably hadn't gone along the same path the convoy had been heading. That led back to Highacre, and the next place for them to turn off the main highway was almost in view of the border. Checkpoint guards seeing the convoy acting strangely would have been a deterrent.

Back toward the mines? Possible. The mines were now under Meridian control and would certainly have space to hide the convoy. But it also meant travelling directly past the Highacren military base. No one there reported seeing or hearing a convoy after this one left on its ill-fated trip.

So, right or left? Jason pulled up a map of the area. There was nothing much over to the left, but that could make it a good place to hide a couple of trucks. On the right,

Jason could sketch out a roundabout way to the facility where he'd met up with Pete and the boys. The PSC's home base. Surely that would be too risky. However, there were a number of other buildings on the map. He had no idea what they were, but there certainly seemed to be a few options that way.

Jason started the car and turned off to the right. He'd been driving for less than five minutes when he saw a checkpoint up ahead. The guards were wearing the same PSC uniform as his buddies. Deciding against driving up to the checkpoint, he turned left and continued on his way for a while, but stopped after seeing another checkpoint.

What don't you want people to find?

Jason continued driving around, marking the area that was being blocked on his map. According to his map and his online searches, there was nothing there, but they were obviously protecting something. On a whim, he drove up to the first checkpoint that he had seen.

"Good afternoon, sir. Identification, please."

The contractor manning the gate was all business. Jason handed over his credentials.

"I've done my fair share of guard duty, mate. You have my sympathy."

The guard didn't acknowledge that Jason spoke. He was not going to be able to build rapport here. Direct approach then.

"You've got quite a few checkpoints over here. What are you guarding?"

The guard finished looking at Jason's credentials and took a photo of them with his phone. At that, Jason started to get nervous. Why did he need a picture, and who was he going to send it too? Now that they knew where Lily was and that she was waiting for them, the pressure had increased. The idea of doing anything that set them back now was sickening. The guard handed his credentials back.

"I'm sorry sir, but you are not authorised to enter this area."

"I'm the head of the Royal Guard." *Or at least I was.* "I'm authorised to go pretty much everywhere in Highacre, or Highacren-controlled territory."

"Sorry, sir, but I do not have clearance to let you through."

"Well, who do I speak to to get clearance?"

"I'm not authorised to tell you that."

Jason looked at the guard in exasperation. "What's your name?"

"Bill, sir."

"Bill what?"

"I'm sorry sir—"

"What is your supervisor's name?"

"I'm sorry sir—"

"Bill." Jason was getting angry now. "You know I'm just going to drive away, have my people look up whatever your contract is for and who arranged it, call the people in charge, and have them give me authorisation. Now, when I do, I can leave out that you were an obstinate turd, or I can express my displeasure that your behaviour has taken the time out of several important people's days. Which would you prefer?"

The guard looked at Jason. His reflective sunglasses meant that Jason couldn't see his eyes, but while he managed to keep his face passive, Jason was sure he was smirking on the inside.

"I'm sorry sir—"

Jason put the car in reverse and sped away from the checkpoint.

31

"So she won't help us until we get money for Elaine and April," Lily finished briefing Ava and Alexei on her visit with Belinda. They were huddled in the living room, trying to keep their voices down so Lily's sisters wouldn't overhear.

April was in her room, allegedly doing her homework, but likely avoiding Lily, and Elaine was getting changed for her night job.

"I think this is fair," said Alexei, looking pleased. "We should try to help your sisters."

Lily stared at Alexei. "I mean, yeah, but don't you think it's messed up that she won't help me? She should trust that I would help them anyway."

"But we weren't going to try to get the gems back," said Alexei in an entirely reasonable way that annoyed Lily. "And if she had given you the device, would you have stuck around to help them?"

"Of course I would!" said Lily loudly before immediately being shushed by Ava.

The three sat in silence for a beat, listening in case they had attracted the attention of Lily's sisters.

"But probably not for long," said Alexei in a quiet,

286

gentle voice. "I get that it's hurtful, but your mother is doing you a favour in taking the decision out of your hands."

"What decision?"

"Having to choose between your family and your country," said Alexei.

Lily didn't want him to be right. She was mad at her mother, and any interpretation that was favourable to Belinda was currently unwelcome. Alexei seemed to sense this and patted Lily's shoulder with a smile.

"Right. So, how are we going to find the gems?" he asked.

"Ava, you're quiet," said Lily. "You coming up with a plan?"

Ava shifted uncomfortably. "I was thinking," she started and then hesitated, looking at Alexei slightly guiltily. "Belinda would keep the device close, right? Like it was probably at the farm with her and then she brought it here. Maybe she took it with her when she left the family apartment? Maybe ..." She glanced between Alexei and Lily. "Maybe she has it with her at the facility."

"That would be good," said Alexei. "She can just hand it over once we help Lily's sisters." His tone held a note of warning.

"You think we should just break in and take it?" Lily asked.

Ava looked tentatively at Lily and nodded. Alexei looked away, as if embarrassed for Ava that she would suggest such a thing, and confident that Lily, like him, would shut her down and focus instead on helping her sisters.

"We could do that," said Lily slowly. Alexei whipped his head around, staring at her.

"Or we could help your sisters, which was the whole point of finding your family in the first place."

"We can still help them even if we get the device," said Lily, not entirely convincingly. She mentally checked herself. She *would* help her sisters before she left. Alexei was right. That had been her plan, and she was not going to abandon it or her family just because things were much, much harder than she had imagined when she was pushing her friends to help find her family.

But meeting with her mother had shocked Lily, leaving her completely unsettled. She was so used to her mum being the pillar of strength in their family. To come home and find her not only absent, but seemingly hiding from the overwhelming tragedy that had befallen their family, was difficult for her to wrap her head around.

Lily was suddenly struck by the parallel. Hadn't she too been fantasising about needing to go back to Highacre? To problems that suddenly seemed easier to manage than dealing with the emotional turmoil and pressure of her family? How was she any better than her mother? She shook the unwanted thoughts away.

Ultimately, Lily was hurt. She had expected to come home to the mother she knew who would hold her and tell her everything would be alright. But everything was not alright, and her mother was not who she thought she was. Lily knew she needed to help her sisters, and she desperately wanted to help them. She loved Elaine and April, and would do everything in her power to make sure they were okay. And should she be sent back before she was able, at the first opportunity, she would return. She would not abandon her sisters.

But her mother demanding Lily help them, and the seeming lack of empathy for Lily's own situation, stung. She knew her mother was desperate about Elaine and April, and David, for that matter. But it felt like Lily was being treated differently.

It's because she knows you're okay. You haven't been living the hell that your siblings have.

But despite the truth in those words, part of Lily couldn't help but think the difference in treatment was due to her not being her mother's biological child. That she was happy to use Lily to help her real children.

"Look." She fixed her gaze on Alexei so that he could see the truth in her eyes. "That was wrong of me. I had a moment of weakness. Faced with this set of problems, the idea of escaping to Highacre seems appealing. I have no doubt that once I was there, I'd be wishing to come back here. And I can't focus on helping my people if I'm feeling guilty about abandoning my family when I could have helped. We won't go until we've done everything we can to set them up." She paused. "I do think Ava has a point though."

Ava sat up straighter and Alexei glared at her before starting to argue with Lily. She cut him off. "I wasn't expecting that from my mum. That she'd put conditions on helping me. And if she does have the device with her, it's possible that she'll try to hide it somewhere now that she knows I want it. I don't think she'll destroy it, but she isn't in the best frame of mind. She could lose it accidentally, or put it somewhere that she can't get it back from once they've kicked her out of that place. We need that device. I believe Giles when he says they're doing their best, but it sounds like they're struggling. They may not be able to help us.

"I think we try to secure the device first. Once we have it, we can go after the gems. We'll all be able to focus better when we know we can get home whenever we need to, and we'll be motivated because retrieving the gems will be the only thing in our way."

Alexei did not look convinced.

"And who knows if Belinda will even give it to us after

we get the gems?" Ava said, standing and beginning to pace. "Maybe she'll have other tasks for us. Maybe she's just not on board with letting Lily go back. We can't know for sure, but what I am certain of is that I need to get back. I've been gone too long. Who knows what might be happening? We need to get back as soon as possible. I mean, who knows if we will even be able to get the gems back at this point? They're likely long gone. If we go home, we can get—"

"I understand how you feel," Lily said firmly, interrupting Ava's rant. "And that you need to get back to your father. But my family is important too. We need to help them. I won't leave here without trying."

Ava blinked at Lily as if coming out of a daze. She shook her head. "I'm sorry, you're right. Of course, they're important and I know we need to help them. I want to help them." She looked imploringly at Lily, clearly needing Lily to believe her. "I panicked. It's just ... a lot."

"So we all agree we need to help Lily's family," said Alexei. "Which is why we should concentrate on the gems first."

Ava's head whipped around toward Alexei, her expression showing she was ready to argue, but she caught herself. "Look, part of my desire to get the device first is to see what we're working with. What if there's enough of whatever it was that powers it—"

"Felixium," Lily supplied.

"That it can sustain multiple trips? One of us could go back to get help while the other two look for the gems. Or we could simply get more resources to bring back and sell here. We could also bring back Lily's ID so we can get the best price. I admit," she cut off Alexei, hands raised as if in surrender, "I am thinking that the person to return would be me, and that I could also sort my personal stuff while I'm back there. But I really think this way gives us the best chance at concurrent activity. If we get the device, we have the control, but we can still help Elaine and April."

Alexei stared at Ava, trying to get a read on his friend. Lily considered her words. It did make sense. And if there was a way for Ava to go back first, she could even get Jason or Giles to sort out the ID and resources while she went to speak with her father.

"This discussion might be premature," said Alexei eventually. "Can we not plan both activities? It may well be that we are not all needed for each task. Maybe, like working and finding Lily's sisters, we could do both concurrently."

"That makes sense," said Lily quickly, before Ava could find an issue with Alexei's suggestion. "How are we even going to find out if the device is at my mother's facility?"

"Or where the gems might be now?" Alexei added.

The questions were met with silence, reminding them all that agreeing to the plan was merely the first step.

"I can't believe my mum was able to mentally block me," Lily said after a prolonged silence. "I've not come across anyone that powerful in Highacre. If I could just read her mind, I could figure out where the device is."

"She's not more powerful than you," said Ava. "You're just out of practise and she's had way more time to develop using her magic here. You just need to work on it."

"That's sweet," Lily said dismissively.

"No, it's reality. You're more powerful than she is. It took you mere months to go from no magic to being the most powerful person in Highacre. Give yourself a break, and some time. Now, let's get to planning."

32

"Okay ... go!"

At Ava's command, both women darted across the parking lot and toward the door. Ava was faster than Lily and managed to grab the handle just before it shut. Lily glanced around, but just like he had every half-hour while the two had been watching, the mental health nurse was hurrying toward the assigned smoking area, solely focussed on lighting up.

The planning the night before had been relatively short-lived. Without much information to go on, the consensus had been reached that they would split up and conduct surveillance on each venue. Alexei had been sent to try and find out if the gems were still at the pawnshop, and if so, gather information about how they might be retrieved. Aside from clearly preferring they focus on the gems, Alexei wouldn't attract the same attention that either Lily or Ava would.

They had agreed that Ava and Lily would similarly watch the mental health facility. Ava had been able to access the building plans using her implant, but while that gave them the layout, it didn't identify what each room was used for.

And so the plan was for them to watch the facility, enabling Ava to try and scan what she could, and for Lily to try and read the minds of any unsuspecting workers. Lily had been surprised when Alexei had agreed that if the opportunity presented itself, the women should attempt to recover the device.

"It's not as dangerous as the gems," he'd said reasonably. "If you're able to find it, and can get it without issue, I can't see why you shouldn't try."

Lily felt slightly guilty that they'd only been watching the facility for two hours before making an attempt to retrieve the device. Using their abilities, they'd quickly discovered where the patient belongings were kept, and the oblivious smoker had provided a handy way in. But it still felt like they were taking advantage of Alexei. Like they'd been planning to go in today from the start.

"Clear to the stairs," Ava whispered, scanning for staff with her implant.

Lily snapped her head back into the game and followed along behind Ava. They were heading to the third floor, but the stairwells weren't aligned. They needed to duck down corridors on each level, winding their way to the next flight.

Ava pushed Lily through a doorway, narrowly missing being seen by the group of people who clomped past them and down the corridor.

"That was close," Lily whispered, still clutching Ava despite the threat having passed.

"Yeah, sorry. I thought they were turning the other way."

"Maybe we don't risk it? We have time. Let's be careful. If we get busted, it's going to be harder to get back in again."

Ava nodded, extracting herself gently from Lily. She

turned back to the door, staring through it, watching people Lily couldn't see.

They exited the unattended office and continued through the building, making slower but safer progress. Eventually they found themselves facing a solid door on the third floor labelled *"Storeroom"* and secured with a bulky padlock.

"What is this?" Ava whispered incredulously, looking at the lock. "I can't pick that. What century is this place in, anyway? Haven't they heard of electronic locks? More convenient for the staff—they can use their ID cards—and more convenient for me, 'cause I can usually hack them with my implant."

Lily glanced suspiciously at Ava. "Your implant seems to be able to do an awful lot of dodgy things."

"*Useful* things," Ava corrected her. "And to be fair, I got it while I was working for the Meridian Intelligence Agency."

"Which, of course, you're not anymore," Lily said in a slightly sarcastic tone.

"No, I'm not," said Ava, slightly defensively. "I'm in the foreign office now. Hence the ambassadorial posting."

"Uh huh," said Lily, unconvinced. "But the MIA just let you keep the implant?"

"Well, it's all government, isn't it?" said Ava weakly, with a slight apologetic note in her voice. "But anyway, it's not going to help us with this door, no matter whose implant it is."

Lily turned back to the lock, not really wanting to drop the discussion about where Ava's loyalties might lie, but agreeing that this was the more pressing issue. She considered doubling back and finding a nurse. If she could remain hidden but read their mind, she might be able to find out where the key was kept.

That all seemed complicated, and more problematically, time-consuming. They had already taken a while to reach the room, and there really wasn't anywhere to hide near the storeroom. Ava could give them some warning, but it would be cutting it close to run back to the nearest empty room once she spotted them.

"I can make myself invisible," Lily mused. "Well, I could in Highacre. I haven't tried here. And I don't know if I could make you invisible, too."

"Probably not the time to test it out," said Ava. "But we won't have to worry about hiding if we can get rid of this lock quickly. You don't have any other handy lock picking powers by any chance?"

"No," said Lily, mentally running through what she knew she could do. "I mean, I could try to make a fireball that could melt the metal."

"That might also burn the house down," said Ava.

"Maybe summon a lock pick?" mused Lily. "I can move little things around, but I can't imagine a pick would be close enough for me to find. Oh!" She grabbed the lock, looking into the small keyhole. "I wonder …"

Concentrating, Lily tried to connect with and move the small pins and springs within the mechanism. It was fiddly, and required her to manipulate each one to different degrees, trying to find the right combination that the key would have pressed on.

Ava didn't question what Lily was doing, content to let her concentrate in the absence of a better plan. However, after about ten minutes, she warned Lily that there was movement in the nearby break room, and it was likely that people would be exiting soon.

"Just a second," Lily muttered, "I think I almost have "

With a small but satisfying click, the lock suddenly popped open in Lily's hands, surprising her. She looked at

Ava, who grabbed the lock from Lily's hands, opened the door and ushered her inside, closing it just as the break room door opened and they heard voices disconcertingly close.

Lily looked at Ava, wide-eyed. "Do you think they'll notice the lock is missing?"

Ava shook her head. "Unless they're coming this way, I don't think they'll pay that much attention."

Ava watched the people descend the stairs, then signalled to Lily that they were clear for now. They turned to take in the room and ascertain the enormity of their task. Relief flooded Lily as she realised each patient's belongings were labelled with their name and room number. Feeling slightly stupid for not assuming this would be the case, she and Ava spread out, looking for Belinda's belongings.

"I think this is it," called Ava quietly. Lily joined her, seeing her lift a small document box down from the top shelf. "Room 102?"

"That's it," said Lily, and she opened the lid. Inside was a worn jacket, a pair of dirty shoes, and a handbag. Lily pulled the bag out and looked inside. It was empty, except for some tissues and a purse. The purse was also empty. Lily assumed that they stored the valuables more securely.

Ava pulled the jacket out and was holding it up. "Belinda has good taste," she said, putting the suede jacket on. It was a little bulky on Ava, but the colouring suited her. Ava smoothed it down and tried to pull it tighter around her. "I think I need the next size down, please," she joked. "Hang on, something in the pocket."

Ava put her hand in and pulled out a small metal rod. It put Lily in mind of the small foam weights that she had seen some ladies her mother's age holding while power walking in the park. But the rod was all metal, the same type as the communicator. Ava handed it to Lily, who noticed a small latch at one end. Flicking it, the top of one end opened, and underneath was a small red button.

The two women looked at each other, smiling in disbelief.

"That was easier than I anticipated," said Ava.

"I know," agreed Lily. "Let's get out of here and go find Alexei."

They moved back through the building the way they had ascended, with Ava scanning and clearing the way, and occasionally ducking into cupboards and alcoves to avoid detection. They got as far as the corridor that led to reception when suddenly it seemed like everyone who worked in the facility decided to congregate in the area. Lily and Ava ducked into a large, long-term pantry near the kitchen and waited there for a few minutes with no sign of the traffic abating.

"We could probably make it out through the kitchen," said Ava, scanning behind them. "There's an exit through to what must be a loading dock. If we can make it to the grounds, we might be able to find a way out. Or at least we can look like we're visiting someone and then leave."

Eager to escape, Lily agreed, and they exited the pantry and moved toward the kitchen. Halfway there, they heard, "Hey!"

"Run," said Ava and the two dashed for the kitchen, bursting through the door and startling the staff inside.

"This way." Ava grabbed Lily's arm and pulled her along, already knowing where to go from her study of the building plans.

Lily could hear footsteps in pursuit and someone calling, "Stop them!"

Lily followed Ava, trying to figure out where they were. They abandoned the loading dock, as the kitchen staff stood between them and that exit, and instead, Ava pulled Lily out into the rear grounds of the facility.

"Here," said Lily, remembering a small alcoved area of trees and shrubs from her previous visit. They hurried into it, protected for a minute from searching eyes.

"She's looking," said Ava, watching their pursuer.

Lily took a couple of breaths, trying to think.

"She's heading this way," said Ava. "We're going to need to move."

"We need to think," said Lily. Ava frowned at her, amped up and wanting to escape. "We're not robbing a museum here. If she busts us, what's the worst that can happen?"

"She searches us and finds the device."

"So?" Lily asked. "She won't know what it is, and she's not going to know it's Belinda's."

"We don't know that," argued Ava. "Maybe she was the one who checked your mum in here. She might have taken her stuff, and wondered what this weird metal thing was."

"Okay," said Lily. "So we hide it in the bushes here and come back to visit my mum tomorrow. That lets us leave now and it doesn't matter what the nurse does to us. Even if we get barred, Alexei can come and get it," Lily added, correctly anticipating Ava's next argument.

"Or maybe ..." Ava looked beseechingly at Lily. "Maybe we use the device?"

"Ava, we agreed," said Lily, shocked. "We're going to help my sisters before we go. And we can't leave Alexei. He might even have the gems."

"Alexei will be fine here. And if he has the gems, even better," said Ava, her desperation now palpable. "Think about it, Lily. We're stronger with someone back in High-acre who knows what's going on. Once we have someone back there, it's only a matter of time until we can help your family. And if Alexei hasn't got the gems, it doesn't matter. We won't need to put ourselves at risk trying to get them back. We can just bring resources back here. Heck, we could arrange to bring your family to Highacre!"

"I don't know that they'd want to come," said Lily distracted and wrong-footed by the intensity of Ava's plea. "And it's probably not safe for them at the moment."

"Fine, not yet then," said Ava, smiling and shaking her head, thinking she had Lily on side. "But it really does solve most, if not all, of our problems."

Lily blinked, trying to think rationally. There was a lot of sense to what Ava was saying. But could she really do that? Abandon Alexei? Abandon her family? Lily's stomach dropped, imagining her sister's reaction to her simply disappearing again.

"They'll understand," Ava urged, seeing Lily's face. "Especially when you come back with everything they need."

That was true, but when would that be? Giles had said it could be months before they had any felixium, and the country was in turmoil. If Highacre and Meridia went to war, they'd never get access to the mines. Let alone be happy with her waltzing back to her home dimension for a visit. And taking a bunch of resources that they probably needed for the war effort with her.

"Someone's coming," Ava said urgently, staring over Lily's shoulder.

"Look, I hear you Ava, I do. And we can revisit this back at the apartment with Alexei, but we can't just disappear. I mean, yes, I absolutely do want to use this"—she pulled out the device—"and run away back to Highacre—"

"Lily!"

Lily whipped around to see her mother's shocked face.

"I have never been more disappointed in you."

Belinda looked a mixture of hurt, angry, and disappointed. Lily was surprised, but quickly felt deeply offended. Of course her mother would assume she would run away. All of the hurt she felt about everything Belinda had hidden from her bubbled up, exacerbated by the pain of losing her father, and the pressure to help both her family and an entire nation.

"Disappointed? What, that I'm not helping your *real* daughters before I go home?"

"Oh, come on Lily," said Belinda, frustrated.

"No, if you cared about me the same as them, you would have given me the device when I asked for it."

"And it looks like I assumed right when I worried that you might simply use it and abandon your family."

"I wasn't abandoning them," said Lily. "If you'd bothered to let me finish, I was telling Ava we couldn't leave."

Belinda looked pityingly at Lily, which only served to make Lily angrier.

"I don't know what happened to you over there, Lily," said Belinda sadly. "But my daughter wouldn't have taken the easy way out and run away from the hard things." She looked at Lily, her eyes piercing Lily's heart. "What would your father say?"

That was too much. Lily felt angry that Belinda would punch so low. Here she was, doing all she could to help everyone. Regardless of everything she was going through. Did her mother even think about how she felt? That she never got to say goodbye to her dad? It had taken all her energy to stand there with Ava, with the means to escape this hell she had returned to, and decide to stay.

But that energy had gone.

"He'd probably suggest that you stop malingering and help your daughters yourself."

And with that, Lily flipped up the cover and pressed the little red button.

33

Nothing happened. Lily pressed it a couple more times, then handed it to Ava, who also tried with no success.

"It needs felixium," said Belinda drily.

"But that's stupid," said Lily, grabbing the device from Ava and futilely pressing the button a few more times. "How does it help to give you a portable portal generator if it needs—"

Lily looked at Belinda, who was smiling sweetly at her.

"You took it out."

"I did."

"And you hid it somewhere else."

"I did."

"And you won't tell me where until I help Elaine and April."

"I won't."

Lily turned away, frustration and anger bubbling up quickly. The brief spike of relief she had felt at the idea of going home turned into disappointment. She felt trapped. Lily knew it was going to be extremely hard when she got back to Highacre. From what Giles said, everything was going wrong, and fixing it—if she could even fix it—was going to be a mammoth and long-term effort.

But it felt like one problem, whereas here … here it felt like she had to deal with both problems; fixing her family *and* finding a way back to Highacre. And with her family, it was different. In Highacre, she was important. People listened to her, gave her advice, and looked to her for decisions. With her family, she was the second youngest child. She had no job or expertise to offer, and looming over everything was the spectre of her dead father, which she really didn't want to acknowledge.

Blinking furiously to banish the tears, Lily focussed the hurt and anger that she felt on her mother. She was stung as much by the assumption that she had intended to run away and abandon her sisters as she was by the fact that her mother was forcing her to help. Why wouldn't her mother just help her? She might not be biologically her daughter, but she had lost her father just as much as the others had. It was cruel for Belinda to be treating her differently, emphasising the differences now.

"Why won't you help me?" Lily exploded at Belinda, hissing to avoid attracting the attention of the staff. "Do you resent me that much? Hate me?" Her voice caught and tears ran unbidden down her cheeks. "Do you blame me for Dad?"

"Oh Lily, no." Belinda reached for Lily, but she wrenched away.

"Is it because I'm adopted then? Because I'm not your biological child? You don't love me as much as the others?"

"Mum! You can talk!" April had appeared in the garden, her eyes wide and mouth gaping.

"Lily's adopted?" said Elaine from beside her.

"Of course she is. She even told us she's a princess in that other country," said April impatiently.

"Oh yeah. I guess—but I didn't really think about it ..."

"But Mum's back!" April ran forward and hugged her mother tightly. Belinda returned it, kissing the top of her head. Elaine also hugged her mother, and they moved over to some benches.

"Guess she told Elaine then," whispered Ava to Lily.

"She must've seen my name in the visitors' book the other day when she signed out. Decided to get in before I told Elaine and busted her."

"Wait, then who are your parents?" Elaine suddenly asked Lily.

"The king and queen, remember?" April answered for Lily, rolling her eyes at her older sister. "They died. That's why they came and took Lily in the first place."

"Oh, yeah," said Elaine, still looking slightly confused. "Sorry, I know you told us. I guess it didn't sink in until now. But then ..." She turned to their mother. "How did Lily get here to start with?"

"Oh, well, that's quite a tale," began Belinda, eager to keep the conversation away from her sudden recovery. "We were living at the farm and one night, out of the blue, we got a knock at the door."

Lily noted that her mother wasn't going to mention that she too was from Highacre. It grated at her. She would be the odd one out, whereas Belinda was preserving her place in the team.

"—bunch of strange men and a pregnant woman. So they came in—"

"What, you just let a bunch of strangers into the house?" asked April, appalled.

"Well, yes, we couldn't just leave a pregnant woman on our doorstep."

"*Seemingly* pregnant," said April. "What if they were there to rob you?"

"What if they were there to kill me?" said Elaine, alarmed.

"Why would they be there to kill you?" asked April.

"Who knows why crazy murderers do what they do?" said Elaine defensively.

"Well, spoiler alert—I don't think they were there to kill you."

Elaine playfully nudged April. Their banter left a hollow spot in Lily's heart. It used to be she and April who teased each other like that. Belinda pushed on with her story.

"Anyway, we let them in and, as it turns out, they were illegal immigrants about to be deported. The woman told us that her country was in a state of civil war and if she were to have the baby back home, it would be killed. Especially if it was a girl. She begged us to let her stay long enough to have the baby and then asked us to keep it and raise it as our own."

"So, not asking much then?" said Elaine. "Of two complete strangers she'd never met before."

"Well, I just looked at you and David and imagined myself in the same situation. I told her that we would take her baby. She was so relieved; she even asked us to put our details on the birth certificate so there could be no risk of the baby being sent back to her home country, and then a few days later, she gave birth on the couch."

"Wait, on our couch?" asked Elaine.

"Yes." Belinda smiled at the memory.

"The couch that's now in my lounge room?"

"Yes, dear."

"But I *sit* on that couch."

"Lily's birthing couch is very comfortable," commented April.

Belinda looked across at Lily, tears in her eyes. "She

gave me Lily to hold, and the moment she was in my arms, it was just like it had been with all of you. She was mine."

Lily looked away, still stung by her mother's actions.

"Mum, I'm so glad you're back," said April, hugging her mother happily.

"Yeah, April told me she'd found you, but you were catatonic. What happened? Did you just get better?" asked Elaine suspiciously.

"Yes, it was so odd. One minute I was stuck inside myself, and then Lily turned up and it was like I was free. It was just like magic." Belinda emphasised the last word, and Lily thought she felt a ripple through the air.

Elaine and April turned and looked meaningfully at Lily. "Thank goodness you visited, Lily," said April.

"Yeah, it's almost like you were able to fix Mum," said Elaine before mouthing "thank you" to Lily. "I just know everything's going to be fine now that you're back, Lily."

Lily knew she could correct them, tell them that their mother had been faking, but that felt needlessly cruel. Especially when she looked at April. Knowing that her mother could have been talking to her and hugging her when she had been visiting all this time would crush her little sister. But their gratitude intensified the guilt Lily felt at even wanting to escape back to Highacre. Certainly she couldn't think of leaving before ensuring they were taken care of now.

She looked over at Belinda, who was smiling at her, and realised that was exactly the outcome her mother had wanted.

34

"WHAT A MANIPULATIVE BIT—"

"Lily, that's your mother," Ava chastised.

"Exactly. That makes it worse."

Lily and Ava were heading towards the alley where Alexei was currently ensconced, undertaking surveillance of the pawnshop.

"Look, there's nothing you can do about your mum," said Ava calmly. "All we can do is try to get the gems back so that she will give us the felixium and then you can go home feeling satisfied that you helped your family."

"Whoever stole the gems has probably sold them by now," Lily muttered grumpily. She was keen to remain angry, as it was much easier to deal with than the hurt she felt.

"Possibly," sighed Ava, "but we need to try, and maybe if they have sold them, they still have some cash."

Lily agreed, deciding that venting to Ava, who had also had her chance to get home snatched from her grasp, was unfair. She apologized and promised to make an effort to be more positive.

"It's okay," Ava said. "I understand. I feel like we keep getting so close to a way home, but the solution keeps moving just out of reach."

"I know what you mean," said Lily.

They walked in silence for a bit, Lily fiddling in her pocket with the device they had stolen from her mother. Close to the shop now, she could see Alexei hidden up ahead, perched behind some trash cans and stacked bags of garbage. She wrinkled her nose, though admired his commitment. If she hadn't been looking for him, she never would have spotted him amongst the trash.

"People coming," said Ava suddenly, grabbing Lily and pulling her into a doorway deep enough to hide them from view.

"—see his face! What a wanker."

Two men moved into the alley, joking and laughing about some poor guy who seemed to have misplaced a relatively large amount of drugs to the displeasure of his supplier. Lily didn't think the response of the supplier was funny, but the two thugs seemed to find pleasure in it.

"What are we gonna do about Hammer?" one asked the other, sobering up slightly.

"Shit," replied his friend, exhaling loudly. "I dunno. How the hell does he think we're going to be able to pull off another job like that one? Not like everyone is wandering around with a bag of gems on them."

Ava and Lily looked at each other. Was it possible? Lily silently thanked the universe and any higher powers that had brought them this gift.

"He's just messing with us," said the first thug. "He's pissed. Thinks we should have got more for them."

"That's bull. Not like we can control how much Fingers will pay for them."

"Yeah, you and I know that. But he probably thinks he could have done better."

"Should have done it himself then, shouldn't he?"

Following this was a round of general verbal bashing of all aspects of Hammer's character and physical attributes, with both thugs occasionally looking around worriedly, making sure there wasn't anyone who could report back to Hammer.

"Do you reckon Fingers still has them?" Thug One eventually asked. "Maybe we could break in and pinch them back. Sell them again. That'd keep Hammer off our backs."

"Don't be stupid," scoffed Thug Two. "You've seen Fingers's security. Ain't no way we're getting in there."

"I heard he got infrared cameras or something," said Thug One, a note of awe in his voice.

Thug Two scoffed. "You'd believe anything, you would. Nah, but he's got the store locked up tight, cameras everywhere—normal cameras—and he's employing Bob and Duncan to watch it overnight."

"What's he doing all that for?"

"What do you think?" Thug Two said with scorn in his voice. "Got a bunch of gems in there, doesn't he?"

"Oh, yeah."

The two men eventually moved off, Thug Two still making fun of Thug One.

Ava beamed at Lily and the two women moved quickly toward Alexei's trash heap, liberating him from the garbage. They all moved a couple of blocks away and waited for Ava to scan the area before sharing what they'd all learned.

"Wait, you tried to use it?" Alexei interrupted.

"I did. I'm really sorry, Alexei," said Lily. "I wasn't intending to, and then my mum assumed I was going to use it. And all I was thinking was if she was going to assume I was going to abandon my sisters then what do I have to lose in using it anyway? I wasn't thinking. I'm so sorry."

Alexei frowned, clearly hurt. "I mean, if that was something we needed to do—send someone back and leave someone here—I'd understand, and I'm even happy to stay if I need to. But I'd like to at least know about it."

Ava cut off Lily's apology. "I was pushing Lily to use it. She was the one who said we couldn't leave you. And of course we can't. I know that. I just lost my head. I'm really sorry, Alexei. You should be mad at me, not Lily."

Alexei stared at the ground, thinking, before he looked Ava in the eye. "Of course I'm mad at you. I don't even like you. You're so annoying."

Ava looked shocked before seeing the familiar twinkle in Alexei's eye and she pushed him, embarrassed to have missed his joke.

"We really are sorry," said Lily, feeling Alexei was letting them off far too lightly.

"It's okay," he said. "I can tell you feel bad about it. And I know you won't think about doing it again."

"Absolutely not," Lily said, Ava shaking her head emphatically.

"Then it's done," he said simply. Lily marvelled at his ability to forgive so quickly. She thought maybe she should take a leaf out of his book with her mother, but the talk turned to the pawnshop and the thought was forgotten.

"Fingers is the guy who owns the pawnshop," Alexei told them after Ava finished filling him in on the discussion they'd overheard. "From what I was able to overhear, I think at least some of the gems are still there. Some of his guys were complaining about extra shifts to protect the merchandise. They were keen for him to sell it all so they could get a break."

After some discussion they all agreed that they needed to confirm that the "merchandise" was, in fact, the missing gems. Ava suggested that the two girls go in alone. They had been in the store before, but it had been Alexei who had done most of the talking. It was less likely the girls would be recognised. Alexei did not like this plan at all.

"You already spoke to the guy. Besides, you're too threatening," she told Alexei. "We're just two sweet little girls. Nothing to worry about."

"Okay," Alexei grunted, "but I'm right out here. Scream if you need me."

With a wry smile, Ava turned and led Lily across the street and into the shop. A little bell tinkled, announcing their arrival. It seemed so incongruous with the whole atmosphere that it threw Lily, and she jumped when a voice from behind asked if they could help her.

"Sorry, I didn't see you there," said Lily, feeling her heart pounding in her chest.

The man just grunted back at her and looked her up and down.

"Er, no. Thank you. I'm fine," Lily finally said, disconcerted.

The man grunted again and moved off toward Ava, who was looking in the glass cabinet that also served as the counter.

"These gems are unusual," Ava was saying. Lily wandered up to have a look, trying not to rush or seem overly interested.

The man appraised Ava suspiciously. "One of a kind. *Very* expensive."

"Are these all you have?"

Lily looked in the cabinet, her breath catching as she saw two of the medium-sized gems and a handful of the smaller ones. It was less than a quarter of what had been stolen, but it was something.

"Oh, sorry," Ava said as she bumped Lily. She continued her conversation with the man.

Taking the hint, Lily moved off to pretend to look at some other wares, then focussed on the man's mind. The rings of light that Lily saw when mind reading were dull, as if dirty. They felt almost sticky to Lily. She wondered how much of that was the individual's personality and how much was her own projection based on how she viewed the person. She thought to ask Lady Octavia about it when she returned home, and then remembered her mentor was missing, likely dead. Lily felt a spike of sadness and forced her mind back to the task at hand.

Feeling like she was wading through garbage, Lily pushed past memories and imaginings—at least, she hoped they were merely violent fantasies—looking for anything about the gems. She tried focussing her own mind on what she was looking for, rather than wading through the man's mind. Lily suddenly found herself in the relevant memories, as if she'd done an internet search.

She saw the thugs bring the gems to the man, who they greeted as Fingers, and felt his excitement spike before he quickly tamped it down to get a better deal. He had pretended that he didn't want to buy the gems, and then felt anxious that they would take them elsewhere. Fingers was exhilarated when they fell for his ploy and sold them for significantly less than they were worth. He had felt pleasure imagining the beating that Hammer would probably give them for being ripped off so badly.

Pushing along, Lily saw him contact three rare gem dealers, trying to play them against each other. Frustratingly, Lily couldn't see the face of the man Fingers had eventually sold the gems to. She was straining to find something that would identify him when she was suddenly evicted from Fingers's head.

"If you're not buying, get out," he was saying angrily to Ava, who was already walking towards the door, tugging Lily by the arm. Lily realised it was Ava grabbing her arm that had severed the contact.

They crossed the road, collecting Alexei, and walked away in silence. Five minutes later, having changed direction several times to try to evade men they thought might be following them, the trio entered a small cafe on the waterfront and grabbed a table by the window, where not only did they have a lovely view, but they could keep an eye on anyone suspicious approaching.

"Well?" said Alexei impatiently. He had refrained from asking what happened while they were walking, but was clearly dying to know.

"He's got some of them," said Ava, eyes scanning their surroundings.

"How many is 'some'?" asked Alexei, turning to Lily.

"Not many," she admitted. "He's sold most of them, but what's left would still be a tidy profit."

Lily tuned out the discussion and tried to bring up the memories she had seen of Fingers selling the gems. She replayed them over and over, searching for something that might identify the buyer.

Frustrated, Lily sat back in her chair and looked out the window, trying to focus but not force anything. There had been a word echoing in Fingers's head when she was in his mind looking at the memories related to the gems. Batton? Battalion? Bat-something.

Alexei and Ava were now discussing strategies for defeating the security system. Lily pulled out her phone, opened a search engine, and typed in "rare gems" and "bat".

Nothing relevant came up, so she started messing around with variations on "bat".

"But if we try to get in the skylight, we still have to go out one of the doors," Ava was protesting.

"No, we can use the shelves to boost ourselves back up."

"That's a terrible position to be in if we're in a fight."

"If we're already in a fight, there's no reason we wouldn't use the door. The skylight would only be viable if we were still undetected."

"Batyola!" Lily said excitedly.

"Is that like 'huzzah'?" asked Ava.

"No, it's the name Fingers was thinking of. I think that's who he sold the rest of the gems to."

Alexei's face lit up as much as Ava's face dropped. Lily knew Ava just wanted to get the gems they had found and go home. But while Lily desperately wanted to do just that, she knew in her heart it was wrong.

"Let's focus on this job first," said Ava before Alexei could get too excited. "I think we hit it tonight. He was a bit suspicious, but probably hasn't had time to really think it through and beef up security. The longer we leave it, the harder it'll be."

"Agreed," said Alexei, nodding enthusiastically.

"Alright," said Lily, butterflies churning her stomach. "Let's go rob us a store."

In the end, they decided that the skylight entry was unnecessarily extravagant, and that good old-fashioned violence would be both effective and satisfying, given how these people had already treated them, and what Lily had seen in Fingers's mind. They waited out back for one of the goons to take a smoke break and Alexei knocked him out with a quick thump to the head.

Ava had already infiltrated the alarm and camera systems with her implant, and as the goon hit the ground, she switched the systems off, eliciting a grunt of surprise from the other goon. Silent and swift, Ava then headed straight for his position and knocked him out using pressure points. Alexei and Lily stared at her, disconcerted, but she just shrugged and indicated they should hurry up and get the gems.

As it turned out, the front counter's alarm was on a different system to the building, and when they tried to open it up, an ear-splitting shriek exploded overhead. Alexei didn't miss a beat and grabbed a baseball bat stored under the counter—no doubt for unruly customers—and smashed the countertop. Lily reached in gingerly and picked out the gems before turning at the sound of the cash register opening. Ava shrugged at her, pulling a couple of hundred dollars out. "It's really ours, anyway."

Alexei, inspired, led them back through to an office near the second goon, who was still out cold.

"We need to go," implored Lily, listening to sirens in the distance heading their way.

"There's a safe in here, though," Alexei said.

Ava jogged over to it and slapped it with her palm. "What is it with you people? Does nobody use electronic security here?"

"Seems just as well they don't," said Alexei with a wry smile.

"Lily, over to you," said Ava, stepping aside.

Lily hesitated, then hurried over. "One of you keep an eye out. We can *not* be caught here."

Steeling herself against the desire to run, Lily forced herself to feel for the inner workings of the safe with her mind. She felt a pin and some latches. But they needed to be in the right order ...

"Lily, they're about two blocks away," said Ava, worry entering her voice for the first time.

"Just a second ... there!" She heard a satisfying click and opened the door. Ignoring everything else, she grabbed a few bundles of bills and the three ran for the door, following Ava, who was plotting their getaway to avoid the incoming police and any CCTV cameras or other systems that might identify them when the police reviewed them later.

Four blocks away, they huddled at the end of an alley, waiting for two police walking down the main street to pass.

"Excuse me, are you alright there?" A voice coming from behind said, making them all jump.

"Oh! Sorry officer." Lily's heart was pounding so loudly she could hardly hear herself.

"What are you doing?" He began approaching them, hand by his waist where Lily assumed his pistol was.

Ava laughed, looking embarrassed. "It's silly, really. Jenny, our friend from uni—well she's not really our *friend*—but we saw her over there." She pointed across the road at the bar. "And, it's just, we told her we had to study tonight, so if she saw us ..." Ava shrugged, smiling at the officer.

Lily thought she saw his shoulders relax and his arm move from his waist, but he still looked like he might not believe them.

"You shouldn't be hiding in these alleyways. There are some dodgy people around. Already been a break-in tonight."

"Oh, really!" Ava looked at him with a mix of shock and excitement. "Where? Oh, you probably can't say. Was it near here?"

A wave of panic hit Lily. He might let them go, but they

were memorable. If Fingers suspected them from their interest in the gems earlier and gave a description ...

She had managed to have some success back in High-acre in getting the guards to do what she suggested, and she could read memories. Could she erase them? Or perhaps tweak them a little? Now was not the ideal time to try, but she really had no choice, so Lily reached out with her mind while Ava still had the policeman distracted.

With a little effort, Lily managed to find the part of the man's mind that was creating memories of the current events. It was like an echo, and Lily could see the previous events running into the background like a roll of film. She thought very hard about erasing their images, but nothing happened. *Maybe if I put all my concentration into it ...*

"Is your friend okay?" the policeman asked Ava, staring at Lily suspiciously, whose face was screwed up as if in pain.

"Oh yes," said Ava. She leant towards the officer and said in a stage whisper, "Cramps."

The officer leant away, looking both embarrassed and slightly disgusted.

Lily tried to ignore all of this. The only thing that mattered was fixing his memory. She was painfully aware that if she failed, she would have definitely cemented them in the man's mind.

She tried thinking of smudging the images of their faces, drawing over them, turning them to silhouettes, but nothing worked. Distantly, Lily heard the officer trying to disengage from Ava, and in desperation, she imagined grabbing the memories of them like a roll of film and ripping them from the reel.

"Lily! What did you do?" said Ava, alarmed.

Lily opened her eyes—she hadn't even realised she had

closed them—and saw the policeman on the ground, unconscious.

"I didn't ... I just—" Ava was by his side, feeling for a pulse.

"He's alive," confirmed Ava.

"I was trying to alter his memory," Lily explained, imploring her friends to tell her it was alright. "If Fingers gave them a description, and then this policeman said he saw us nearby acting suspiciously—"

"You did the right thing Lily," said Ava.

Alexei grunted in agreement, but Lily felt he didn't entirely mean it.

"Physically, he seems fine," said Ava, standing.

"We can't leave him here like this," said Lily, still crouched by his side.

"We have to." Ava pulled Lily to her feet. "You're right. If we're seen so close by, we'll probably be caught. Then we are stuck here permanently and your sisters don't get any help. If anyone finds us by an unconscious cop with unknown brain issues, we'll probably be more memorable than we were to him, and whatever you've done to his mind was for nothing."

Lily knew she was right, but she stared down at the man's blank face. She had done that to him. Whatever damage he was suffering, she had caused it. Guilt engulfed her, but she let Ava and Alexei guide her away and out into the street.

It wasn't the first time she had hurt someone; her mind flashed back to the terrorists she had burned with her fireballs at the arena attack. But they had been killing people. They would have killed her. She was protecting people. Just like the policeman was trying to do.

They had all told her to be careful with her magic. Giles, Addison, Lady Octavia. Told her not to experiment when it could be dangerous. And now some innocent policeman who was just doing his job had been hurt. And she did it to get away with a crime. No matter how they dressed it up in helping her sisters, or getting back what had been stolen from them, they had done the wrong thing, and Lily had hurt someone innocent to get away with it.

"I'm sure he'll be fine," Ava tried to reassure her.

Lily nodded, because she didn't want her friends to worry. But long after they fell asleep that night, she was lying awake, thinking of the slack face of the man whose mind she had broken.

35

CLAIRE PACED the length of the tiny apartment, glaring at her watch and willing time to move faster. She crossed to the window, glancing out at the street through a chink in the blinds, considered sitting on the couch that looked suspiciously broken, and then began pacing again, her nervous energy in overdrive. Claire had cracked the case. She had found the evidence proving beyond doubt that Austin was the insider, and that he was doing everything at the behest of the mysterious Patriot.

She had then turned her attention to uncovering the Patriot's identity, but after spending half a day chasing leads, Claire had conceded that she needed help and had contacted Hudson.

Intelligence is a team sport. There's no room for individual glory.

The words of her mentor echoed in her mind. She briefly wondered where he was now and if he was safe. It seemed unlikely with the number of arrests and disappearances. And now she had someone else to worry about. Hudson normally responded instantaneously, but she'd heard nothing for a couple of hours.

Initially, Claire had allowed that he may need to go to the bathroom, or perhaps run errands. But then she started getting nervous. Hudson had been infiltrating so many systems, it was probably only a matter of time until he was caught.

He might still be okay.

Claire stalked back to the window. If they had Hudson, then it was probably no longer safe to stay in this apartment. Immune now to moving, Claire had only remained in place to limit her time on the street. It was a precarious balancing act. With Hudson seemingly out of action, Claire knew she needed to contact Naomi and Jason. She had to let them know Hudson might be in danger, and share what she'd found. Indeed, it seemed only a matter of time until she was found, too.

But you have the training to escape and evade.

Naomi should be continuing with the surveillance effort on Austin, and Claire had considered heading to the nationalist movement offices to try to link up with her. But if they had found Hudson, they might have found Naomi. And if not, Claire could lead them right to her. Jason was due back from the Disputed Region soon, though. No doubt Naomi would head to the palace for his return to debrief with him. Claire would meet them both there.

Claire checked her watch again. She had a little under an hour before she had to leave in order to arrive at the palace before Jason was due back. That would give her time to surveil the area and find a location on his path from the vehicle bay to the ops room where she could hide, knowing Naomi would still be able to see her.

Claire sat back at the uneven table she had used as a small desk and shuffled her papers, deciding to look over them one more time before she left. Without really thinking, Claire plugged a tiny hard drive into her computer and started copying the files. It was more of a chip, really. Barely the size of her little finger's nail. She had already copied the information onto several drives, but it couldn't hurt to have more copies. Led by her gut, Claire decided to transfer all the information off her computer altogether. It was probably safer to keep it mobile. She laughed without humour, imagining what the Claire of six months ago would think about how paranoid she was now.

Claire scanned her files again. She had used the information that she and Naomi gathered from the nationalist movement offices and, working with Hudson, conducted targeted searches of emails, chat boards, and websites. Claire didn't want to know how, but Hudson had been able to gain covert access to expansive military archives, and had also somehow obtained access to the impressive, if not disconcerting, amount of surveillance footage that Highacre's CCTV, drone, and satellite networks gathered.

Vaguely thinking that Highacre's citizens might not be happy if they knew the extent of the government's surveillance abilities, especially given who would have access to it now, Claire reorganised the fairly solid pack of evidence she had put together showing that Austin had become radicalised during the war by other members of his regiment and had committed a number of atrocities.

As Jason and Naomi had suspected, Claire now had evidence that Austin had killed General Mortimer, the previous queen's father and leader of the Highacren war effort, and then destroyed the evidence. Or so he thought. Hudson had been able to recover data that Austin would have thought deleted or destroyed, and with Claire able to direct him as to what files and folders to focus his efforts on, together they had unravelled Austin's secrets remarkably quickly. Perhaps there were benefits to intelligence agents and the military working more closely together after all.

At any rate, it seemed that Austin had settled down when he went to the palace and largely cut his ties to his military mates. There was no evidence of him speaking with them, or anyone else from the nationalist movement for a number of years. But then, for some reason, he had re-established links in the last year or so. This is when the Patriot reached out to him and enlisted his services. Austin had been providing the Patriot with information and doing his bidding within the palace. His actions had more than likely enabled the assassinations of the royal family and culminated in pushing Lily through the interdimensional travel machine.

Claire's computer beeped insistently, breaking her out of her reverie. She assumed that there was an error in copying the documents onto the drive, but instead found an email containing the results of one of the searches that Hudson had been running for her through an HIA server. Relieved that it had worked despite Hudson's concerning silence, she opened the attachments and scanned the information.

It was a bunch of data that made little sense to an untrained eye, but Claire could see that it contained financial information and transfers. Scrolling back up to the top, she looked for the identifier to tell her who the information belonged to. Claire's heart stopped. *Ezra Brown.*

Oh my goodness. Ezra is the Patriot!

Claire checked the information again. And then checked her notes and then checked what they had actually searched for. She couldn't believe it. Surely it couldn't be this easy?

At any rate, she couldn't wait to tell Jason.

Bugger, Jason!

Checking her watch, Claire swore. She was going to be late. Hand on the doorknob, she paused.

You can never be too careful.

Worried about something going wrong before she could tell Jason, Claire sent him and Naomi a brief email, hurriedly ejected the drive, grabbed her papers, and ran out of her apartment.

Claire arrived late to the palace, dashing her plans to wait outside and ensure it was safe. She couldn't risk being caught before she spoke to Jason or Naomi. Of course, Claire's strong preference was not to be caught at all, so she settled for chameleoning and pausing strategically to try to avoid or identify any tails.

She didn't think she was followed, but she hadn't been as careful as usual during her trip to the palace. If she was going to get caught, it would be better to make a scene within the palace walls than be captured outside while watching.

Ducking into alcoves and behind statues to avoid the seemingly increased HSP presence in the palace, Claire headed straight to the ops room, hoping that Jason would head there to report in before he and Naomi went somewhere else to really talk. She felt in her pocket, making sure she had brought the disrupter to jam any listening devices.

"... managed to get—Claire?" Naomi looked up in surprise at Claire's entrance. Jason looked around in confusion, unable to see her, and jumped when Claire unveiled herself right next to him.

"Listen, I don't think I have much time—"

The door smashed open and the Highacre Special Police burst into the room, yelling and brandishing their weapons and pushing Jason and Naomi back against the wall.

Well, that was an understatement.

She looked around, biting back an urge to laugh. With the number of pistols and rifles crammed into the room, if any of the HSP needed to use one, it was highly likely that they would all wind up shooting each other.

"Claire Jones, you're under arrest on suspicion of treason."

Jason and Naomi started arguing with the officers and positioning their bodies to prepare to fight if required. Claire was touched. She couldn't think of anyone that she had worked with before who would be willing to take on a room full of armed fascist police for her. There was no way that they could win, but she saw Jason and Naomi squaring up nonetheless.

But Claire knew how this went. Either she went quietly with them, or they would all be arrested, or worse, killed. It was better that only one of them was taken out of the fight. The others had to remain free to keep going. To finish uncovering the plot and bring the queen home.

"Okay! It's okay. I'll come quietly." Claire felt the guards on either side of her relax. She then threw herself forward at Jason, wrapping her arms around him. Jason caught her, bewildered.

"Oh, Jason!" She kissed him passionately. She felt his stunned body freeze and could hear the shocked gasps in the room, though a few of the officers also laughed and whistled. Good, that would buy them the seconds that she needed. Jason seemed to come to life, and she could feel him start to push her off him. She grabbed him tighter, and finally he understood.

Claire could feel the conflict within Jason as he realised she was passing him her tiny drive with her mouth. He was no longer struggling, but he also didn't want to play along and kiss her. He would make a terrible spy. Claire smiled as she finished the kiss, lingering for an unnecessarily long time with their lips together.

She felt hands grab her arms and pull her away from Jason.

"Now that Hudson's out of the way, we can be together!" she said urgently, fighting the officers. Jason continued to look stunned by the whole situation, but Claire sensed that Naomi understood.

"I really loved that email you sent me, babe," Claire called as the officers manhandled her out the door. "Wait for me!"

"I'm married," Jason spluttered, slightly confused and still shocked.

Claire could hear Naomi chuckling as the HSP dragged her out the door.

36

"What are you going to tell your wife?" Naomi asked in mock horror. Jason looked at her, still in a state of shock, and Naomi burst into laughter at the expression on his face. "Relax. Claire just needed to get you the drive. And surely your wife must know that you are literally the only married man alive not even vaguely thinking about cheating on his wife."

Jason was taken aback, and took a moment to be appropriately offended on behalf of all the other married men out there.

"That's a bit of a harsh indictment of men everywhere. Bad break up?"

Naomi squirmed and blushed uncharacteristically, making Jason feel bad for asking, but also extremely curious. Her face became more serious.

"With both Claire and Hudson gone, we're going to have to be more careful."

That was an understatement, but Jason didn't protest. Well aware that their already small team had just been halved, and that anyone he would trust to get them out of trouble seemed to have already been arrested, Jason and

Naomi had gone to the mess following Claire's arrest as if everything were normal. They spoke loudly about the arrest, which would have been of interest whether they were involved with Claire or not, and then retired to their respective barracks rooms.

They had then moved separately to a previously agreed-upon meeting point—a disused basement room in the old Royal Guard barracks, that rumour said used to be a safety bunker for a slightly mad king.

Jason had been hiding electronics and supplies there in case of emergency. Though, looking at the ration packs stacked in a corner, he now couldn't think of why he might need those. This was not somewhere he ever planned to live long-term.

"Look, the point is, the girl had to get it done, and she did." Naomi snatched up the drive, pointedly wiped it on her pants, then plugged it into the standalone computer Jason had acquired. It had no connectivity to the internet. The drive began to load, and they watched as several files appeared.

"Oh, there's an immersion file," said Naomi excitedly.

Jason stood and located the immersion device he had squirrelled down here weeks ago and brought it back to the table. Naomi pulled out the chip and placed it in the device. They both pulled up chairs. Naomi looked at him, eyebrow raised, asking if he was ready. He nodded, and she tapped the button.

The room around them disappeared, and with a jarring feeling of déjà vu, Jason looked around at the recreation area of a forward operating base during the war.

"Oh wow," said Naomi, looking at Jason in alarm. "It's a memory. How the hell did she get someone's memory? That's illegal ..."

Before Jason could think to reply, the scene around them began to play.

———

"I win again!"

"That's bull, you're cheating!"

"You're a sore loser!"

"You're just a loser."

Austin gleefully wrapped his hands around the commissary items that he'd just won and pulled them towards him. Owen tried to swipe a chocolate bar, and Austin smacked his hand away.

"Get off! Win your own." Austin pushed his friend gently.

"Geez, you're as bad as a bloody Meridian!"

The banter from the soldiers around the table turned to some good-natured Meridia bashing.

"Stuck up tight arses. All they care about is money."

"And they're so bloody secretive. Your deal, mate."

"Yeah, mad at us for not sharing our tech, as if they'd tell us what they've got."

"The only good Meridian is a dead Meridian."

"So true."

Austin felt a familiar sick feeling starting in his stomach. Harry and Jack kept joking about killing Meridians, and at first it was funny, just soldiers blowing off steam. But lately, as their deployment dragged on, there was something he couldn't quite put his finger on. Maybe their tone? Whatever it was, it made him uncomfortable. He mentally kicked himself for being such a wimp. They were only joking. Jack was a good bloke, and their patrol's second in command. They'd been friends since they were kids. He wouldn't actually do anything.

Austin was an officer, and was to be the unit's officer commanding, working directly for the commanding officer. But this CO liked his officers to understand the patrols and how they worked, and so had assigned Austin to Jack's patrol to get some experience. While he was with them, he was just one of the guys and not to be treated as an officer.

"Anyway, enough of that," Owen broke into Austin's thoughts. "Focus on the cards before you lose all your stuff!"

The weeks passed in a similarly light-hearted fashion. Well, as light-hearted as it could be in a war. The routine became comfortable. They patrolled, they came back, they played cards, they worked out in the makeshift gym that they had put together. And then they did it all again.

Austin was out on yet another patrol. He was looking around, alert and watching for movement, or any sign of the enemy, but he was more relaxed than he'd been when they first moved into this area. Their patrols had been fairly benign, a few firefights, but nothing major.

On this particular patrol, they were pushing deeper into Meridia than they had gone the last few patrols. Austin really liked the landscape in this part of the country. It was all green rolling hills and forests, not too hot and not too cold. And so far it hadn't rained while they'd been out on foot, which was a bonus.

Austin turned his face, enjoying the sun on his cheek and listening to the birds.

"Contact!" bellowed George.

The patrol broke from their formation and all hit the ground, rolling and crawling for cover. Austin dove towards a pile of rocks that looked like might protect him. He landed heavily, rolled, and crawled, his heart pounding in his ears. The rocks barely covered his face, but he glanced around furtively, trying to get his bearing and figure out where his buddies were and where the gunshots were coming from.

"Two enemy, up the hill behind trees!" screamed Owen, the patrol's leader.

"One enemy, behind the hut!" called John.

Austin glanced up the hill to his left and then over to the hut that John was referring to on his right. Unless it was just the three enemies, this was going to be a mess.

"Medic!" Harry screamed, his voice higher than usual. "Ethan's been hit."

Austin noted the patrol's medic crawling over to where Harry's voice had come from. Austin forced himself to focus. This was what he was trained for. He covered the ground in short bounds, catching up with Owen.

"You lay down some fire to cover me. I'll head up that way." Austin pointed to some cover on their left. "I'll flank him. Then we have the high ground and can sweep down and take out the one by the hut."

Owen grunted and nodded his agreement, then turned to his right to pass the plan along. Austin wasted no time. He ran and crawled his way up the hill. His breath was so loud, he was sure the enemy would know where he was and what he was doing. After what felt like an hour, he reached the cover and took a second to catch his breath, peering out to see if he could spot the shooters. They were behind two large trees. One man was on his knee, peering out, watching the patrol below, the other on his belly.

Suddenly, the sound of his entire patrol firing up the hill erupted, deafening Austin and making him jump. He rushed out of the cover, heading farther up the hill to get the drop on the two men. Austin propped himself behind a tree and took aim. Steadying his breath, he focussed his power. Austin could magically direct his bullets, but it took a lot of concentration. With two shots, he dispatched the enemy. He called to his team, and they stopped firing up the hill.

Austin headed cautiously towards the Meridians,

keeping his rifle trained on their bodies. He kicked them over one at a time, making sure they were dead. The one who had been on his belly was still alive, but wouldn't be for long. He looked at Austin with pleading eyes as he tried to stop his insides leaking out.

"All good?" Jack suddenly popped up beside Austin, his focus towards the hut.

"He's still alive."

"Well, fix it."

Austin looked at Jack. Their rules were clear. If someone was injured and no longer a threat, they couldn't be killed.

Jack glanced at Austin and rolled his eyes. "He's dying, dude. We can't help him. Are you going to let him suffer?"

Austin looked back at the man on the ground, who now looked panicked.

"Austin, come on! We need to clear that hut so we can get Ethan out."

Austin focussed his mind on the mission. Ignoring the man, who was now softly muttering "No, no, no," and raising a hand as if to defend himself, Austin raised his rifle and shot the man in the head.

I ended his suffering.

Telling himself there was no time to dwell on it, Austin turned towards the hut and followed Jack's lead back into the fight.

Austin took a gulp from his bottle as he watched George and the medic patch up Ethan while Owen spoke to someone over the radio, trying to organise a medical evacuation. Turning away, he wandered back towards the hut. His patrol were all still hyped up and alert. Some of the guys were facing out, away from the group to make sure that they weren't ambushed again. He walked behind the hut and heard some noises from the bushes between the hut and a small stream.

Approaching cautiously, Austin peered through the branches. Jack and Harry were there. And so was a young girl and an older man, who was bound and gagged and on his knees. Both were crying.

"What are you doing?" Austin asked.

"Hey Austin," Harry greeted him as if nothing was amiss.

"We're just doing to these Meridians here what they did to poor Ethan," Jack said. Austin met his eyes. Jack's stare was hard, and his eyes were weird. Flat, in a dead kind of way.

"I don't think they were in the fight, guys," Austin said, looking at the girl who was sobbing quietly, snot mixing with tears and running down her face.

"They're all in the fight." Jack was facing him now. His look was warning, daring Austin to step in. "You think they didn't tell the fighters that we were coming?"

Harry suddenly slapped the girl's face. "Stop crying." He then broke into laughter before ripping her already torn shirt off her body. She screamed. A short, terrified scream, and then resumed her sobbing. Austin figured she'd been told to keep quiet.

The older man flinched, closing his eyes tightly. Jack put his pistol to the man's head. "No," he pushed the muzzle into his temple, turning the man's head toward the girl. "I told you to watch."

Austin left. He ignored the sick feeling that he should have made Jack and Harry let them go. He'd tell Owen and he'd sort it out. Those guys would have never listened to him, anyway. As he approached, he saw the medic doing chest compressions on Ethan, and Owen was now yelling at whoever was on the other end of the radio. Austin hurried over to see if he could help.

"No, you need to hurry the fuck up!" Owen was running one hand through his hair in frustration.

"Don't worry about it," said the medic sadly. "He's gone."

Austin stared at Ethan. He was a good bloke. And had a wife and two kids at home.

A shot rang out from over towards the hut. Owen and the rest of the patrol whirled around, rifles ready. A second shot echoed.

"It's okay," Austin reassured Owen, feeling nauseous. "It's just Jack and Harry."

Owen looked at Austin, confused, and then Jack and Harry wandered back out towards the group.

"Whoa, relax," Harry smiled at everyone, raising his hands in mock surrender. The two men saw Ethan, and the grins left their faces. Jack turned back towards the bushes and spat on the ground.

The mood around the patrol base was morose. Ethan had been well liked and respected. Most people were moving around in a state of introspection. It could easily be any of them at any time. Austin went to his bunk and pulled down the sheet that gave him the only privacy available at the base. All he wanted was to go to sleep.

An explosion rocked the base. Austin fell out of his bunk, already reaching for his rifle and pulling on his boots. Outside was chaos. Yelling, running, gunfire. The patrol base was under attack. There was panic and the smell of gunpowder everywhere. Austin saw some of his friends being carried back inside, covered in blood. He ran towards the recreation area. That was where his patrol usually hung out. He jumped over the exercise equipment and finally saw Owen and the others at the fence a couple of hundred metres away.

"Austin." The voice came from his right, and was weak, pain etched into it. It was Jack. Austin rushed to his side.

"Show me. Where are you hit?"

Jack shook his head, blood coming from his mouth as he coughed, and Austin could see that Jack had taken a large piece of shrapnel to his stomach. He wasn't going to make it.

"Mate." Jack took Austin's hand and squeezed it. His grip was weak. "Remember when we were kids, and we used to ride our bikes at the lake?"

"Yeah mate, I remember."

"I was so happy back then." Jack's eyes misted, focussed on something Austin couldn't see.

"They were good times."

"Tell my mum I love her, will you?"

"You'll tell her yourself, mate."

Jack shook his head. "Nah. Tell her I love her, and tell her I died well." He looked at Austin, his eyes pleading. Austin was sickeningly reminded of the shooter on the hill.

"Tell her I was a good soldier." Jack nodded to himself.

"I will mate," Austin whispered. Jack's hand stopped gripping Austin's, and Austin realised he was gone. Austin took a minute to close Jack's eyes and wipe his own tears. Then he snatched up his rifle and sprinted towards the fight.

"Which way, boss?" Owen asked, his voice tight. Austin knew Owen resented his presence in the patrol. As acting commanding officer, Austin should remain at the patrol base, planning the missions, not carrying them out. Austin didn't care. He was a soldier. He wanted to fight. He wanted to kill the enemy. The enemy who had killed so many of his friends.

Austin didn't answer Owen, instead giving him a hand signal indicating that they would head up the hill to the left, then gave the order to the rest of the patrol. He could tell Owen was pissed that Austin was doing Owen's job, but he didn't care. It wasn't Austin's fault that he had distinguished himself in the defence of the patrol base and that he had been chosen to replace the CO who was killed in the initial explosion.

They patrolled towards a small town before settling down in the high ground and watching the people below. Simple Meridians going about their day. Or as Austin now understood, helping the war effort by supplying the Meridian forces and providing information, enabling the killing and maiming of his friends. They were all the enemy. Austin had come to hate these enemies more, though. The soldiers fought bravely in the open. These cowards kept to the shadows and stabbed their foes in the back.

"We should move on, boss," Owen said, kneeling behind Austin. "There are no targets here."

"Sure there are. They're all walking around down there."

Owen looked at Austin, clearly trying to decide if he was serious, or if this was just big talk. The new unit was a bloodthirsty bunch who usually tried to patrol their way into a fight, regardless of the mission they were given. Though, if Austin didn't join them and left Owen in charge, they did seem to toe the line. Austin wondered what that said about him. He shook the uncomfortable thought from his head, deciding to better choose his patrol commanders in future, and focussed on the town, figuring out which way to approach it.

"They're not targets, Austin." Owen touched Austin's arm, trying to make Austin look at him. Austin slowly moved his head, staring pointedly at Owen's hand. Owen dropped it and moved in front of Austin.

"Mate, come on. You know this is wrong." Owen looked very agitated. "Austin!"

Austin wheeled around on Owen at his raised voice. "Shut it," he hissed. "Are you trying to give us away? You a Meridian sympathiser now?"

"This is wrong." Owen looked Austin in the eye. "I won't be a part of it."

Austin looked at Owen for a beat. "Harry," he finally called over his shoulder. "Take this traitor away. Tie him up so he can't warn the enemy."

Owen kept looking at Austin in disgust as Harry and John appeared on either side of him and led him away.

"This is wrong, boys," Owen called to the patrol. "You don't have to be a part of it. But god help you if you are."

"Shut him up," Austin called to his men, then went back to planning the attack.

***

"And so before he gets in here, you need to make sure the map is clear, his tea is ready, and the daily intelligence reports are on his desk."

Austin looked around the command tent. It was sparsely furnished, the comforts kept to a minimum. Not at all what he had thought the brass would be living like. He had figured they'd be in hard standing accommodation with all the modern conveniences. From what the general's military assistant had said, the general was down-to-earth and big on keeping it simple. If the fighting men didn't get it, the higher command didn't get it, and if it was available, it was to be sent to the front.

"Austin, did you get that?"

The assistant had been talking about something else that needed to be ready before the general finished his morning briefing. Something that was about to be Austin's job, since he had been pulled from the front and given new orders. He hadn't yet figured out whether this job was a reward, since Austin's regiment had become the most successful, making significant headway into Meridian territory, taking and holding ground, or a punishment. But if it was a punishment, then they'd have to know about his regiment's attitude towards Meridians, and if they knew that, then he was sure he'd be in a cell somewhere, not given a plum job with the general.

"Intelligence reports, then casualty reports, then proposed missions. Got it."

"No, casualty reports first." The current assistant sighed and ran his hand through his hair. "You need to pay attention. I'm out of here tomorrow."

"I'm sure I'll figure it out," said Austin coolly, looking at the reports on the general's desk.

"I have every confidence that you will," a deep, confident voice sounded from the entrance to the tent. Both men started and then braced up, stiff as boards.

"As you were lads, rest." The general waved the compliment away. "Now, you're Major Austin Wilcox. I'm Angus Mortimer." The general approached Austin and shook his hand, looking him in the eye.

"Pleased to meet you, sir." Austin returned the general's firm grip and tried to maintain eye contact. The general was indeed down-to-earth, but he was still intimidating.

"Rick, why don't you leave us to get acquainted? I'm sure you have things to pack up."

Rick brought his heels together, bracing up again, and left quickly.

"Well, Austin." The general indicated to a chair in front of his desk and sat in his own. "Your regiment has been highly successful. You've led it to some great victories out there on the northern front."

"Thank you, sir." Austin felt nervous, but reminded himself that if anyone believed half the rumours about his regiment, he'd be in a cell. It was strange—now that he was this far away from the guys, the action and the danger, he was struggling with justifying what he had done while with his unit.

"You, of course, would be aware of the rumours, though." The general was still looking at Austin, his blue eyes piercing. Austin tried not to squirm. He shrugged instead.

"Sure, I've heard things. I don't pay them any attention, sir. People are either jealous of our success or don't understand the realities of war."

The general considered Austin for a beat that felt like hours. "Of course. Nonetheless, we couldn't leave you in charge. We're getting all sorts of heat from human rights groups. And certainly, you couldn't remain in command while the inquiry is ongoing."

Austin's stomach fell away. An investigation? It would be fine. What could the investigation find, anyway? "Of course, sir."

"I mean, three unaccounted for claims of civilian casualties draws attention, as it should, but no doubt it will all be cleared up." The general was watching Austin closely for a reaction. Austin was determined not to give one, but he was surprised by the comment. Only three claims? They didn't know the half of it.

"Yes, sir."

"So, you will work for me, and learn how to lead an army. If your success on the northern front was a clear demonstration of your talent as a military professional, this will help you as you advance, and maybe one day you'll have my job."

"Thank you, sir."

Austin hadn't thought that he would like being an assistant to a general, but as the days turned into weeks, he found he was enjoying himself. The general let him attend high-level strategic briefings and read reports, and discussed his thoughts and strategies with Austin. He even asked Austin's opinion, and more than once, had taken his advice. Austin couldn't help but like and respect the man. He was smarter than anyone Austin had met before, and he wanted not only what was best for Highacre but also his men. Austin had watched him argue with the politicians more than once about ideas they had that would put the troops at risk.

The more Austin learned about the strategic picture, the worse he felt about his actions in the field. He didn't regret what he'd done. They were still the enemy, but now he realised the impact that reputation had on everything from the support for the troops at home to the international support for Highacre over Meridia.

Sometimes the things he'd done felt like a dream, and he began to wonder if he'd ever really done them. It had been so extreme out there. Maybe his mind had invented these ideas in response to the deaths and injuries of all his friends. Deep down he knew that wasn't true, but it helped him fit into his new role, and sometimes he was even able to sleep for a bit without nightmares.

As Austin was coming up on five months as the general's assistant, the general called him into the tent. Austin thought it was to discuss the intelligence they had received about Meridia looking to mount an assault in the Disputed Region. As he sat in his chair and looked at the general's face, he realised it wasn't. Whatever the general was reading was clearly upsetting him. Had there been a battle with heavy losses?

The general put down the document and looked at Austin, his eyes sad. Austin looked at the document. It was the inquiry report.

"Austin." The general's voice was quiet. "Is this true? Did you really do all of this?"

Austin panicked. He could feel his world beginning to fall down around him. How could he get out of this? Could he convince the general that it wasn't true? Maybe he could argue that the person who did the inquiry got it wrong?

"All of what, sir?" He decided to buy some time. And better to know what they knew before he said anything that could get him in trouble. Maybe they didn't know everything.

"Murder. Wounded enemy combatants, innocent civilians, women. Children."

"Uh. Well, what does it ... what does it say about—"

"It says," the general's voice was cold now, "that you committed, ordered, and sanctioned murder, rape, and torture of those who were not in battle. Those you should have been protecting."

"Meridia deserves no protection," Austin snapped back, thinking of his dead comrades.

"Those not in the fight do." The general sat back in his chair and rubbed his eyes.

"You don't get it, sir. Safely back here away from it.

They are all involved. They help the army, they report on us. They get us killed!"

"They are not combatants!" Austin had never heard the general yell before, and it silenced him as easily as a slap to the face would have. "You killed children." His voice was ice.

"No, I ..." Austin flailed about for the words, but there were none.

"Austin. You have broken the law in the most heinous way. You will be arrested and taken back to the capital to await charges and your trial." The general stood, getting ready to call the guards in to take him away.

Three explosions hit in quick succession. Bizarrely, Austin wondered if it was his comrades here to bust him out. The general ran out of the tent, pistol in hand and yelling orders to his men. Austin followed, walking, everything feeling like a movie he was watching, like he was removed from it. He watched the general calling orders and protecting his men. The general pushed a soldier into cover just as a bullet hit where he had been seconds before, then fired into the enemy with his pistol to enable his men to get to cover. He was a better man than Austin.

There was yelling to his left, and Austin looked over, seeing two military policemen kneeling with their pistols out, unsure whether to leave who they were guarding and fight, or remain. They were in the open, and Austin didn't understand why they wouldn't at least get to cover. Then he saw who they were guarding. It was Harry and his old team. Harry spotted him and began yelling, though Austin couldn't hear him. A rocket screamed through the air, landing behind the prisoners and killing them all, as well as their guards. Austin stared blankly at the burning mound where his friends used to be.

"Austin," the general said as he pulled him back into the

tent. "Here, grab these." He tossed Austin a rifle and a pistol, keeping a rifle for himself. "Come on, we're needed."

"Wait." Something in Austin's voice made the general stop and turn to look at him. He stared at the pistol pointed at his head in bewilderment. Austin could understand his confusion. The enemy was supposed to be outside.

"Austin, come now ..." The general trailed off after seeing Austin's expression. Austin watched as the general considered talking him down. The older man looked Austin directly in the eye and tightened his grip on the pistol, but before the general could raise his weapon, Austin pulled the trigger. The general's body fell to the ground. Austin felt everything freeze around him. "I'm sorry," he whispered.

* * *

Austin looked around his new room in the palace. It was fancier than his usual accommodations. He could get used to this. When he first arrived in the capital, he'd unpacked the basics, but hadn't wanted to get too comfortable until he was sure he would stay. Now, since it had been two years, he was considering how he wanted to decorate his upgraded room. He might be here for a while. He proudly placed his beret on a shelf and reached back into the box. He pulled out a photo that one of his buddies had taken of him, lying prone behind his rifle, looking out with the mountains in the background. That would go on the shelf, but his Star of Honour for his actions in saving the command post would stay in the box.

He liked it here. It was relaxed, and the royal family was very nice. He avoided the queen, of course, but he felt like she preferred it that way. He was simply a reminder of her father. He didn't miss the strict routine and discipline of military life, but he did miss the friendship. The bond that could only be forged through shared hardship.

He sat on his bed and, on a whim, sent one of his buddies a message. Kieran had been in Austin's first patrol, but had rotated out before things went south. Surprisingly, Kieran responded quickly and invited Austin to the pub later. *Why not? What harm could there be?*

Austin hadn't expected to feel like no time had passed, but immediately it was like those early days. Kieran took him from the pub to a rally that he and his friends were going to, and Austin felt like he had found his people again. He laughed and joked, and enjoyed being able to say out loud that he thought the government was bending to their trade partners too much, and should focus more on fixing things internally. He hadn't wanted to go to the nationalist rally. He had heard some pretty extreme things, and that wasn't for him. Not anymore. But now he realised that he could just hang out with people who felt and thought like he did.

He was getting ready to go to his fifth rally when the note turned up. It appeared in his room, which was really weird, and was from someone calling themselves "the Patriot". Austin threw it in the bin. Some random guy wanting him to spy on the royal family could go jump. All he wanted was to hang with his buddies and get drunk.

But he mentioned it to his friends all the same, and when they were clearly impressed and a bit jealous, he reconsidered the note. Maybe he could drop the guy some information here and there. What was the harm? Plus, he felt important again. He hadn't realised he missed that.

For the next couple of years, Austin kept carrying out the tasks whenever he got the mysterious notes. He and his buddies tried to guess who the mysterious Patriot was. Kieran thought it was the opposition leader. Austin joined in the guessing, but really, he didn't care. He had his mates, and they seemed to think the Patriot was helping Highacre. That was enough for him. Perhaps this was how he atoned. A nonviolent way to help his country.

Austin read the latest note from the Patriot that had turned up in the wake of the attack on the royal family. It told him that the attack was clearly Meridia's fault, and that he was to keep a close eye on Lily, the sole surviving royal who had been brought back from another dimension. He was to protect her, and eventually the Patriot would give Austin the information he needed to convince Lily that the Meridian influence permeated even the highest levels of government. And then he would help Lily purge it from their country. Austin crumpled the note in his fist. He would do his duty.

Silence had fallen over Jason and Naomi as they watched Austin's past. It hung over them like a silent spectre, the dead asking what they would do now that they knew the truth.

"I'm getting the police," said Jason, pushing back his chair and going to stand.

Naomi put a hand on his arm, stopping him. "Which police?"

Jason settled back into his chair. She had a point.

They sat in silence for a minute before Jason said, "We need to find that email. Remember Claire's comment as they dragged her out of the room?"

Naomi went to get a laptop that had internet connectivity.

"I bet it's about Hudson vanishing. Maybe an idea about what happened?" Jason suggested hopefully.

"But she already mentioned Hudson. She wouldn't have bothered if she sent that information in an email. Ten bucks says she's figured out who the Patriot is."

Naomi sat back down, opening the laptop and stabbing at the power button. Nothing happened. She rolled her eyes and sighed heavily as she heaved herself back out of her chair and plodded off to retrieve the power cord.

"It's got to be Ezra," Jason said. "She didn't look surprised enough for it to be someone other than him. He was her obsession."

"But what does he get out of it?" countered Naomi. "War with his own country?"

"Wars are profitable. And he's a businessman."

"Seems like a very risky way to make money. And besides, it's been months now, and all we have is Highacre turned into a police state."

"Maybe that was his aim. Maybe he hates Highacre and wants to destroy it."

Naomi plugged the cord into an outlet and sat back down, glancing at Jason as she plugged the laptop in.

"Unlikely. He's hardly some fairy tale villain out for the destruction of the world."

"He might be," Jason muttered defensively, thinking he'd never trusted Ezra and found him smarmy.

"It's got to be someone who benefits from a regime change. That's what the Patriot seems to be after," said Naomi, pushing the power button and smiling with satisfaction as the laptop began to boot up.

"Okay, well, who does that leave?"

"It could be one of our own politicians," said Naomi. "But thinking out of the box for a minute—what about Austin?"

"I thought he was the insider?"

"Any reason he couldn't be both?"

Jason raised an eyebrow and considered Naomi's suggestion. It was frustrating that the immersion device didn't include thoughts. They were left to impute meaning from what they saw and heard. Could Austin be behind the entire nationalist movement? That didn't feel right to Jason. Austin just didn't strike him as a strategic leader or a mastermind. Though perhaps that would be a reason to invent a shadowy persona. If no one was taking him seriously, he may have created a figurehead for them to get behind.

"How about Minister Toot?" Naomi suggested.

Jason snorted the water he had been drinking. "Are you serious? Toot can't manage anything other than his whiskey, and you think he's staging a coup?"

"Haven't you noticed he's surprisingly efficient now the PM's given him a bunch of power? He's here all the time, overseeing operations. He's the one running the HSP. Maybe he's pulling the prime minister's strings and just letting Toth think he's the one in charge."

"Fair call," said Jason, now realising that Naomi was right. Toot *had* been more engaged than he'd ever seen the old man. Sure, he was rude and dismissive to Jason, but now that he thought about it, Toot was being very hands-on in running the HSP, and the palace security.

"But for the record, if it's one of the politicians, my money's on Bellingham."

"She was arrested," said Jason incredulously.

"Sure, but have we seen her since? No. Listen, what better cover for a shadowy anonymous leader than to have herself arrested and retreat from view? She could then run everything without suspicion because we're all busy feeling sorry for her, thinking she's locked up in some cell somewhere."

Jason considered this. It didn't sound as crazy as it

might have a few weeks ago. Rather, to him, it sounded like the perfect plan.

"Then," Naomi continued with her theory, "once she's set whatever conditions she's aiming for, she returns, the hero having endured goodness knows what while in captivity at the hands of the evil Patriot, who she's now defeated. She then gets elected in a landslide victory, and everyone loves her."

Jason looked at Naomi with renewed respect and a small twinge of fear. "If you ever decide to become an evil mastermind, we're all screwed."

"Thanks." Naomi smiled. "Now, let's find that email and see if I'm right."

Naomi turned her attention to the laptop, her fingers gliding over the keys. Her frown gradually increased before Jason finally asked, "Not there?"

"No, but not only is there no email, I can't find her in the system at all."

"What do you mean?"

"Claire's email address is gone, and even old emails she sent to me from her account back when we thought she was the etiquette advisor are gone." Naomi looked up at Jason, fear in her eyes. "It's like she never existed."

37

"THAT WASN'T THE DEAL."

Lily and Belinda glared at each other from their respective benches in the garden of the mental health facility. Belinda would be there another week, after which time she would move in with Elaine and April, and Lily couldn't help but think, somewhat cynically, that this was partially behind her current stance.

Though Lily was intending to recover all of the gems, she felt that having recovered some of the gems, along with "acquiring" what turned out to be a little over three thousand dollars, she had fulfilled her side of the deal, at least in essence if not in actuality. At least enough for Belinda to provide the location of the felixium to enable concurrent activity.

Belinda, on the other hand, was sticking to her position that she had told Lily she would reveal the location of the felixium only when *all* the gems were handed to her eldest daughter.

"Look, even at a poor price, the gems bring the total amount we recovered to around five thousand. That's a pretty good boost. And with you now being recovered, you should be able to get a job, which means Elaine can cut back. That was the outcome you wanted."

"What I asked for was all the gems, which you and I both know are worth significantly more than five thousand."

"Are we looking for a solution to help Elaine? Or one that means you don't have to work?" Lily spat bitterly.

Belinda looked genuinely shocked at the venom in Lily's tone, and Lily could see hurt in her eyes. She felt a little guilty, but reminded herself that her mother was essentially holding her hostage.

"Lily," Belinda began, her tone much softer. "I ... I only want what's best for you and your siblings. The gems mean a break for Elaine, yes, but they also mean maybe getting some help for David. Not to mention doing something nice for April—she's been through so much. I know you want to get back. I'd be lying if I said that selfishly I didn't want some more time with you. Once you go ... I know I probably won't see you again."

The tears in Belinda's eyes were real, but Lily still felt hurt by her mother's actions. She hadn't expected her mother to act like this, demanding action from Lily before she was willing to help her. And then having learned about her mother's past as a Highacren spy, Lily couldn't help but feel suspicious. At least, that was how she justified to herself her desire to find out if her mother was being genuine.

Lily hesitated. She had spent all morning searching on her phone, trying to find out what had happened to the police officer whose mind she had damaged. Though she'd found nothing, she wondered whether that was because the media only reported when they thought the injuries were suffered in the line of duty. Perhaps they assumed the poor guy had suffered a stroke or something.

Trying to convince herself that there had been no reports because the police officer was fine, Lily reminded herself she was just going to observe the thoughts, not change them, and she reached out tentatively, trying to make contact with Belinda's mind. She took a couple of deep breaths, steadying herself. Her mother was an expert in mental barriers and would likely notice any incursion that was anything but subtle and precise.

Lily felt for the rings that she saw when mind reading and managed to make contact, feather light; it was possibly the most subtle penetration she had ever achieved.

Belinda's head snapped up. "You don't believe me." She stated it as fact, looking at Lily sadly. "I suppose I can't blame you. I kept a lot hidden, and it's all been dumped on you at once. If it helps you in any way—if it helps you begin to trust me again, here."

Lily felt the mental barrier lift and found she had complete access to Belinda's current thoughts and emotions. She quickly scanned around inside. Belinda was being genuine, however, Lily noticed that her mother's barrier had not disappeared, but simply moved. Lily had access to Belinda's current thoughts and feelings, but not her memories.

So much for establishing trust.

Lily felt resentful at having to prove herself yet again, and this made her reckless. She had access to her mother's mind. Why not test her powers against the best? Claire had explained to her about mental barriers. The easiest way to deal with them was to blast through. This gave you access to everything behind them and you usually gained a few useful seconds to examine the person's mind while they futilely tried to repair their defences.

But the downside of that approach was that they knew that you knew. The real art of mental penetration came from breaching a barrier without the person realising you had done it. This, Claire had told her, was something they spent a lot of time and effort in teaching in the intelligence agencies, but very few could achieve it. If you could, then you would have access to your opponent's information without them being aware of it.

Lily had, in fact, been able to achieve this level of breach, but only against those able to erect rudimentary barriers. She had tried a handful of times against someone she had been told had modest skills, but she'd been detected every time. Belinda was a master of mental magic, but Lily told herself that she had come a long way since her early attempts. And her experiences back in this dimension had only strengthened her skills.

When Lily was first trying to learn magic, Addison had told her that self belief was often the key. If you genuinely believed in yourself, you were more likely to succeed. However, having that level of faith in your own abilities—unless you were a narcissist—was often akin to not thinking of an elephant after having been told not to.

Immediately, Lily's devastating failure the preceding evening filled her head. She tried to dismiss it, focussing only on her successes and the great progress she had made in a relatively short period of time. Predictably, this didn't work, and instead Lily found herself focussing on her failures and setbacks.

Ava popped into her head, and Lily remembered her saying that learning from her mistakes would propel her further forward than perfection ever could. She held on to that thought, now turning all her errors into successes, thinking instead of how she had overcome her obstacles.

I can do this.

Lily took a steadying breath and imagined piercing Belinda's mental barrier like a needle through water. She hesitated once, then went for it, trying not to display her shock on her face when she succeeded and found herself in Belinda's mind.

The experience of everyone's mind was different. Some people lived mainly in words, others in pictures or sounds. Belinda's mind was full of impressions. As Lily accessed memories, she saw some images while hearing certain words in her own mind, and she noticed feelings associated with the memories. She saw Christmas from when she was five, and as the family sat around the tree, Lily heard laughter. The word "love" floated across her mind, and she felt a happiness that was separate from her own emotions.

Lily flittered through more of her mother's memories of Lily's childhood, indulging her childlike need to reassure herself of what she already knew. Her mother loved her very much. Finally, and with an effort despite knowing she had very limited time, Lily tore herself from those memories and looked for what her mother had done with the felixium.

She found the memory of her mother arriving at the facility and the staff taking the device. Her mother had let them have it, and Lily couldn't find any memories of accessing the device after that. So she returned to that memory and followed it back. Her mother's memories prior to arriving at the facility were fractured, and she realised that her mother had been telling the truth about her mental health.

Not that I thought she was lying.

Although, she did realise that she had felt perhaps that Belinda had been exaggerating. Now she felt horrible for that assumption. Of course Belinda's mind was fractured. She had been devastated. Her daughter had disappeared, and they lost her home. And then her husband died.

This drew Lily like a magnet to Belinda's memories of her husband. Lily saw her dad leaving their new city apartment, heading out to continue the search for Lily. There was an overwhelming sense of guilt attached to the memory and she felt her mother's conflict—wanting to ease her husband's mind and tell him where she suspected Lily was, but scared to reveal the lie that had existed for their entire relationship.

The stress was extreme. Belinda was terrified that her lie would ruin her relationship. At first, she had refrained from saying anything, thinking that Lily might reappear at any moment. She was unwilling to risk her marriage, and was more worried at first that something bad had actually happened to her daughter.

As time went on, Belinda became more certain that Highacre had taken Lily, but now she had to explain, not only that she had lied about who she was, but that she'd had a good idea of where their daughter had gone, and had kept it to herself. She oscillated on a daily basis between deciding to tell her husband everything, and resolving to remain silent.

The memories flashed to Belinda waiting near the door, anxiety permeating from her final decision to tell her husband the truth. But then the memory morphed into Belinda being informed of her husband's death. Lily flinched away and back to the memories of the device, but not before feeling the overwhelming grief, pain, and disbelief of her mother's loss.

Feeling nauseous and sure that if her mother hadn't already noticed the incursion, she was sure to soon, Lily scanned the memories of the device, looking for the felixium. Finally, she found it. It was an image of her mother removing the felixium from the device with an attached feeling of achieving her task.

That's it?

Lily felt panic rising. She examined the memory again, noticing that her mother was younger. She had removed the felixium a while ago. There had to be more to it, but she didn't have time to explore. She focussed on the memory, trying to use all her senses. She saw a flash of her mother's favourite emerald ring, and then she heard it. Just a whisper. *Lake.*

"Sorry, what?" Lily snapped out of her mother's mind and back to the present. Her mother had been talking to her, but she didn't know what she'd said.

"I asked you if that helped at all? Helped you understand where I'm coming from?"

"I do understand, Mum," said Lily, thinking back to the extreme emotions she had felt while in her mother's memories. "I want to help you all too. I really do. But I also need to get back. I guess ... I guess it feels like I want to help you, but you don't want to help me."

Belinda visibly stopped herself from whatever retort had been on her lips. "I can understand why you'd feel that way," she said eventually. "No matter how we've acted so far, I think it's clear now we both want to help each other. We both want to help your sisters, and we both want to get you back to Highacre. Can we put the rest behind us and move forward together to achieve those goals?"

"Yes," said Lily guiltily.

Alexei and Ava had been looking into the feasibility of going after the rest of the gems. She would be happy to hear what they'd found, and if possible, retrieve the gems.

But she now knew where the felixium was.

Whatever else happened, she was going home.

Claire blinked and looked around the room, squinting. It was dark and fuzzy. Was that her eyes? She moved her head to see if she was hooded. No hood, but a sharp pain reminded her of yesterday's interrogation session. Was it yesterday? She blinked and looked around again, unable to find any indication of the time of day. How long had she even been here?

Following her arrest, Claire had expected to be taken to a police station, or wherever it was the HSP operated out of. But then they had handcuffed her to the inside of a van, hooded her, and brought her here. Wherever here was. She recalled being driven around for a long time. Either it was very far away from the palace, or they had driven her around to disorient her. She had tried to keep track of turns and distance as she was taught in training, but doing so had proven more difficult in reality.

She sniffed and tried to stretch. It felt like she was in the interrogation room they used, rather than the cell she had been largely confined to since her arrival. And stretching told her that she was strapped to the small uncomfortable chair, as was usual for interrogations.

Bugger.

Had they even taken her back to her cell after last time?

Clearly they were trying to disorient her, make her lose track of time. And it was working. It could have been days, or it could only have been a few hours. At first she had tried to tell the time from the intervals at which something changed. The weedy little rat-faced man brought her mouldy bread and stale water. They emptied the bucket she had so generously been given for relieving herself. She was taken to and from interrogations.

But eventually it became obvious that they were purposefully mixing things up to keep her confused. Plus, they were drugging her through the food and occasionally injections. The drugs knocked her out quickly, leaving her unconscious and unaware of the passage of time. She might have been out for a minute or days each time.

Occasionally, they would pull her from her cell, bring her here, and strap her to this chair. Sometimes they would just leave her there for a bit. Sometimes a masked guy would come in and question her. So far, she had managed to remain silent. Sighing, Claire thought about how much she had hated this part of spy training.

She focussed on the dripping off to her right, trying to use the sound to clear her head and focus, rather than being irritated by it. She heard some voices outside the door. Short, sharp orders were being given. People were moving around in haste. Her door opened, momentarily blinding her with the light in the corridor. When her eyes finally recovered, she saw a guard standing off to her left. He was alert, rigidly straight. Someone important must be here. *Shit.*

Her masked buddy entered, more wound up than usual. He was obviously putting on a show for whoever was watching. He shouted the usual questions at her, and, barely waiting to see if she would answer, struck her across the face for refusing to do so. He was hitting harder than before. Showing off for whoever was here.

Claire didn't recall passing out, but as she came too, she felt kind hands gently pressing a cool cloth to her wounds.

"There, there. Don't move too quickly."

She was disoriented, and her head throbbed. She felt jumbled and unsure.

"Now, how are you feeling?"

Claire squinted up at the face hovering in front of her. Concern was in his eyes. The face gradually came into focus.

Ezra!

"Ezra!" Claire felt hopeful. "Are they watching?" she whispered, trying to look around.

"There now, everything's going to be alright."

"No, we need to get out of here." Claire tried to remember where "here" was, a new wave of confusion taking her. She shook her head. That didn't matter. All that mattered was that she and Ezra needed to get out of there. "They'll be back soon."

Something was niggling at the back of her mind, but it was trapped in the fuzzy part, and she couldn't see it. Claire blinked rapidly, trying to clear her brain. Whatever drugs they'd given her this time were no joke. Or maybe she was concussed from the enthusiastic questioner.

Panicked, Claire tried to stand, and found herself bound to a chair. Everything snapped back into focus in her head. Ezra didn't need to get out of there. Ezra was the big boss that they were all showing off for. He was probably the one who ordered her arrest. She stiffened, and Ezra noticed.

"Ah, good. You *do* know. Saves us a lot of pesky revealing of secrets and unveiling of plots."

"Oh, come on now. It's traditional. You tell me everything you've been up to in unnecessarily long and incriminating detail. I'm shocked that someone like you would do something like that. You explain your backstory and why you're really a good person. I realise that you wouldn't be telling me all this if you were going to let me live. You then explain that you're going to kill me in a bizarre and unnecessarily complex way that includes opportunities to escape. Which I do."

Ezra laughed genially, but his eyes were dead. Claire's insides froze, but she tried to keep up the bravado.

"Somehow you strike me more as the simple, shoot-them-in-the-head kind of guy. But can I still get the background information? I really want to know if I'm right."

Ezra pulled up his chair so that he was sitting in front of Claire, but now a reasonable distance away. "Why don't you tell me what you think I've been up to, and I'll tell you if you're right?"

Claire's mind was in overdrive. She tried to calm herself. She had to think. She had to be smart about this. He wanted to know what she knew. What she had found out and how compromised he might be. She couldn't give him all the information. Then she would have no value and he'd kill her. But maybe she could give him parts of it and try to use that to get more information out of him. Obviously, he knew that she knew enough to know he was bad.

"May I have some water?" Claire was very thirsty, but she also wanted to see how he was going to play this interrogation, as well as buy herself some time to strategize.

"Of course." Ezra nodded at the guard, who immediately crossed to the door and spoke with someone outside. Ezra smiled pleasantly at Claire as they waited, occasionally picking some lint off his sleeve. "Ah, here we are."

Another guard entered and placed a tray on a small table. It held one glass of water. Claire eyed it suspiciously.

"Would you like me to take a sip first?" Ezra asked. He was smiling at her, finding her paranoia amusing.

"No thank you. I was just contemplating how I might drink it with my arms restrained as they are."

Ezra nodded at the guard again. Claire's spirits lifted. If she could free her arms, she had more options. Her heart sank as a guard entered and placed a straw in the glass.

"Now." Ezra sat back and crossed his legs. "What exactly do you think I've been up to?"

"You're the special advisor to the prime minister. No doubt you played a key role in the creation of the HSP, which explains why you're here questioning me." Claire had decided to start out lightly, providing Ezra with a plausible reason for his being there that had no implications of his being involved in anything untoward. If he bought it, he might let her go. Or at least live a little longer.

"But of course." Ezra's dead eyes remained locked on hers.

Claire suddenly felt very uncomfortable. She cast around her memory for information on Ezra's cybernetic implant. As far as Highacre knew, he had an implant that could somehow boost his charm and likability.

He certainly isn't using that right now.

But they were almost certain that his implant could do other things. They just didn't know what. All reports on cybernetics agreed they couldn't replicate the mind reading or mind control abilities that some Highacrens possessed. But who knew what Meridia was able to hide? And if anyone would have an implant that could do something like that, it would be Ezra. If he could read her mind, then it was game over. She focussed on her mental barriers, vaguely wondering if they would work the same with cybernetics as they did with magic.

"Why were you meeting with Jason and Naomi?"

"We were working together to try to unveil the identity of the palace insider. What are you really doing for the prime minister?"

"I am his special advisor. But he also relies on me for the kind of advice he might seek from the director of the HIA. If you still had one. Did you discover the insider's identity?"

"Yes. What is your end game here in Highacre?"

"Oh, poor question, Miss Jones. And asked too soon in the dance. I expected more from you. Who is the insider?"

"You know who the insider is. You recruited them."

Ezra sat back, eyes fixed on Claire, expression unreadable. She wondered if he was using his implant. After what felt like an age, he turned his head, getting the attention of the guard by the door, and nodded once. The guard left and Claire felt her anxiety rising.

"Were you involved in the assassinations of the royal family?"

Ezra looked Claire dead in the eye. "Yes."

Claire's heart dropped. She was not getting out of here alive.

"Oh come now, don't worry. Political murder is so crass. Much more Reginald's flavour than mine. No, I won't kill you. Instead, my people will hack into your life, take over your social media, your email, and we'll turn you into a conspiracy theorising crackpot. Then you can say whatever you like. No one will believe you. It might actually work in my favour if you go around accusing me of being involved in the deaths of the royal family."

Claire had felt a spark of relief when Ezra said she wouldn't be killed, but it fizzled and died as he described what he had planned instead. She prized her reputation. What would she do with it trashed? For a beat, Claire couldn't decide which outcome would be worse.

Don't be ridiculous. If you're alive, you have a chance.

The guard re-entered the room, this time carrying a small box that he gave to Ezra. Ezra thanked him and the guard left. Ezra stroked the lid of the box as if it held priceless gems. He picked up his chair and strolled around behind Claire, settling himself close enough to speak quietly in her ear.

"Now," he said softly. "Who do you think is the insider?"

Claire felt a sudden blast of pain exploding from her fingers. It was so sudden and overwhelming, she could focus on nothing else. And then, just as suddenly, it was gone. Ezra waited patiently as Claire tried to think. Should she tell him they knew it was Austin? He likely already knew they knew anyway. But before she could answer, the pain exploded again.

"Come on Miss Jones. It's not a difficult question." The pain ceased. Claire again tried to gather herself. "Let me make it easier for you. Is Austin compromised?"

Claire sat up slightly, surprised that Ezra had named Austin. Ezra grunted, satisfied with her reaction. And then the pain returned.

"It would seem he is. Not to worry. Probably safer to find a new lackey, anyway. Austin will no doubt still have his uses."

The pain ceased and Claire slumped forward in her chair, sweating, heart racing, already exhausted. The interrogation continued, with Ezra asking question after question. He mainly seemed focussed on determining what Claire knew about his operations and whether she had passed some or all of that information over to Jason or anyone else. That she didn't know what he was doing behind her to cause so much pain added to the growing terror rising inside her. The pain changed from hot to sharp to focussed to all-encompassing. Claire lost all sense of time, and started to fret that he would keep her here, torturing her for days.

Ezra kept asking questions in his calm, genial voice. Claire answered none of them.

"I'm impressed, Miss Jones. So few can withstand that level of ... discomfort for so long. I would have liked to have had an agent of your calibre under my command back in the MIA."

Ezra strolled back around in front of Claire. She was vaguely aware of an interaction with a guard. Perhaps he passed him his torture box for safekeeping. She jumped as the straw appeared by her lips, offered by Ezra. Tempted though she was to ignore it, she was dehydrated and gratefully took a couple of mouthfuls.

She looked up. Ezra was cleaning his glasses, preparing to leave.

"Pity it was all wasted effort on your part. I just need to hold fast for a little while longer and then everything will be in place, and it won't matter whether you or your friends shout your theories from the rooftops."

What does that mean?

Claire tried to commit his exact phasing to memory for dissection later, but her mind couldn't help trying to figure it out now. What could he possibly do that would mean they could reveal his role in the assassination of the royal family and it wouldn't matter?

Ezra opened the door and then turned to the guard. "Take her back to her cell. Leave her there for now. She won't be troubling us anymore."

39

"Those were some ... interesting people," said Ava, getting off the bus and falling into step beside Lily.

"You do meet a lot of diverse people on the bus," Lily agreed with a smile.

"I would never have thought of some of those hairstyles on my own. Your people are very creative."

"I mean, technically these are not my people."

The banter continued as they walked along the road. Lily felt more relaxed than she had in ages. She knew that she and Ava had a job to do, but she couldn't escape the feeling that they were on vacation. She got the impression that Ava felt the same way. She was smiling more than she had been recently and was joking a lot. This was the Ava she knew and was friends with.

Lily frowned at the thought. Ignoring the bigger question, she wondered if this made her a fair-weather friend, only wanting to be around people when they were at their best.

No. I still enjoyed being around Ava when she wasn't happy. I just wanted to help her feel better.

"What's going on in there?" Ava asked, gently tapping Lily's head.

"Oh nothing. Just trying to remember the last time we were here."

Ava's face fell sympathetically. "It must be hard coming back. You know, not that—well, with your dad and all."

Not actually having been thinking about that, it was now front and centre of Lily's mind. They were at a lake about three hours east of the family farm. It was a popular holiday spot for her family and their neighbours, but people in the city usually went a few hours in the other direction to go to the beach. The lake was very large and blob-shaped with many inlets and coves. This meant that the cabins scattered around its edges were relatively secluded. When holidaying there, often Lily hadn't realised who else was visiting until they met in the water.

It had been a few years now since the last family trip to the lake. Lily realised with a drop in her stomach that trip would now be the last ever for the whole family. She had been sixteen, like April was now, and David had been at the age where playing in the water with his sisters wasn't cool. He had split his time between indulging his younger siblings and trying to talk crop futures with their father.

Lily could picture her dad in her mind. Sitting on a chair by the lake's edge, near enough to keep his children safe, but engrossed in his book, a beer in his hand. She remembered he had been reading some spy novel because he'd laughed at David's eagerness to talk business.

"I admire your enthusiasm, son," he'd said, patting David proudly on the shoulder. "But this time is about relaxing. You need to be able to switch off. Life's about more than work."

David had argued that the farm *was* his life, and hadn't someone said that if you do what you love, you never work a day? Nonetheless, he had dropped the business talk and relaxed. Straining to remember if it was that trip or a previous one, Lily thought maybe he had gone inside shortly after to take over dinner preparations from their mother so that she might relax with Dad.

Lily was hit with a wave of sadness for her brother, and guilt that she'd been so focussed on helping her sisters that she'd barely given him a thought. She told herself that there was so much on her plate; that it was okay to focus on the problems she had a hope of solving, but a small part of her knew it was an uncomfortable problem that she didn't want to face, and so she'd ignored it.

Lily felt Ava's arms around her and realised she'd started crying. She began apologising, but Ava shushed her and held her tightly.

"You're allowed to cry, Lily."

Lily held Ava back and allowed herself a few more tears, before commenting that, given the quality of their fellow bus travellers, perhaps they shouldn't remain crying on the side of the road. They may attract some unwanted attention. Laughing, Ava wiped Lily's face gently, and they both resumed walking in the direction of the lake.

"So your mum took the felixium out years ago? Why?"

"I don't know," said Lily. "I didn't have time to really look into it. But I mean, if she had the device with her at the farm, she may have taken the felixium out when she had kids. What if one of us had found the device, hit the button, and turned up in Highacre as a random toddler? She'd have no way to warn Highacre or get us back."

"Fair enough," said Ava, smiling at the idea. "So she takes it out and puts it in a ring."

"That's what I think." Lily had come up with her theory on the way home from the facility. "She'd want it close by, since that was the whole point of the device, and felixium is a stone. Dad always used to say her emerald was too dull for her and that he should get her a new ring."

Ava gave Lily's arm a squeeze, and they walked in silence for a bit.

"So you and Alexei couldn't find a way to get the rest of the gems?"

"No. As you'd expect from a rare gems dealer, their security is pretty tight. Not like Fingers's shop. This guy basically has his own underground bunker. It's locked up tight and inside are safes and lockboxes and probably alarms and lasers and an army—"

"Okay, I get it." Lily laughed. "That sucks though. I'd feel a lot better about securing our way home if I was still going to be able to help my family."

"I know," said Ava sympathetically. "But think of it this way. We're just not going to be able to get the gems back. Which means your mother is not going to willingly give us the felixium. So if we want to get back, we'd need to just take it anyway. This way Alexei is stocking all the shelves and cleaning all the break rooms possible to help Elaine. I mean, your family."

Lily laughed. Alexei really was taken with her older sister. But in his defence, he was right in that retrieving the felixium was unlikely to need all three of them, and of the three, he was less useful in locating the ring. So he had opted to remain behind to keep working and get as much money as possible as a show of good faith for when they broke the news to Belinda.

"Wow," said Ava, coming to a halt.

The lake stretched out before them, the same deep blue as the sky and surrounded by the bright green leaves of the trees that stretched from the water to the distant mountains.

"Lily, this is beautiful."

Lily had to agree with Ava, though she remembered

being similarly struck by the beauty of Highacre when she first saw it. It had seemed so much more beautiful than this. Perhaps she had taken the lake for granted, and Highacre seemed so much prettier because it was new and exotic.

Lily led Ava off to the left, heading for the cabin that her family had always stayed in. They arrived in front of it about half an hour later. It looked smaller than Lily remembered. And more run-down.

"Cool!" said Ava, heading up the steps to the door.

"Ava! It's not ours. There might be someone staying there."

"One way to find out." She wiggled her eyebrows at Lily and knocked loudly on the door, calling out a greeting. When there was no answer, she went to each of the front windows, cupping her eyes to block the light and peering inside. "Looks like no one's home."

"Okay, but we can't just—"

"You're kidding!"

"What?"

"Here? In the middle of nowhere. This is where you people decide to use electronic locks?" Ava gestured to an electronic pad, currently displaying a thin red light. She looked at it for a beat, then tapped it with her finger. The door beeped, and the light turned green.

"Ava," Lily began, hesitation in her voice.

"It's fine," Ava reassured her. "We're not being dodgy. We're just going to check it to see if your mum's ring is here."

Lily looked at her suspiciously. "You couldn't just scan from outside?"

"I mean, I could, but I'm tired." She said the last part in a whiny voice. "And if we need to go in the lake, I'm going to want a shower before we head back to the city."

Lily followed her reluctantly inside. It occurred to her

that she was much easier to convince when it was Ava suggesting something. Deciding not to dwell on why that might be, Lily instead looked around the cabin. It was similar to how she remembered it, but there were some small differences. A different coloured throw rug on the couch. New kitchen appliances. She moved around, casually opening and closing drawers. It was an inefficient way to search, but she didn't really want to use her magic. She was yet to be able to push back that far into a location's memory, but the idea of going back and seeing her family, happy and whole, was too much.

"No jewellery." Ava bounded down the stairs. "But that's not a surprise. Your mum probably wasn't going to store something that valuable in a shared house owned by someone else."

Both exited and stood on the deck, looking at the lake. It was a nice day for a swim. Warm—not too hot or too cold. But it was a big lake, and if the ring was in there ...

"Of course it is," said Ava, who was staring intently at the lake.

"It's in there?"

"Yep. Right in the middle. Belinda must have tossed it as far as she could. How she thought she'd get it back—"

"Probably like this," Lily said cockily, winking at Ava. She concentrated on the lake, ordering the ring to return to her. She could feel the ring in there, but it was farther away than her magic could reach effectively. And it also felt stuck somehow. Maybe in mud, or possibly caught on something.

"That—whatever it is—seems to be an ineffective retrieval method," said Ava seriously. Lily gave her a gentle shove.

"How's your diving?"

The women walked down to the lake, and Ava stripped to her underwear before performing a perfect racing dive off the jetty. Lily stood watching self-consciously. Ava surfaced, whipped her hair off her face, and turned to face Lily, treading water.

"Come on then."

Lily considered keeping her T-shirt on, but chastised herself. Now was not the time to be prudish. It made no sense for her to get her clothes wet, and it'd only bog her down when she dove for the ring.

Still. She was certainly not in as good shape as Ava. *She's not looking, idiot.* Though, as Lily quickly discarded her clothes and jumped in the water, she felt her friend's eyes on her.

They swam out until Ava announced that they were right above the ring. Wanting to distract from her hesitation to get in, and possibly to impress Ava, Lily immediately dove down, kicking as hard as she could, driving toward the bottom.

How deep is this lake?

Lily's lungs started to feel enormous pressure, and she began to worry about getting back to the surface, so she turned and kicked back up, breaking the surface and gasping for air.

"Your turn," she panted at Ava, who was staring at Lily, a smile on her face.

"I mean, I could," Ava said happily. "But we're closer now. Can't you just magic it up here?"

Feeling decidedly stupid, Lily let herself recover a bit longer, telling herself that she hadn't tried because of how stuck it had felt from the shore. However, directly overhead, it was easier to move, and with some mental jiggling and tugging, the ring finally squelched free of the bottom of the lake and Lily carefully brought it to the surface, immediately putting it on to avoid losing it.

Ava turned onto her back and began casually floating back towards shallower waters.

"You needn't have gotten wet after all," Lily said, copying Ava.

"One in, all in." Ava smiled. "Besides, I fancied a swim."

They floated quietly back until they were able to stand in the water, and Lily stood for a bit, giving her arms a rest. Ava floated over.

"Nice work back there, Your Majesty."

"Shut up," said Lily good-naturedly, and she splashed at Ava for good measure.

Ava splashed back and before they knew it, the two women were laughing and splashing and then Ava ran at Lily, tackling her into the water and dunking her before bringing her back to the surface.

"Ava!" Lily squealed. "You bi—"

Ava kissed her. Lily, stunned, at first did nothing, and then feeling panicked that Ava would pull away, kissed her back. Their arms went around each other, and the kiss deepened. Eventually, Ava pulled away, and though Lily didn't know how long they'd been locked like that, it definitely felt too short.

"Sorry," said Ava tentatively in a voice that didn't sound sorry, but sought confirmation that Lily had wanted the kiss and had enjoyed it.

"No, I—it was—I liked it," Lily finished shyly.

"Me too." Ava smiled, then looked meaningfully at Lily. "I like you."

Lily's heart fluttered enthusiastically. "I like you too."

They stayed in the lake for about an hour, then returned to the cabin to shower and dry off. While Ava was in the shower, Lily pulled up the bus schedule on the internet.

"Bugger."

"What's wrong?" Ava asked, appearing in front of Lily, drying her hair with a towel.

"No buses until tomorrow."

"Oh no," said Ava insincerely with a smile. "We have to stay here? Whatever will we do with our time?"

Lily's stomach butterflies went mad, and she felt herself blush.

"Relax," said Ava, sitting beside her on the couch. "I'm joking. Unless you want to. And then I'm up for it. But otherwise I was joking."

Lily smiled, but looked around the cabin, concerned. "We can't stay here though."

"Why not?"

"Because we haven't paid for it."

"We'll write them a good review."

"Ava," Lily said more seriously. "It doesn't feel right."

Ava looked back at Lily. "I know, but I mean, we're already inside and we've used their shower. We should at least clean up after ourselves, and in that case, why not do it tomorrow instead of right now?"

"What if someone turns up?"

"It's, what? Four in the afternoon on Wednesday? It seems unlikely that anyone's coming. But if they do, we'll apologise profusely and tell them we mistook their cabin for our own."

Lily felt uncomfortable about the plan, but she had no alternative to suggest. And she didn't really want to sleep outside. Not knowing that there was a comfy bed right here. *Or at least a couch. No need to use more linens.*

"Come on, grumpy," Ava said, pulling Lily to her feet and into an embrace, planting a quick peck on her lips. "Let's get you some food."

40

"Unit One, in position."

"Copy Unit One." Jason could feel his heart pounding in the familiar way it did before an operation. Everything had happened so fast. After what felt like months of complete lack of progress and total inaction, suddenly he felt like there was barely time to breathe.

Following the discovery that Claire's email account had been obliterated, and without a Hudson to go looking for it, Jason and Naomi had turned their attention to the rest of the files that Claire had passed them. For all their hypothesising about the identity of the Patriot, as Naomi said, they had the information Claire had, so if she was able to figure it out, they should too. There was logic to that argument, but Jason had wondered whether they would be able to put the pieces together in the same way as Claire.

After about two hours of silent scrolling, Naomi had commented offhand that she'd found nothing even hinting at the identity of the Patriot, and the only item of vague interest was that one of Ezra's companies had bought an abandoned warehouse facility in the DR. Jason had practically jumped into her lap to look at her screen.

"Woah there, cowboy."

"Where is it? Where in the DR?" Jason was frantically scrolling through whatever document Naomi had open on her screen.

"If you give me a second"—Naomi pointedly pulled her mouse out of Jason's hand—"I'll reopen the relevant document."

"Sorry." Jason's embarrassment was dwarfed by his excitement. "It's just that, those checkpoints I told you about? What if this facility is behind those checkpoints?"

Naomi looked at him. "You think he stole the felixium? He shouldn't even know what it's used for."

"And yet he was in the room with the machine when Lily was pushed through. Maybe he knows more than we think."

"I suppose he was a top-level spook," Naomi conceded, returning to her screen. "I'm just not clear on the motive."

"We won't find that out 'till the end," Jason said. Naomi raised one eyebrow. "You know, right at the end, the baddie will give some long speech explaining everything and neatly tying up loose ends."

Naomi stared at Jason.

"Don't stop looking for the document."

Naomi continued staring.

"What?"

"For someone who never seems to have a day off, you clearly watch too many movies."

"My kids are into superhero movies."

"Uh huh. 'Your kids' are."

"Someone has to supervise."

"Oh, here it is."

Jason gently rolled Naomi's chair away from the screen, earning him a scowl. Moving his own in front, he eagerly scrolled the document, looking for the location.

"It's not here."

"What's not there?"

"The location."

"Yes, it is."

"No. There's no map, no description. It doesn't even mention the DR." He'd done a quick search of the document.

"No, but these funny little numbers and symbols are called coordinates," Naomi explained as if to a small child. "I thought military folk knew all about them, but I guess I was wrong."

Jason scowled, having missed them in his haste. He pulled up a search screen, ready to type them in, but Naomi pushed her phone under his nose, showing a map with the location highlighted.

"I knew it! Look, it's smack bang in the middle of the checkpoints. I'll bet my house that Ezra's warehouse is storing the stolen felixium."

After that, it had been a flurry of activity. Jason reached out to some trusted contacts within the military and managed to get a small squad assigned for a covert operation. He'd even found a good buddy who was looking to quit the military and so was happy to be responsible for notifying the defence minister *after* the operation had occurred.

Before leaving, Jason had rushed to his quarters and pulled his grab bag out from under his bed. It had everything he would need, other than weapons and body armour, but those he'd pick up down in the DR. Exiting his room, he came face to face with Naomi.

"The answer's no."

"You don't even know the question."

"You can't come. You need to stay here and run the operation as overwatch."

"This is such horse manure. What, do you not think I'm up to it?"

"Actually, I think you're more than up to it, and there's no one else I'd rather have by my side down there carrying out this mission. But what if I'm taken out? Claire's just been arrested. Hudson is missing. If we both get captured or killed down there, who will carry the operation on and retrieve the queen?"

Naomi looked placated. In fact, she was blushing. Jason made a note to provide more regular feedback. She needed to know that she was top-level material.

"Look, if—no, when we get the queen back, there needs to be at least one of us here to keep her safe. I wouldn't trust that role to anyone else. I will be able to do what needs to be done down there to get the felixium only because I know that you're here and can keep running with everything if I go down. Besides which, who here do you think we can trust to be our eyes in the skies? Richard?"

"Well." Naomi cleared her throat. She blinked a couple of times. "I mean, when you put it like that. I guess I can stay and run things here."

———

"Overwatch, all teams in position. Operation Blue Ferret is green light. Awaiting your go."

"Copy Zero Alpha. Overwatch has eyes on. Be advised, Little Birdy has investigated the unusual activity at the mines. Mines are operational."

"Ack." Jason considered Naomi's message. When he arrived back in the DR, he'd headed to the base to be issued his kit and had noticed a lot of activity around the felixium mines that Meridia had taken. Meridia shouldn't have a use for felixium, and so he had asked Naomi to use one of the drones she had been given command of to check it out.

Used to tough codenames, like "Reaper" or "Eagle", he smiled at Naomi's choice of "Little Birdy". It suddenly made him think of Edmund, and his smile slipped, wondering where he was now, and if he'd managed to enlist.

The radio chatter brought him back, and he steeled his mind to his mission, only permitting his thoughts to drift to wonder why Meridia would be mining felixium. Sure, the prime minister had let the interdimensional travel machine secret out of the bag, but there was no way Meridia could have built a machine this quickly, right? The only Meridian who had seen the machine was Ezra, and they had closely monitored him while he was in the room with it. Unless he had been in there before ... it suddenly occurred to Jason that Ava had also seen the machine, though she couldn't do much with that information from her current location.

Maybe they were mining it to study its properties. See how it powered the machine, and maybe what else it could do. Or maybe they were mining it to sell back to Highacre at a ridiculously high price. Or both. Whatever the reason, it was bad. But it could wait. Jason needed to keep his head in the game.

"Zero Alpha, you are a go."

"Copy, out to you Overwatch. All teams, move out."

Naomi nervously clicked her pen, watching the drone feeds and listening to the radio chatter. She felt so helpless, not being there, but what Jason had said made sense, and she could call in information from the drones as required. She probably wouldn't have to, since Jason said one of his team could magically access feeds from any surveillance equipment in a hundred-metre radius. But she could only focus on one feed at a time, so Naomi would have to keep an eye on the bigger picture.

She watched and listened as Jason and his team moved through the outer perimeter of the facility. They were like ghosts, gliding through abandoned shipping containers and pallets, neutralising any PSCs they came across. So far, they looked to have been able to take them down non-lethally. There were two paralysers with Jason, but they could only deal with one person at a time each if they were to paralyse the PSCs for the duration of the operation. And no one wanted them to suddenly wake up and come at the team from behind.

Naomi heard shots ring out and excited but clipped radio chatter. She checked the footage. It looked like Jason had met a small pocket of resistance. They overcame it quickly and continued their rapid progress toward the building where they had assessed the felixium was being stored. She watched Jason and two of his team enter like a well-oiled machine, while the remaining soldiers provided cover from outside.

"Overwatch, this is Zero Alpha."

"This is Overwatch. Do you have the package?"

"Negative Overwatch, nest is empty."

Naomi sat up in surprise. *Empty? But then, where is the felixium?*

There had been no other building that they had seen either on the plans or from the pre-operation surveillance that could house two trucks of felixium. Unless they had broken it down into smaller packages.

"Overwatch, I'm moving to—" The transmission cut out and Naomi went to try to raise Jason before he came back on the line. "Contact! We are under attack."

Naomi could hear the firing and explosions in the background. She clicked through a few of the drone feeds, checking the bigger picture. *Oh shit.*

"Zero Alpha—"

"Little busy, Overwatch."

"I see three teams of ten, in addition to those currently in contact with you. Teams are northeast, north, and northwest of your position. They are manoeuvring in your direction. Possibly attempting to flank."

There was a pause before, "Copy."

"Three armoured vehicles to your east." Naomi fought to keep her rising panic from her voice as she watched the operation turn into a disaster. She muted her microphone and swore.

Watching the feeds, Naomi felt nauseous. It was like watching a train wreck and being unable to stop it. This was an ambush. They must have been compromised. Should she call someone for back up? She had no idea who she would call, and if they had been compromised, it might make things worse. *Could things get worse?*

Naomi saw two of Jason's people fall and remain down. He was manoeuvring his team west so the PSCs wouldn't be able to envelop them. At first she thought he was moving west so they would have access to the other main buildings on the property. That he was still going for the felixium. Then she realised he was heading for the only defensible position for his team against a force that size.

She suddenly knew without a doubt that there was no felixium at that facility. They had been set up, and this was all for nothing. She broke out in a cold sweat. They had been lured in to be slaughtered. A panicked voice in her head screamed at Naomi that Jason would be killed and they'd never get the queen back. That she should run, hide, save herself.

Naomi closed her eyes and took a deep breath. She

muted the panic and watched Jason and his team move into a defensible position behind some shipping containers. Naomi assessed it from the drone footage. It was a good spot. The PSCs wouldn't be able to get the vehicles close enough to really use them, which evened the odds somewhat. She watched the PSCs taking up positions around Jason's team and picked up the handset that provided a direct link to the base commander in the DR.

Jason finished giving his quick orders, and his section commanders hurried back to their positions to brief their people.

"Come on, Jase," Pete's voice called out from behind a rusted forklift. "Give it up mate, you're not going to succeed."

Jason swore at him under his breath but didn't respond.

"There's no need to die here, mate. Think of Gwen and the kids."

Jason did not like Pete mentioning his family, but he needed to focus and not give in to the distraction. His plan needed to be timed right, and he could only try it once. He checked his watch.

"You always were stubborn. But don't worry, if something does happen to you I'll make sure she's—"

"Now!"

On Jason's command, the team on his right opened up with everything they had, both ammunition and magic. He'd put an emotional amplifier over there to increase the feelings of fear and anxiety, and a bloke who could make the enemy think that more munitions were coming at them than what was real.

His team on the left pushed forward, sweeping the

enemy and pushing them back. Jason and his team would sweep around to the rear, securing a withdrawal route.

"Go!" he commanded his team.

Naomi watched, on hold and becoming increasingly anxious. She saw Jason and his team fall back and into positions where they could provide fire for the others to withdraw.

"Brigadier Garnet." The voice pulled Naomi mentally back to the bunker where she was sitting.

"Brigadier, hi, this is Naomi Faulkner. I work with—"

"I know who you are, miss, and I'm hearing reports of gunfire from over by the abandoned warehouse in the PSC sector."

"Yes," said Naomi, exhaling in relief. "Jason—"

"As far as I know, there are no sanctioned operations in that area."

Naomi froze, her heart sinking. "Brigadier, Jason needs—"

"And as such, there can be no sanctioned assistance if anything goes wrong."

Naomi watched the drone feeds, watching Jason's team trying to withdraw. Three of their people fell as she watched. None of them moved. She felt numb.

"Brigadier—"

"No *sanctioned* assistance, Ms Faulkner. Now please excuse me, I think I have an unscheduled appointment."

The line went dead. A small flame of hope ignited in Naomi's chest.

Hang on, Jason. The cavalry's on its way.

She watched as the fighting intensified. Jason's team stopped their bunny hopping toward the exit and hunkered down behind cover, returning fire and trying to halt the relentless advance of the mercenaries.

Naomi wondered how long help would take to arrive. The onslaught couldn't last forever, could it? The members of Jason's team closest to the PSCs began laying down fire as they moved, one at a time, painfully short distances, trying to escape. With the rate of fire, the PSCs couldn't advance, but what would happen when they ran out of ammunition to sustain that rate? She didn't have to wait for long. The barrage started dying down, and she saw the mercenaries again begin to advance.

Jason's team began taking bigger risks, running farther and with less cover to try to escape. For many, this didn't work.

A helicopter exploded into view, causing Naomi to jump. She jumped up, crying out in excitement and punching the air before feeling slightly foolish and sitting down again. Thank goodness. They were going to be okay.

"Man down!"

"Medic!"

"Get the stretcher."

That was Jason's section! Naomi frantically clicked through drone footage, trying to locate one with eyes on Jason. She knew they wouldn't say who was hurt over the radio, but she needed to see.

It took all her restraint to keep from trying to raise Jason on the radio. If he was fine—and he had to be—then he'd be focussed on evacuating the casualty. But the minute they got on the helicopter, she was calling.

Screw it.

"Zero Alpha?"

"Overwatch, this is Zero Bravo. Zero Alpha is down."

41

Alexei stood as the girls entered the apartment.

"Well?" Seeing their furtive looks toward the bedrooms, he added, "We're alone."

"We got it," said Ava excitedly.

Lily showed him the ring, and Alexei examined the stone with interest.

"It's quite dull, isn't it? I thought it'd be more impressive. Shinier."

"It doesn't need to be impressive. It just needs to work," Ava said, moving past Alexei to her backpack, from which she retrieved the device.

"How did things go with you, Alexei?" asked Lily. She was nervous seeing Ava's enthusiasm. Now that her return to Highacre was imminent, she was suddenly more worried about her family, and had an overwhelming urge to remain here to help them.

"Actually," Alexei said, beaming. "I managed to get most of the gems back."

"You *what?*" Ava gasped.

"Really?" Lily asked excitedly. "How did you manage that?"

"Well, we'd decided that I should find as much work as I could before we leave," Alexei said, leading them to the lounge to settle in for the story. Ava looked slightly put out by the delay to their return, but seemed too interested to interrupt. Lily wondered briefly if Ava thought that Lily would entertain leaving without saying goodbye to her family.

"And I presumed that there would be gardeners at Batyola's property, so I went and asked if they needed an extra pair of hands. They did, but what they really needed was someone to clean the pool. So I headed around the back and grabbed the gear from the shed, and when I returned to the pool, Mrs Batyola was there."

"Alexei!" said Ava, guessing where his story was going.

"The other workmen—they weren't laughing when they offered you the pool cleaning job, were they?" Lily asked.

"Yes," replied Alexei, surprised. "Why?"

"No reason," said Lily while Ava tried not to laugh.

Alexei decided to ignore the girls. "Anyway, as it turns out, she's not *Mrs* Batyola. She's his mistress. I have a lot of experience with mistresses. My *father's* mistresses," he explained to Ava and Lily's shocked expressions. "I mean, talking to them. Honestly, your mind, Ava. What I mean is, I know how jealous they get. How resentful when they realise that they'll never be legitimate. Never be allowed to officially be on their man's arm at fancy events. Always be hidden, like a dirty secret."

"I mean, if the shoe fits," said Ava.

"Speaking of secrets," said Alexei, looking pointedly at Ava's hand resting on Lily's leg.

"It's not a secret," smiled Ava. "we're legit."

Alexei looked over at Lily and seeing her happy breathed an exaggerated sigh of relief. "She said yes? Thank goodness. Now I don't have to listen to Ava's fretting about whether or not you'd be interested in her."

Ava threw a cushion at Alexei and Lily suggested he continue with his story.

"So I was cleaning the pool—"

"Shirtless?"

"I didn't want to get it wet," Alexei said reasonably, oblivious to the girl's giggles. "And she starts talking to me. Once I realised she was the mistress and not the lady of the house, and that she was lonely, I knew what I had to do."

"You didn't!" said Ava, shocked.

"I did."

"But how will Elaine feel?"

"She will understand."

"I know you were doing it for money for her, but ..." Ava looked at Lily, lost for words.

Lily turned to Alexei. "When you say you 'did what you had to do', what do you mean, Alexei?"

"Well, I charmed her and led her to believe I might be interested in her, and then helped her believe that if we stole her lovers' gems, it would hurt him and we could run away together. She thinks we're meeting at a bar tonight after I sell the gems." Alexei looked quite conflicted about leading the woman on.

Ava dissolved into laughter. "Oh Alexei," she gasped. "You gigolo."

"What's so funny?" asked Elaine, leading April and Belinda into the apartment.

"Mum!" said Lily, surprised.

"I've been discharged," said Belinda. "And the girls are being kind enough to let me stay here."

"It might be a bit of a squeeze," Elaine said apologetically to Lily.

"Or maybe it won't be," said Belinda, spotting her ring.

Her face fell, and she said to Lily, sadly, "I guess you'll be leaving."

"What? No, she's not," Elaine said, staring at Lily in confusion.

"I am," Lily said quietly, staring at the floor. "But we did manage to get most of the gems back."

Lily took the bag of gems from Alexei and gave them to a bewildered Elaine.

"These should help quite a bit. Mum can help you make sure you get what they're worth."

Belinda looked gratefully at Lily, tears in her eyes.

"Wait," Elaine said, shaking her head, trying to make sense of things. "What do you mean, you're leaving?"

"I need to go, sis. Remember what I told you about the stuff going on in the other dimension? I need to get back there and help fix it."

"But what about us?" Elaine asked.

April pushed past them, fleeing to her room, head down to hide her tears.

"Let her go," said Belinda as Lily went to go after her. "I'll talk to her when she's calmed down. I'll make sure she understands."

Lily wasn't sure that was the best plan, but she saw the reassurance in Belinda's eyes and nodded.

"Understands what?" Elaine asked, starting to get angry. "And what's this? You think we need money? We need *you*, Lily. Our family's lost enough—" Elaine broke off, her voice cracking and tears running down her cheeks.

"I'm sorry," Lily said, and hugged Elaine tightly. Elaine resisted at first, but then grabbed Lily just as tight and sobbed into her shoulder.

"She has to go, love," Belinda said, rubbing Elaine's shoulder. "They need her, and no one else can help them."

Lily and Elaine broke apart.

"I will come back," Lily promised. "And maybe, if I can fix things so they're safe, you can come and visit. Maybe move to Highacre with me if you wanted."

Elaine nodded, seeming unsure of whether to believe her. Lily turned to her mother, and they hugged too.

"I'm so proud of you, Lily," Belinda whispered. "Thank you for helping us. And be safe."

Lily saw the fear in her mother's eyes and promised she would be. She turned upon hearing wet smacking sounds.

"Ugh."

"It's not goodbye, my sweet bumblebee," said Alexei before kissing Elaine again. "I will come back for you."

Elaine nodded, crying, and they kissed again.

Ava coughed pointedly, and Alexei and Elaine broke off their farewell. Ava handed the device to Lily. "Are you ready?"

Feeling conflicted about not going to resolve things with April, Lily nodded. She flicked the cap off the device and prepared to press the button.

"Wait!" April flung herself at Lily, wrapping her arms around her waist, almost making Lily click the button, which would have resulted in taking just her and April to Highacre. Lily replaced the safety cap and heard a sigh of relief from Ava.

"Don't go," came April's muffled voice.

Lily hugged her little sister back and whispered through tears she hadn't felt come, "I have to. They need me, kiddo."

April looked up at her big sister. "I need you."

Lily felt her heart break.

"It's hard, my love," said Belinda, placing a hand on April's shoulder and one on Lily's. "But we need to let her go. A whole country needs Lily. A whole world, really. We have to be brave and share her with them. And she'll come back if she can."

Belinda smiled sadly at Lily, and Lily realised her mother did not believe she would see her daughter again.

"I *will* come back," she said, meaning it. It seemed to be enough for Belinda that Lily wanted to.

She hugged each of her family again, told her mother to let David know she loved him too, then turned back to her friends. Alexei broke away from another final farewell with Elaine. Lily looked at them, and they nodded.

Before she could reconsider, Lily flipped back the cover and pressed the button.

42

"Ooof."

"Ow, get off—"

"Once again, that is *not* my arm, Alexei," said Lily, with a sense of déjà vu.

"It's not Alexei," came Ava's playful tones.

Smiling to herself, Lily got to her feet and felt her way to the wall.

"Some light would be good," suggested Ava.

"Yeah, but I can't just—oh." Lily summoned a small fireball with her powers and with its help, found the light switch. She flicked it on. Nothing.

"Can you make your fireball a little brighter?" asked Alexei, both so that he could see what he was doing, and to subtly remind Lily that she didn't actually need the light switch, now that she had fire.

Blushing, Lily increased the fireball's intensity and located the door.

"Wait," said Ava as Lily went to open it. "Do you know where we are?"

"No, I was going to have a look."

Both Ava and Alexei moved closer, concentration and concern on their faces.

"Remember what Giles said," Alexei cautioned. "Even your palace may not be safe."

He had a point, and the joy that Lily had felt at being home was tinged with sadness. Returning home never seemed to be positive.

"Ava, can you see anyone out there?" Lily asked, bringing her head into the game.

After a pause Ava replied, "There are two people, I think a man and a woman, that way. But I think they're in another room."

Lily nodded and, dimming her fireball, cracked open the door, peering out. There was a dark hallway, and a door on the other side about where Ava had pointed out the people. At the end of the hall, Lily could just make out some stairs leading up, but to where, Lily had no idea. If they were in the palace, she hadn't been to this part.

Closing the door again, Lily faced Ava and Alexei. "I should have asked Belinda where we'd arrive. Never mind, too late now. I don't know where we are from that quick look, but there's a hall leading to some stairs. We'll head out and listen at the doorway where Ava saw the people, see if we can get any information, and then head up the stairs with Ava scanning ahead."

The others nodded and Lily led them out into the hall and pressed her ear against the opposite door.

"—might lose the eye, but they think he could keep the leg. His arm's just broken, but it might be awhile until he's up and about."

"Thank goodness he's alive, but ..."

"I know. Without the felixium, it was all for nothing. They led us straight into a trap and Jason very nearly died because of it."

Ignoring the hisses of alarm from her friends, Lily pushed open the door and demanded that Giles and Naomi tell her exactly what had happened to Jason.

"Your Majesty!" Giles moved to hug her before catching himself and settling for clasping his hands in joy. Lily saw tears in his eyes. "You're home."

"But how?"

Lily could see the regret in Naomi's eyes, despite her clear excitement at Lily's return. Lily gave a very brief overview of how they had returned before Naomi let her know about the failed raid and Jason's injuries.

"Gwen's with him," she finished before sighing. "She's pretty mad. Stopped taking my phone calls. My information about his condition is a couple of weeks old now." She shook her head. "Not only was the felixium not there, but you didn't need us anyway."

"You didn't know that," reminded Lily. "And besides, I did need you all looking. It was only luck really that we were able to get ourselves back here."

Giles and Naomi seemed to notice Ava and Alexei for the first time, and looked immediately uncomfortable.

"Is there a problem?" Lily asked pointedly.

"No ma'am," said Naomi quickly, "but in the current climate, your being seen with them could be problematic."

"How so?" Lily asked, offended.

"It may be all the justification the prime minister needs to claim you are a traitor and have you locked up."

"He can't do that," said Lily, not entirely certain it was true. But it seemed unlikely politicians would have the power to detain royalty.

"I mean," Naomi said, shrugging, "all he needs is enough reason to keep the HSP on side. I don't know to what extent the Royal Guards have been infiltrated, and without Jason here to rally them ... the prime minister could certainly detain first, ask questions later."

"But we can't leave them here," Giles said, addressing Naomi. "They'll have to come with us."

She considered this. "I suppose if we can keep them out of sight until we get to the Tower, it's feasible that as ambassadors, they would want to witness the vote."

"Vote?"

"Sorry, Your Majesty," Naomi said as Giles turned away, making a phone call. "As we speak, the prime minister is preparing Parliament to vote to declare war on Meridia. The only one who can intervene is the sovereign. And we *need* you to intervene. The emergency powers that Toth pushed through after the Trials? They stipulate that if a successful vote sends Highacre to war during the enactment of the powers, the sovereign cannot revoke the decision without the support of the prime minister."

"Well, let's go then," said Lily, moving to the door.

"It's just, well, you need to *be* sovereign first," said Giles, hanging up and moving to the door to exit first. He turned to Naomi and said, "He'll meet us at the first corner past the gate."

Naomi and Giles led them up the stairs. They paused at the door, Giles listening while Naomi explained the current situation in the palace and told the newcomers that they would need to move through without being seen.

"Let Ava go first," Lily said. Giles and Naomi hesitated. "She can scan with her implant. Let us know if there are people ahead."

Reluctantly, Giles and Naomi moved aside to let Ava through. Lily noticed Naomi watched her like a hawk, but decided now was not the time to deal with that.

Luckily there wasn't a lot of traffic around the old

barracks area. Ava easily spotted threats and Naomi led the group around them, and finally out into the grounds.

She removed a tarpaulin, revealing a van, and urged them all to get in the back.

Lily, Ava, and Alexei ducked down as they approached a gate manned by several HSP officers. Luckily, they showed little interest in a van leaving the palace grounds, and even less when Giles tried to explain the household goods they were allegedly going into town to procure.

Naomi drove them away from the gate, turning down a side road, then pulled over.

"Why are we stopping?" Lily asked. Before anyone could answer, the side door opened and a middle-aged man hopped in, beaming at Lily.

"Your Majesty," he said, trying to bow in the tight confines and almost falling as Naomi pulled the van back out onto the road.

"Your Majesty, this is Lord Philipe," said Giles. "He is the one with the power to effect your coronation."

"But isn't the prime minister still claiming that I wasn't successfully confirmed?"

"He is, but he's produced no evidence to back that up. Whereas before your last coronation, we found significant evidence stating that the judges were within their authority to declare that you completed the Trials," replied Giles. He huffed. "That man seems to think he can just say whatever he wants in the media and people will just believe it."

Lily briefly met Naomi's eye. Toth did seem to think that, and unfortunately it seemed to work better than it should.

And so, bouncing along in the back of a van, Lord Philipe began the ceremony that would make Lily queen of Highacre. She much preferred low-key to pomp and ceremony, but thinking of what had been planned for this occasion, did feel sorry for Giles.

"... and so it is my great pride and honour to declare you queen of Highacre! Rise, Your Majesty."

Lily, who had been awkwardly kneeling in the narrow aisle between the seats in the van, now struggled to her feet, balancing as Naomi took corners at the fastest speed she dared and hunching so as not to hit her head.

"You can sit now, Your Majesty," whispered Lord Philipe, still beaming, apparently oblivious to the mood of the rest of the passengers.

Lily fell back in her seat, feeling no different than when she had knelt. She knew that nothing had actually changed, and so she shouldn't feel any different, but in a way, everything *had* changed. When she had pictured her coronation, often worrying about it as she tried to get to sleep at night, Lily had imagined this part of the ceremony as her standing, overburdened by a heavy cloak and crown, and turning from the raised platform to see hundreds of her loyal subjects cheering and clapping.

She looked now to see the anxious faces of her closest friends. Notably absent were those arrested or injured on her behalf.

Heavy is the head, and I'm not even wearing an actual crown.

"Congratulations, Your Majesty," said Giles, offering a tense smile. The others murmured their congratulations too. Ava reached over and gave her hand a quick squeeze.

Arriving at the Tower, Lily noticed the stark difference from her last time there. No crowds, no media. Just a dozen armed men in body armour and helmets stationed outside looking entirely unwelcoming. Lily expected trouble and so was surprised and unsettled when the officer in charge simply smirked and waved her through.

Lily, Ava, and Alexei broke out ahead of the group, entering the doors to the Parliament chamber first. Lily's mind was full of what she would say to halt the prime minister's warmongering.

They pushed through the crowd at the back, emerging in the rear of the area for elected members. She saw Minister Jeremy Toot sitting off to the right of the prime minister. He was relaxed and smiling, sipping on his ever-present whiskey. Lily couldn't help but wonder how he was allowed to have alcohol in Parliament, let alone during a vote about going to war.

She turned her attention to the prime minister. He was standing at the lectern, smiling out over the floor of assembled politicians. They were applauding in a sombre though enthusiastic way. His gaze met Lily's, and her stomach dropped. His eyes hardened, and a cruel smile spread across his face.

"Thank you Mr Speaker, I confirm the vote." He gave Lily a final, triumphant glare, then looked down the barrel of the camera directly in front of him.

"Highacre is at war."

BOOKS BY K.T. HOLDER

The Highacren Prophecy

Regent (free prequel novella)

Royal

Return

Reign

Rogue (free bonus chapter)

The City Chronicles

Rise of the Divvinium (free prequel novella)

City of Stone

City of Shadows

Echoes of the Divvinium (free bonus novella)

City of Sorrow

ACKNOWLEDGMENTS

Here we are again! This book was as difficult as I've heard second books are to write. It didn't go through as many iterations, but let's just say the chapters about what Lily gets up to at home went through a bunch of different versions!

I wound up writing a lot of this book as I was completing my transition to my new life which involved a career change and international move, and writing this story really helped me through that time. If only in being able to put imaginary people in significantly worse situations so I could feel better by comparison!

But I'm so pleased with where it wound up, and I couldn't have done it without my wife. I don't know how I managed to get the most amazing, supportive and beautiful wife, but I did and all I can say is: no take backs! You're stuck with me :).

My dogs helped again with snores and imposed writing breaks for exercise and snacks. I don't think they care for the story so much, but they indulge my pretence that there is something more interesting than food and chasing a ball.

Thank you again to Courtney at Elevation Editorial. Courtney is a master at fixing stories and encouraging writers to be their best. If she didn't give me suggestions for a better direction, she provided inspiration with little comments, that wound up becoming major storylines.

Thank you to the team at GetCovers for another amazing cover. The team there is so easy to work with and their designers are exceptional!

And again, the biggest thank you is for you! I can't tell you how grateful I am that you're still reading this series! You're support means everything and I hope you enjoyed Return.

If you did enjoy the story, please consider leaving a review on Amazon or Goodreads, or really anywhere you like! They really can make a difference, especially in helping other people find my books, and it'll go a long way to letting me keep writing stories for you.

Feel free to to head over to my website (www.kthold er.com) where you can sign up to hear about book releases and other fun things! If you sign up, you get Regent, an exclusive prequel novella, for free!

You can also get updates by following me on Facebook and Instagram, and I'm also on Goodreads and BookBub!

Thanks again!

www.ingramcontent.com/pod-product-compliance
Lightning Source LLC
Chambersburg PA
CBHW021405310726

48971CB00005B/1211